2236

A

Novel

By

Milton McGriff

Published by AMM Publishing LLC, P.O. Box 13017,
Philadelphia, Pennsylvania 19101 U.S.A.

Library of Congress Cataloging-inPublication Data

ISBN 13: 978-0-9793782-9-4
ISBN 10: 0-9793782-9-X

Printed in the United States of America

Ruchell Magee's quote is used with the permission of Claude Marks from Freedom
Archives in San Francisco, California.

Author's photograph, book cover and book layout by: LaVell Khepera Finerson;
www.lavellfinerson.com

PUBLISHER'S NOTE
This is a work of fiction. Names, characters, places, and incidents
either are the product of the author's imagination or are used
fictitiously, and any resemblance to actual persons, living or dead,
events, or locales is entirely coincidental.

ii

DEDICATION

To the memory of my mother, Alverta McGriff,
and the memory of my son, Wayne Jordan,

and

for the uncounted millions —
those who survived the journey,
and those who didn't ...

Each ripple in the ocean
is the grave of an African
who refused to be a slave *

* from "For the Millions," The Last Poets

ALSO BY THE AUTHOR

And Then We Heard The Thunder, a three-act play (based on the novel by John Oliver Killens)

T.C.B. (Takin' Care of Business), a one-act play

The Nigger Killer, a one-act play

The Path of the Night (A collection of poetry by four writers)

If we must die, let it not be like hogs
Hunted and penned in an inglorious spot,
While round us bark the mad and hungry dogs,
Making their mock at our accursed lot.
If we must die, O let us nobly die,
So that our precious blood may not be shed
In vain; then even the monsters we defy
Shall be constrained to honor us though dead!
O kinsmen we must meet the common foe!
Though far outnumbered let us show us brave,
And for their thousand blows deal one deathblow!
What though before us lies the open grave?
Like men we'll face the murderous, cowardly pack,
Pressed to the wall, dying, but fighting back!

Claude McKay

Never doubt that a small group of thoughtful,
committed citizens can change the world:
Indeed, it's the only thing that ever has.

Margaret Mead

The greatest weapon of the oppressor is the mind
of the oppressed.

Steve Biko
South African
freedom fighter

Until the lion writes the tale of the hunt,
the hunter will always emerge victorious.

African proverb

ACKNOWLEDGMENTS

"Writing is something you do alone in a room" is a quote from Michael Ventura, one of my favorite writers.

However, once that book is finished, it must find a reading public. Seeing that book through to completion, and then marshaling resources to get it to the marketplace, requires the love, help, kindness, encouragement, and skills of many, many people. You will note that some did double- and even triple duty. I feel the blessings, thank you for them, and hope I have returned the love in some small measure.

I first thank the Creator for everything involved in bringing this book into being.

I must first thank those who stepped up when the decision was made to form AMM Publishing. Christopher Chaplin, a gifted MBA, said he had my back. These brothers (yes, Howard) helped make it happen: Howard Braitman, Kedrick Bellamy, Sulayman Muhammad, Andrew "Duke" Jenkins, Joe Idokogi, and LaVell "Khepera" Finerson. Thank you for believing in me.

Two of them—LaVell and Kedrick—then joined Chris and me to become what I have dubbed the AMM Team—Christopher Chaplin, LaVell "Khepera" Finerson, Kedrick Bellamy. Recently, a dear friend, Marie

Grossett, became the company's administrative assistant. All have been indispensable in making this happen.

I must thank my editor, Toisan Craigg, both for her skillful eye and for saving me from my excesses.

I had two primary "offices" where I wrote daily. Gila Williams (and all of her staff at the Well Grounded Coffee Shop), was warm, supportive generous and encouraging. The same holds true for Audrey Elam, Trish Duke, and the staff who put up with me for hours on end at the Cereality Café.

Barnett Wright, a direct and forthright friend, gave valuable feedback on the first draft, and acted as a cheerleader throughout the process. The Reverend Frank Tyson and Michael Dabney also suffered through that first draft and provided helpful suggestions. Kedrick, Howard, and Marie, thank you again for serving as efficient copyreaders.

In the early stages of writing, the then-vacant convent at St. Luke's Episcopal Church was made available to me for brief periods. Thank you, Dana.

When quiet solitude was needed during the final draft, and again during the editing phase, all of the friars at St. Anselm's Abbey in Washington, D.C., were warm and generous with their hospitality.

Author Karen E. Quinones-Miller was generous with advice when I told her I wanted to emulate her successful self-publishing effort.

Thank you to my spiritual adviser, John Walker, for being a voice of calm whenever I needed to hear one.

I had more cheerleaders than I can name—and would probably omit someone—but thank you to all my friends who believed in me.

Thirty-five years ago, there were many—actors, directors, co-producers, stage managers, venues, and so on—who helped a modest, angry one-act play called *The Nigger Killer* become my most-produced dramatic effort. I never dreamed then that the story would become fleshed out in a novel. But then, in those heady, idealistic times when all things seemed possible, I never dreamed that in this new milenium violence and neglect would still be visited upon those of African descent by a right-wing government that is both mean-spirited and inept, as most recently and vividly witnessed in the aftermath of hurricane Katrina.

2236

TIME: *The Near Future*

PLACE: *A U.S. City*

LOVE YAHWEH YOUR ELOHIM WITH ALL YOUR HEART, AND WITH ALL YOUR SOUL, AND WITH ALL YOUR MIND

LOVE YOUR NEIGHBOR AS YOURSELF

THIS IS MY COMMANDMENT: LOVE ONE ANOTHER, AS I HAVE LOVED YOU

PROLOGUE

nh!" *Whap!* "Unh!" *Whap!* "Unh!" *Whap!*

"Now! What you got to say about that?" Big Larry sat back, looking very pleased with himself. "Did you just take a butt whipping or what?"

Mister Jake stared at the board, dismayed. He cursed under his breath. How in the world did he let that happen? He never got triple jumped. Mister Jake knew he'd be hearing about this one for a while. At least until he could put a real hurting back on Big Larry.

"Yeah, well, everybody gets lucky every now and then," Mister Jake said. He started setting up a new game to keep proof of his humiliation from remaining in evidence. "Even you. That's the last time you triple jump me."

Big Larry snorted. "You got some nerve talking trash after I've put a whupping on you, and a bad one at that."

The other two men were tickled. "I think you're slipping, Mister Jake," Varnell said. "He really did a job on you."

"Don't y'all make Jake mad," Mister Otis said. "Big Larry won't win another game 'til next year, you watch." Two years Jacobin Robinson's junior, he was the only person in the entire Dock Street neighborhood, and in Sam Butler Center, who didn't preface "Jake" with "Mister." Not that Mister Jake cared. It had been that way so long he didn't really notice.

They called themselves The Checkers Gang. No one employed at the Sam Butler Center, where they held court, or any of the young people who played there, could remember when The Checkers Gang hadn't been seated by the front window on weekends, talking trash and playing checkers.

Mister Jake and Big Larry ran through their rituals in preparation for the rubber match. Mister Jake turned his ever-present kufi skullcap around for a moment on his silver white Afro, and then turned it back, as he always did after a loss. He wore his white hair and walrus sideburns like a warrior's helmet. In the kufi, his wizened face resembled that of a dark-skinned Elijah Muhammad. Big Larry just rubbed his palms together rapidly for a few seconds and then held them palms up like a surgeon preparing to operate. Then he turned them over and shook his fingers.

The front window overlooked the center's basketball court on an uneven asphalt surface. The older men looked up as a hard foul by one teenager nearly sparked a fistfight with another boy. Cooler heads in the pickup game separated them.

"They play like they playing for money," Mister Otis said before turning his attention back to the checkers game.

The Checkers Gang played on the painted surface of a scarred white Formica table with one leg shorter than the other three. A wad of napkins more or less evened the short leg. The table had been there ever since they had. They usually listened to an oldies station that played what they referred to as "Moldy Oldies" from the Fifties. At other times they let the television set drone in the background. Sometimes, like today, it was both. As Mister Jake regrouped for battle with Big Larry, the Spaniels doo-wopped, *Baby, It's You*, on the oldies station blaring from the portable radio at Otis' side.

Varnell stood up and started doing the slow drag with an imaginary partner. "Man, this girl named Betty used to give me fever when we danced on this song," he said. "I wasn't no more than thirteen. It had been out a few years by then, but all the older kids still played it. My brother had a copy and I'd take it to our blue light basement parties. Man, Betty would rub it up against me and I thought heaven was right there. I'd tell people, 'Don't throw water on me, just let me burn!' And Lord, Betty could kiss like nobody's business." He twirled his imaginary Betty, large hazel eyes closed, smiling.

"Aw, sit down, fool," Mister Otis said. "I guess y'all heard they let them cops off out in Los Angeles. The ones that killed that young girl."

"Yeah, I heard," Mister Jake said. He looked through his coke bottle glasses at Big Larry. " It's your move. What you expect? They white cops and she's a Negro. I know you didn't think they was going to jail."

"Things have been for real crazy since this fool Bruder got in the White House," Mister Otis said. "He's worse for black folks than Reagan and the two Bushes put together, don't you think?"

"Why do you still say Negro?" Varnell asked for the umpteenth time since they had started playing checkers twenty-four years earlier, missing only a dozen weekends or so in all that time.

Mister Jake always gave the same answer. "Negro, colored, black, Afro-Americans, African-Americans, what difference do it make? White folks ain't gonna treat you right, regardless." Then, a new coda: "And President Hugh Bruder is white the last time I looked."

"I thought these cops might go to jail," Mister Otis said, pulling at the silver puff of hair directly below his lower lip. "I mean, they had no reason to shoot that girl." He paused. "You know, the cops shoot a lot of women out there in Los Angeles. She's the third one I know of in the last four or five years."

2

"You are lying," Big Larry said as he moved a checker. "I didn't see anything on television about them shooting black women."

"You better keep your mind on the game, that's what you better do," Mister Jake said, moving a piece.

"Killing black folks isn't news no more," Mister Otis said. He was well read and the preeminent researcher among them. "You need to read more. That television rots your brain," he said to Big Larry.

"Yeah, one happened a while back, before all these recent killings," Mister Otis continued. "Name was Eunice Valentine. A housewife, I think she was about thirty-five or forty. The sister got behind in her gas bill and cussed out the people come to turn her gas off. They come back with the cops. She had a kitchen knife in her hand. She got upset and threw it toward the cop, and he emptied his gun on her.

"Now, this was a little overweight lady who was unarmed after she threw the knife, and the knife didn't even come close to the murdering bastard who shot her. I mean, they could have arrested her, they didn't have to kill her." He paused, shaking his head as if he'd been there.

Mister Jake made a double jump. "White folks ain't gonna treat you right, regardless," he said.

"The other one, young woman named Delores Olds, just happened last year," Otis went on. "It wasn't L.A., but it was somewhere near L.A. Cop didn't kill her but he killed her baby."

"Yeah! Yeah! They did have something on about that," Big Larry said. "A white cop who did a whole bunch of funny shit, tried to set her up or something." He moved and realized his mistake as soon as he took his hand away.

"I'll take that... and that... and that... and that!" Mister Jake said with his cigarette-stained grin. "Boy, where you learn to play checkers?" He looked at the other two men. "C'mon, Otis, you my next victim."

Mister Otis moved to the table. "Now, I ain't no Big Larry," he said. "I got something for your ass."

"Just set them up and play," Mister Jake said.

Mister Otis continued with his story. "After the mess was over, he claimed he thought she was selling drugs and he wanted to make the bust." He held up a forefinger at Mister Jake. "Jake, let me finish this before we start the game. Anyway, it came out that he was the only deputy on duty in her area that night, and it's about one in the morning and he fakes a call to his station, and tries to sound like one of us, saying there's a disturbance going on, knowing they'd send him to investigate. He gets there and fakes his voice again, knocking on the door and trying to sound like us again, yelling that the cops are after him. This young lady, Delores Olds was her name, eight or nine months pregnant, had just come home with a girlfriend and she don't know

3

who the hell's knocking on her door sounding stupid. So she goes to the door with an unloaded rifle in her hand, thinking she'll scare them off. That motherfucker blasted her in the stomach as soon as she opened the door. Shot her baby in the head."

"But he did get arrested, didn't he?" Big Larry asked.

"Yeah, but I think that's because he was such an embarrassment after he had to admit how he got there," Mister Otis said. "I have to tell you, I was surprised that he got charged. I don't think he's had a trial yet though."

Mister Otis lost his first game and won the second. During the second game, they paused when the voice of Minister David Walker, a leader in the Covenant of the New Commandment, came on the radio. Walker was holding a news conference in Los Angeles. The Covenant, headquartered in their city since being founded there more than forty years ago, was a local institution. Its leaders, David and his father, Johnnie "Black Label" Walker, were local celebrities.

"We are here to monitor the trial of this murdering deputy who killed Delores Olds' unborn child and seriously wounded her," Walker said. "It was a heinous crime, and we will settle for nothing less than the full weight of the law finding Deputy Milford Sales guilty of second degree murder as charged." The newscaster said the trial was expected to last at least two weeks; Sales was free on $2,500 bail because he was not considered a flight risk.

"What do you think of these folks, Covenant of the New Commandment?" It was Mister Jake. Asking the question was another routine for the Checkers Gang. Mister Jake posed the question several times a year. Opinions had both changed and remained the same over the years, depending on what was going on.

Mister Jake had been a supporter of the Covenant since a summer night in 1973. Around dusk that steamy August night, a Covenant member stoked the fury of three police officers by refusing to stop selling the organization's newspaper, the *Scabbard*, after being ordered to do so. The trio beat him to within an inch of his life, and then arrested him for assault on a police officer. Minister Johnnie "Black Label" Walker, the Covenant's founder, took ninety-two well-dressed members of the Covenant's paramilitary arm, the Swords of the Master, to the precinct. Lined up in military formation, they stood at parade rest when Minister Johnnie ordered them to do so. Although unarmed, their bearing and discipline startled the policemen. They had thrown their battered and bleeding colleague into a cell to languish. Hundreds of nearby residents, told that some angry Negroes were lined up outside the police station, came into the streets to watch in disbelief. Minister Johnnie, then a young Turk of twenty-eight, told the police in quiet tones the Swords had no intention of leaving unless and until their comrade received medical attention.

Four Swords rode in the ambulance with their injured comrade; once he was under medical care, the Swords called Minister Johnnie Walker. Within minutes, the squad of Swords at the precinct disappeared.

Black barbershops and beauty parlors buzzed about it for weeks. Some people (and a dismayed nearly all-white police force) hadn't even known an organization that big existed in their neighborhood that was so well organized. Attendance, and membership, spiked at the Covenant meetinghouse.

Even though Jacobin Robinson wasn't a religious man, he came close to joining the Covenant that year. He attended their weekly community meetings for over a year. Eventually though, all the talk about Yahweh and Yahshua wore him out. He wasn't really big on their "wake up, clean up, stand up" pronouncement either. The waking up and standing up he liked, but he knew the "cleaning up" meant his pack of Viceroy cigarettes and weekly pint of Vat 69 or Cutty Sark would have to go. They didn't talk about it being a sin or anything; they just didn't smoke or drink alcohol. One brother did tell him that poisons kept the temple of his body from functioning at capacity, or something like that. Even though he didn't join, Marcus Garvey, Elijah Muhammad and Malcolm X were the only black men Mister Jake admired as much or more than Minister Johnnie "Black Label" Walker.

Mister Otis always said the same thing. "They all right, but they talk tough more than they act. They do say what needs to be said, though. Black Label don't bite his tongue, that's for sure."

"They stand up for their own," Mister Jake said. "That's where their name comes from, loving God and loving each other. We sure need more of us doing that."

"Not God, they say Yahweh," Mister Otis said. "And I got you. Unh! And unh!" He jumped Mister Jake's last two pieces. "You on a losing streak, Jake."

"That's all right, I need a break anyway," Mister Jake said, rising from the table. "God, Yahweh, Allah, Jehovah, it's all the same. And whatever you think, they all we got, unless you think the NAACP or the Urban League are saying what needs to be said." He ambled off to the bathroom.

"I'm with you, Mister Otis," Varnell said as he took Mister Jake's seat. He called after Mister Jake, "They all right, but they never *do* nothing."

One

We hold these truths to be self-evident, that all men are created equal, that they are endowed by their Creator with certain unalienable Rights, that among these are Life, Liberty and the pursuit of Happiness. . . . That to secure these rights, Governments are instituted among Men, deriving their just powers from the consent of the governed, --That whenever any Form of Government becomes destructive of these ends, it is the Right of the People to alter or to abolish it, and to institute new Government, laying its foundation on such principles and organizing its powers in such form, as to them shall seem most likely to effect their Safety and Happiness. Prudence, indeed, will dictate that Governments long established should not be changed for light and transient causes; and accordingly all experience hath shewn, that mankind are more disposed to suffer, while evils are sufferable, than to right themselves by abolishing the forms to which they are accustomed. But when

. . . a long train of abuses . . .

and usurpations, pursuing invariably the same Object evinces a design to reduce them under absolute Despotism, it is their right, it is their duty, to throw off such Government, and to provide new Guards for their future security.

ONE

Andy dozed, slipping in and out of slumber...

The river gently rippled and flowed between them. A smiling Jhanae —at least she looked like Jhanae — stood on the far bank. With no face. How did he know it was Jhanae if she had no face? How did he know she was smiling if she had no face? He just knew. Even with no face, she looked like Jhanae, had her Hershey chocolate coloring. She moved like Jhanae, curved the way Jhanae curved. One of a kind curves. She had Jhanae's height; tall with long lean legs that stopped short of being skinny. Full bosomed with sista girl hips. It was definitely her ... for one thing, she was wearing Jhanae's wedding dress ... he sat at his computer watching her, watching her become many people, men as well as women...and people were shooting, why were they shooting? All the people shooting wore police uniforms and they were smiling...the people being shot looked like Jhanae, even the men...they were smiling, too...

"... and gentlemen, the pilot has requested that you please return your seat to the upright position and fasten your seat belts. In a few moments, we will begin..."

Andy blinked, tried to focus the bleariness from his eyes. The flight attendant's singsong voice nudged him toward wakefulness. The pinging seat belt sign punctuated her message. Andy pressed his armchair button and straightened his seat. His seat belt had remained fastened during the impromptu nap. He closed the half-read airline magazine on his lap, replaced it in the net basket behind the seat in front of him. Flight Lite reading, he called it. Airline magazines took bland journalism to a whole new level.

He stretched, pushing his arms above his head and to the side. He'd been dreaming about Miss Ex-wife. Whoopee. He stared out the window at what he could see of an enormous cumulus floating beside the plane. The five years since the breakup and divorce felt like five months on days like this. Time flies when you're having fun. Now here he was, leaving the pain of Debora behind in L. A., and thinking about his ex-wife. What was that about?

He liked California, but he liked coming home better. When Romeo had offered full time work with the *Scabbard*, it was a chance to move back and he accepted immediately. Working for the *Bugle*, a black weekly, had been bearable and almost fulfilling. The City Hall beat in Inglewood and Hawthorne, two suburban towns, kept him busy, along with occasional drama and entertainment reporting. But being senior correspondent for an advocacy paper whose organization was already in his life seemed as good as it got.

It would be good being back with George and Romeo, too. He wondered what baby brother's surprise was. "Come on through when you get here," was all George would say. "Come on through, and you'll find out when you get here."

George had given him a dose of mock attitude when he told him Romeo was picking him up. "I really thought you were working, George," Andy said. "Romeo lives closer to Uncle Sherman's place anyway. When I lucked into Uncle Sherman being away for the next couple of weeks and letting me crash there, I called Rome. Stop giving me shit."

"I was all ready to come get you," George said. "If Romeo wasn't like family, I'd smack you upside the head when you did get here," George said.

Andy laughed. "You still don't weigh enough to be hitting me upside the head, little brother." The voice on loudspeaker called his flight again. "I'll call you when I get in. I have to get to the gate. See you tonight."

"Bring me and Marian some cheese steaks and I might forgive you," George said, feigning sternness.

"It's a deal," Andy said. "Play all fly balls to the wall."

"Yes, sir," his half brother said. "And line drives safe."

He turned his cell phone off and hurried to the line for his flight. The baseball metaphor valediction was an old one for them, dating back to adolescence, when they still thought they were cousins and didn't know they shared a common mother.

George was an absolute baseball fanatic at the time. He was not only current on major league baseball, he was a virtual encyclopedia of Negro Baseball League history. As an all-city high school second baseman, he'd been close to the team's coach.

Both he and George figured out quickly that "playing all fly balls to the wall," which he got from the coach, meant they should not give up easily on anything they tried to accomplish. More than twenty years later, they still analyzed the possibilities of meaning in "playing line drives safe." Andy's most recent philosophizing thought it meant that in sudden, unexpected happenings, one should not take big risks. George, far less analytical than he, would only say, "Yeah, maybe. Coach Bernardino was a deep dude."

As always when flying, Andy was glad to have opted for comfort over styling and profiling. The charcoal gray running suit and T-shirt felt good, the next best thing to traveling in pajamas. He slipped his feet into his worn no-name white sneakers and tied the laces.

The plane began its descent toward the airport. Andy's mind returned to the jumble of feelings he had fallen asleep to escape. Feelings about returning to his hometown; feelings about Jhanae; feelings about L.A., a city he liked; feelings about his new, raw memories of L.A.; feelings about the specific raw memory named Debora; feelings about working for the Covenant full-time. Shit, feelings about his feelings.

Two years ago, there was no thought of returning home to live. What was it folks said about life being what happened while you made other plans?

Moving to the West Coast had surprised him as much as his move back. One day he'd been eating a quick sandwich, minding his own business. He looked up and there was fine Debora Benson, his college love, having lunch four tables away. And sitting alone, no less. A big hug had followed a big, surprised smile. She said she was in town from Los Angeles attending a seminar and visiting relatives.

The tentative smile, enhanced by the tiny birthmark above her upper lip; the invitational softness in her dark eyes; the brimmed porkpie-styled hat, cocked just so, styling as only Debora could style; their reminisces about the good parts of their college days. Designed by both of them to tease the other, their rummaging through memories succeeded in a big way.

They started with a long phone call, tried another lunch, progressed to a candlelight dinner, and transformed it all into four semi-magical weeks while she completed the executive training seminar.

Debora actually lived in Santa Monica, in a pricey high rise not far from Third Street Promenade. Andy visited for the Christmas holidays. She surprised him with a visit on Valentine's Day weekend. On a warm weekend in May, he caught a bargain flight. Because he had vacation time, he stayed five days. They treated her two children to a day at Disneyland. One morning, they drove up the Pacific Coast Highway and had breakfast at a funky little restaurant in Santa Barbara that served huge portions. Later, between kisses on the beach, he said he'd always wanted to live in California anyway. After interviewing and getting a job with the *Bugle,* he packed his clothes and books, sold his furniture, and moved in with Debora that fall.

A year of less magical communicating and miscommunication followed. Her two pre-pubescent daughters warmed to him on the Christmas visit and again on the springtime one. But from his first day there as a resident, they reminded him at every turn that he wasn't their daddy. Understanding they came first for Debora didn't make it hurt less when both of them realized it wasn't going to work out.

The plane bumped down, interrupting his mawkish reverie. Andy stretched again, felt the tension in his thirty-nine-year old body. He knew he needed to get back in the gym, or start jogging again, or something. He retrieved his carry-on bag and laptop computer from the overhead compartment. Because the plane was half empty, it took no time to disembark.

Romeo Butler stood near the inert baggage carousels, grinning. "Whassup?" he hollered. "Whassup?" Andy hollered back. The two men grinned and embraced.

"Hey, Rome, how you doing?" Seeing his old friend, Andy knew he was really glad to be back. It was always good to see anybody from back on the block, but especially this brother who was like a blood brother.

"I'm great, Any. Glad to see you back, man."

Andy chuckled. He hadn't heard his childhood nickname since the last time he'd seen Romeo. Only his boys from his old 'hood ever used it. Once, when they were about sixteen, Romeo, Andy, and a few other brothers had pooled their money and bought three seriously cheap bottles of wine through an older intermediary. They were cheaper than cheap: a bottle of Tokay, another of Thunderbird, and one big half gallon of Gypsy Rose. Separately, the wines were barely bearable. Then one of their partners, Barry, came up with the bright idea of mixing them. The result resembled a putrid chemical dreamed up by a mad scientist. No one could take more than a swallow. Except Andy. For reasons he could never explain, the concoction hadn't tasted all that bad to him. Andy had chug-a-lugged several large gulps as his buddies looked on in disgust and wonder.

"Damn," Barry said, "this nigga will drink *anything*." His buddies had whooped and hollered. He'd almost choked laughing himself, spewing the cheap wine in every direction. First, he became "Anything Andy," which gave way to "Anything," and finally to "Any." It was good hearing it from Romeo.

His homeboy seemed to be taking care of himself. But then, that was like a mantra from Minister Johnnie for all members of the Covenant. Take care of your body and treat it like a temple, the minister said. As a boy, Romeo's long eyelashes and smooth brown skin, although not feminine, nevertheless had a degree of prettiness. As a boy, his good looks had gotten him into more than one fight. Now, his close-cropped hair edging toward salt-and-pepper, his bearded chin, and life's lessons had erased most of the youthful soft features away. His rimless eyeglasses masked the length of his eyelashes. As always, he was sartorially immaculate. He wore a chocolate brown pin-striped suit, a light blue dress shirt with a brown, blue and pale yellow patterned silk tie. Expensive midnight brown suede tasseled shoes set the combination off. On his lapel he wore a black, red and green stylized oval with two crossed swords below it.

"After you get over your jet lag, we'll start trying to find you a place," Romeo said "A new member of the Swords owns a building with some furnished one-bedrooms."

"If he's got a two-bedroom, I'll probably want that," Andy said. "I want a room for an office. I've got a lot of books being shipped from L.A. How's Fredericka?"

"Growing like a weed. She's almost twelve, going on twenty-two, she thinks. She'll be glad to see 'Uncle' Andy." He slapped his homeboy on the shoulder.

"I'm glad to be back. Speaking of uncles, do you remember where my Uncle

Sherman lives?"

Romeo smiled. "Bro, you haven't been gone that long. How long is he away?"

"Two weeks. Although he said I can hang there a while, if I don't have a place."

"Why don't you crash at my place tonight? Malikah and Fredericka would love to see you. I'll take you over to your uncle's place in the morning."

"Sound like a plan to me. I'm tired and I'm hungry. Oh, I called George while I was at LAX. He wants us to stop by, and he said to bring them some cheese steaks."

Romeo laughed. "You have to fly in from Los Angeles to take your brother some cheese steaks? What's up with that?"

"It's a joke thing, about you picking me up instead of him. I said I would."

"Yeah, we can do that." Romeo tapped his friend on the stomach. "Although you look like you don't need to be eating cheese steaks, if you ask me. Debora sure fed you well while you were out there."

Andy's smile had no humor in it. "Yeah, she did do that," he said.

Romeo looked at his friend as they walked. "I'm sorry, I was just messing with you. Too bad you two weren't able to make it. That was a big move on your part. You okay with it?"

Am I okay with it? Andy cocked his head as they approached the baggage carousel. "I wish it could be different, I want it different, but it is what it is, you know? Her girls might have eventually accepted me, but getting to that probably needed more patience than either of us had. And that wasn't all of it. We're both carrying baggage from school."

The carousel lurched and began to spin. After retrieving his two suitcases, they made their way to the parking lot. Andy placed his bags in the trunk and back seat of Romeo's Honda Accord. They played bi-coastal catch up during the drive through the city.

"Did you see Minister David?" Romeo asked. "He went out to monitor the opening of the trial of that deputy who shot the pregnant sister."

"No, we crisscrossed, I guess. I wanted to stop at the courthouse yesterday but I just ran out of time. Wonder what this shooting of sisters is all about? She's the second one out there this year."

"Black men *and* women have no rights they are bound to respect," Romeo said, his face suddenly cold with memory. "Back in 1857 when they wrote that, they just didn't have to even mention women is all that is. Hey man, the piece you wrote on the Tanya Morris shooting was first rate," Romeo said as they started out of the airport. "And the sidebar summary on wrongful shootings going unpunished. I'm really glad you'll be working here with us full time. So is Minister Johnnie. He was really impressed. Said you've grown into a strong reporter."

In the throes of an epileptic seizure in her car, Tanya Morris had managed

2236

to pull off the road and lock her car doors. She took a pistol from her purse and placed it in her lap, and then used her cell phone to summon help from relatives. An uncle had called the sheriff's station. Three deputies responded. One spotted the pistol and shouted "Gun!" The other two fired three times from behind, killing the young woman instantly. City authorities ruled her death justifiable homicide. In their analysis, the deputies had good reason to believe their lives were in jeopardy.

Andy smiled at the compliment from the Covenant's founder, Teacher and soon-to-be Teacher Emeritus. His son, David, was his successor, currently called the Teacher-Designate. Minister Johnnie Walker, now in his mid-sixties, was the youngest old man Andy knew. "Thanks, I appreciate it. From what I read, the Minister seems busier than ever. I thought he was retiring. He doesn't know how to retire, does he?"

When Romeo didn't say anything, Andy glanced over at him. He sensed that Romeo was taking his time with a response. He spoke after they were in traffic and moving along the freeway. "It's partly that, and partly something else that's been hard for me to pin down. He's said he's turning the leadership over to David, but..." He fell silent again. "If I didn't know better, I'd almost say he lacks confidence in David. I think he doubts his ability to lead the Covenant."

That puzzled Andy, too. He, and almost the entire national Covenant membership, assumed that David Walker had been groomed from childhood to succeed his father.

"David's not as political as his father is," Andy said. "He talks the talk, but it's just not deep down in him."

"Yeah, a lot of Covenant people realized that when he wanted to go to Penn State instead of Howard, where Minister Johnnie has such a legacy and connections. Not that Howard is a bastion of militancy." They both laughed. "I hate to say this, and I wouldn't to anyone but you, but it's not like David is ultra-spiritual either. I mean, it's hard to fill Minister Johnnie's shoes, but so many Saturdays I hear David saying all the right things but it feels mechanical, you know?"

"Rome, I thought it was just me feeling that way, which is not something I would say to anyone but you either," Andy said.

"Maybe David has to grow into it." Romeo fell quiet again. Finally, he said, "Andy, you are my best friend, practically family. There's more to why I feel this and I can't discuss it now. I will when I can. It has nothing to do with trust."

"You didn't even have to say that much," Andy said. "I understand it's like that sometime. You supervise the *Scabbard*, you're chief of staff, and I'm rank and file who doesn't need to know a lot of stuff."

"That's another thing. I'm no longer chief of staff. Minister Johnnie just placed me in a new job. Basically, I'm Minister Johnnie's special assistant. It's like being chief of staff with more work. I believe the Swords commandant will get the chief

14

of staff job, and that they'll promote somebody, maybe Glenn Greene, to replace him."

"You okay with that?"

"Oh, hell yes. I love working with Minister Johnnie. I would lay my life down for that man. He saved my life." Romeo turned off at the Liberty Heights exit near his home. Andy wondered how deep the political intrigue went. It's better I don't know, he thought to himself.

"How's Jhanae?" Andy asked, deliberately changing the subject. Plus, no need trying to front and pretend I don't want to know, he thought.

"I'll just give you the short version for now and explain the details later okay?" Romeo said. He turned into a mini-mall and parked in front of a steak and pizza shop doing vigorous business. There was a line at the takeout counter and several people waiting for seats.

"Jhanae has started back in the Covenant," Romeo continued. "Not like when you two were together, but she's back." He paused. "She's seeing a brother named Wardell Keyes, which is a story in itself. If David has his way, I'll be working with him some. I think she's back because of him. They're engaged."

It had been five years, he had been in another relationship, and still he felt heaviness in his stomach at the news. He tried to ignore the residue of jealousy still lingering over his ex-wife.

"I am starved," Andy said. "Let's eat our sandwiches here and you can give me the gory details."

That would be Jhanae, he thought. If some man told her to come back, she'd be listening to him instead of herself. Her submissiveness had been interesting and ego satisfying on one level, boring on another. He'd joined the Covenant because she was there, but stayed because of himself. He felt, but couldn't prove, that she left to create distance between them.

"I thought you were over it," Romeo said after they had ordered their sandwiches and a pitcher of homemade-style iced tea.

"I thought I was over it, too, Rome," Andy said after a while. "And I am over it. I'm just reflecting, I guess. I wasn't all that religious, and I came to see what the Covenant was about because it was part of her life. I mean, even you couldn't get me but so interested." He smiled without mirth. "She was just plain 'Janet' then. I didn't join to please her, but I did come because of her interest. So now she's back, possibly to please somebody. It's just funny, man."

"I hear you," Romeo said. "There's not that much more to tell, actually. Wardell has worked his way into the leadership of Swords of the Master. He's part of David's security detail. Now David wants to start something new, where all leadership has security with them virtually all the time. He wants Wardell with me and I'm resisting. It's not very spiritual of me, but I don't like the man. And that has nothing to do with Jhanae. I felt that way when he first showed up about four years ago."

Andy sipped his drink. He vaguely remembered Wardell Keyes. A tall man, about thirty, who looked as if he worked out a lot and had something of a military bearing, which would be good in the Swords of the Master.

Romeo decided to change the subject. "As senior reporter on our modest staff, you're going to have a really tough workload. There's all the regular daily stuff. And Minister Johnnie and Minister David both want us to look into these shootings of unarmed black folks with as much depth as we have resources for. I have an assistant named Claudia Greene who'll be a big help with the research." Romeo cocked his head and smiled, as if he'd just thought of something clever. "You'll like Claudia," he said.

"Does Minister Johnnie believe there's any connection between the shootings?"

Romeo emptied his glass of iced tea, refilled it. "No, he doesn't. I don't, either. We've found nothing at all to make us think that, other than the climate in the country since Hugh Bruder became president. I don't have to tell you, this man makes both Bushes look like flaming liberals. I think it's much simpler than a connection or a conspiracy. More like an unspoken license to kill."

The waiter arrived with their food. Andy immediately started wolfing his sandwich down. Not only was he famished, it was his first authentic cheese steak in two years.

"I think it's what it's always been historically," Romeo said, picking the conversation up again. "Contempt for black people, and not much regard for our lives.

"For instance, Tanya Morris," Romeo said. "If that had been a white woman with a pistol in her lap, she'd still be alive. Those deputies would have taken that extra moment, and would have seen she was sick. They *knew* she was sick, her uncle's call said so. They would have fired only if she had pointed it at one of them. Witnesses say Tanya never pointed the gun.

"Now take the story you covered last year, the one on Delores Olds. To my surprise, Sales is about to go on trial for murder two, and could do as much as ten years if he's convicted. And you know the brothers in the joint will have something for his ass when he gets there!"

"They will literally have something for his ass," Andy said. They both chuckled at the sordid image.

"This messed up system may actually work every now and then," Romeo said. "But the downside is there's an all white jury. The suburb where Olds lives is in a county that's overwhelmingly white. So maybe we shouldn't celebrate just yet."

He looked at his watch. "As soon as he brings the cheese steaks for George and Marian, we can roll."

"Yeah, I've caught a second wind," Andy said. "It'll be good to see old Nappy Head. That's what I used to call him when we were kids, just to make him mad."

About the same time the two friends sat down with their sandwiches, iced tea and memories, Carl Harris, who lived three doors from George on Dock Street, got involved in a fender bender on nearby Dock Place with a man named Michael Patrick.

TWO

Black homeowners in the unit block of Dock Street, with two exceptions, refused to sell their property when gentrification edged into the Riverfront District.

They liked their manicured block of old red brick row homes, white marble steps, and cobblestone streets. The Dock Street Homeowners Association had always fought mightily against developers, the city, and anyone else who even thought about wanting their homes or tearing up the nearly two-hundred-year-old cobblestones on their block.

On the north side of Dock Street were the backyards and heavy boxlike oak fences of the neat brick row homes on Bay Street, the next street over. The Dock Street homes were similarly situated except their backyard oak fences and gates on the south faced an alley even narrower than tiny Dock Street. "No parking" signs policed the alley. Although the narrow thoroughfare had no street sign, city records officially listed it as Dock Place. Full-sized automobiles could negotiate the narrow thoroughfare if drivers moved slowly with caution and care.

Thirty-one garages lined the south side of Dock Place; many belonged to Dock Street and Bay Street residents. But several rented out to anyone with four hundred dollars monthly for the rent.

Garage 031 rented to Carl Harris, a deacon and God-fearing man, and also a longtime homeowner on Dock Street. He and his wife, Amanda, kept the family car, a Toyota Camry, in a space on Dock Street. (Only residents with permits could park there.) Amanda Harris usually drove the Camry. Carl Harris kept his black Mercedes Benz, purchased almost six years earlier as his retirement present to himself, in 031.

On this night, he backed out as he always did, and cut his wheel quickly, as he always did. The crunching noise behind him, in front of Garage 030, made him grimace. His Mercedes had its first dent.

"God damn it! God damn it to hell!" a voice inside Garage 030 said.

Michael Patrick, already in a foul mood, boiled over when he heard the crunch and saw what caused it. His fight with Kathy had started his day off wrong.

18

His game plan was to go out on the lake, get a little bit, at least get some head, and then take her out for the evening. But, no, she didn't feel well, she said. And then her phone rang. The tone of the conversation told him it was her ex-husband. Supposed to be ex, anyway. When she hung up, the two of them argued, and he left. He bought a fifth of Red Mountain and met up with his friend Garth Wilson. He and his buddy had been tasting from it off and on since. They had almost made it to the halfway mark. Now this shit. Now this goddamned shit.

Wilson, a tall, taciturn man who looked amazingly like a young Gary Cooper, tried to calm him down as the two of them came out of the garage. They had a double date coming up and he tried to tell Mike to let it slide. But Patrick wasn't having it.

He should have known better than to rent space over here with these jungle bunnies anyway, he thought. He had nothing against black people; hell, he worked with quite a few of them and they all got along fine. But, in hindsight, he should have spent the extra hundred a month and rented near the Marina Boat Club. He's here three months and look what happened.

Carl Harris stopped and got out. As he looked at the point of contact, Michael Patrick stormed out of 030. The Mercedes' right taillight was shattered, right next to an ugly foot-long gash scarring the black paint. The frame of the boat trailer pushed in, twisted awkwardly where it met the Mercedes. The boat, a twenty-two-foot fiberglass, was undamaged.

"Look, I'm really sorry," Carl Harris said. "I'm really sorry. It was my fault. I didn't see your trailer. I have insurance."

"Fuck insurance! What is your fucking problem? Do you know how much that trailer costs? Do you know how much that boat costs?" Michael Patrick ran his hand over his slicked back black hair. He was a large man, about two hundred pounds. His ruddy face scowled as he strode close to the shorter man. Carl Harris instinctively stepped back, but not before catching a whiff of stale alcohol on Michael Patrick's breath. Wilson stood back, quiet. He knew his friend's temper, especially after he'd had a couple.

"Look, I thought I had enough room," he said. "I'll call my insurance company as soon as you give me your information. The trailer looks expensive, and I'm really sorry." Discomfort kept his words softer than usual. He went out of his way to avoid trouble. He wasn't a wimp, just a quiet retiree who liked to keep peace on their mostly quiet street.

"Yeah, well, I'm sorry, too, you know? I am really fucking sorry." As Michael Patrick paced and waved his arms, his windbreaker opened. For one heart stopping moment, Carl Harris thought he saw a holstered pistol on the man's right hip. Maybe it was a shadow. "So what are we going to do about sorry, huh? What should we do about sorry? Man, I am so pissed at you right now. Do you know how much this trailer costs?"

Mister Harris, his black Tyrolean felt hat pushed back on his sweaty forehead, backed away slowly as he spoke to the angry trailer owner. "I told you, I'm willing to pay ____"

"But what am I supposed to do tonight?" His voice grew louder, higher-pitched. "I have a woman waiting to go out with me, and what am I supposed to do about that? You are a real pain in my ass right now, you know that?"

Windows opened. The first window open belonged to Mrs. Saunders, a one-woman Neighborhood Watch. She was also a woman who took no tea for the fever.

Amanda Harris, arms folded across her ample bosom, stood at the back gate of their home. She had walked out as soon as she heard the commotion and her husband's voice in the middle of it. Mouth in a tight line, she started toward the two men. Her son Richard, a man about forty, appeared at the gate as she left it.

"Carl, get his information and let's go on in the house," Amanda Harris said.

"Mom, what's going on?" Richard asked.

"What's going on down there?" Mrs. Saunders called from her window.

"Your father's having trouble with the white man," Amanda Harris replied to her son.

Michael Patrick turned in her direction. "Shut up, you goddamn nigger bitch!" he said.

A shadow of anger passed like an apparition over Carl Harris' face. His mouth tightened. He started moving toward his wife. Anger tightened her son's features. More second floor windows opened.

"Who do you think you're talking to?" Richard said as he moved toward Michael Patrick and his father.

"Richard, stop, don't make it any worse, please," his mother said. She had stopped at the sound of his voice. She blocked his path as he tried to confront Michael Patrick. "Please," she said again, placing her hands on his chest.

"Now that wasn't necessary," Carl Harris said. "That wasn't necessary at all."

"Ask God why he made her a nigger bitch and you a honky," Mrs. Saunders shouted. "Get your white ass away from here!"

Time seemed to stop as Michael Patrick reached under his windbreaker. He withdrew a Glock 9mm automatic pistol. Carl Harris and his wife both stopped in mid-stride. Michael Patrick pointed the barrel upward. "I want to kill a nigger," he said. His voice was flat, matter-of-fact. "I want to kill a nigger so goddamned bad I can taste it." Michael Patrick's flushed face glistened with perspiration, despite the coolness of the fall evening. His friend, Garth Wilson, grimaced but said nothing.

"Someone call the police," a voice said, softly but firmly. Another voice: "I'll do it." The suggestion was loud enough for Garth Wilson to hear, and he quietly moved toward the corner to look for police.

Almost half the back doors on the block were open now. Most, but not all, of the occupants were black. There was a white graduate student from the university. He rented a room from a friend of his family. A murmur followed the charged moment of seeing Michael Patrick's gun. The low collage of conversation along the small street carried a texture of its own, voices familiar with each other, neighbors trying to comprehend what they were seeing. Mister Harris was a good man who never, ever started trouble. What in the world was this mess?

Michael Patrick placed his left hand below his right hand gripping the pistol, his forefinger extended along the side of the trigger guard.

"What's going on, Richard?" George Bascomb, wearing a blue T-shirt, asked as he walked up to his neighbor. He, too, had been attracted to the commotion.

"Hey, George. Damned if I know, man," Richard said, his voice low. "I'm just coming from the video store and the Seven-Eleven, and heard this white dude giving Dad some shit about hitting his boat trailer. He needs to put that gun away, that's what he needs to do."

"You people back up, this is none of your business!" Michael Patrick moved the gun in an arc, first to his right, then to his left. He moved backward, trying to keep anyone from getting behind him.

George looked to his own left, and eased away from the others, beyond Patrick's peripheral vision. He took what looked like a wooden slat about two feet long from a tall silver trash can sitting just inside the Harris' gate.

The white man gestured with the gun toward Harris. "C'mere, we got to settle this. Come here, you hear me?" He pointed the barrel toward the sky again. The sudden *pop!* split the air, loud and angry. People flinched; several audible gasps raised the fear level, tightening everyone's breath.

Later, in court, Richard Harris would be the only one to testify that he saw a man, later identified as Raymond Hayes, get out of a white pickup at the corner with his gun already drawn. At first, Richard would testify, he thought the tall, slender white man in the dark blue uniform with his gun drawn was a police officer. Harris would testify that Patrick's friend, Garth Wilson, left the scene briefly and came back with Hayes. Wilson, too, drew a licensed pistol at the sound of his friend's shot.

"All right, all right, move back! What's going on here?" Raymond Hayes barked, his gun pointed in the air. He moved into the small street with a sense of authority. "Sir, you okay?"

Michael Patrick glanced quickly at the newcomer, smiled a faint smile. "Yeah, I'm fine, as soon I get these people back off me." He gestured to Carl Harris, his son, and a third man. "You, you, and you, put your hands against the wall. I mean you—move, goddammit!"

Confused and reluctant to turn their backs on him, the three men nonetheless moved toward the closest wall.

In turning to see the uniformed man rendering assistance—who everyone now realized was a rent-a-cop—Michael Patrick didn't see George Bascomb move quietly behind him, clasping the slat. Nor did Raymond Hayes or Garth Wilson.

Others did; the murmur dropped, imperceptible but definite. Those who saw George, even as they tried not to watch, held their breath.

George raised the slat. Raymond Hayes, glancing over his shoulder, shouted almost simultaneously. Michael Patrick pivoted just as George swung; the slat struck a glancing blow on his shoulder. George backed away quickly, chagrin visible in his eyes and wrinkled forehead.

Raymond Hayes tried to watch the crowd and the new drama simultaneously. The barrel of his gun now pointed at Richard Harris and those standing near him. Wilson stood frowning, the barrel of his pistol pointed at the ground.

Michael Patrick's eyes narrowed. He planted his feet into a firing stance. A woman's voice wailed, incongruously commingling love and fear, her words high and trembling. "Baby, leave it alone, please! C'mon now, leave it alone, George."

"Drop the stick. Drop it, goddammit!" Michael Patrick said in a voice bloated with tightness and fear disguised as anger.

George, holding the stick, continued to backpedal, widening the distance between them.

"Oh dear God! George!"

"Drop it, I said. One__"

George crouched, continued to back away, his left hand holding the slat extended perpendicular to his body.

"Two__"

The report of the gun somehow sounded louder, more horrible, than the first shot. George's eyes filled with disbelief as shock quickly suffused his nervous system. His legs buckled; he dropped to his knees.

People screamed. One scream rose like an eagle above the rest. The uniformed white man struggled with the woman who screamed, but she broke away and fell on her knees next to her stricken husband. She moaned his name in unholy sobs, embraced him, and rocked his head against her chest as he collapsed in her arms. The uniformed man reached for her but her aura of unrestrained grief slowed him, made his movement awkward. She shook him off as the shooter leveled his weapon at the crowd, swung it in an arc of containment. Wilson, too, had his gun leveled now.

"I've got fifteen more! Who wants them?" he yelled. Michael Patrick's face twisted into an almost feral snarl. "Get out of here, you black bitch!" he yelled as the uniformed man struggled to pull the sobbing woman away.

A red blotch, wet and silent, grew on George's pale blue T-shirt, staining a stylized California sun glowing above the name of the state.

Michael Patrick looked down at his chest, expecting to see his badge. He cursed under his breath and reached into his breast pocket. With his free hand, he threw the lanyard around his neck; the leather holder settled against his chest like a miniature shield. In the holder was the oblong silver badge of the city's police department.

He grabbed the holder, held the badge like an exorcist using a cross in front of a vampire. He moved to George Bascomb as his life fluids leaked from his body onto the ancient cobblestones of Dock Place. He kicked the moaning man in his rib cage.

"Shut up, dammit," he growled. "Shut up."

Sounds and images coalesced, bleeding into, against, through each other: sirens, frantic and growing louder ... everything suddenly awash in flickering, blinking reds and blues ... a high-pitched scream rending the night and her neighbors' souls ... George Bascomb moaning, his eyes rolled back in their sockets ... cursing people ... crackling static and voices murmuring matter-of-factly on a radio: "Shots fired ... officer needs assistance ... suspect wounded ... emergency ... .

The police placed Carl Harris, handcuffed, into a cruiser. His son, also handcuffed, went into another patrol car. George Bascomb, no longer moving, was also handcuffed.

"They killed George! They killed George! Why? Why?" The word drew itself out, quivering with pain bordering on dementia. Two women stood with Bascomb's widow. The crying woman held her stomach, bent at the waist,

23

keening her helpless lament to no one in particular, and to everyone.

Someone un-spooled yellow crime scene tape and started cordoning off the area. Six police officers created a human barrier around two angry men.

"Naw, that ain't right! What the fuck's wrong with y'all? They didn't do nothing! You ought to be locking up that cracker cop! No, get your hands off me, I'll say what I want . . . Look, don't touch me . . . TAKE ME TO JAIL, I DON'T GIVE A DAMN!"

A tall officer in a tweed sport coat with a badge draped from its breast pocket approached them. His chocolate skin glistened with perspiration. The human barrier separated for him.

"I have not been having a good day, and it's gotten worse. If I touch you, I'm going to jack you up," he said to the short loud man, who wore a baseball cap turned backward. The cop pointed his finger close to the target of his wrath. Over six feet tall, the cop towered over the squat, broad-shouldered man.

Baseball Cap started to say something, seemed to measure his chances, and then closed his mouth.

"Now you keep it like this. Don't make me come back over here, or you'll have an interfering with an officer charge, along with anything else I can think up." The squat man glowered but said nothing. The cop pivoted and walked back to the area around George Bascomb, now covered by a white sheet.

Anger swept through Dock Place like a slow moving storm. One man turned toward a telephone pole as he felt the contents of his stomach moving upward. He leaned over just as his stomach contracted violently. Salty, oatmeal-looking liquid spilled from him with a will of its own.

"They killed my husband! They killed him!" The sobs, and her loud, anguished, achingly raw exhalations of breath tried to expel the pain. For many of her neighbors, her pain drowned out everything else.

The first ranking detective on the scene, the man in the tweed sports coat, took Michael Patrick's gun, placed it in an evidence envelope, and had him escorted to a police cruiser out of sight of Dock Place. Walking to the cruiser, Michael Patrick asked one of his escorts if he had any chewing gum or mints. The officer looked at him. He produced a package of mints; Patrick took two.

Inside the cruiser, the reality of his first shooting started to sink in. Michael Patrick inhaled deeply, and then let it out. He leaned his head back against the car seat. He remembered a bottle of Visine in his trousers pocket. He held it up and saw that he had half a bottle left. Tilting his head back, he placed two drops in each eye. Eyes closed, he savored the momentary coolness.

Officer Michael Patrick's thoughts tumbled over one another: The man shouldn't have come at him with that stick. They could have settled everything if only the man hadn't come at him. What was it Bulldog had told him? "My boy, you can't trust any of the scum out there." Bulldog said it at least once each time he saw him. At least, it seemed that way. A man attacking a cop with a stick was certainly scum. He willed himself to ignore the feelings in the pit of his stomach.

He opened the cigarettes in his windbreaker breast pocket and asked a colleague standing outside the cruiser for a light. The first drag moved his mind away from the tension in his gut. He opened his cell phone, punched on the speed dial directory and selected Kathy's number.

"Kathy? Hi, babe . . . No, I'm still in the city . . . Look, we've got a crime scene, babe, and I'm not going to be able to get back down there . . . It's going to be a while, because I'm involved . . . I was assaulted by this black guy, he came at me with a piece of wood . . . Yeah, I'm okay. But he's not . . . Do me a favor, will you? Call your father and tell him what's going on, will you? . . . It's in the Riverfront area . . . Thanks, babe . . . I'll call as soon as I can. Bye."

Knowing that Bulldog Hudson knew made him feel better right away. He knew how to handle things like this. In his time, Bulldog hadn't become a chief inspector without knowing his way around the block.

THREE

There is no time.

When Andy first heard the esoteric theory in one of Minister Johnnie's signature sermon/lectures, "There's Only Eternally Now," his mind found it a difficult concept to wrap around.

The phenomena called time slows, accelerates, stops, and does none of these things because the mind is doing them all, Minister Johnnie would expound on the Saturday mornings he plugged into discussing what he called "temporal illusion." Andy called them "occasions when the minister felt like getting deep."

As Romeo drove toward the sea of blinking red and blue lights between Dock Street and Dock Place, time felt for Andy as it always did. He wasn't thinking of Johnnie Walker's views. The pseudo-psychotic ambiance created by the police lights was familiar to both Andy and Romeo from attendance at dozens of crime scenes.

Romeo parked almost a block away. It was only as his friend locked the car that Andy whiffed a premonition, an uncertainty, felt a slight temblor low in his stomach. Once before, similar feelings had descended without warning: that summer day in 1990, in the moments just before he learned that his mother had collapsed after an aneurysm exploded the wall of an artery in her brain. He and Debora were lovers the first time around then, sophomores at John Upton Church, walking with arms around each other to his tiny studio apartment near campus. When they approached his building that day, time suddenly stopped for him when he saw his landlord, a note in his apartment door, and his next-door neighbor calling out to him simultaneously. The images shook his being before he even knew what was wrong.

On this balmy October night, it was the simultaneity of the yellow tape sealing off Dock Place, the remains of someone covered by a white sheet, and a woman's hoarse, choking sobs coating the overall turbulence of the moment. He knew.

Time stopped.

Andy felt as if he were part of a still photograph. A heightened sense of unreality saturated his next hours; events unreeled in slow motion, making it feel more like a day.

"It's George, Rome, I know it is." He heard terror in his own voice as he started under the yellow tape.

Romeo grabbed his arm. "Easy, Andy, let's see what happened. C'mon, man." He looked around for an officer in charge and pulled his press credentials from his pocket.

Andy's certainty unnerved Romeo; he was afraid his friend was right. Just then he saw Lieutenant Carvel Thomas, or rather recognized his familiar tweed sports coat and trademark police shield tie clip holding down a paisley-patterned tie. He had met Thomas on several stories. He knew him as a fair brother, considering he was a cop, a profession Romeo had held in contempt for almost a quarter century. "Carvel!" he shouted.

Thomas looked up, recognized Romeo, and signaled to give him a moment. He had similar feelings of respect for Romeo. The Covenant for the New Commandment was anti-cop in Thomas' eyes. But Butler seemed intelligent, unlike some vitriolic supporters who liked the Covenant's militancy.

Andy saw his sister-in-law. Seeing that she was the source of the anguished wails, he closed his eyes tight.

"It's George, Rome, I'm telling you, it's George." Hysteria welled in his chest. "What in the fuck has happened here? Who killed George?" Loud and high now, his voice knifed the night air and already existing pain. Heads turned, including Thomas'. Andy shook his head, struggling to comprehend his surroundings. "Who'd want to kill baby brother?"

Romeo saw Marian moments after Andy did. Heat seared his own chest.

Thomas, his visage grim, walked over to the two men. "Hey, Butler," he said. "What can I do for you?" He glanced at Andy as he shook hands with Romeo. His eyes had the cautious, alert tone that Romeo had long ago dubbed "the cop look."

"This is my friend, Andy Blackman. If the deceased is a man named George Bascomb, we're here for personal reasons more than professional ones," Romeo said. "We can talk later. And we'd like to come inside the tape, as a personal favor."

Thomas frowned. "You related to Bascomb?"

Something crumbled inside Andy. "I knew it! I knew it!"

"George is Andy's brother," Romeo said.

Thomas sighed. It was a part of the job he could never get used to. "I'm sorry, I really am," he said. He lifted the tape. "I can't let you near the body. And if your friend loses control, I'll have to have him escorted out. You understand."

"Deal," Romeo said. "What happened?"

Thomas looked uncomfortable. "It's an officer-involved shooting, that's all I can tell you now. We've just started our investigation."

Tears welled in Romeo's eyes. Officer-involved. Here we are again. He put an arm around his friend's shoulder. "C'mon, Andy. Marian needs us, man."

Andy half heard the conversation. Dazed, he let Romeo lead him under the tape. They headed straight for Marian Bascomb.

Marian seemed near collapse. She still cried but tears no longer came. Inconsolable, she sat on the curb, her head on a neighbor's shoulder, rocking back and forth. George's blood stained her white running suit.

At first Marian recognized neither Andy nor Romeo. When she did, she tried to greet them. Only a strangled, exhausted cough commingled with sobbing came from her contorted face. Andy hugged her tight. Romeo scowled, removed his glasses, and pulled a wall down around his emotions.

A muted anger hovered over Dock Place. You heard it in the low rumbles of conversation. You saw it in the hunched postures of onlookers, in the sullen sideways glances directed at anyone appearing and looking official.

Andy's reddened eyes glanced at the white sheet lying over his brother's body ten yards away. Two small cardboard tents with the numbers "1" and "2" on them sat on the ground next to chalk circles surrounding the shells from Michael Patrick's pistol. Not far from that, a wooden stick about two feet long had chalk marks around it.

Romeo followed Andy's glance and leaned over to his friend. "I'm going to see what I can get from Thomas," he said. "You stay here with Marian, okay?"

Andy nodded. Romeo looked around, saw the lieutenant and happened to catch his eye. When Thomas moved his head up and down imperceptibly, Romeo extracted a reporter's notebook from his inside jacket pocket and walked over to Thomas.

"How much can you tell me?" Romeo asked.

Thomas looked around. Other reporters clustered at the yellow tape, waiting for the briefing he had promised them. "Do me a favor. Put your notebook away," he said. "They're already feeling dissed because you're on this side of the tape and they're not. I don't have much anyway. You can memorize it. How's your friend doing?"

"As well as can be expected," Romeo said. "Carvel, I knew George Bascomb. It's hard to believe he's on the receiving end of an OIS."

Thomas remained stone-faced. "Earlier this evening, at approximately seven p.m., there was a verbal altercation here between another individual, not the deceased, and an off-duty police officer."

"Names?" Romeo asked.

"Carl Harris was the individual in the altercation," Thomas said. "We're not releasing the name of the officer yet. Probably in the morning. During this altercation between Harris and the officer, the deceased—Bascomb—took a piece of wood, a board, and attacked the off-duty officer. When the suspect refused to drop the wood, the officer fired one shot."

"Was the officer in uniform, in plainclothes, on duty, what? What were the circumstances of the officer being there?"

Romeo thought Thomas' eyes narrowed. "The officer was in plainclothes," he said. "He had a dispute with Mister Harris. It appears there was a traffic accident with Harris' car and the officer's boat trailer, a fender bender. One thing led to another, and then Bascomb got involved. Look, Butler, that's all we have now. If you call the Horseshoe in the morning, we can fax you a news release."

On one level, Romeo knew Thomas was giving him what he could. On another level, his gut told him there was more to this. He remembered the early official statements coming in from the West Coast on Tanya Morris. The authorities tried to keep the emphasis on the gun in Tanya's lap. But Andy's reporting from interviews with eyewitnesses—every eyewitness—said that Morris appeared almost unconscious and in no way made threatening moves.

"Thanks, Carvel," Romeo said. "I owe you one, man. I'll call you in the morning." He looked around at the crowd. A middle-aged woman stood off to the side, speaking with agitation to two neighbors. A good place to start.

Amanda Harris had her arms folded as if she were hugging herself. "Why? Why would they arrest Carl? This mess don't make no sense at all!" She shook her head in anguish. "Why don't they arrest that no good cop? He started all this mess. He killed George. He didn't have to shoot him! He started it all!" Her voice broke. She shook her head. Romeo saw that she'd been crying.

The woman to her right placed an arm around her. "Amanda, it's going to be all right," the woman said. "They can't charge Carl with anything. Probably just took him down for questioning. Come on now, you have to trust Jesus." Her voice was calming but unconvincing.

"In handcuffs? They have to take him for questioning in handcuffs?" Amanda saw Romeo at that moment, looked at the press card hanging on a lanyard around his neck. "Yes?" she said, her eyes wary. "Who are you?"

"Romeo Butler, ma'am," he replied. "I write for the *Scabbard*, the newspaper of Covenant of the New Commandment."

"I know what the *Scabbard* is," Amanda Harris said. "At least you'll tell the truth about how they treat black people."

Romeo said nothing. He took out his notebook and a ballpoint pen, kept it out of view by holding it close.

"There's no reason that white racist cop had to kill George," she said, spitting the words through clenched teeth. "No one knew that dog was a cop, and even if they did, he was out of control. Am I right, Theresa?"

Theresa had dropped her arm from Amanda Harris' shoulder. She held her hands in front of her mouth. "Completely out of control," she said. "He acted like a crazy man. Then he comes pulling his badge out after he shot George. Almost like he was saying that the badge made it okay, you know what I'm saying?"

"You're sure he showed his badge after he shot George?"

"Of course I'm sure. I was standing right there," Theresa said, pointing.

"That man will answer to his Maker when judgment comes, believe me," Amanda Harris said. "My God will deal with him. He will pay for this night."

She told Romeo about the accident and her husband's willingness to cooperate with Michael Patrick. "But he was just so ugly! So belligerent. I'll never forget what he said when he pulled that gun out. 'I want to kill a nigger,' he said. 'I want to kill a nigger so bad I can taste it.' Then he shot George. And they take my Carl to jail in handcuffs."

Romeo thanked the women. He looked around at the knots of people. He interviewed several, aware of the morose eyes of all who had witnessed the shooting. One man said he had cursed the police and almost been arrested. As people talked, Romeo not only saw what they saw, he felt what they felt. What are the chances? Two friends, and two brothers, suffer the same fate? But there was something else, something more ancient.

The sullen eyes veiled a centuries-old rage. He saw the look so many times in the eyes of those who felt like he did. A look that surely was in the eyes of millions after being snatched from their ancestral homes. The look, the rage, had been chained down on the ships, looking for an escape at every turn. Eyes like these looked at strange people with weapons stronger than their own weapons. Eyes glared on countless ships, eyes praying for a moment to disarm and kill. A few got the chance; most did not. In the cotton fields, the rage in these eyes simmered as sweat poured like rain, burning the eyes, but not burning as hot as the rage. A sheen of fear coated the rage when armed white-sheeted devils wearing the cross of Christ on their breasts rode roughshod over their unpaved roads.

Sometimes, when their rifles were present, the rage spoke, expressed itself, and maybe even managed a grim smile. Sadists had muffled the rage on auction blocks like the one standing less than two miles away in this northern city. Shame and rage mingled in those eyes as strange pale beings looked at them as if they were sheep or cows. These same eyes once sulked in cotton fields, once witnessed loved ones pulled from their homes in pre-dawn darkness. These eyes knew countless George Bascombs. If the goddess of justice of their adversaries was indeed blind, she somehow winked at their captors, assailants, and murderers from beneath her blindfold.

As Romeo closed his notebook, he saw Andy coming toward him. "Hey man, how you doing?"

"It's still sinking in, Rome," Andy said. "I told Marian I'd come by tomorrow. She's in bad shape. Look, I want to cover this if it's okay with you."

"Do you think you're up to it?"

Andy nodded. "I want to keep busy. And I think George would want me to. I need to do this, Rome."

The two friends embraced. "I was just thinking about your brother," Andy said. "Getting blown away by a John Wayne cop. The same damn thing, twenty-five years apart. What are the chances?"

"I was thinking the same thing a little bit ago. It's unreal."

As they started toward Romeo's car, a portly young man in his twenties approached. "I saw you talking to Miss Amanda and Miss Theresa," he said to Romeo. "You a reporter?"

"Yeah, I am." Romeo extended his hand. "We both are. I'm Romeo Butler. This is Andy Blackman."

"Jonathan Gardiner," the young man said. He wore a baseball cap turned backwards, a pullover sweater, and the straight-legged jeans that had started to replace the baggy look about two years earlier. Jonathan looked around, lowered his voice. "I live over there. I saw the whole thing. If you can come by tomorrow, I want you to check out something."

"What is it?" Romeo asked.

Jonathan looked around as he spoke. He kept his voice low. "I don't even want to talk about it now. I'm not trying to sound paranoid or anything, I'd just rather you stop by tomorrow if you can. After these damn cops are gone."

The young man's earnestness impressed Romeo. "Checking out things" led to dead ends more often than it did to stories. Still, he made it a habit to follow through until he saw the dead end. You never knew.

"Here's my number," Romeo said. He handed Jonathan a business card. "Let me have yours. And your address."

"When I was small, I wanted to be a cop, you know?" Jonathan said after they made the exchange. "But I've been looking at what's been happening these last couple of years, things like what just happened to Mister Bascomb. Cops ain't shit, you know?"

"What makes you think it's been only recently?" Andy asked.

"Well, maybe I just started paying attention because it seems to be getting worse, you know?"

Romeo promised to call in the morning. "Andy will probably be the one coming by to see you," he said. They shook hands with each other and parted.

As they walked to the car, Romeo shared his briefing with Carvel Thomas with Andy, as well as his interview with Amanda Harris.

"Sounds like my brother was trying to do what too many of us don't do," Andy said. "Defend his neighborhood against a crazy who turned out to be a cop."

"And he didn't choose his weapon well," Romeo said.

They thought about the information they had, and the information they didn't have. Romeo remembered a tart comment from Theresa as he said goodbye to her and Amanda Harris. George's death, she said, was part of a "new open season on black people."

Romeo's phone rang; he looked at the incoming number. "It's Minister Johnnie. He's probably heard about it on the news." He clicked on. "Hi, Minister. Yes, sir, I know. I'm just leaving the crime scene now. The murder victim was Andy's half-brother. We were just coming over to see him, and he was dead when we got here . . . Yes sir, I will . . . I believe we can . . . Okay, fine."

Romeo clicked off. "Andy, Minister Johnnie not only sends his condolences, he'd like to see you. Do you feel up to it? "

Andy felt strange, almost euphoric. He didn't understand it or try to figure it out. It was probably some form of shock settling in. "Yeah, we can do that," he heard himself say. "It might be good for me."

"We won't stay long," Romeo said. "I know you're exhausted."

FOUR

hen Romeo drove onto the deserted headquarters meetinghouse parking lot, it occurred to Andy that, in all his years with the Covenant, he'd never been to a meetinghouse campus at night unless an event was taking place. The long rectangular lot was empty except for a black SUV sitting quietly in the shadows of an aging sycamore tree about fifteen yards from the building entrance. Romeo flicked his headlights three times. The headlights of the SUV flicked once.

The stone structure almost a century old, the narrow ribbon of lawn surrounding the corner building, and the near-deserted parking lot exuded a quiet air of sanctuary. Although the building had a security system, the SUV signaled the presence of Minister Johnnie, Minister David, or both. Although Minister Johnnie insisted on calling Covenant buildings "meetinghouses" instead of "churches" or "temples," this headquarters building nonetheless felt like a church. In fact, it had been an austere Jewish-American school/community center until the Covenant bought it in 1973 after "the neighborhood had started changing" about five years after the organization's founding.

Andy and Romeo both heard the muffled voices of anger as soon as they got out of the car. Both men looked toward the sole window spilling light onto the parking lot. Minister Johnnie was in Minister David's face, animatedly making a point about something. David tried to turn away; his father grabbed him by the shoulder and turned him back. Andy and Romeo weren't close enough to hear what was being said or see expressions. Perplexed, they looked at each other, said nothing, and walked to the building. Romeo had a key and opened the front door.

Minister Johnnie's office was in the corridor that ran to the left of the entrance. As Andy and Romeo approached, they heard Minister Johnnie, talking over David, say something about "handling your liquor." The voices stopped when Romeo knocked on the reinforced wooden door to Minister Johnnie's study.

"It's open," Minister Johnnie said. He was already at the door when they opened it. Without a word, he first embraced Romeo.

He looked at Andy, his eyes questioning. "How you doing, man?" he asked with a deliberate casualness.

"I'm not okay, Minister," Andy said. "No need lying about it."

Minister Johnnie engulfed him in one of his patented bear hugs. He was a big man, an imposing presence at six foot, four inches, who, at sixty-four, looked as if he might still crank out a four hundred meter run in well under sixty seconds. In his glory days at Howard, he'd consistently hit forty-four flat.

"It's an awful welcome home. I'm so sorry. But the Covenant is glad to have you back. I know Romeo's told you how much I appreciated the work you did in Los Angeles. You're one of our best reporters anywhere in the country."

"Thank you, Minister."

"You ask George's widow if there's anything we can do, anything at all."

"I will, sir."

David sat quietly, his back to them, looking out the window. He turned but didn't stand as his father waved the two men to seats on an oversized black leather sofa in front of a ceiling-high bookcase that was filled to overflowing.

"Hello, Andy," the younger Walker said. "I know of you but somehow I don't think we've ever formally met. I'm really sorry to hear about what happened to your brother," David said. "My condolences."

"Thank you," Andy said. He wondered why this sensation that felt like euphoria, but wasn't, was still with him.

David looked at Romeo. "How's it going?"

"It's going good, David," Romeo said, sinking down on the sofa and settling back. "How you doing?"

"I'm making it."

Minister Johnnie had placed a compact disc in the player of his handsome mahogany entertainment center. European orchestral music softly and slowly entered the room.

"It's called *Les Preludes*," Minister Johnnie said. He wheeled his black leather desk chair from behind his desk until he was near the three men. He sat and stretched his long legs out before him. "I've loved it since I was in high school. It's by Franz Liszt. I often play it when death visits. I play it because it's not morbid; it's triumphant. Andy, I hope it comforts you as it almost always comforts me."

He made a tent with his fingers. "When I was a boy, I sang with a community choir at Tubman Community House on the Avenue. It's not there anymore. Someone put lyrics to this and we sang it as *Preludes to Eternity*." He paused. "There is a line that says, 'Whence is our life but from God in heaven above?' The song is about all of this—this thing we call life—being a prelude, an introduction to something far more important."

Minister Johnnie closed his eyes as the melodic line became more muscular. Andy understood his leader was offering him spiritual comfort. He let the unfamiliar music wash over him.

He tried to adjust to Minister Johnnie's new look. For years, the older man had worn a striking Afro of moderate length. As he grew older, it became more impressive as it earned patches of grey. Two years ago, a bald spot began at the crown about the same time his hairline began to recede. Six months ago, Minister Johnnie startled his flock one Saturday morning by showing up at meeting with his head shaved clean and polished until it glistened.

Romeo gave the Teacher and his son a summary of the tragic events that had transpired on Dock Place earlier in the evening.

"Romeo, how many OIS deaths with black victims have you researched?" Minister Johnnie asked.

Romeo's response was immediate. "Before George's murder, there were twenty-six, Minister," he said. "Twenty-six in just under two years and four months. It's almost one a month."

Minister Johnnie scowled. "A century ago, we were being lynched at the rate of at least one a week. I guess some would say that things are better for us, that we're making progress." He looked at Romeo. "This is the second one in this city, is that correct?"

"Yes, sir. Nineteen months ago, an officer shot an unarmed black security guard leaving work about eleven at night. Some undercovers approached him about buying drugs. When the young man, Prentiss Dotson, got an attitude about being called a drug dealer, a fight broke out and one officer said he thought Dotson was reaching for a gun. Incidentally, the shooters were Puerto Rican, not white, as is usually the case. We also had a near fatal earlier this year. Two plainclothes rookies drew their guns on an almost routine traffic stop; the young man got scared and drove off. Said he didn't know they were cops and thought they were trying to jack him up. They shot him in the back and almost killed his nine-year-old niece sitting in the back. He survived but can't work; his niece is getting psychiatric care. No charges in either case. And here's an interesting note on the near fatal. An Internal Affairs investigation said the shooting violated policy almost every step of the way, but still no punishment or charges."

"The other homicides have taken place in just four states, all in the North," Romeo continued. "So these stats don't include the South, where we're certain there's a resurgence of terrorism being underreported and brushed aside as rumor and speculation.

"The rumor is that a spin-off group from the Conservative Christian Crusaders doesn't think the CCC's doing enough to thwart what they call 'black demands.' But we don't have any hard information yet. We have our Fellowships in Monroe and Atlanta investigating, but we just don't have the resources to pin too much down in that region. And mainstream media hasn't been reporting anything."

"We've never attracted people in the South," the Minister said. They heard the regret in his voice. "Just two Fellowships in forty-one years." He looked at Romeo, shaking his head. "Twenty-six murders."

"Yes, sir. And I need to stress that these twenty-six are African-Americans who were in no way involved in criminal behavior. I have a separate list of incidents where a crime was either in progress or there was a question about a crime. I call these twenty-six the 'Amadou Diallo Syndrome.' The closest case you could make for criminal conduct would be one of the three women killed in the L.A. area about two years ago. Her name was Eunice Valentine."

Minister Johnnie frowned. "I remember the name," he said. "She was the one with the gas bill?"

"Yes, sir, it was," Romeo said. "A little plump lady in her mid- to late thirties, distraught and frustrated because they wanted to shut her gas off. She threatened the gas company employees, and they came back with the cops. She threw a kitchen knife at the officer and missed by a wide margin. He and his partner could have arrested her easily at that point instead of shooting her. Coincidentally, Valentine's death was the only one I've found where the shooter was black, by the way."

Liszt's tone poem moved with grandeur now. Andy thought it almost sounded like a tribute to George. Fatigue and grief weighed him down; he felt almost groggy. "Romeo, do you have that seven-year-old shot in Arcadia, California, about nine months ago on the list?" Andy asked. "I wrote a brief when it happened, and I sent you the research afterward but I somehow never got back to writing the story after I learned all the heartbreaking details. It seemed like an exception to this other madness that's been going on."

"I don't have it on the list," Romeo said. "I don't think it belongs, as horrible as it was. Do you remember, Minister Johnnie?"

"If the *Scabbard* didn't have a big story, I don't think so," he replied. "I've gotten so I still read the dailies out of habit, but if it's a OneCorporation news account, either print, television, or the web, I take it with a grain, make that a basket, of salt."

"Tell him what you found, Andy," Romeo said.

"A suburban police officer got a call about a prowler. He went to the home and found the door ajar. He drew his weapon, went in and started securing each room. He came to a dimly lit bedroom, saw a figure in the shadows pointing a gun at him. He fired and killed a seven-year-old boy holding a toy pistol. It seems the mother had stepped next door to talk with a girlfriend. She had intended to stay two minutes and had been gone maybe fifteen, twenty minutes at the most. The police never said publicly why the prowler call was made; a concerned neighbor may have seen the door open, we don't know."

"The officer should have called for backup before going in," Romeo said. "But the tragedy still could have happened. I didn't put him down because I think he deserved to be absolved."

The minister's smile was wan. "Coming from you, my brother, that's a strong and powerful testament on the officer's integrity. What happened to the officer?"

"He was devastated and couldn't work anymore," Andy said. "He resigned from the force and was receiving professional counseling last I heard."

"I understand now why you had not forwarded that one to me on the confidential list I requested when you first came back from Los Angeles."

"What list is that?" David's voice was terse.

"It's not a list that concerns you, David," his father replied. "It's something I've been discussing with Romeo."

"I'm the Teacher-Designate, and it doesn't concern me?"

"Son, I said it doesn't concern you, and that should be sufficient," Minister Johnnie said, his voice even and controlled. "As far as you being Teacher-Designate, that can change. There are others who are capable of stepping up." He looked at Andy and Romeo. "Before you arrived, David and I were having a conversation about the future. His future, and the future of the Covenant of the New Commandment. I was expressing my displeasure about behavior I've observed."

The room grew quiet with discomfort.

"Why don't you say the rest of it?" David said finally. His words were tinged with bitterness.

"Because I made a choice not to go further, David," Minister Johnnie said, keeping his voice even. "You are my adult son and I love you even though you're behaving like a petulant child. I've said what I want to say about my feelings. The conversation is over. Don't make me go street on your ass."

When there was no reply, he looked at Romeo and Andy. "I wish you didn't have to hear that. I have given forty-one of my sixty-four years to building a haven, a sanctuary, a fortress for those of our people who want it. My son has the skills to take us to the next level, but he's got to do some serious self-examination." Minister Johnnie leaned forward. "David, pull your chair closer. We have some important decisions to make."

When they formed a square, the Teacher spoke again. "Yahshua commanded his disciples to love one another as he loved them. He also told them when he sent them to preach to avoid the Samaritans and Gentiles, which I've always taken to mean: help your own first. Now, you know well how I have tried to use Yahshua's model; but I have not tried to make us Jews. Or orthodox Christians. I have worked to have us love one another, because our folks have so much self-hatred among us. We cannot love Yahweh if we can't love ourselves, and vice versa, because it's the same thing."

The minister's smile was warm when he looked at Andy. "When you first joined the Covenant, you wrote an op-ed piece defending nonviolent direct action. Do you remember?"

Andy was impressed and flattered at his leader's recall. "Yes, sir, I remember it," Andy said. "I said that armed struggle for African-Americans, and even self-defense in terms of protecting ourselves from law enforcement, was suicidal. You had quoted Malcolm X in one of your talks about living peaceably, but putting anyone in the cemetery who tried to harm us or our loved ones."

"Do you still feel that way after the events of tonight? No, wait, that's very unfair, I know better, and I apologize," he said, holding up a hand. "I do want you to answer, but not tonight. Your feelings and emotions are too raw right now. When you've finished grieving and are more centered, get back to me and let me know if your thoughts and feelings are the same."

Minister Johnnie turned his attention back to all three men. "It's not just defending us against brutal cops," he said. "We're not defending us from living in America!" He slammed his hand down on the coffee table between them, and then pointed the index finger on one of his large hands. "We are the only people I know on the planet who don't seem to believe we have an inherent right to defend ourselves against enemies. We'll kill and hurt each other but won't do a thing to those who mean us no good."

As frequently happened, Minister Johnnie's hands became animated as he warmed to his subject. "We won't defend ourselves from a brutal government that has never meant us well; we accept policies clearly designed to brutalize and impoverish us, like the prison-industrial complex, like the decimation of our schools and neighborhoods; we allow the importation of drugs, and allow dealers to run rampant; and we say nothing about the political empty-headedness of so-called representatives wearing blinders to all of it. For the past year black folks have let this madman in the White House, Hugh Bruder, send all kinds of signals that we're headed back to antebellum days, and we have said virtually nothing publicly, except for me and one or two others. There are some whiners, but they ain't condemning it. We are not defending ourselves from any of it. Just because we've got a few more middle-class black folks than we had when I was a boy, many of us have convinced ourselves that we've arrived, that this empire works for everybody. Or else they fling up their hands and say there's nothing that can be done. Well, damn it, I won't allow those in the Covenant to think like that. Have you noticed how our members, if they've been to jail before they join us, don't go back? Or how our children don't act out the way too many kids do in public schools? I'm preaching to the choir; of course you have. But has anybody come to us asking, 'How do y'all do that? What's your secret?' "

The older man leaned forward and placed his head in his hands. "It's late and I'm sure you're both exhausted," he said. "Get some rest. Call me in the morning." He looked at Andy. "Romeo speaks highly of you. I have some special plans for you if you're interested."

"I want to help the Covenant anyway I can, Minister," Andy said.

Minister Johnnie smiled his warm smile again. "Be careful what you wish for, Brother Andy."

Later that night each man retreated alone into his own thoughts, his own perceptions, and his own prejudices, based on what he knew or didn't know. Each man reviewed the meaning of the meeting through emotional filters that helped protect what he already believed about himself, and about the others.

David felt humiliated. He didn't like being called out like that. He was a grown man. True, his father had withheld the source of their argument from the others. Still, he had no right to talk to him like that. Only Johnnie, no one else, thought he had a drinking problem. His wife never said anything. Johnnie really had other concerns about him. For one thing, he wanted the Covenant to remain militant and angry. His father thrived on being divisive. He had refused to go to a black college, specifically to *his* black college, and now he tried to talk to his paranoid father about some kind of détente with people he said were harmful to black people's interests. Some of their stuff was harmful, no question, but his father didn't see they have the power. This was the twenty-first century, and sometime you got to go along to get along. Johnnie Walker was still stuck in the Sixties. True, some things had to be said, and Johnnie said them. But it would take him, as Teacher, to bring the Covenant into the present. Johnnie wielded influence with the board, but when all was said and done, he only had one vote. And by bringing them into the present, those who were trying to harm the Covenant simply wouldn't be able to.

Johnnie's thoughts were more with Romeo and his friend, Andy Blackman. Romeo had gradually become the spiritual son he wanted David to be. He had watched Romeo's bitterness over his brother transform itself over the years. If one had to fight, he had to do so because he loved those he protected, not because he demonized and hated those who brought them harm; Romeo understood that now. Despite his pain, or maybe even because of it, he saw good things in Romeo's friend. He felt dumbfounded over the awful coincidence of their lives. Maybe now Andy would see that King's tactics, used correctly, could overwhelm an adversary when the conditions were right. But used as a way of life, they could be detrimental and stagnating. And, as they took this thing to the next level, Andy might be able to start meeting with the police source they had to help develop whatever intelligence they received.

Romeo moved quietly around his bedroom, trying not to awaken his wife. He understood David's jealousy and he didn't. Minister Johnnie was supporting his son as his successor, but that wasn't enough. He suspected something. Romeo had never cared much for David and David sensed it. His father had done so much that his son seemed—what?—intimidated. He didn't think he would measure up. He couldn't, or wouldn't, internalize what his father taught and so he created a self-fulfilling prophecy. He wished he could tell David that he had no reason for jealousy. The Minister had him doing exactly what he wanted to do, and he certainly had no desire to assume the role of Teacher. He knew Andy wondered why he had been in Los Angeles without stopping by; the Minister realized his mistake in bringing it up, but it was good to just let it pass. If Andy asks, he'd explain that there may come a time when he could explain.

Andy sat on the bed in Romeo's guest room and decided he would unpack in the morning. He wondered if maybe his grief and fatigue were feeding his bewilderment. He knew two things. Minister Johnnie seemed to like him, but he knew that started with Romeo. He wouldn't be this close to the Teacher if Romeo weren't close to him. But something else was going on that he was too tired to think about. His attention had gone in and out of the meeting. He had only known David as Minister Johnnie's son and a public speaker before tonight. He seemed more insecure up close. That whole thing between him and Minister Johnnie, did it have something to do with Romeo? And why had Romeo come to Los Angeles and not let him know? He'd started to ask on the ride from the meetinghouse. But he trusted his friend to tell him if he thought it important.

He was going to insist that he write the story about George. He knew Romeo would let him rest if he wanted to. He didn't want to.

FIVE

I n eleven years of newspaper reporting, Andy placed interviewing grieving families first on his distasteful list. He knew that interviewing—he called it invading—a suffering person was as much a part of the story as the victim's death that sat at the story's center. As a rookie just out of John Upton Church University, he remembered the queasiness he felt watching colleagues thrusting microphones, holding poised notebooks and shouting questions at newly bereaved family members.

During his sojourn in Los Angeles, a child's death took him to a playground in South Central down in the Eighties, east of Normandie. During a resurgence of gang warring, an eight-year-old boy in a swing was caught in the crossfire of the two factions. Andy and other reporters stood near the empty swing where the child had sat when a high velocity bullet tore open his brain. "Leave me alone! Just leave me the fuck alone!" yelled the boy's incoherent mother, tears streaming from her eyes as detectives took her home. One colleague took exception to being cursed at; another impulsively cursed back. He remembered standing there, feeling ashamed for not saying anything in the woman's defense.

He also remembered not wanting a trial for the two warring gangs, latter-day versions of the 1980s Crips and Bloods. His anger as he stood on the playground wanted both gangs lined up against a wall and summarily executed. The power of the feelings caught him by surprise.

Today was different. His pain melded with Marian's. He was interviewer and interviewee. He needed to be with his sister-in-law. He needed to hear her talk about George.

He still found it hard to believe his brother was dead. Less than twenty-four hours ago, they were bantering about cheese steaks; now George lay in a drawer on a metal slab with a tag on his toe, all because of a trigger-happy cop. If he had called George for a ride from the airport, he might still be alive. If he and Rome hadn't stopped for cheese steaks, they might have gotten to Dock Place before the mess got out of hand. And done what? If, if, if.

Stop with the "ifs" already, he told himself. He still felt disoriented, confused. The reality of his suddenly altered world kept sinking in.

He looked at himself in Romeo's full-length bathroom mirror. Once a Buppie, always a Buppie. He wore tasseled loafers, khaki slacks, a button-down shirt, and a navy blue pullover sweater.

The tensions and pain of the previous night remained. He saw it mostly in his dark eyes. He'd shaved the stubble from his dark skin and neatened his beard, where salt was just starting to gather among the pepper. He ran a finger through his unruly moderate Afro. He needed a haircut. At least he felt clean, if not relaxed, for the first time in two days.

Romeo had taken Malikah's car after driving her to work, leaving his own Honda for Andy to use.

As he drove to Dock Place, Mary Bascomb pushed into his consciousness. He had been trying not to think about his natural parent. He knew that she and the reverend would be coming in for the funeral. He wondered if they were here yet. Andy was certain she was devastated. Grimly, he wondered if she would have been devastated at his death. Once, while living in Los Angeles, he had flown to San Francisco to see her. "Cordial" seemed like such an odd word to describe the interplay between mother—he still said "natural parent"—and son, but it was the best he could come up with. He hadn't seen her since.

Andy rummaged through his mind for something to think about instead of Mary Green Bascomb. He focused on officer-involved shootings, instead. In the jargon of police and reporters, they were "OIS incidents." He'd become even more conscious of OIS incidents since researching the investigative piece that Rome had assigned to him the year before. He tried to remember a conviction of a single police officer for shooting an African-American in the years he'd been a reporter. He couldn't. He tried to think of a white victim in an OIS when no crime was being committed. He couldn't.

The only convictions that came to Andy's mind weren't for fatalities. In his early years as a journalist, a cop in New York had been sentenced to some serious time, twenty-five or thirty years, for sodomizing an arrestee with a broomstick. Andy saw the irony of heavy jail time for a non-fatality, no time at all for blowing black men and women away. The sodomy incident had been an embarrassment that couldn't be explained away as justifiable. If he had killed the man during the arrest, regardless of the circumstances, he would have been doing his job and probably still be on the force. But the sadism of sodomy without cause had to be made an example of.

And there had been Rodney King, a man beaten half to death and seen by the world on videotape, no less. The initial acquittal had been America's real sentiment. But after black, white, brown, yellow—everybody—tore up a sizable piece of Los Angeles, the feds convicted the four cops for "violating King's civil rights." Indeed, they had done that.

He parked the Honda at the corner of Dock Place and closed his eyes. After a moment, he got out and walked to Marian's house. A ragged piece of "do not cross" yellow tape dangled from a telephone pole. Shortly after George moved in, the two of them, grown men, had sprinted half the block in a race like teenagers to prove they still had it, although neither of them did. George's blood stained the street near the imaginary finish line they had created that August day. Someone had made an unsuccessful attempt to wipe the ugly reminder away.

Theresa, the woman standing with Amanda Harris the night before, opened the door of Marian's home. Her eyes were momentarily wary until Andy introduced himself.

"It's been a terrible time for her," Theresa said. The apron around her waist and the aromas that greeted him indicated adherence to the tradition that black people grieved best on a full stomach.

Several people sat in the living room with Marian. A well-dressed older man in a dark suit and bow tie sat on a large sofa with a younger woman. Both bore a resemblance to Marian. Andy had met Minister Isaac Muhammad and Vera Muhammad, Marian's oldest sister, when George got married. He hadn't seen either of them since then. They smiled wan hellos at each other. Two women about Marian's age bustled about in the kitchen.

In serious moments, the brothers had marveled at the religious polyglot that shaped their lives. "We're a little bit of this and a little bit of that in our family, huh?" was how George put it. He called himself "a lapsed COGIC," having been raised in the Reverend Harry Bascomb's Church of God in Christ Church in Richmond, California. Marian still considered herself a Muslim although she had stopped attending mosque after matriculating at Iowa State on a full scholarship. Andy had been raised as an AME in the church his mother—Madeline, Mary Bascomb's older sister—attended. Like George, he had dropped out and lost interest in organized religion. Then, six years ago, he had met Jhanae and found his way into the Covenant of the New Commandment. More than once, he and George had discussed how the Covenant was regarded as unorthodox in Christian circles in much the same way the Nation of Islam was viewed among Sunni and Shiite Muslims.

Marian Bascomb sat upright on the edge of her sofa, staring at thoughts in the deepest recesses of her being. She didn't really see the people coming and going in her two-story row home and was unaware of the aroma of fried chicken and other gastronomic preparations in her kitchen. She was totally oblivious to the television newscaster's warning of the possibility of terrorist strikes in their city before the end of the year. She looked up at Andy when he entered. Her lips moved into a smile of affection. Andy leaned over and they embraced.

A russet stain resembling a Rorschach blot and several other dried streaks of George's life fluids stained the jacket of her sleek white running suit, mute testimony on the dull pain now settled inside her chest. She had endured the police precinct for several hours, until Carvel Thomas glared at the detective who brought her down and said she could return the next day, although he knew it would be no easier then. A sedative had helped her doze off for a few hours. She had meant to change and simply forgot.

When she awakened, she insisted on going to the medical examiner's office for the formality of identifying her husband. Touching his cold cheek, she promised that, somehow, justice would be done. When she returned, neighbors began coming by to embrace her, to bring food, to murmur condolences, knowing they affected her raw pain about as much as new snowflakes disappearing on a heavy winter coat. Theresa, who had gone to the precinct with her, suggested she change when they first arrived home; they had moved on to doing other things. In the scheme of things, it didn't seem important.

Her wide grey-gold eyes, usually stunning against her golden brown skin, now reddened and wet, looked into a private universe no one could enter. "How you doing, big brother?" she asked, forcing a smile. Andy smiled back. She had never called him that; he knew she was saying it for George.

"It hurts bad, but I'm hanging in there," Andy said.

"The first time he kissed me, George told me we were going to be together forever," Marian said. She frowned at Andy as if she were pondering something, and then looked away.

"George," she said suddenly, speaking to no one in particular, "forever was supposed to be longer than this." The intimacy of her vulnerability created an embarrassed silence, but it was a warm and affectionate embarrassment, not awkward and uncomfortable.

Andy thought she was willing herself to focus on the moment. She balled her hands into fists.

"Mom and Dad are flying in," she said. "They should be here this evening. I called them last night. She's taking it pretty hard."

Andy nodded. He found it ironic that she could call Mary Bascomb "mom" and he couldn't.

"Daddy, can you and Vera move closer?" Marian said. When they had done so, she looked at her father.

"Daddy, you're not going to be happy about this, I don't think, but I want to ask the Covenant to officiate at George's homegoing. He wasn't a member but I know he had been thinking about it." She turned to Andy. "He was so proud of the work you were doing."

Andy swallowed. "I'll call Minister Johnnie," he said. "He'll be honored, I'm sure."

"Marian, if it can't be us, I'm glad it's them," Isaac Muhammad said. "I do understand. And I want what you want."

She paused. "I'm two months pregnant," she said. "George won't get to see his only child." Her voice quavered. "Andy, that was the surprise he had for you."

For several moments, there were no dry eyes in the room. The words hung like quiet in the wake of a summer storm.

It was Andy who broke the awkward silence. "Do you feel like talking, Marian? I wanted to get some remembrances from you. But we can do this at another time."

She smiled suddenly, and it was a bright one. "No, let's talk now. All I'm thinking about is him, so it might do me some good. Did he ever tell you how we met?"

Andy took a small tape recorder from his pocket, pressed the "record" button, and placed the machine on the coffee table. "I know some of it," he said. "Tell me about it."

"I have a friend named Pat who lives in Baldwin Hills. You know, that la-de-da part of Los Angeles for black folks." She smiled. "Pat would beat me up if she heard me say that. Seriously, it's a nice area."

As his sister-in-law talked, he saw that the memories indeed seemed therapeutic, at least for now.

"Pat and I go back forever," Marian said. "So I went out there for the Fourth of July week that year. She and Roland decided they wanted to have a cookout. And it was nice, but it was just like any other holiday cookout. I was stuffing myself, and then George walked in. I locked eyes with this skinny man"—she giggled—"We looked at each other and kind of nodded.

"He called me Miss Marian the first time he said anything to me," Marian said. She seemed to be watching the memory on a screen in her mind. "Roland introduced us. And George said, 'Hi, Miss Marian.' The way he said it, it didn't sound at all formal. And that was my nickname from then on."

A shadow crossed her face. It was the first of many moments of remembering and loving a habit, an intimacy, a place, a movie, a song, and then understanding that it had happened for the last time.

"Roland and Pat told me later they looked at us and saw what it took us a few weeks to catch up to, that there really was such a thing as love at first sight, or almost. I stayed an extra week, used all of my vacation, but I was working as a bank management trainee in Des Moines and had to go back. George had been at UCLA on a track scholarship and bruised his Achilles tendon. He drove an airport shuttle, and was taking night courses in criminal justice because he was thinking about going into law enforcement." The irony resonated through the tastefully decorated living room. "If things went right, he was even thinking about law school."

Andy let her talk. Much of it he knew he wouldn't use. But some of these small moments she revealed would humanize the portrait he developed of his half brother seen through the eyes of this woman who loved him.

"Like most people, he said"—she tried imitating him—"'I didn't know any black folks were actually born in Iowa.'" She looked at Andy. "Everybody black always said that to me, and it had gotten old. But it sounded fresh when George said it, probably because I wanted it to. We talked about everything that day." A thought started a giggle that expanded into a full-blown laugh that made her clap her hands in delight. "We discovered we were both Spiderman junkies and had been since we were kids! Can you imagine anything so stupid and silly?"

Andy saw that she was out of her pain for just a little while. Marian said they both kept changing their cell phone plans to add additional minutes. Her bank was nationwide, a subsidiary of OneCorporation International, and she was able to transfer to Los Angeles six months later. She and George married almost a year to the day after they met. They relocated to the East Coast about a year after that so that George could drive for a nationwide trucking company. His income and benefits, a declining rarity, were good. He got a lot of overtime, enough to buy the home on Dock Street. They both were thinking about going back to school full time, with her doing the first shift in graduate school while he saved money. The three years, one month and sixteen days on Dock Street together they both saw as, in George's words on their wedding night, "The beginning of forever with each other."

Andy watched her looking at yesterday. He turned away to look out the window. The Harrises and a couple of men he didn't know were coming up the steps.

To those who knew him, Carl Harris seemed to have aged five years. His jaws were sunken; his pain constricted his small frame. He stood in the doorway, his hound's tooth skinny-brimmed hat in hand; his shoulders slumped from the enormous weight sitting on them. His eyes darted back and forth, then looked down. He tried to raise them to speak to Marian, lowered them again. Amanda Harris' hand stroked his back through his trench coat.

Marian focused her energy as she looked at the gentle neighbor she regarded almost as an uncle.

"Mister Harris, this was not your fault," she said, her voice carrying across her living room. She enunciated each word carefully, stressing "not" firmly in her Mid-western tones. She stood up, very erect, as if her body understood the dignity of the moment. She walked with a quiet regal bearing to her elder. Amanda Harris dropped her hand from her husband's back in appreciation of her neighbor's gesture, so necessary both for Carl and herself.

The room was still, even with the chattering of the television set, as she placed her arms around Carl Harris' defeated shoulders. He gave an audible exhale and placed his arms around her in turn. They held each other in a long embrace. Then the two women embraced.

"Thank you," Amanda Harris whispered, her eyes moist. "Carl so much needed to hear you say that."

While Carl and Amanda Harris settled in with the others, Marian walked over to stand by the stone mantel shelf above her faux fireplace. She stared at the framed photographs that book-ended the other knick knacks. She smiled at George styling in their wedding photograph, sartorially immaculate in his black dinner suit, white shirt, and kinte cloth bow tie. "Miss Marian," he reminded her frequently when he had glanced at the picture, "you sure looked delicious that day." And she had been a vision to George and her guests, her white scalloped gown eliciting more than rote murmurs of appreciation.

In the other picture, they were dancing at a friend's party to a Jeffrey Osborne ballad that became "their song." She wore a favorite pink dress with spaghetti straps; George was dressed in a beige double-breasted suit set off with a dark brown shirt and dark brown patterned tie.

When they were courting, George had bought her a mahogany jewelry box with a large Egyptian ankh engraved on the top and smaller ones on each of its four sides. Now she wanted only two pieces of jewelry in it from now on. She would get George's wedding band from the funeral director and place the two gold rings in the box. She would place it here.

She wanted them to rest between these two moments frozen in time.

SIX

In almost a half century of practicing law, Ike Erlickson never had a client he didn't like. Just as remarkably, when a magazine reporter wrote an in-depth feature about him as he eased into semi-retirement a half dozen years earlier, the journalist couldn't find a single client Erlickson had defended who didn't have some measure of avuncular feelings for the venerated attorney. Regardless of race, age, gender, or sexual orientation, each, without exception, spoke well of "Uncle Ike."

Isaac Orville Erlickson had specialized in the defense of murder suspects during his long storied career. Nearly four dozen times he had gone before the bench to defend people accused of murder. As the man from the Bronx became wildly successful and extraordinarily wealthy, fact and legend blurred.

Legend had it that Ike Erlickson had never lost a murder case. The legend, although wrong, grew from a remarkable statistic that was right. Courtroom observers bent the statistic as if they were playing a game of Whisper Down the Lane.

In fact, Isaac O. Erlickson III had lost several cases. But not once had a client been convicted of first-degree murder. On several occasions, Erlickson pleaded clients down to manslaughter. And once he lost a client to a second-degree murder conviction. But no one who ever got "Uncle Ike" to defend them ever went to jail for murder one.

For several years, Erlickson had been taking life a little easier. Even though he made his reputation and much of his money defending accused murderers who law enforcement usually wanted put away, he was paradoxically admired by law enforcement. He personally thought highly of peace officers. Thus, part of his semi-retirement included a relationship with the Police Officer's Benevolent Association. He quietly let POBA presidents and executive directors know that he was available as a consultant, *pro bono*, if any "difficult situations" came along and officers needed competent counsel.

When the call came from his old buddy, Bulldog Hudson, about Michael Patrick, he was ready. He had just finished a racquetball game at the city's plush Federal Club. Erlickson spoke with Bulldog on his cell phone as he toweled off.

"Bulldog, if they do change their minds and charge this young man, I'm ready to saddle up and ride in to do what I can," Erlickson told him.

"I talked to Tom and, since he didn't want to file charges against Mike anyway, it was easy to have a meeting of the minds. But Mike needs someone watching his back," Hudson, a retired chief inspector, said. "Looks like he may be marrying my goddaughter, so I hoped you might help us out."

"Of course I'll help. I'll have Mary re-work my schedule so we can dig right into this thing. Let's have lunch over at the club about twelve-thirty."

"We'll be there, Ike," Hudson said. "Mike's a great kid, I think you'll like him. I'm sure you can understand he's a little antsy about all this. Him knowing you're there watching his back will calm him down."

"See you at the club."

And so it was that the legendary lawyer, the retired law enforcement icon, and the awed young police officer sat down in the city's most exclusive private club to break bread on the last day of September.

The Federal Club, founded in 1862 by abolitionists to help support the Union effort in the Civil War, featured a dining room that was all mahogany, crystal, fine china, expensive silver place settings, and rigidly appropriate waiters. Bach, Haydn, Johann Strauss, and other pre-Beethoven composers comprised the playlist that wafted through speakers discreetly placed and kept out of sight.

They ordered chilled martinis, straight up, with two olives. On Erlickson's recommendation, they all ordered prime rib.

"So, young man, tell me a bit about yourself," Uncle Ike said as he straightened his monogrammed shirt cuffs to expose his diamond cuff links. "What took you into law enforcement?"

Michael Patrick knew an opportunity when he saw one. Even though he wasn't being charged, Bulldog said it wouldn't hurt to have legal representation, "just in case." Not only was this famous lawyer doing free work for POBA, he was a personal friend of his mentor! Talk about prayers being answered.

"Well, I grew up in a household full of Boston blue," he said. "Both my granddad and my dad were cops there. I don't think I ever wanted to be anything else."

He felt tongue-tied talking to this dapper man with a national reputation. He bet the suit Mister Erlickson wore cost more than all of his suits put together.

"I came here in '96 to go to John Upton Church University," Michael said. "These days you need some college to be on the force. My granddad talks about that a lot. He reminds me all the time about how things have changed. 'Mike,' he says, 'in my day all you had to do was be willing to bust the heads of commie kikes and uppity niggers.'" He looked around nervously. The older men laughed.

"It's okay, son," Bulldog Hudson said. "I came along the same time your grandfather did. Ike and I understand. Things were a lot simpler then. You wouldn't be going through this if you had been on the force when I was your age."

"How'd you do at Church?" the barrister asked. "And what else have you done? Or have you done anything else?"

"Well, I dropped out of Church in my junior year," Michael said. "I wasn't real focused at the time. I kicked around on a few odd jobs until I got on at OneCorporation International with their security agency. If you're not on a police force, they're as good as it gets, you know that. I've been trying to finish my degree in night courses when I'm not working the swing or the overnight."

Bulldog Hudson took out a solid gold cigarette case. He offered but was the only cigarette smoker at the table. "Talk about a crack outfit," he said after lighting up. "Their commander, Charlie Burr, is an old friend of mine. Runs a tight ship. Shit, in some places OCI is better than the city police forces."

"And larger, if you count Charlie's worldwide operation," Erlickson said. "Go on, Mike."

Michael Patrick told Ike Erlickson what he already knew. He met his fiancée, Kathleen, through a mutual friend he worked with at OCI. Kathleen's godfather was Bulldog Hudson. Although Mike Patrick's test scores were borderline acceptable, Hudson made a couple of calls and got him into the academy. "I've been a cop for a little over four years," he said.

Robert Hudson said grace when the three orders of one-inch thick prime rib, rare, arrived.

"Let's enjoy our lunch, why don't we?" Hudson said. "Then I want you to tell Uncle Ike everything about this incident." He took a manila folder from his briefcase and slid it across the table to the attorney. "I called a favor and got a copy of Mike's personnel records for you. He's a good cop. " He shook his head. "It's sure not like the old days when we knew there were the good guys and the bad guys, and which was which."

When they finished their prime rib, Ike Erlickson leaned forward and looked his new client in the eye.

"You've got to let me in your head, let me know what you were feeling that night. And call me Ike."

"Call him Uncle Ike," Hudson said. The attorney smiled.

Each man ordered a third martini. After the drinks came, they listened to Mike Patrick. Erlickson lit a Cuban cigar, part of a stash he had obtained through a discreet connection; Hudson smoked another cigarette.

Mike Patrick clasped his hands together, looked away as if looking in the distance. He tried to ignore the cigar and cigarette smoke.

"It had been a bad day, sir," he said. "Kathy and I had been on the boat that Bulldog gave her. We'd argued and I was just feeling like shit."

"What did you argue about?"

Patrick reddened. He looked at his mentor.

"It's okay, Mike," Hudson said. "Kathleen and I have talked. She told me her side of it. She's my goddaughter but I understand. I'm a man. And, to hear her tell it, it's not like you tried to rape her. Then I'd be kicking your ass myself." He smiled to try and ease the sting of his last words.

"I'd come on to Kathy, and she wasn't interested. Her ex-husband called her, and I didn't like the way they talked. We yelled at each other a bit, and I left. I didn't try and force her or anything; I just left.

"When I got back in the city, I stopped at the Roundtable and met my buddy Garth, who I've known since college. We had some shots of Red Mountain. They didn't make me feel any better so we left and bought a fifth. When we got to Dock Place, I called Kathy. She reluctantly agreed to go out, but then hung up on me. Garth and I were sitting there talking about it when I heard my trailer get hit."

He fidgeted, looked away. "When this guy Harris hit my boat, it just seemed like one more thing in a real fucked up day, you know? Now, in fairness, he didn't give me any guff, none at all. If it had just stayed between him and me, things might have been okay. But people started to gather and that made me nervous, it upset me. When you're out on the street, sir, you can't let these people take charge of the situation. Not under any circumstances, my granddad used to say. I guess it's just ingrained in me. When I drew my service weapon, it was kind of like my training just kicked in. I was outnumbered. I needed to regain control, you know? And shortly after that, this Bascomb came at me."

Erlickson kept his voice soft, non-accusatory. "Mike, even though you haven't been charged with anything, your enemies are going to make a big deal out of something you allegedly said. They're already making a big deal of it. You and I need to confront that right now. 'I want to kill a nigger,' you supposedly said. 'I want to kill a nigger so bad I can taste it,' or something to that effect."

Blood appeared to drain from Patrick's face. "We say things like that sometimes when we want to intimidate. Bulldog, you know how it is."

Hudson nodded but said nothing.

"I mean, I didn't have anything against this man, nothing at all. In my mind, he was a suspect, and I wanted him to back off. He kind of did, but he wouldn't drop the stick and that still made him a threat. I was the only one who was supposed to have a weapon, as far as I was concerned."

"Some witnesses claim you didn't identify yourself as a police officer," Erlickson said. "Is that true?"

Mike grimaced. "Sir, I swear to you, I thought I had my badge on! I really did. Everything happened so fast." His eyes widened, pleading with the attorney to believe him. "I mean, my training kicked in, and I was just trying to stay in control of the situation. I mean, he could have dropped the stick!" His voice rose, both in volume and pitch. "Why didn't he drop the stick? I didn't have anything against him. I don't have anything against blacks at all, sir. I work with them and we get along fine, we really do." He suddenly became aware of himself. A few patrons had glanced in their direction. "He should have dropped the stick," he said in a lower voice.

Ike Erlickson sat his Cuban cigar in a crystal ashtray. He looked his potential client in the eye. "Son, I want you to be totally honest with me now," he said. "Talk to me as if I'm your priest. What is said will not leave this table. Does any part of you feel that what you did that night was wrong? And, if so, why?"

Mike told his attorney what, in fact, he had told a priest at confessinon that morning. "Sir, I was mortified when I realized I didn't have my badge in view. It was just so, so unthinkable to me that I would have my gun out without my badge on. I've never shot anybody before. And not being, you know, a plainclothes cop, I haven't had a lot of times to be in that kind of situation." His voice grew quieter. "Afterward, when I saw that I didn't have my badge on, I kind of understood what this fellow Bascomb was trying to do. He was doing what I might have tried to do if I had been in that kind of situation without my Glock." He looked down at the table. "Even though I'd gotten upset and all, I still thought I was being a cop out there. But I know he didn't know that."

Bulldog and Uncle Ike looked at each other. Bulldog lit a cigarette; the attorney re-lit his cold cigar. The air became acrid with smoke again; Mike coughed but said nothing. Bulldog spoke first.

"Mike, do you understand the concept of the thin blue line?" his elderly mentor asked.

"Yes, sir, I think so. We are the first line of defense between order and chaos. Without us, it would sometimes be difficult for government to function."

Uncle Ike took a big puff on his cigar. "What I think he's pointing out to you, son, is that you are, and have been, a part of that thin blue line. Government needs you there, as you said, and sometimes they must give you the benefit of the doubt."

He took another puff. "When I was in law school a lot of years ago, I remember looking at the Declaration of Independence. Something struck me when I was reading the part about how the people have a right to throw off government when it becomes destructive of certain ends. I saw that, even then, we really need the thin blue line to stop these populist notions, or we might end up with something worse. It's just the way things have to be constructed, Mike. Somebody always feels the government's being destructive of this thing or that thing, and so government creates the thin blue line to keep these notions of so-called "destructive government" on the other side of that line. You protect our way of life, Mike. It swings to the right sometimes, and sometimes to the left —not too often, thank God—but it's still the greatest government ever put on this planet."

Ike Erlickson smiled at the young police officer and held up what was left of his martini. Bulldog did the same, and then Mike held his up, too.

"I'll drink to that," Bulldog Hudson said.

They clinked glasses and drank.

SEVEN

Andy smiled as he watched Jonathan Gardiner bustle around the chaos that was his workstation. The young brother ate well, and a lot, that was obvious. He was also intellectually curious. One look around the Gardiner's lived-in sitting room told a visitor that if an audio-visual gadget, gizmo or thingamajig existed, young Jon had it, had tried it, or was looking for it.

After fixing Andy a cup of coffee, Alberta Gardiner insisted that her son show off his new second generation HoloScreen, a laptop computer attachment that transformed photographs and videos into convincing three-dimensional illusions. The Gardiners had bought their first computer just ten years ago, a year before Jon had graduated from grade school. Now Alberta referred to the son who towered over her as "my little genius," which invariably embarrassed him. She had created the phrase years before after Jonathan's technical prowess garnered first place in a statewide contest for middle school students.

Like so much else, the HoloScreen was now a OneCorporation International product. OCI's I-Tech Division had recently acquired exclusive rights to the HoloScreen by buying the patent for two billion dollars. Andy was awestruck by the realism of the laptop's images. Mimicking the top of a convertible automobile, a shell slid into place on the laptop case to complete the illusion of depth.

Jonathan hurried through the demonstration, anxious to get to the business at hand. "This is nice, but that's not why I asked you to come by," Jonathan said, snapping off the display. He took two DVDs from his cluttered desk and handed them to Andy. "I made these for you." He took a third disc and inserted it into his player.

Andy braced himself. Jonathan hadn't told Romeo what he had. Now he realized he was going to watch his brother die.

Images sprang to life on the wall screen television monitor. They were clear enough to identify almost everyone. "I apologize for the jerkiness," Jonathan said. "I'm still working on my handheld technique. The camera's so small." He held up a video camera about half the size of the palm of his large hand.

It was a low flying bird's eye view. The camera's vantage point looked down on the turmoil of the night before from the Gardiner's window overlooking Dock Place. Michael Patrick stood almost directly opposite their window. The voices below on Dock Place were distinct although distant. The Gardiners' voices, unwittingly louder, provided additional commentary.

"But what am I supposed to do tonight?" It was Michael Patrick, in his whiskey-slurred voice. "I have a woman waiting to go out and what am I supposed to do about that? You are a real pain in my ass right now, you know that?"

"Early, call the police." Mrs. Gardiner's voice was close to the camera.

"I was just running my mouth, I wasn't thinking," Alberta Gardiner said. Andy waved a hand to dismiss the apology.

"Bert, I'm watching the game," her husband's voice said off camera. "They just having a few words is all. Stop overreacting."

"Your father's having trouble with the white man." Andy recognized Amanda Harris' voice.

"Shut up, you goddamn nigger bitch!"

"Who do you think you're talking to?"

"Ask God why he made her a nigger bitch and you a honky. Get your white ass away from here!" That was Mrs. Saunders, the woman upstairs, Andy remembered.

"Oh dear Lord," Alberta Gardiner said off camera. "Jonathan, you keep that camera on, I have a bad feeling about this. I'll call the police myself."

A groan came from Early Gardiner's voice. "Aw shit, what did you drop the damn ball for? You're a wide receiver, they pay you to catch the damn ball!"

"I want to kill a nigger," Michael Patrick said. The flat, matter-of-factness with which he said it surprised Andy. The words rubbed across him like coarse sandpaper. "I want to kill a nigger so goddamned bad I can taste it."

"Jesus! Police? Yes, there's a man out here with a gun! You better get somebody here quick. No, I'm in my house, he's outside, on Dock Place, and I think he's getting ready to shoot somebody."

"Bert, who's got a gun? What are you—?"

"I don't know! What's he look like, he's a white man and he's calling people out of their name and he's got a gun!" A pause. "I told you, the unit block of Dock Place. It's a large alley next to Dock Street in the Riverfront District." Her voice sounded both plaintive and excited, all mixed up together.

Andy felt a chill. He closed his eyes, unaware he'd done so, remembering, not wanting to. Him, and Romeo, and Sonny . . .

"__ C'mere, you hear me?" Patrick's first shot rang out.

"He's started shooting, you better hurry! What do you need my name for? Just get somebody here!"

Andy opened his eyes, momentarily bewildered. Without willing it, he'd found himself back in the bank, fifteen years old, with Romeo and his older brother, terrified. He swallowed, the inside of his mouth dry and sticky at the same time. He tried to push his feelings away.

The videotape unfolded, the ultimate reality show. Alberta Gardiner, off camera, mumbling for the police, trying by force of will to get them there faster. Early Gardiner, finally able to leave the football game alone; Alberta asking her son to zoom in if he could.

Andy heard the security guard that people mentioned, Raymond Hayes, join Patrick, asking Patrick if he's all right. He noticed another lanky white man standing silently, almost as if he didn't want to be there. Why did the guard assume Patrick was in the right? He had no way of knowing at that point that Patrick was a cop. Was it just a white man coming to help another white man, regardless, because of course the black folks were messing up, doing something?

"Yeah, I'm fine, as soon I get these niggers back off me," Patrick said.

Andy lowered his head. Somehow, as he got ready to see George die, he had an epiphany. Michael Patrick, and what he was doing, would never, ever go away until someone did something. Writing about Tanya Morris and all the others was fine but it wasn't enough. But what? What was he supposed to do?

"Drop it, I said. One____"

Andy looked up again. Alberta, Early and Jonathan's voices were still.

"Two____"

Then Alberta Gardiner, chanting the negative over and over, a litany, a prayer, one destined not to be answered: "No, no, noJesusnononononononono!"

Pop!

Screams. Cursing. Sirens.

Andy looked at Jonathan. "You did a good job, it was quick thinking on your part," he said. "Good job."

"I was afraid to give it to the cops," Jonathan said.

"They'll have to get a copy," Andy said. "But first I'll show it to my editor, and to the Walkers. Then we'll take it to the police. And we'll give you credit in the story, and of course a byline on the photographs."

"I'm proud of my son," Alberta Gardiner said. "The camera was a

Christmas present from his father."

"I'm proud of him, too," Andy said. "George was my brother."

"Oh dear Jesus!" Alberta Gardiner said. "I am so sorry."

"Thank you." He turned to Jonathan. "If Patrick's charged with anything, you may be asked to testify. Are you okay with that?"

"Sure," Jonathan said. "I'm really sorry about your brother, Mister Blackman. But you said 'if.' You mean, even with the video, he might get away with shooting Mister Bascomb?"

Andy nodded. "And even if he's charged, they may not find him guilty. Almost twenty years ago, around the time you were born, there was a tape like this of four cops out in California brutally beating a man named Rodney King. Someone did just like you, Jon, and taped the beating. The jury found all four of them not guilty. People rioted in the streets, they were so angry. The feds got a conviction on violating his civil rights later but, without the riots, who knows?"

Jonathan's face told Andy that he didn't know about Rodney King. He would have been an infant. He was just a young man who liked to videotape things. Andy asked a few questions, took some notes, and thanked them. "We could use a young man with your skills in the Covenant," Andy said as they shook hands. "We're trying to strengthen our technology program."

"I'll think about that, Mister Blackman, I really will," Jonathan said.

"Maybe you and the family will come to one of our Saturday morning lectures," Andy said.

As he walked to Romeo's Honda, the images of George being shot played and replayed in Andy's head. He felt glad and sad about the oversized man-child who had captured the murder with his digital video camera. It was scary that black boys like Jonathan were becoming more and more atypical. The gangsta role model continued to grow, like a virus, as young scholars like Jonathan moved toward endangered species status. Prison statistics kept climbing; the new drug on the street, Sweetness, was doing what crack cocaine had done before it: aiding and abetting self-destruction. President Bruder promised to help incarceration numbers climb even more with a recent pledge of tax breaks to help the private sector build more prisons. Private prisons needed "product." Thirteenth Amendment slaves. From what he heard, the euphoric explosion in the head caused by Sweetness, a synthetic opiate, made crack cocaine seem like soda pop.

He started to call Romeo, and then remembered he was out of town until tomorrow. He knew his friend would be excited when he saw the DVD. The *Scabbard* had a hell of an exclusive. And black people had a decent chance at justice.

A long buried memory—a decision, really—arose and brought a bittersweet smile. His youthful idealism had spurred a promise to himself, one that had brought him to this moment of interviewing the young man who witnessed his brother's death. A complementary memory followed the first one: his mother, saying, "When that boy makes up his mind to do something, he's like a pit bull and won't turn it loose until it's done."

He made the commitment to himself two days after Sonny's death. There had been video of that horrible moment, too. The security camera videotape had captured it all. The robbery had also been taped, but treated by the authorities as a separate piece of evidence for a separate crime.

They had met Romeo's older brother in the lobby of the suburban bank, with plans to tag along with him to Lawton, a little, mostly black town just on the other side of the river. Sonny, newly discharged from three years of active duty in the Army, wanted to visit a favorite aunt and uncle he had lived with briefly as a boy.

The bank was in a high-rise building with long escalators to the second floor. The building's atmosphere was sterile, with an intimidating quality in its glass and metal façade and sea of mostly white faces. The trio joined the shortest of three lines and waited silently.

Andy remembered it almost as if he were watching a movie . . .

A man with dirty blonde hair and angular face had turned from the line next to them and jogged toward the front door. Not real fast, not in a hurry, but jogging. He carried a dark cloth bag in one hand and pushed his glasses firmly up on his nose as he loped toward the door, stuffing the cloth bag in his pocket as he ran. Almost every head in the bank rotated slowly to follow him. He disappeared through the front door and down the steps next to the escalator.

No one spoke at first, but everyone knew. They had just witnessed a bank robbery. A buzz of conversation hummed among the customers. Heads swiveled back, almost in unison, toward the counter.

The teller who had been held up, a plump woman with salt-and-pepper hair and a beaklike nose, looked dazed. Activity darted around her. A bespectacled blonde woman embraced her, another silver-haired woman talked animatedly to another employee. The buzz hummed, grew louder.

Andy and Romeo drifted toward the front door with the curiosity of youth. People stood on the up escalator, business as usual, oblivious to what had just enfolded.

Four policemen burst through the front door, guns drawn, faces grim.

"Romeo!" Sonny shouted.

"Hands in the air! Now, goddammit!" One cop, a beefy, gruff-sounding man, shouted, pointing his gun at Andy. His hands went up without him thinking about it. He remembered how huge the hole in the barrel seemed.

"But we're not the ones___" Romeo started. The cop next to Gruff Voice, a tall man with lanky movements, was on Romeo in two strides.

"Officer, please, wait, they didn't do ____" A white man's voice called from across the room.

The cop slammed Romeo to the ground. "Keep your nigger mouth shut and stay down, you got that?" he screamed, his gun pressed on Romeo's cheek. Andy was there again, in the bank, holding his breath, seeing Sonny with his peripheral vision, seeing him close the distance with long strides.

"My brother didn't do anything! What the fuck's wrong with you?" he yelled. The white man in the background yelled something; other voices joined, a jumble.

"Hold it! Hold it goddammit!" Gruff Voice roared.

Sonny dipped low toward his brother. "You okay, Romeo?"

The tall cop raised his pistol, swung at Sonny's head. Sonny's responded reflexively. In one fluid movement, his head ducked to one side, his right arm blocked the blow. His left fist caught the cop high on his temple, sending the startled man's navy blue wheel cap flying.

"He's got a gun!" one of the other cops shouted. Andy shut his eyes, knowing, not wanting to know.

Bap!

Like a loud firecracker.

Bap! Bap! Bapbap! Bap!

Andy squinted through tears filling his eyes. Sonny looked surprised, then pissed off, then frightened as his life and death and the moment coalesced, trembled in fusion, separated. The front of his shirt blushed a furious red, moist and damp like tears. He went down on one knee, looking as if he were trying to figure it out. Then his eyes rolled back in his head and he pitched forward on his face because nothing mattered anymore.

When Andy read the front page news account the next day, he planted the seed of his decision, watering it with the anguish of what he had witnessed.

The news story began: "One man was killed and a policeman injured during an aborted holdup yesterday at a Maple Village bank, authorities said.

Police shot and fatally wounded Crispus Thomas Butler, 22, after officers trapped him in the suburban branch of . . ."

He had closed his eyes, unable to read further for a full minute. He looked back at the newspaper. He and Romeo were "thought to be teenaged accomplices of the dead man."

The day after that, on page twenty-two, the same newspaper cleared Sonny in a three-paragraph brief:

"An unidentified man who robbed a suburban bank yesterday escaped with more than $3,000, authorities said. The suspect is still at large.

"Crispus Thomas Butler, a 22-year-old black man killed by police during an altercation at the Maple Village bank shortly after the holdup, was not involved in the robbery, a police spokesman said. Butler was shot to death after he attacked officers.

"Police officials ruled Butler's death justifiable homicide."

That day, Andy knew he would learn how to report the news, and get it right, even as he balled the newspaper up and threw it in the trash . . .

This time, with this black man's death, the story would be told right. At that moment, Andy became aware that he was crying.

EIGHT

The man walked along the water's edge, his gleaming shaved head bowed, his hands folded behind him. His long black double-breasted trench coat fell almost to his ankles, swaying as he walked. The coolness off the water felt good, as always, on his dark skin. The night air soothed his body as the water's presence soothed his spirit. Here, in the pre-dawn darkness, he never failed to feel the Holy Breath course through his entire being. For more than four decades, this stretch of beach on the Atlantic Ocean had been his place of refuge. Forty-one times he had driven here on the anniversary of his Calling. What he described as "life being in session," and the tribulations that sometimes resulted, determined his other visits.

He had to make a decision.

Forty years he had ministered, always knowing he must speak truth to power when necessary, as an example for those who followed him, who came after him. In the fifth year of his ministry, he had ordered nearly a hundred Swords of the Master into the streets to stand vigil outside a police station after several officers almost killed a Sword who refused to stop selling the *Scabbard* when ordered to do so. The incident had created a public face for his little known congregants; his ministry sprouted. Many who didn't join applauded the Covenant's militancy. But it was 1973, and it was clear that the revolution would not be televised, or even take place any time soon.

Twenty years into his ministry, images of himself going to the brink of death in a showdown with the city filled his memory as he walked.

The city had decided to take almost a mile of homes through eminent domain, along with a historic African-American cemetery, to build a new freeway that would provide faster access to the suburbs. Most of the tombstones, dating back to 1871, had already been torn up and the bodies were next. A smaller Jewish-American cemetery less than five hundred yards away from the black one was going to be spared.

City officials called it a lawful use of eminent domain; Minister Johnnie "Black Label" Walker condemned it as a debasement of African ancestors that must not go unchallenged.

On that occasion, he invoked the techniques of King, of Dick Gregory, of Gandhi. He even quoted "Letter From Birmingham Jail" in a Saturday lecture, teaching how the civil rights leader had responded to unjust laws. Create a crisis, King said; heighten tensions until you bring a resolution.

"Black Power!" Minister Johnnie's voice, hoarse and impassioned, had soared over his congregation the day he announced his hunger strike.

"Black Power!" came the throaty response from the hundreds of his Saturday morning faithful on that day in 1988.

The adrenalin-pumping call and response had lasted for more than a minute, a civil rights anachronism past its heyday, some said at the time.

"I've said it before, I'll say it again. They—your government—has taught y'all that you should never, ever, *ever,* put those two words—'black' and 'power'—together again, and then act like you mean them. You scare them, and they don't want to be scared, and I guess you don't want them to be scared, so you don't use them together anymore. And they find ways to distract you with, you know, bling bling, and television and football and basketball, and blunts and forties, and other things, and because you don't know any better, you buy into being distracted. Well, I still say those two words together, because I know who it scares, and I don't care what they think about me or feel about me, and I will never stop saying, and exercising my black power! Black power! Black power! Black power!" The congregation chanted with him

He explained to his audience that power meant being able to get people to do what you wanted, even when, and if, they didn't want to. "And you exercise power by any means necessary!" he shouted.

First, Black Label went to community meetings and listened. Listened to the earnest complaints and the bitching and moaning and posturing. The homeowners were pissed about their homes, most of which, although old, were well kept and neat. But they were just as angry about the disrespect planned for their ancestors. Both cemeteries, already under eminent domain, had been closed for close to thirty years and had fallen into disrepair through neglect. People had grumbled for years about the city's lack of interest, but none had expected them to come in and callously dispose of people's remains, as they proposed.

Minister Johnnie told city leaders that the people had three demands. One, the proposed freeway would be re-routed along the river. It would cost several million more, but "it bee's that way sometime," Walker said. Second, if a Covenant-led fundraising campaign were successful in raising half the cost, the city would provide matching funds to place an African-American Ancestors memorial park on the present site where the remains were interred, and would remain interred. They would honor those whom they had all neglected. Three, the eminent domain decree would be rescinded and none of the homes would be touched. He would not eat any solid food until the city complied.

The city had been unhappy with Minister Johnnie Walker and his upstart Covenant of the New Commandment organization. They were getting everything, the city was getting nothing, and that was no way to negotiate, they said. They were strange ones, this Covenant bunch. If they followed Jesus, or Yahshua, as they called him, how come none of them wore crosses?

For forty days, Johnnie Walker fasted on water, juices, and broth, and led daily pickets lines in front of their councilman's office. The councilman, allied with the mayor, opposed Walker's proposal. The numbers grew to more than a hundred daily. On the forty-first day, he began sitting on a special platform made just for him outside the councilman's office, and did so around the clock under a makeshift tent to shield him from the elements. It was the first time many people saw the Swords of the Master. Sartorially immaculate in business suits and ties, at least four of them stood guard over their leader at all times. They'd been part of the demonstrations all along but informally dressed, mingling with the other pickets. Minister Johnnie's young son came after school and helped lead the picket line. On the fifty-third day, Minister Johnnie Walker collapsed and was hospitalized. Against the advice of his physician, he refused to eat, and told a growing assemblage of reporters that he preferred "to join the ancestors, if that is to be the outcome, before I will allow this city to defile those on whose shoulders we stand."

A few courageous black ministers, and one white one, though not thrilled with Walker's theology, decided he was right and cobbled together a committee. Five hundred pickets (about forty whites among them) showed up the next day, more than triple their largest picket line up to that time. The story led the news that night, with ten-year-old David Walker pleading "not to let my dad die." More than eight hundred showed up the next day, the same day city officials announced they would meet Minister Johnnie's demands.

Now, this time, "the barricades going up" would not only be a metaphor. Eventually, he knew they would be a reality.

He must make a decision.

The sea soothed his soul. He sometimes caught a fleeting glimpse of the eternal as he walked alone and close to the ocean. Solace came when that was needed; serenity blanketed him on other occasions when thoughtful decisions were required. He liked describing his Calling to others by telling them his Creator had "knocked me up side my head and said, 'Now pay attention to Me'." He told people that Yahweh's head knocking came while walking along this beach, next to the watery highway that millions of his forebears had traveled unwillingly into captivity. He walked then, as he walked now, looking at the unruly waves rolling in, awed by the mystery of never ending ebb and flow, tides predating the most ancient civilizations of humanity.

He didn't know any of God's names in those days when he first went to the beach to walk, except for Allah from the Nation of Islam and, of course, the generic word, God. Even before he understood the stillness that connected him with the ocean, he knew that quietude provided the best time to make life-changing decisions. While tossing down his namesake's Black Label scotch whiskey on a regular basis back in the day, he still had enough sense to put the liquor aside when he wanted thoughtfulness and quiet to enter. He told those to whom he ministered after his Calling that he had drank a lot of liquor in his time but never allowed it to make decisions for him.

On this night, walking under a full moon, he prayed to his Maker. He prayed . . .

Who will defend my people, who will protect them? . . . My Elohim, You have placed the spirits of the Reverend Gabriel Prosser, the Reverend Denmark Vesey, the Reverend Nat Turner, and General Toussaint L'Ouverture inside me, even as You have demanded that I be Your servant . . . Your Son, the Great Teacher, Yahshua, has said we should render unto Caesar that which is Caesar's, and render unto You, Yahweh, that which is Yours . . . Yahshua commanded us to love You with all our hearts and minds and souls . . . You see my heart better than I do, You know I have done my best to comply . . . He commanded us to love one another, to love our neighbors as ourselves . . . You see my heart and know I have tried to love not just those to whom I minister, but all of my people, even as so many fail to love themselves . . . He told us to love our enemies, too . . . You see my heart and know I have always had far more trouble with this than with the New Commandment . . . My Elohim, I see today's Caesar as Yahshua saw the Caesar of His day, as an oppressor, as a demon . . .

Do our lives belong to Caesar, or do they belong to You, Yahweh? The man leading this country has signaled an open season on us . . . he may well send thousands of our young men and women to South Africa—as his predecessors have sent them all over the globe—to die for the greed of the rich . . . Do their lives belong to Caesar or to You?

The man walked in the pre-morning darkness, listening inside himself for an answer, heard the quietness of his footsteps in the wet sand, the soft crashing of the waves over and over . . . heard the name of his Lord over and over in the quiet place that was his mind:

YAHWEH . . .

The man remembered something he had read or heard somewhere: "The government has convinced almost everyone that only they have a legitimate right to be violent. Everyone else is deemed criminal or insane, or both, if they even dare to think of such a thing."

This man who walked thought about the new president, who had been in office not yet three hundred days. To this man walking, President Hugh Allen Lewis Bruder gave every indication of being both criminal and insane. Yet, many citizens applauded him for his murderous behavior and intentions. A large percentage of white Americans loved him. Red staters, they called themselves, priding themselves on their moral uprightness. He had included five black Americans, a record, in his cabinet. (Some wry pundits nicknamed the quintet "Bruder's Black Brigade," saying they served as the president's insurance against charges of racism for anything else he did or said.)

Adversaries called Bruder the "emperor of euphemisms" even as he developed a reputation for being plainspoken. He made it clear the U.S. was a far better country a century ago than it was now, because, in his words, "everybody understood everybody else then." He invoked the spirit of Booker T. Washington's "understanding" in his historic nomination of the country's first African-American to be Chief Justice of the Supreme Court. The man was so servile that even a majority of black conservatives questioned the nomination. He made former Secretary of State Condi Rice seem like a radical, his critics said. As Bruder expected, it created the spectacle of the Congressional Black Caucus— the only blacks (except one senator) holding office in the three branches of federal government—leading the charge against his nominee. White politicians, especially Bruder supporters, fell over each other to support the appointment to show the nation's racial progress.

Do our lives belong to Caesar or to You? . . .

The same day Bruder made the chief justice nomination he told the world that South Africa's Preston P. Lumemele was deluded if he thought his nationalization of his country's diamond and gold mines would go without a response. Nor would he be allowed to continue nuclear reactor research and development. He had tricked South Africans into giving him eighty-three percent of the vote, Bruder said. If Lumemele intended to challenge the United States, it might become necessary to restore real democracy in South Africa. Lumemele might well meet the same fate as other enemies of America, like Maurice Bishop and Jean Bertrand Aristide and the Sandinistas, Bruder told reporters at a Rose Garden news conference. "The United States Empire is the true successor to the British Empire, and I'm not afraid or reluctant to call us an empire. We are the democratic light of the world. Nuclear weaponry in the hands of Lumemele, along with his blueprint for a United States of Africa, is inimical to the interests of the United States Empire."

Do our lives belong to Caesar?...

Bruder, of German descent, personified the relationship all of Europe had with Africa. In one of his most famous sermons (he called them lectures), this man with the shaved head walking by the ocean described it as a "vile and satanic relationship, trailing the blood of uncounted millions across the centuries." Whenever he gave a version of this sermon/lecture, he always quoted the Last Poets: "Each ripple in the ocean is the grave of an African who refused to be a slave..."

...or to You, my Elohim?

The man walked and he prayed:

From this day forth, I give Caesar only that which is Caesar's and teach those with me to do the same... I place not only my life, but I place my very soul before You in this work I am about to undertake... My people have enemies within and without... I can no longer allow Caesar to ravage my people... I will search for soldiers in the streets, in the jails, in the schools, and even in churches and mosques, if any will choose to stand with me... I ask that You bless the lives You trust to my care, and that they be strong in Your sight...

A field commander couldn't have a better adjutant than Romeo for what he was about to do, this man thought. And his chief instructor, the man code-named "Robert," was as good as they got. Romeo's longtime friend, Andrew Blackman, felt right to him deep down in that still place inside that he had learned to rely on. And of course there were others.

The Fourth Star wanted his decision. He would contact the Fourth Star tonight.

Elohim, the first thing you taught me after my Calling was not about the death of Your Son or His resurrection... You first told me to go among my people and teach them to "Love one another." To "Love one another" and to "Love Yahweh, their Elohim, with all their heart, and with all their soul, and with all their mind...

I have tried to live and teach your New Commandment by example . . . Still, there is more self-hatred and distrust among my people today than love . . . I have tried to live the Commandment among those you brought to me to minister to . . . Some have scorned me, but most have been faithful . . . Now, in humility, I ask You how I can love my people and yet not defend them from their enemies? I ask if I am loving my neighbor when I allow others to brutalize and murder my neighbor, as they have done for centuries . . . You have placed the spirit of Nat Turner and Toussaint L'Ouverture within me . . . You have taught me there can be neither love nor peace if there is not justice and righteousness . . . If, somehow, what I do now is not pleasing to You, I beg Your forgiveness . . .

It has begun . . .

Another man from the Covenant of the New Commandment needed to make a decision, too. He poured three fingers of bourbon into a glass, drank it down and poured another. He drank half of that. The initial warmth descending in his chest usually comforted him. This time it didn't.

He knew he could still back out because he hadn't told them anything yet. Actually, he had nothing to tell them.

If he backed out, he knew they would expose his indiscretion. His fuckup. There would be hell to pay, both with his family, and with those who looked up to him in the Covenant. There would probably be publicity, all of it bad. He tossed down the rest of the bourbon.

He'd made his bed and now he had to lie in it. He winced at the aptness of the hoary metaphor. The phone rang. The handset felt heavy in his hand as he lifted it.

"This line is secure," the nasal and reedy voice said on the other end. "You can talk freely."

"Meaning only you will have a copy of what I say."

"If you have anything useful. Do you have anything useful?"

"No. I don't know why you're bothering the Covenant. We're a religious organization, we're law abiding, and we're peaceful. I told you that when you first contacted me."

"The Director believes otherwise. He believes you're a bunch of troublemakers. And, frankly, so do I. And the Director's usually right. You people live in the greatest country on earth, the greatest in the history of the world, and you have absolutely nothing good to say about it, ever. Because we haven't found anything on you people doesn't mean we won't."

The discussion aggravated the tension headache already snaking behind his left eye. What a crock of shit. But he suspected his caller believed every word.

"Okay, here's what's going on," the caller said. "We have someone inside the Covenant who will make himself known to you. He'll identify himself by letting you know that he knows this phone number. All you need to know is he's on loan to local law enforcement, and he's not an informational like you. Your job is to put him where he's in a position to see and hear things."

The man sat in the dark of his home office for a long time after hanging up. After placing the phone on its charger, he finished his glass and poured three more fingers of bourbon. Outside, an ambulance siren repeated short blasts of urgency en route to a life saving emergency somewhere with someone. He closed his eyes, trying to will the pain away. He sipped, hoping the drink might anesthetize his headache a bit.

The Covenant had been good to him. But, despite where he was, he felt passed over. Because he was sure *something* was going on, and he felt excluded. He felt like he wasn't trusted. With his responsibilities, how could he not be trusted? The thought made him feel as if he'd shot himself between the eyes. *What you're doing now doesn't make you very trustworthy, now does it?*

The twin memories surfaced so quickly, so vividly, that an anxiety attack flooded his being. The pain behind his left eye seemed more acute. He tossed the rest of the drink down, poured another. He closed his eyes . . .

He was a freshman. Her name was Tamika. She thought he was studying with some of his Pi Phi brothers. However, another frat brother had told his cousin the truth. The cousin had told Tamika. He and his boys were going down to see some sweet things in the nearby town of Bellefonte. "You better check your man," the cousin told Tamika.

They sat in her dormitory sitting room as he tried to explain or, in truth, lie his way out of it. Tamika sat rigid, silent, and listened. She was a quiet person, and now her quiet way informed her fury.

"Baby, I swear, I didn't know. When I got in the car, I thought we were going to Sharif's place to study. If I'd known, I wouldn't have gone."

After he finished his weak explanation of his betrayal, Tamika left the room without saying a word. His Pi Phi ring sat on the sofa cushion where she'd just been. He never saw her slip it from her necklace. He went back to his fraternity house and got drunk.

Although they made up two days later, she never trusted him again.

And there had been the scholarship. A sizable endowment to the

Covenant in 1988 in celebration of its twentieth anniversary provided eligible Covenant Academy graduates with full scholarships to pay tuition, books, and room and board. The denial of a scholarship had been bad enough; the scathing dressing down from Minister Johnnie in front of the scholarship board he chaired had been one of the most humiliating experiences of his life.

"No one gets a Covenant scholarship who doesn't earn it," the Covenant founder had said that awful day. "I'm Pi Phi, too, but my grades didn't go down to a 1.7 when I pledged, so I really don't want to hear it. We have high expectations at Covenant and that's the end of it."

Now, again, he felt certain he was being passed over for something important. And now the feds wanted to know about things that didn't exist, or at least didn't exist in the Covenant.

His stomach felt warm and his body more relaxed; his headache had lessened some. He poured three more fingers of bourbon.

NINE

As much as he liked to bowl, Sheriff's Deputy Steven Hubble was glad he was going back to work in the morning. He had done enough bowling to satisfy him for a year.

"One more game?" he asked Josh Krueger as he steadied his bowling ball for his final shot. Josh was the second of the Three Musketeers, a nickname they had acquired at the sheriff's sub-station. Wally Crawford, the third "musketeer," and the only African-American currently at the sub-station, hadn't bowled with them since they'd had to shoot that girl.

"Nah, I'm beat," Josh said. "You know, it's been funny bowling without Wally. Wonder what he's going to be saying tomorrow?"

Steve took his steps and hooked his ball down the lane. He just missed the pocket and got eight pins. He looked at his buddy.

"I don't know and I don't care what he's saying," Steven said. "He's been Mister Self Righteous because he didn't fire and we did. He wants to forget he's the one who yelled 'Gun!' We did what we had to do. Right?"

"Yeah, right," Josh said. "Speaking of black people." He nodded toward the front desk. A well-dressed black man was at the counter. The clerk gestured as if he were giving him travel directions. Then he stopped and answered the phone.

"Steven Hubble, you have a phone call at the front desk," the clerk's voice boomed over the loudspeaker.

"What the hell? Why can't whoever it is call me on my cell?" he wondered aloud, "Be right back."

When he got to the phone at the counter, all he heard was a dial tone.

He told Josh about the call as they packed their bowling balls. In the parking lot, the man who had been at the counter was studying a map with another black man on the hood of a black Pontiac Sunbird. Hubble had never liked seeing black people in his neighborhood. It was not the only reason for selecting this suburb, but it had been a factor when he and Ashley had picked their home.

He parked his SUV in front of their ranch style house and walked to the back of the vehicle to get his bowling gear. As he did, a car slowed down next to him. He looked up; it was the Sunbird. Both driver side windows slid down.

"Steven Hubble, you have been sentenced to death by Unit 2236," the driver said, pointing a pistol with a silencer directly at him. The man in the rear seat fired first.

They were the last words the sheriff's deputy heard before both shots struck him just above his eyebrows.

As police sirens began wailing on the DVD soundtrack, Romeo clicked the remote's off button.

"I don't trust the prosecution as far as I can throw them, but we have to give them a copy," he said. He stroked his beard with a forefinger and thumb. "I think this case will be like watching two defense teams trying to get the defendant off, with no prosecutor really trying to nail his ass.

"This is big." Romeo took out his cell phone. "We have to get this to Minister Johnnie as soon as we can. I called his police source. He's pretty sure they're going to do the 'justifiable homicide' bit with Patrick. Said they pretty much had their minds made up within about four hours. Incidentally, they're not happy with Carvel Thomas. He had the nerve to want to use civilian witnesses in the final report, and I understand there was a big argument. Only police officers' comments are in the final report, he said. Still, with this tape, it will be hard not to charge him."

"Probably. But, like you've said yourself, charging him and convicting him are two different things. Do you think mainstream media will pick up the story? It's clear that he didn't have to shoot George."

"Don't count on it," Romeo said. He took what he called "brainstorming notes" as he talked. "Our paper gets treated like an unwanted stepchild, regardless of how well we do our work. And with OneCorporation controlling more than sixty percent of all print and most television news in the country, they'll ghettoize it. Definitely won't be page one or a television lead. If the cops are saying 'justifiable,' that will be the story's lead.

"Consider this: Last year, some flaky former supporter of our brother on death row, Malik Al-Amin, claimed that Al-Amin confessed to him during a private conversation when he visited the brother in prison. Of course the local dailies ran it big on page one. One of our reporters got his hand on a letter the flake had written *after* Al-Amin's alleged confession. We documented the letter's authenticity thoroughly. In the letter the flake expressed faith in Al-Amin's innocence. Not only did they *not* pick up our page one exclusive catching the flake in a lie, but also, the same day, most OneCorp papers ran a virtual love letter-type story about the widow of the cop Al-Amin supposedly killed and how much she was suffering. They just weren't interested."

Romeo called Minister Johnnie and told him what they had. "We'll be there," he said, turning to Andy as he hung up. "He wants us to bring the DVD up tonight." The intercom buzzed and Romeo picked up. "Hey, Claudia. He is? We'll be right out." He looked at Andy as he hung up.

"The brother out in the front office with Claudia is the infamous Wardell Keyes. Like I told you, this security thing is Minister David's idea. He wants all leadership to have some security detail from the Swords with them most of the time."

"Claudia, I didn't expect you back so soon," Romeo said as they stepped into the outer office. He walked over to her and gave her a hug.

"The videoconference didn't take near as long as I thought," Claudia said. She flickered a glance at Andy. "My little darling F.L. had a brief bout of homesickness and the headmaster thought we should talk about it. We both think she'll be fine, and she got real goofy, in a nice way, when we got a chance to talk on the video. 'This video is cool, Mommy,' she said." She shrugged. "Growing pains."

"Andy, this is Claudia Greene, my administrative assistant," Romeo said. "Claudia, this is the reprobate friend I talk so much about that I can't get out of my life."

They all laughed. Wardell smiled as if he were too cool to laugh.

"And this is Wardell Keyes," Romeo said.

"I've heard a lot about you from Jhanae," Wardell said as they shook hands.

"How is Jhanae?" Andy asked, releasing his hand from Wardell's. He didn't like Wardell either. And it did have to do with Jhanae.

"She's doing great, just great," Wardell said with a broad smile.

"Boss man here speaks very highly of you," Claudia said. "You guys go waaay back, I understand."

Andy thought—hoped—he saw her eyes sparkle as she spoke to him. Be cool, he thought. It doesn't have to be about you. "Waaaay back is right," he said. "Even farther than that. And I was the saintly one growing up. Rome was the ungodly one. He needed this turn around in his life badly."

The phone rang as they laughed again. "This is the *Scabbard*. How may I help you?" Claudia answered. "Oh, hi, Michael. Hold on." She pushed the hold button. "It's Mike in Los Angeles. He says it's important."

"Wait here, I won't be long." Romeo disappeared back into his office.

Andy sat on the side of a vacant desk that he assumed would become his when he settled in.

"Andy, I was so sorry to hear about your brother," Claudia said. "You have my condolences."

"Thank you," Andy said.

"Yeah, Andy, that was too bad," Wardell said. "These cops are out of hand, man."

A series of incoming phone calls took Claudia's attention. It gave Andy time to take a good look at his friend's assistant. He hadn't really stopped looking since coming out of Romeo's office. *You're just going to have to bust me for staring, you and your fine self,* he said to himself. *Claudia Greene, you are mean, mean, mean.* He smiled at his juvenile rhyme scheme. Claudia glanced up at that moment. Her eyes met his; she smiled a quizzical smile of her own.

She placed her call on hold and walked past him to a file cabinet. Her fragrance, flowery and light, trailed behind and melted something inside Andy. He recognized the scent but it had never smelled like it did on her. Then came a light bulb moment.

Claudia reminded him of Uncle Bad Cat's second wife, Helen. "Bad Cat" was his personal nickname for his Uncle Sherman. Sherman had belonged to the Black Panther Party forty years earlier. The nickname was Andy's creation; no one else called him that. Andy vaguely remembered being the ring bearer at their wedding when he was about four or five. Helen had called him her "little boyfriend," creating the kind of bashful crush only a four- or five-year-old can have. Uncle Bad Cat and Helen both gave the Party about four years of their lives, leaving about the time Panther Minister of Defense Huey P. Newton started to derail his own political vision and direction.

The marriage lasted a year. Except for the dim memory of the wedding, Andy's impressions of Helen came from pictures Uncle Bad Cat still kept. The energy of one photograph in particular he remembered. It was the memory of that photograph he connected with Claudia's resemblance. In the picture, Helen, a full-bodied woman like Claudia, sported a huge Angela Davis-type Afro. Hands on hips with plenty of attitude, she stood, radiant and styling, in navy blue bell bottoms, a fringed navy blue vest, a pink turtleneck, and navy moccasins.

Andy absorbed Claudia Greene's light brown complexion a few tones above walnut, her round face and full-lipped easy smile, her ample but shapely figure. "Something to hold on to," Andy remembered old folks saying when he was a boy. She wore her hair in a full-blown look that resembled an Afro except that it had been frizzily straightened.

"Wardell, turn on the television set," Romeo yelled from his office. "The OC Eye-Span." He came out still holding his handset. "Thanks, Mike. I'll tell the Minister. It is an interesting development. Let me know anything else you get."

A newsreader came into focus speaking on a muted television screen mounted on the wall near the door. A moving banner beneath her said that OneCorporation International private security forces had taken heavy fire from terrorist teams trying to wrest control of the oil fields in Iraq from them. Other terrorists in suicide trucks had attacked conventional U.S. forces at three locations along the border with Iran. The U.N. Security Council was in emergency session. "I have not ruled out the use of nuclear weapons if these forces of unholy terror continue to resist the forces of freedom," President Bruder said on the moving banner. "We will never surrender the Middle East to evil terrorists."

"They used to be 'insurgents,' at least in news reporting," Romeo mused. "Bruder has changed all that. People are 'terrorists' even while defending their own country."

Suddenly a photograph of a police officer appeared behind the muted newsreader. Above his head was a banner that read: ASSASSINATION? The man's shirt collar, insignia, and uniform tie differentiated his picture from a mug shot. The officer was swarthy with slicked-back hair and a perpetual five o'clock shadow.

"Turn up the sound," Romeo said.

. . . "Angeles area deputy sheriff was found shot to death outside his Arcadia, California home. Steven Hubble, a four-year-veteran of the force, died of two gunshot wounds to the head. A sheriff's spokesman said Hubble was returning home from a nearby bowling alley. Neighbors said they heard no shots. Hubble was one of three deputies involved in the controversial Tanya Morris incident earlier this year. Morris was killed in San Bernardino, California, when three deputies surrounded her vehicle and saw a gun in her hand. Hubble and another deputy are believed to have fired the shots that killed Morris. Authorities ruled that death justifiable homicide, saying the deputies had reason to fear for their lives. Investigators have no motives or leads yet, and a spokesman said they have no connections between Hubble's death and the Morris incident." The face of the sheriff's spokesman, blonde, young and military looking, filled the screen. "Of course, we're exploring all possibilities. Connections between the Morris incident and Deputy Hubble's murder have not been ruled out, but it's just too soon to say," the spokesman said. The pretty blonde newsreader's earnest face returned. "Deputy Hubble is survived by a wife and three children. Funeral arrangements are pending, " she said. "In other news . . ."

Wardell muted the sound. "I'm glad somebody shot him," Wardell said. "All these racist cops need to be taken out." He looked at Romeo. "We need to write an editorial endorsing his death."

Romeo stared at his security man. "I don't think so," he said. "Get the car and bring it around. Andy and I are going to Minister Johnnie's home."

After Wardell left, Romeo turned his attention to Claudia. "Call production and let them know that we'll need a banner for the Hubble shooting. Patrick is still front page with as large a still of him about to shoot George as we can lift and blow up from the DVD. The South Africa stuff is still both sides yakking, so we can move that to page four or five. Also, look over the editorial I wrote and give me some notes."

"Got it," Claudia said, jotting notes as Romeo talked. "Did you look at that envelope I gave you that was in the mail slot this morning?"

"Yes, I did," Romeo said. " A group calling themselves Unit 2236 is claiming responsibility for killing that deputy we just saw. I'm checking with Minister Johnnie to see if he thinks it's authentic and we should run anything. I haven't heard anything from other news shops. I even called a reporter at a daily; he hadn't heard a thing. If we use it, we'll pull something else off of page one and run Unit 2236 between Hubble and Patrick."

Claudia looked at Andy. "It's a pleasure meeting you finally. I'm looking forward to working with you."

Not as much as I am, Andy thought. "My pleasure, I assure you," Andy said.

Andy thought—hoped—he saw her eyes sparkle as she spoke. Be cool, he warned himself again.

After they were outside, Romeo looked at his friend, pursed his lips, and then cackled.

"My homie wasn't paying attention, but I told him he'd like Claudia." His face became serious again. "She's a great person. Take your time, Any. If you guys manage to hit it off, she's the kind of strength you need nearby right now. You don't need me to tell you that you've got a lot going on in your life. You don't need to be rebounding into nothing."

"True that," Andy said.

"I think she's checking you out, too."

"You saw more than I saw," Andy said, remembering her eyes. "But yeah, she is fine."

Wardell pulled up in the Covenant vehicle, a two-year-old Toyota

Corolla. "Yes, and we'll talk more later," Romeo said, placing a finger to his lips.

Johnnie Walker was gone when they arrived. Ila, his soft-spoken wife, invited them in. The Minister's modest lifestyle had been one of the deciding factors for Andy when he first started attending Covenant Saturday morning meetings. His two-story brick home spoke of comfort but not wealth, as did everything about Minister Johnnie Walker. He earned what he needed to provide for his family and funneled everything else back into the ministry. After some initial tension in the early years, Ila came to not only support but also embrace her husband's position on material things.

"Johnnie said to tell you an emergency came up and he'll have to meet with you this evening," his wife said. She was a light-skinned slender woman with a soft voice and elegant silver hair cut short. She moved with the bearing and grace of a professional dancer, which she had been. "There's a protest meeting at Washington Memorial tonight. He suggested that you meet him here about seven and go over together."

Wardell drove them back to the office. "You can leave, man," Romeo told his security aide. "There's a protest at Washington tonight. I guess you want to be there, but you can take off if you want. We'll have a large security detail there."

"I'll see you at Washington," Wardell said. "Nice meeting you, Andy. I'll tell Jhanae I saw you."

"I don't like him either," Andy said after the aide drove off.

"Didn't think you would," Romeo said. "But, as the Minister teaches, we may not all like each other but we better learn to love each other for our mutual survival."

"Yeah, right." Everything felt jumbled again.

"Claudia's been divorced about six years now," Romeo said "I think they split about a year or two after she joined the Covenant. She had an excellent background as a legal secretary. I hired her almost immediately.

"She has an eight-year-old daughter she adores who just started attending a private school in California. She named her after Fannie Lou Hamer and calls her F.L. It was a tough decision for her to make. Fannie's smart, going on brilliant; she got all A's when she attended our school, and we're tough."

"Why did she send her to a school out there? Our school goes to twelfth grade."

Romeo looked at his friend. "I can't get into that," he said. "If I could, I would."

Andy said nothing. If Romeo was withholding information, he had a reason. "Can you drop me at a car rental? I need something until I can buy something. Then I'm going over to my uncle's and finish unpacking."

"Let's go."

As Andy got out at the car rental, Romeo snapped his fingers. "I know what I meant to ask you," he said. "Have you ever read *Song of Solomon?*"

"In the Bible?"

"No. Toni Morrison's novel."

Andy shook his head. "I've read a bunch of her stuff, but not that one."

"Do me a favor and read it real soon."

"Done," Andy said. He made a mental note to pick up a copy.

TEN

ndy negotiated the winding, sloping curves of Martin Luther King, Jr. Drive carefully. It had been a while. The drive snaked through one of the largest parks in the country; the bends seemed less treacherous than he remembered, and much easier than torturous Mulholland Drive in L. A. But then, he'd grown up with King Drive—it had been Germanville Drive then, named for the river running parallel to it less than two hundred yards to the west. City fathers had changed it during his junior year in college. For him, Mulholland amounted to foreign territory, driven only twice during his stay there with Debora. He pushed her from his mind before she could settle in.

Even as a boy, Andy admired the large, majestic homes nestled among the verdant foliage now segueing to autumnal tones of gold, red and orange. Then they represented wealth and the city's elite. Although far more egalitarian and middle class in ownership now, the mostly Tudor architectural grand dames still retained an old money look. Less imposing areas of Germanville had declined since his high school years; the homes along the Drive had not. Unlike most of the city, this section of Germanville had not succumbed totally to white flight. It now housed several racial ethnicities, avoiding the historically clannish self-segregation and economic apartheid that had long been city characteristics.

He turned off at Roosevelt Lane, waxing nostalgic during the drive to the Minister's home. He still thought of streets and areas by the gangs of his day who had claimed an illusory control over turf, control that was quite real to peers who didn't live there. Baines Street (although the gang called itself Bainez Street). The Coalyard. Winterville Warriorz. Wolftown Esquires. Roaming these streets, and chasing pretty honeys had been an avocation for him, Rome, and a few other homeboys who lived across town on the North Side in less moneyed tenements. Those streets now had new generations of legendary gangs like the Crosstown Exiles, Death Valley, and the notorious Algerian Quarter Bandits. As a teenager, Minister Johnnie had been a "runner," or leader, with the original Exiles' junior division in the early Sixties, almost a decade before Andy was born.

Too late, Andy realized his reminisces had caused him to pass Minister

Johnnie's modest colonial-style two-story home. He made a U-turn at the next corner and came back on the side where the Walker home sat. He slowed as he saw a parking space on the side he had just been driving on. He decided to turn around in the Minister's driveway.

He pulled the rental car into the narrow Walker driveway adjoining his garage and shifted into reverse. Before he could back out, two men materialized from high shrubbery lining the wall of the brick façade structure. He slammed on his brakes as he saw a black SUV move into position behind him. A third man well over six feet tall, a mobile mountain of a man, moved toward him on the driver's side. The headlights of a vehicle parked on the other side of the street came on; the car turned slightly, blocking traffic, headlights trained on his car and the SUV. The blazing light in his rear view mirror made it difficult to see those in front of him.

He should know as well as anybody: the Swords of the Master did not play. Andy knew there was security at Minister Johnnie's home without knowing the details. His unexpected turn into the driveway, in an unfamiliar car no less, violated the Minister's space. The Swords security detail knew the Minister was expecting company, but had no instructions for letting anyone park in the garage driveway.

Andy kept his hands in sight on his steering wheel. Officially, they were unarmed. But whatever they had or didn't have, Andy knew with certainty that any adversary would have to kill them all to breach Minister Johnnie's home. His heart thumped with the realization that membership in the Covenant was the only thing that kept him from being scared shitless.

The football tackle-looking brother leaned down. Andy didn't recognize him. He wore a blue jeans baseball cap with the name of Andy's alma mater in neat white script across the front of the crown: *John Upton Church University*. He motioned with one hand for Andy to roll the window down.

"Yes, sir, thank you," Football Tackle said. His voice was quiet, close to a whisper. Andy saw the silhouettes of the other two men watching. One stationed himself at the car's left headlight; the other stood by the right front fender. "You're on private property."

"I apologize, my brother," Andy said. " 'I come not to bring peace but a sword.' My name's Andy Blackman. I write for the *Scabbard*. I just moved here from the West Coast."

Football Tackle's noncommittal gaze relaxed slightly to acknowledge Andy's use of the Covenant's watchword. "Yes, sir," he said in his quiet way. "May I see your identification?" At the instruction, the man standing at the right front fender moved down so he could see into the car on the passenger side without obstruction. Football Tackle looked at Andy's driver license. At that moment, the headlights went off behind him. "Yes sir, Brother Blackman, I've read your stuff in the paper. You can park across the street. The Minister is expecting you. Peace and blessings to you."

"Peace and blessings." Andy hadn't seen it happen, but the SUV behind him had moved. He didn't even *see* the SUV.

Minister Johnnie opened the door of his home wearing a smile of amusement. "I hope the brothers didn't startle you too much," he said. The older man escorted him to his study, a large, comfortable, lived-in kind of room. Romeo was seated on a huge plush sofa. The masculinity of the furnishings made it clear that this was Minister Johnnie's sanctuary. Several stacks of books sat in front of bookcases chock full of other tomes.

Minister Johnnie went behind his desk and sat in his large worn leather high-backed chair. He fiddled with a fountain pen lying on the blotter of his desk. Behind his chair, a portrait of Malcolm X looked down impassively on the conversation. It was the famous photograph in which the Muslim minister's forefinger was extended and resting on his cheek; his ring finger bore a large ring with the star and crescent symbol of his faith. Minister Johnnie saw Andy looking at the portrait.

"At least you don't have that slight frown that strangers and white folks get when they see Malcolm sitting up there," he said, flashing his famous smile. "I see them wondering why I, who follow the teachings of Yahshua, pay this kind of respect to a man who followed the teachings of Prophet Muhammad. That's the kind of stupid, divisive world we live in. It's so simple, really. Malcolm was a warrior for his people, a warrior who loved his people, a warrior who said, 'If you see a church or organization fighting for black liberation, then join that church or organization.' 'A greater love has no man than he lay down his life for his friends,' our Great Teacher said. Yahshua was talking about men like Malcolm; I don't give a damn what others say about the picture. I am a warrior for my people; I love my people, too. Except for Yahshua, he's the closest role model I've found. He submitted his life to God, whom he called Allah; I submit my life to God, whom I call Yahweh. Same God with a different name from different cultures, as far as I'm concerned. I notice especially the white folks who sit where you're sitting don't seem to get that part, especially if they're fundamentalist Christians." He picked up the pen and started to doodle. European classical music played ever so softly in the background. Andy guessed that it was Brahms.

"You've been in the Covenant how long? About five or six years, isn't it?"

"Six years, Minister Johnnie."

The Minister's look was direct. "Why did you join? And more important, have we done anything for you? You've made a strong contribution to us, and I hope it's reciprocal."

Best to go with what the Minister taught: the truth, unembellished, as best as you know it.

"I started coming to Saturday meetings because of my ex-wife," Andy said. "Jhanae was quite zealous about your teachings at the time, and I was trying to make an impression, so I came along because of her. Had no intention of joining, quite frankly."

"You thought we were a weird cult, like a lot of folks?"

Andy laughed. "Yes sir, I did," he said. "I'd never thought one way or another about God having a name, or the obvious, that the word 'god' isn't a name but a description. I didn't see it as important. The irony is, by the time I decided to join, Jhanae and I were starting to have trouble in the marriage."

"And you joined because of what? Did you become full with the Holy Breath?"

"No, sir. I was as fragmented as most, maybe more so. Minister Johnnie, to be honest, I don't think religion had as much to do with it as the Covenant's political views. The religion came later for me." Andy thought for a moment, remembering. "You gave a talk about how we no longer lived in a democracy, how we had been under non-democratic corporate rule for some time. And you talked about how the corporate sector had hijacked the Fourteenth Amendment from black Americans. And you provided indisputable proof. I didn't know any of this stuff you were talking. There I was, almost thirty-three years old, and I knew things weren't right, but I don't think I understood what I was feeling. I was working for a daily newspaper, the best job I'd ever had, and something wasn't right. I think I got what you call the 'slap up side the head' when you spoke that day. But it was a politicized slap."

"I take that as a compliment, young man. And I don't hear it as flattery." Minister Johnnie sat back in his chair. "I'm glad I could be a part of your development. For me, the political is spiritual, and the spiritual is political, always has been. Some folks say I'm too political, but I don't give a damn. If people can't eat, if they can't be treated when they're sick, if children are getting a third-rate education, if they're not being respected on a daily basis, it has to affect the spirit. If a person's most important part of the day is getting high on whatever, it's got to affect the spirit. I say that as someone who got high back in the day. And I say that Yahshua saw it that way, too. He saw the Romans as oppressors, the Sadducees and Pharisees as collaborating Uncle Toms, and he worked for the liberation of our people." He looked at Andy. "I hope you've drawn closer to Yahweh. You had quite a temper when you got here, I understand. You seem to be calmer in your spirit."

Andy was surprised that the Teacher knew about his temper. There was more to Minister Johnnie than was apparent even in his charismatic leadership. "I like to think I've grown spiritually, Minister," he said.

"I'll say this, and then we'll get to the business at hand," Minister Johnnie said. "When I was in seminary at the Interdenominational Theological Center in Atlanta, one of my first mentors was a fierce professor named Frank Beatrice. Reverend Beatrice was big on the Old Testament prophets, had no patience with white people, and very little patience for what he called 'those corn bread and chicken eating, Uncle Tom, Maryland Farmer preachers who are sellouts of our people.'" He grinned remembering his mentor's salty appellation for appeasers. "He was fond of saying this: 'some churchgoers want love and peace, but the saints want justice and righteousness.'"

He looked Andy directly in the eyes. "Your friend Romeo is a saint. I'm looking for some more saints. Are you a saint, Andrew Blackman?"

The sudden question surprised Andy. "Well, sir, I want justice and righteousness, if that's what you mean," he said. A sudden thought struck him with a certainty rooted in intuition: *I'm being interviewed. For what?* He glanced at Romeo; his friend's eyes revealed nothing, and his mouth gave only the slightest hint of a smile.

Minister Johnnie smiled. "Hard to call yourself a saint, isn't it?" he said. "I like that." He paused. "Romeo said you have a DVD from a young man who videotaped your brother's murder."

"Yes sir." Andy took the disk from his briefcase and gave it to Minister Johnnie. "He said he didn't trust giving it to the police himself."

Johnnie Walker didn't reply. He placed the tiny silver disk in his DVD player; the three of them watched Michael Patrick gun down George Bascomb.

Once again Andy felt fear and anxiety surfacing, the kind he had first felt on that spring day almost twenty-five years ago when Romeo's brother was killed. Now, though, he felt something else, something unfamiliar, something hard to identify. This feeling had not been with him that day in the bank, that day with those cops, with Romeo, and with Romeo's brother, Sonny. And his next thought was this: *I bet Rome felt this . . . thing . . . that I feel.*

Minister Johnnie clicked the disk off at the moment police hustled Mike Patrick away from the crime scene. He leaned back, clasped his hands, and pressed his extended forefingers together and against his lips. So long ago that he no longer remembered why he did it, Johnnie had taught himself the gesture as a reminder to think about his words before speaking.

"I want to kill a nigger," Minister Johnnie said, speaking to no one in particular, speaking to millions. "I want to kill a nigger so goddamned bad I can taste it." He closed his eyes, which were wet. He grimaced, as if in pain, and shook his head from side to side.

Finally he spoke, his eyes open again, looking away from both men. "The Covenant has built a school to care for the minds of our children. We have created a credit union for our economic well-being. We own a few successful businesses that provide a small measure of independence. We have a strong prison ministry. We provide information to our people through the *Scabbard*. But, with all these works from a committed congregation after forty years"—he gestured toward the television monitor—"We have built no protection against the nigger killers.

"We have fifteen meeting places in this country, with ten thousand people who study the work of the Great Teacher, Yahshua. We have a branch in South Africa," he said, still reflective although his voice rose. "We do pretty well, on the whole, with the New Commandment from our Great Teacher. As groups go, we love one another. But we have no defense against the nigger killers."

He turned his chair toward Andy. "I assume you've been following the shooting of that sheriff's deputy in California yesterday."

"I know the basic details."

"The six o'clock news said investigators are theorizing that it was an execution, that there may be some connection to the death of our dear sister, Tanya Morris." Minister Johnnie pursed his lips. "You know, of course, that Hubble will be given a large hero's funeral by his colleagues, whatever the reason for his death. He will be praised as a fallen hero. Tanya Morris' family, on the other hand, did not even receive a letter of condolence from city officials. None of them attended her funeral; none of them wondered if a young white woman in the midst of an epileptic seizure—information officers had when they arrived on the scene, by the way—if a young white woman with epilepsy who had a gun in her lap would have been gunned down. I think not. I think they would have correctly surmised that she had it for self-protection. Witnesses said at least one deputy, and it may have been Hubble, made inappropriate remarks of mock remorse immediately after the shooting. But then, in our legal system, and in discussions with law enforcement, black witnesses never seem to have the weight of law enforcement witnesses. No one witnesses for us."

The Minister stood up suddenly. "If it's proven that Hubble was executed, the people who did it will be characterized as criminals, as terrorists, as demons. There will be a massive manhunt for them. No one will believe they were right to kill Hubble. No, I take that back. There will be some in our barbershops and beauty parlors and on our street corners and the like who will applaud them, but only in that environment. And Tanya's horrible and unnecessary murder will be mostly forgotten, mentioned only at the bottom of news stories about Deputy Steven Hubble." He walked back to his chair, sat down.

"And now, even as we wait for the verdict on the scumbag who killed Delores Olds' fetus, we have Michael Patrick." The Minister looked at Andy. "You understand, of course, that Michael Patrick is not the real nigger killer."

"Well, maybe," Andy said. "But he's a member of the army for those who are the real nigger killers." He thought he saw the minister's eyes twinkle.

"What do you mean?"

"My uncle and I used to have these discussions. I hated cops for quite a while after what happened to Rome's brother, Sonny. One day I was yelling about how rotten the pigs were. He listened for a while and then he broke it down for me. Showed me that they were doing what they were hired and paid to do. In other words, he showed me that the nigger killers were the ruling elite, the Hugh Bruders of the world, if you will, and the CEOs of places like OneCorporation International, which, of course, Bruder used to be. He said the Michael Patrick types might be the ones we have to fight, but they were just doing the bidding of their masters."

Minister Johnnie smiled. "Your uncle's a smart man. That's exactly what I mean. President Bruder has not ordered a single one of these killings by police. But if he wanted to exercise a different kind of leadership, he could set a tone that said these murders wouldn't be tolerated. He could see that an example was made of someone like Michael Patrick. If he wanted to make ending drug traffic a priority, it would be done. But that's never in their best interests."

"And black life has always been cheap," Romeo said. Andy looked at his friend. The two men had received that lesson early in life and seen little to dispel it since. Andy suddenly saw the Covenant in a new light. He realized how truly dangerous the Covenant of the New Commandment was.

The Covenant valued black life. They had no monopoly on doing so, but valuing black life seemed in short supply when one walked along streets like the Avenue. Andy saw it even in the eyes of children. Not all, but far too many. They had stopped valuing their own lives. And they understood the cost of confrontation with the law by the time they were twelve years old. Any black male, banger or not, knew he would be blamed for his own death if a cop took him down for any reason. Fighting and killing each other might not be acceptable but it was tolerable to those who decided the consequences of such things.

Those who valued black life, and considered black lives equal to white lives, had historically been considered dangerous, even anti-American. Andy saw this as he looked at Minister Johnnie and saw danger in what he did and said, as he had not seen it before. Before him, there had been Huey P. Newton and Bobby Seale... H. Rap Brown... Kwame Ture... Karenga... Malcolm... King... Robert F. Williams... Elijah Muhammad... Garvey. The Federal Bureau of Investigation had hounded them all and many others who thought like them.

"Are you okay?" It was Minister Johnnie. Andy explained where his mind had drifted. "He does understand," he said when Andy finished. He looked at Romeo as he said it. Andy heard the approval in the older man's voice.

It had started to rain. Minister Johnnie looked out the window, then at his watch, as the rain quickly became a stormy downpour.

"We have to get over to the protest meeting." He looked at the two younger men. "The way of life in this country has always sanctioned nigger killers and nigger killing, from the first day captive Africans were pulled off a ship in chains. The killer can wear a sheet, a uniform, judicial robes, a corporate business suit, sit in the Oval Office, it don't matter. He can even be black, wearing a gang banger's clothes.

"You have to understand, it probably never occurred to Michael Patrick that he couldn't get away with what he was doing. He possessed a badge and a gun, he was facing an uppity nigger who dared to raise a hand to him, to try and disarm him. How dare he raise a hand to a white man! Patrick didn't hesitate to take him out. *Because... he... could.*"

The study fell silent. Andy looked at Romeo. His friend's eyes were moist. He was sure he was thinking of Sonny. *The way of life in this country has always sanctioned nigger killers and nigger killing, from the first day that Africans were pulled off a ship in chains.*

"Romeo, did Wardell bring you over here?"

"Yes sir, he did."

"Let's ride with him. I don't feel like driving. I'll call David and tell him to meet us at the church. Andy, leave your car here and pick it up after the rally, okay?"

"Yes sir."

Andy thought about what had transpired as they walked to the car. Even though Minister Johnnie had done most of the talking, and Andy had said little, the feeling still had not left him that he was being interviewed.

But for what?

ELEVEN

Big Larry heard about the protest rally first and called his Checkers Gang comrades. Of course, he started with Mr. Jake.

"They're holding a rally over at Washington Memorial tonight over that shooting," Big Larry said. "I'll pick you up if you want to go."

Mister Jake had answered the phone with a mouthful of a bite from his pork chop and mayonnaise sandwich on wheat bread and swallowed before he spoke. "It's just going to be a whole lot of talk but, yeah, I'll go," he said. "Especially if you're driving. Have you talked to Otis?"

"I'm calling him next."

"You know they ain't going to do a thing to that cop, don't you?" Mister Jake took another bite of his sandwich. "They let y'all have your little rally and blow off some steam while they just go about their business."

"I don't know, Mister Jake," Big Larry said. "Folks are upset. I hear they're expecting a few hundred folks out there tonight. Let me call Mister Otis and Varnell. We'll talk about it when we get together. Varnell's just bought one of these electronic checker players and he said he's going to bring it. That man never gets tired of playing."

Mister Jake snorted. "As far as I'm concerned, you need real checkers to play checkers. I don't know what that is he's talking about. So c'mon, I'll be ready. But it's like I tell you, white folks ain't gonna treat you treat you right, regardless."

Two

We hold these truths to be self-evident, that all men are created equal, that they are endowed by their Creator with certain unalienable Rights, that among these are Life, Liberty and the pursuit of Happiness. . . .That to secure these rights, Governments are instituted among Men, deriving their just powers from the consent of the governed, --That whenever any Form of Government becomes destructive of these ends, it is

. . . the Right of the People . . .

to alter or to abolish it, and to institute new Government, laying its foundation on such principles and organizing its powers in such form, as to them shall seem most likely to effect their Safety and Happiness. Prudence, indeed, will dictate that Governments long established should not be changed for light and transient causes; and accordingly all experience hath shewn, that mankind are more disposed to suffer, while evils are sufferable, than to right themselves by abolishing the forms to which they are accustomed. But when a long train of abuses and usurpations, pursuing invariably the same Object evinces a design to reduce them under absolute Despotism, it is their right, it is their duty, to throw off such Government, and to provide new Guards for their future security.

TWELVE

hen the Checkers Gang arrived at the church, the crowd was still quite sparse. Mister Jake insisted, as he usually did at such gatherings, on sitting up front. The four of them had occasional social outings, usually to gatherings of a political bent like this one, and, on rare occasions, a movie. Although it was Big Larry who called this time, more often than not it was Mister Jake who gathered the others. A widower for eight years, and without an active partner for seven years before that—Alzheimer's Disease had first claimed his wife's mind and then her life—Mister Jake refused to go quietly into what he called the dark night of old age.

"You talk to Varnell?" Mister Otis asked.

"Uh-huh. He finally broke down and got a cell phone. Said he had to work late but that he'd be here." Big Larry looked around the cavernous church. "I sure hope more folks get out here. It's a shame what they did to that brother. Word on the street has it that cop's going to get off."

"You ought to know that, Mister former Black Panther," Mister Jake said. "They can't prosecute him because it would be bad for morale. And even if they do prosecute him, they can't do it like they mean it." He glanced at his watch. "What time does this thing start? I can't be up all night, I need my beauty rest."

Mister Otis guffawed. "Jake, you ought to quit. We're early, it's going to be a half hour or more."

Varnell bustled up the aisle. "What's up, y'all?" he said as he sat down in the pew with them. "Larry, thanks for letting me know, man." He glanced around the sanctuary. "Do you notice anything?"

The other men looked. The crowd was considerably larger and coming in at a steady pace. "What are we supposed to notice?" Larry asked.

"It looks like young folks are way outnumbered by people over fifty," Varnell said. "Over half of this crowd are old warriors. When we came up, it would have been the young people filling this place, with a smaller amount of us older folks. Am I right?"

Big Larry turned to look at the other attendees. "You know, you're right,"

Big Larry said. "Well, we've got a couple of generations since the Civil Rights Movement who never saw that overt racism these folks used to put down."

"As usual, I have to give you all some perspective," Mister Jake said. "See, my grandparents had my father late. Grandfather Robinson was forty, and I think Granny must have been mid-thirties. Grandfather Robinson was born in captivity. He was a teenager when captivity ended in 1865." Mister Jake never used the word "slavery" if he could help it.

"My grandfather told my father, and my father told me, that if we ever tried to get this lousy system to start educating our children, they would refuse. They would let the schools fall apart first, he said. My father said Grandfather Robinson was a self-taught man and brilliant. If he had gotten a formal education, he probably would have ended up a professor at a university somewhere, like Du Bois. Instead, he ended up drinking himself to death. But he always said we must teach our own first before we sent them off to other schools, that is, if we got the chance. That's how I ended up with the Honorable Marcus Garvey's movement.

"My father was conflicted over the Civil Rights Movement. He wanted those young people to stomp out segregation. But he said the Brown court decision would never become reality because people didn't want it to. And, of course, he was right. The schools are more segregated now than ever.

"I'm saying all this to say that young Negroes are not being taught what they need to be taught." He paused. "I'm done."

They digested Mister Jake's brief homily, no longer surprised by his unrelenting fierceness and antipathy toward all things American.

Varnell took out his small electric checker set. "Anybody up for a game?"

Mister Jake rolled his eyes, snorted, and pretended to study the program an usher had given him. Mister Otis took Varnell on and beat him twice while they waited for the program to start.

THIRTEEN

or more than forty years, Washington Memorial Episcopal Church had been at the barricades with the dispossessed, the neglected, the lost, the despised, the forgotten, and all the others that Jesus would have hung out with. For the first twenty or so of those years and before, the church, then known as Church of the Exemplar, ministered under the shepherding of a blunt spoken man named the Reverend Warren Walden Washington, who had since gone home to be with his Maker. If a rumble of any consequence took place anywhere on behalf of black folks during his lifetime, he was smack dab in the middle of it. Like one of his heroes, Frederick Douglass, he fought right up until the day of his death. Ironically, like Douglass, he was attending a women's meeting, a group called Sisters Sick of Violence, when he collapsed.

The unquestioned centerpiece in his church was a twenty-foot by thirty-foot mural that dominated the pulpit. The mural was framed by the Sacred Desk at stage right of the pulpit and a blonde mahogany lectern on stage left. The mural, four years in the making, depicted the Last Supper with a dreadlocked African Jesus flanked by twelve disciples culled from the winds of North America's tortured history.

Malcolm X sat at Jesus' right hand, and the Rev. Dr. Martin Luther King, Jr., sat next to him on the other side. Fannie Lou Hamer was there, too, and Harriet Tubman. W.E.B. Du Bois stood in the back, next to the Reverend Nat Turner. Elijah Muhammad sat at the table; on his left was Mary McLeod Bethune, and next to her was Frederick Douglass, looking fierce. Marcus Garvey and Sojourner Truth were at the other end of the table. Standing a little apart from the others was Booker T. Washington. There was no Judas figure, although some hardcore nationalists insisted the artist had placed Booker T. in the picture for just that reason.

Diminutive in stature, the Reverend Washington had been a giant of a man who marched with King, held counsel with Malcolm, and talked theology with Howard Thurman. He allowed Stokely Carmichael, H. Rap Brown, Eldridge Cleaver and others to hold forth with revolutionary invective during the turbulent, unruly Sixties. A story, possibly apocryphal, said that on the night that Panther Minister of Information Cleaver spoke, Washington had stood on the church steps with him before his talk.

"Brother Eldridge, I've heard recordings of several of your speeches," the cleric said, looking up at the leather clad Panther official towering over him. "I enjoy them. You have a gift. You use the word 'motherfucker' with a lot of wit and attitude. I laughed out loud when you rhetorically told the authorities, 'And I don't want those motherfuckers telling me not to say motherfucker.'"

"Right on," Eldridge replied with a smile. "You're my kind of reverend."

"I'm glad, brother," the Reverend Washington said. "Still, you need to know that in the Church of the Exemplar, I am telling you not to say motherfucker, or use any other profanity in this church. I will personally stand up and tell you to sit down if you use that language in my sanctuary. I hope we understand each other."

Eldridge didn't say "motherfucker" that night.

Now, nearly a score of years after Washington's death, the beloved cleric's spiritual presence and authority still permeated the aging stone building. The flat coolness of the air conditioning system chilled the large room, made larger by its vaulted ceiling. Despite the sizable attendance of four hundred, there were still available seats in the three dozen pews on both sides of the center aisle that seated about ten people each. Volunteer ushers scurried about, urging those seeking justice for George Bascomb to move closer to the front.

Out of sight and facing the speaker, for his or her eyes only, a small post card sized plaque sat framed on the Sacred Desk. The Reverend Washington had placed it there in his sophomore year as the church's minister. The worn card, which he had laminated after it became dog-eared, read, "Know before Whom you stand."

On this night, the room hummed with an aliveness the church's namesake would have liked. A palpable expectation shimmied in people's conversations and greetings of each other as the gathering grew larger. It was an expectancy often felt around assemblies either motivated by tragedy or celebratory uniqueness. Such expectancy ran bounteously through the 1963 March on Washington; a similar energy, writ large, permeated the first march of millions in 1995, when over a million male descendants of Africans and others reflected their true selves, dumbfounding everyone, especially their enemies, with both their extraordinary quantity and magnificent quality. The Reverend Washington had put the rhetorical question to his congregation on the following Sunday: How many times and places can a million plus of *anyone* come together *anywhere* for *anything* without a single arrest or disturbance, minor or major? When Minister Johnnie arrived at the church, he left his aides and joined the Reverend Doctor J. Wellington Thibideaux, the Reverend Washington's successor, in his office. Romeo went directly to the pulpit to do a sound check, prepare the Sacred Desk, place water, and do other chores for his leader. With a view of the audience, he tilted his head in the opposite direction from which he had just come and grinned. When Andy followed the direction of his friend's tilt, his line of vision bumped into a smiling Claudia Greene. With sign language and self-conscious facial gestures, he asked if there was a vacant seat. His pulse raced, which he did not take as a good sign. Andy's experience told him that his conversation with women flowed more easily when he was at ease and unconcerned about the outcome.

Romeo's assistant sat at the end of a pew, holding her purse and an organizer. She slid over to make room for him. She wore a waist-length brown leather jacket over a beige button-front tailored blouse; form-fitting blue jeans that hugged her full thighs; and dark brown patent leather sling-back pumps. The light floral fragrance that smelled so natural on her made him want to take her face in his hands. After he settled in, she said, "You guys have had a full day. How are you feeling?" Her smile, slight but one that included her dark brown eyes, was encouraging.

"I'm holding it together," he said. "Being busy is good." He gestured at the crowd. "Seeing that there's some anger over George's death is encouraging." He wished his pulse would slow down.

"I admire what you're doing, and how you're doing it," Claudia said. "It's the best tribute you can give George."

Andy saw that she had a small birthmark next to her full lips. "Thank you. I've been meaning to tell you that I think you're the Covenant's best-kept secret. I'm surprised that we haven't met before now."

Her smile grew. "We do have ten thousand members," she said. "Until recently, I've just been a rank-and-file kind of girl. I've only been at headquarters about two years," she said. "I joined the Covenant in San Francisco after I saw my brother turn his life around."

"That explains it. I moved to Los Angeles about two years ago." He deliberately avoided saying why. "Do I know your brother?" He snapped his fingers. "Are you Glenn Greene's sister?"

"Yes I am. We don't look alike, so many don't make the connection. My parents adopted him as an infant."

Glennville Greene was a textbook example of Minister Johnnie's work with brothers off the block. He had terrorized the streets of Detroit as a precocious, baby-faced drug dealer and gang leader who carried two guns at all times. Unable to reach either weapon during a sneak attack when he was sixteen, Glenn was hit in the head with a tire iron while making a call from a public phone. He spent three weeks in the hospital. His concussion was severe but miraculously there was no brain damage. Unable to afford plastic surgery, a jagged scar parted his hair and ran like an ugly part along the left center side of his skull. He concealed it with a large collection of skullcaps that became his trademark. A year after the beating, he learned who his assailant was, found him, and pistol-whipped the older man to the point of death. He was arrested for aggravated assault. A good lawyer got him tried as a juvenile, and his sentence allowed for release at age twenty-one. By that time, he had connected with the Covenant of the New Commandment after Minister Johnnie came to the Youth Facility and spoke. Glenn started a meeting at the YF that grew quickly and reduced the institution's recidivism rate dramatically. Glenn got an early parole, ostensibly for good behavior. Minister Johnnie saw his leadership skills and groomed him for the hierarchy of Swords of the Master when he was released.

A flurry of activity made them turn to the aisle next to their seats. "Speaking of the devil," Claudia said. A quartet of security, two in front and two behind, escorted the ministers Walker and the Reverend Thibideaux toward the pulpit. One of the lead Swords was her brother.

Glenn, two Swords, and a Magdalene Society sister were immaculate in black three-button suits with discreet red and green epaulets on the jackets. Glenn wore a black knit skullcap. Walker *père* and Walker *fils* wore identical black calves' leather three-button sports coats with tiny black, red and green metal flags on their lapel, charcoal grey trousers, and black tasseled loafers.

Andy looked around the sanctuary. While he had been immersed in the brownness of Claudia's eyes, other Swords had quietly moved into security positions in the large room. Two Swords had quietly ushered Ila Walker, Minister David's wife, Judith, and Marian Bascomb to front row seats. A squad of ten Swords stood at parade rest in front of the communion rail. The Reverend Thibideaux moved to a seat on the right side of the pulpit, his eyes mildly approving the Covenant's pageantry; the Walkers sat behind the lectern on the left side.

Applause rolled through the high-ceilinged room as the Walkers and Thibideaux saluted the audience and took their seats. Thibideaux was a small wiry coconut-colored man in his early fifties; both Walkers were tall, chocolate, broad shouldered men who looked like football wide receivers.

Although Andy had sat and talked with the elder Walker no more than an hour ago, he noted how there seemed to be so much more of him when he was on, when he was getting ready to do his thing and bring his message to his people. His presence dominated the pulpit.

The host cleric nodded to a slender pale-skinned woman sitting quietly in the front pew whose immaculate makeup bordered on the theatrical. The woman stood and walked with the bearing of a fashion model to a microphone just inside the pulpit on its lower level. She removed the wireless microphone from its stand and tapped its head with an expensively manicured finger.

"Good evening," she said. Her tones were strong, big and confident. Her voice spoke each weekday morning from WRAP, a once African-American owned radio station now under the umbrella of OneCorporation International's Communications Division (OCI/CD). "I'm Martine Rideau, your hostess for this evening's very serious business. How's everybody doing?" A rumble of "okays" returned her greeting.

"C'mon, c'mon, *my* people can do better than that. I need to feel your energy. How's everybody doing?" The "okays" came back louder, sounding more like a chorus.

"Despite my new employers, I had to be here because, once again, the law has indicated that there's one kind of justice for white folks and a long train of injustice for black folks. When they say justice, they mean 'just us.'" It was an old saw but the crowd laughed anyway because it was their girl Martine saying it. She knew the OCI buyout had not been received well in the black community. And she knew her days at the station were numbered, regardless of what she said.

She introduced a quartet of female poets, The Poet Company, who brought the crowd to their feet stomping and shouting with a stirring, conga drum accented adaptation of Claude McKay's "If We Must Die," firing words and rhythms through the sound system like bullets. At the end, the entire audience chanted, again and again: "Fighting back! Fight, fighting back! Fight, fight, fighting back!"

Andy enjoyed Claudia's animated response to the syncopations of the four spirited griot sisters. She swayed back and forth, eyes closed, smiling, her hands aloft, clenched in fists, following the beat. Andy jotted a note to quote McKay's poem in his story.

When they finished, the younger Walker signaled Rideau, then stepped down and whispered in her ear. She nodded as David handed her a piece of paper.

Rideau introduced Marian Bascomb, who waved wanly to the crowd.

"I want to thank all of you from the bottom of my heart for coming out to honor my husband," she said. "My doctor advised me not to come, but I had to. Because George always fought for the right thing, I know he would have wanted me here, and I'll keep fighting for the right thing, too. God bless all of you because you give me strength."

Minister David Walker surprised everyone after Rideau introduced him. "I know you see me listed as the main speaker, and that's the way it was supposed to be. But I stopped by my dad's this morning. He tells everybody he's about to retire." There were a few chuckles sprinkled across the room. "Well, we were drinking tea and he said, 'Son, would I be imposing if I asked to say a few words this evening?'" More chuckles. The junior Walker crossed his arms in mock exasperation. "So am I supposed to tell my father, who taught me everything I know, well, *almost* everything I know, that he can't 'say a few words?' I ain't crazy!" He stoked the crowd slowly, playing off of their reverence for the firebrand who said things other preachers wouldn't dare say, and who had been doing so for almost forty years.

"And some of y'all have been to our Saturday morning meetings, so you know what 'a few words' means. It means I better save my remarks for another time or we'll be here all night!" Everyone laughed openly now; Johhnie's wide smile said he probably enjoyed the gentle roasting the most. "So let's hear from the brother who has always been a voice for those without a voice, a man who has implored us to wake up, clean up, and stand up for as long as we can remember, the man who has never forgotten where he came from, a man of power, my father, Minister Johnnie 'Black Label' Walker!"

The Swords in front of the communion rail, who had been seated since the program began, leaped to standing attention in one move, surveying the wildly applauding crowd giving Black Label a standing ovation. The Swords patrolling in the aisles also went on alert as their leader walked to the lectern, first waving, and then turning his large open hand into a clenched fist.

The crowd stood, shouting for the man some had started to compare to Malcolm. Walks it like he talks it, old folks said. Sure hope that boy David be as stand up as his daddy, they said.

At sixty-four, Johnnie Nathaniel "Black Label" Walker was at the top of his game, even though he made noises about "retiring" as Teacher and turning leadership of the Covenant over to his son.

Walker had honed his speaking skills during the crucible of the Civil

Rights Era, finding his voice as demonstrations, protests, and rhetoric morphed into the Black Power Movement.

"I want to thank my good friend, Father Jerry Thibideaux, for graciously allowing us to gather in this very spiritual sanctuary. Washington Memorial is a home for us all, and it's certainly a home away from home for the Covenant. It's a place filled with the energy of so many ancestors who struggled and gave so much of themselves that we might be here. We indeed stand on the shoulders of giants when we are here at Washington Memorial. I also want to thank my son, David, for allowing me time to say a few words." He smiled and paused for the wave of gentle laughter. "That sure was a Walker introduction."

He segued into a brief biography of himself although everyone there knew who he was, providing the autobiographical information as a covert history lesson. Both Andy and Claudia could almost recite what came next.

"I'm from Monroe, North Carolina. David makes you think I'm tough, but none of you knew my father. I'm not tough; that man was tough. Whatever I got I got honestly, and I got it from him. You see, my daddy was a member of the NAACP in Monroe." He could hear the puzzled murmur since the venerable civil rights organization was not known for militancy, or at least not Johnnie Walker's brand of militancy.

"Who knows who Robert F. Williams was? I call him Saint Robert, although I don't think he would have liked that." Of course, all of the Swords and all Covenant members raised their hands. Less than a hundred other hands went up, and most of those belonged to people who had heard Walker before.

"Williams was president of Monroe's NAACP in the mid-fifties, about the same time that a young preacher named Martin Luther King, Jr., was turning things upside down in Montgomery, Alabama," Minister Walker explained in the cadences of a charismatic university professor. "As NAACP president, and to the organization's consternation, Robert F. Williams organized an armed cadre to fight back against the Ku Klux Klan. In North Carolina! In the Fifties!"

A rumble of surprise rippled through newly informed listeners.

"In Monroe, the Klan had to bring some if they intended to get some because Williams, my daddy, and several others didn't play that," Minister Walker said. He enjoyed shifting back and forth between academic sounding phrases and street colloquialism, sometimes in mid-sentence. "They got their rifles, loaded them, and waited for any racists who even thought about taking black life, do you hear me?" His voice thundered, a modern day Jeremiah imploring his people to action.

"Now, I know I'm here to talk about George Bascomb, and we're going to talk about our brother, but I'm telling you these things for a reason, because I want you to know where I'm coming from. When those virulent racists in Monroe saw that Brother Williams and his men weren't afraid of them, it made them crazy. This was 1954, 1955, and all Negroes were supposed to be afraid of all white people. They had to frame Brother Williams to get rid of him. I'm not going into all the details but they had to frame him, and he chose exile over jail."

His chocolate skin glistened with perspiration. He perspired easily, and Walker often made his audiences laugh by saying he was getting "dewy," a line he had stolen from Lena Horne decades ago. He removed a white handkerchief from the pocket of his black leather jacket and patted his salt-and-pepper beard and glistening dome.

""Let's talk about George Bascomb and what we have to do for him. I didn't know Brother George, but I feel like I knew him because of his actions. I feel like I know him because *I* am George Bascomb. *You* are George Bascomb. *You* are Amadou Diallo and Tanya Morris and the unborn baby of Delores Olds. Minding your own business and here they come, guns drawn, thinking they're the Terminator or some damn body.

"George was a young man trying to protect an elder in his community, and the community itself, from a crazy acting white man. The only thing he did wrong was not going to get his piece, if he owned one." Several "ooohs" and "hmmms" and someone shouting "Tell it! Make them understand!"

"Yeah, I said it!" Walker roared. "If I'd been there, Officer Michael Patrick wouldn't have to worry about a trial or nothing else. I'm a peaceful man, but the lessons of this country tell me that when people like this Patrick start shoving our people around the way he did, he's supposed to be on his way to the graveyard to keep him from doing it again! You tell me, why should people believe in and follow a god that tells them they should do nothing but take a whipping from their oppressors? I would have done to him what Moses did to that Egyptian he saw beating up on one of his people. He looked around and saw no one was looking and he took him out! Yeah, I said it!" The crowd rose as one, stomping and hooting and hollering and talking about what a mouth Minister Johnnie had on him. Minister Johnnie patted his right hand in an impatient gesture on the lectern. He took a glass from beneath the lectern and sipped water.

When they quieted down, the minister became conversational again. "All of us know that Patrick would not have behaved like that in his own community, even if he did exchange words with somebody. He would have identified himself.

In closing, I just want to say that if George had lived in Monroe when I was a boy, I know he would have been cleaning a rifle along with my father and Robert F. Williams." There was long, sustained applause that made Marian Bascomb's eyes mist in gratitude.

Claudia lived about a half mile from the church. They walked slowly by unspoken mutual agreement.

"What did you think of the minister's talk?" It didn't quite sound like a test question in an examination, but almost. The top of her head came to his chin; he felt her looking up at him. Their hands bumped as they walked, and he restrained himself from taking hers in his.

"I always get something from Minister Johnnie when he speaks," Andy said. "Tonight, maybe even a little more because it was about George. Listening to the minister tonight, I found myself aching inside to do something more than I'm doing."

"About George?"

"About George. About them shooting us down anytime they feel like it."

"Romeo says you're more political than spiritual." Test question number two. He tried to deflect it lightly. "You two been talking about me?"

"Yes, we have," she said, looking him directly in the eye and smiling. "I asked him to tell me about you. If we're going to be working together, I want to know who I'm working with." Answer my question, Mister Man, her eyes said. It's important to me.

"I grew up in a Methodist church," Andy said, looking straight ahead, as if a Teleprompter might be there to help him. "I was active, I liked it for the most part, but as I grew older, a part of me knew that I went because my mom said I had to. I didn't feel any real spiritual connection all those years, except maybe once. I could get excited or involved while singing with the youth choir, but it just seemed like less than I thought it should be about. Once, at a youth conference at Morgan State during the summer, I had some kind of spiritual experience standing outside under the stars. I remember we were singing 'Jacob's Ladder.'

"Then a favorite Sunday School teacher of mine got killed suddenly in an accident. I was about fifteen, and it didn't make sense, because she was one of the most Christian Christians in the church. And when I prayed, it all seemed very arbitrary to me, as far as getting answers. So when I was eighteen, and my mother didn't try and make me go anymore, I stopped going."

A quiet breeze wafted across them. In some way that made no sense, the moment seemed somehow more intimate because of the slight wind caressing them. Claudia's spiked heels tapped a tattoo on the sidewalk. They passed two teenage boys smoking and exchanging a joint. They made no attempt to hide it as Andy and Claudia passed.

"But you seem committed to the Covenant." It was a question although it sounded like a statement.

"I am committed to the Covenant," he said. "I'm older and I see deeper into things than I did as a boy. I think there are a lot like me. We like Minister Johnnie standing up for black folks, and we want to fight that fight with him. I'm just not a Bible thumper." He paused. "Do I have to pass a litmus test on ideology?"

"I'm sorry, we just met, and I'm doing a first degree on you," Claudia said. "It's a bad habit I've acquired since—" She stopped and it was quiet again, except for the clack-clack of her footsteps.

"I met my ex-husband about the same time I became involved with the Covenant," Claudia said. A shadow of wistfulness crossed her face, flittered away. "I know now he was just not a nice person, but I had the zeal of a new believer and pushed, probably too hard, to get him to join, and it was like a wedge that grew between us. He was more interested in the politics, too, than he was in a spiritual life." They walked for a long moment without saying anything, the silence drawing them closer. "I guess I'm using my faith like it's a defense mechanism, aren't I?" It was a statement although it sounded like a question.

"It's okay," Andy said. "They call it getting to know each other."

Their hands bumped again. This time, he took her hand in his. He felt her hesitation, and then her acceptance.

As they walked, a feeling of vertigo washed over Andy. And then it was gone. For a fraction of a moment, he'd felt disoriented, off-center, as if in a boat, spinning slowly, moving at an untried speed through unfamiliar water, getting no response from attempts to guide himself in the direction he wanted to go.

FOURTEEN

Nearly every police officer in the Twenty-third Precinct sensed the animosity on the street. They inhaled it as they patrolled, a rancid effluvium hanging in the streets, over intersections, and along sidewalks. They saw it in the eyes of grandmothers as well as the sullen glances of young bangers. They heard it expressed in insincere politeness. These things passed, the old-timers on the force said. You just ride it out. And just because things were tense didn't mean you had to take any shit from anybody. Use common sense, but don't lose the upper hand.

Mike Patrick felt the tension in the precinct, too, although not as much as in the streets. A thin, almost imperceptible layer just below the surface at roll call. He tried to ignore it; they all did. Divisiveness could be fatal, Bulldog always said. On patrol, there was no room for white, black, brown, or yellow—just Blue.

Everyone had not been pleased, though. Detective Lieutenant Carvel Thomas, for one. Carvel was a good cop, Mike thought as he and his partner rolled out of the parking lot to start patrol. A little arrogant and bossy sometimes, but a good cop. The night of the incident had been a little problematic, but things would work out.

Just before Bulldog and the chief brought him the good news that night, he had heard Carvel sounding close to insubordination. The office door was closed and Mike froze momentarily before knocking.

"I've rewritten the report like you asked." Carvel's voice, just short of shouting, had come through the door loud and clear. "What do you mean, do it again?"

"Carvel, look, the chief said you have to change a few things, that's all." It had been a woman's voice, probably from downtown. He didn't recognize the voice. "Don't make this any tougher than it has to be. He said he'll look at the eyewitness stuff you have next week, but he doesn't need it in this report. And if you didn't actually see Mike drinking, well, you don't know that he was."

Mike remembered taking a deep breath, knocking, hoping he and Carvel wouldn't get into it. The downtown investigator had opened the door.

She was tall, lanky, and wore her salt and pepper hair in a page boy. The three of them had looked at each other.

"Hey, Patrick."

"Lieutenant."

Thomas had picked up his jacket and walked toward him. He remembered tightening up, ready for . . . whatever.

"Mike, maybe you should write my report for me."

Without another word, Carvel had brushed by him and slammed the door. He frowned at the memory. Bastard, he thought.

When Mike Patrick slid the patrol car to the curb in front of the Chinese takeout restaurant just off the Avenue, the young bangers standing outside stood their ground. There were five of them. To cops on the beat, punks standing their ground usually meant they had stashed anything they were dealing or smoking, or were just being brazen. (In this case, there was no Sweetness, cocaine, or weed within a half block of the restaurant. The word had come down from their supplier: he had received a directive from *his* supplier to do phone orders only until things calmed down from this Bascomb thing.)

Mike Patrick and his partner got out of their patrol car. Both officers adjusted their weapons belt as they moved slowly toward the teenagers. It was Patrick's first night back at work since the "incident." Bulldog Hudson had been the first to call it that. He remembered what Bulldog always said: "You're a cop first, so be that. Don't get distracted. Being distracted can cost you or your partner his life. Or these days, her life." Bulldog was still adjusting, decades later, to the concept of female officers.

Bulldog had gotten an Internal Affairs "justifiable" ruling on the Bascomb shooting in record time. Four frigging hours. If Mike had been impressed with his mentor before, he damn near worshipped him now. He'd been at the station, huddled with the IA CO, when Mike came in from Dock Place. Then, boom, it was "case closed," and Mike was back on the street. He smiled at the memory. You have it like that when you're a legend.

Mike's partner, Jorge Rodriguez, walked up to the banger who appeared to be the baddest. Out of the academy six months, he told classmates that he preferred to be called "George." He'd even engaged in some gallows humor with his partner while they were getting dressed for the street.

"Damn, brother, why'd you have to shoot somebody with my name?" George asked Mike with a crooked smile. Mike had shrugged but said nothing.

Now Officer George Rodriguez looked this black young man, who appeared to be about eighteen, directly in the eyes. The banger wore a hooded sweat shirt with the sleeves rolled up, exposing large tattoos on his left forearm: a large Gothic C, below it a B, and below that the Roman numeral III.

"Don't you think you're out a little late, homeboy?" George asked.

Cornbread the Third knew the drill. Walk the line between dissing this punk Rican cop and his redneck looking partner, and being punked out in front of his boys. Walk that motherfucker and don't step down on either side.

"First of all, I'm old enough to be out as late as I please," he said. His voice was low; one had to listen hard for the rancor. "The other thing is, you probably from the East Side, so I ain't your homeboy." He said it all without blinking.

"I see we've got a smart one on our hands," Mike Patrick said. "What's your name?"

His grandfather had schooled the young man well. "Even when you think you may have to throw down with the pigs, know the law for your own sake, not theirs," Big Bread had told him. "If they ask who you are, the law says you have to identify yourself. Name, rank and serial number, as they say in the Army. Think of it like the Geneva Convention of the streets."

"My name's Willis Jamal Richardson," the young man said.

"You have ID?"

"May I take out my wallet? I don't want to be shot at forty-one times just for reaching for my wallet. It does happen, you know." Watching the white cop's jaw tighten made young Richardson smile. His grandfather had schooled him well.

Two of his boys snickered. "You tell him about it, Bread," one of them said.

"Keep it up smart asses, you just keep it up," Rodriguez said. Both officers had their hands resting on their belts just above their nines. "Let's see your goddamn ID."

Slowly, Cornbread the Third took out his wallet. He handed it to Rodriguez, who made a show of examining it. Cornbread the Third and Patrick stared at each other.

"I don't like your attitude, boy," Patrick said as he moved toward the younger man.

"I'm not a boy," Cornbread the Third said, his tone even, walking that line.

"If I say you're a boy, you are a boy," Patrick said. He moved his hand to the butt of his nine-millimeter pistol, the gesture unmistakable.

Cornbread the Third didn't blink.

"Mike, cool, my brother, cool," Patrick's partner said. He handed the wallet back to Cornbread the Third and looked at him. "I'm going to cut you some slack."

Cornbread the Third returned his gaze. "Thanks," he said. "Y'all a little late getting to that 'good cop, bad cop' bullshit, ain't you?"

Rodriguez and Patrick backed away. "We'll see you again," George Rodriguez said. "Count on it."

"Jive punk asses," one of the young men murmured under his breath as the officers got in their car.

The patrol car pulled away. Mike Patrick looked at the streetwise young bloods staring at him and George. He knew in his heart that he had nothing against these people, despite what had happened the other night. Colored people —or Afro-Americans, whatever—had the same rights as anybody else. But people can't be allowed to just do what they want.

And, like Bulldog always said, scum are scum, whatever color they are.

When the patrol car turned the corner, the quintet relaxed. They did their ritual exchange that served as a greeting, a compliment, or a celebratory exchange: a light tapping of the fist on the shoulder with a downward motion and the thumb facing upward.

"Big Bread done taught you some shit," said a sixteen-year-old they called Bugeye. "You sure didn't take nothing from that Blue."

"I see why they call you Cornbread the Third," said Drugbucket, the one who had encouraged him. "You just like your Grandpops, talking much shit."

"You my nigga even if you don't get no bigga," Bugeye said with a laugh. It was an ancient compliment Big Bread had passed to his grandson, one that Big Bread said he had heard from Cornbread the Third's great-grandfather.

They tapped shoulders again.

FIFTEEN

George reaching in the trash can for the wooden slat, George creeping up behind Michael Patrick, Hayes shouting, Patrick turning, George backpedaling, Patrick aiming, Patrick firing . . .

The images kept recycling on a screen in Andy's mind during the drive to the 10 A.M. news conference at the 'Shoe. The ache inside came and went. Familiar and unfamiliar territory. He felt something extraordinary about his brother's death, something vague and indefinable. This wasn't like that day at the bank, when he and Romeo's innocence ended abruptly, ripped from them like a purse being snatched without warning; somehow he knew, deep in his gut, that George's death was only the first in some series of events leading him into a future he might not otherwise have chosen. He felt swept away into something he didn't understand.

"It was personal." The comment sprang into his mind. He knew the history but he hadn't known the comment: Four young black men had gone into what was called a Five and Ten Cent store on February 1, 1960. They sat at a lunch counter where white folks said they couldn't sit. Employees wouldn't serve them. Law enforcement was called. They came back the next day, reinforced by other students, and the day after that. Television news, then in its infancy, spread the protest images across the country. The demonstrations took on a mercurial life of their own. The fire that was the beginning of the end of segregation—started five years earlier in Montgomery—caught a new wind and roared out of control across the South.

What surprised Andy was the comment of one of the original four instigators. They hadn't planned to start a movement; it was personal. They weren't activists, they were freshman students going to school, and they didn't like being treated as if they were "less than." He and his comrades had decided they wouldn't allow people to treat them like that.

"It was personal." Now, the pain swimming through Andy was personal. Was it one more link in a chain of events stretching across a quarter of a century? Romeo had joined the Covenant, and evolved eventually into its leadership, because of his own pain. It was personal. Now here he was.

He parked, glanced at his watch. If they started on time, these folks, at least those who wanted to, would be able to get to the Covenant meetinghouse news conference by eleven. The police department news advisory faxed to the *Scabbard* said only that "an important announcement" in the Bascomb shooting would be made at 10 A.M. That son-of-a-bitch Patrick, at the very least, deserved murder two, but would probably be charged with murder three. There was no way this district attorney would file first degree murder charges against him.

The flat gray fortress-like building's official name was the Carmine L. Pecsi Police and Fire Administration Building. Officially named in the former police commissioner's honor, it unofficially remained "The Horseshoe," a nickname Pecsi himself ad-libbed at the ribbon cutting after thanking them for "giving me my flowers while I'm still here." The sleek, low-slung five-story monstrosity, with its glass and gray concrete exterior, occupied the entire city block bounded by Fourth Street, Main Street, Fifth Street, and Rose Street. The curve of the Horseshoe followed the contour of the nearby four-lane RFK freeway that led into the city from the south. The 'Shoe's curve housed the coroner's office, the morgue and, incongruously, the Department of Health Services. When the freeway straightened out past Main, the building curved again. The fire department's administrative wing then occupied the entire block parallel to its police counterpart, moving from Fifth and Rose down to Fourth and Rose.

The Horseshoe was the crown jewel from Pecsi's tenure. Like current Commissioner Timothy Kaheel, he was a local cop who had climbed through the ranks to the top cop job. It inadvertently became a memorial for its abrasive champion when he died of a massive heart attack a scant nine weeks after the ribbon-cutting ceremony. Originally planned as police administration only, other municipal services were added by a cost-conscious City Council.

Andy noticed the absence of cables littering the floor, which he still hadn't gotten used to seeing. The no longer new wireless technology now so commonplace meant an era had passed, a passing he had witnessed. Andy counted six television cameras, over a dozen still photographers, and at least two dozen print and television reporters, including stringers, several foreign reporters, and a handful of wannabes.

He crossed the lobby just as the police commissioner, the district attorney, a police inspector he didn't recognize, and two men in dark suits emerged from the elevator. The entourage walked directly to the battery of microphones on the podium. The suits hovered behind their superiors. The lobby's buzzing of voices dropped immediately into a quiet anticipation. A few throats cleared. Commissioner Timothy Kaheel stepped forward. A large, imposing man, Kaheel knew he was a presence in his full dress blues and wheel hat with gold braid—the military called it "scrambled eggs"—covering the patent leather brim. He wore the uniform the way it was meant to be worn. At fifty-nine, he still worked out at least an hour every day, except for Sundays. The band over his scrambled eggs was absolutely parallel with the ground: the gleaming brim stopped just a fraction above his dark, piercing eyes. No one had ever seen his shoes in other than spit shine condition. He had paid from his own pocket to have his shirts custom tailored when he was a rookie. Kaheel's no-nonsense manner had been honed over thirty-one years of movement through the ranks from walking a beat to the commissioner's office.

"Good morning," Kaheel rumbled in his deep baritone. "I'll provide you with a statement based on our investigation at this point, and then District Attorney Lynda Jacobs will provide you with the findings of her office. After that, we'll take a few questions."

He tilted his large head down, pulled out a pair of bifocals, perched them on his wide nose, and read: "Last Tuesday, September 29, at approximately 8:10 P.M., police Officer Michael Patrick was involved in a minor traffic accident in the unit block of Dock Place. Officer Patrick was off duty at the time.

"Words were exchanged with the owner of the other vehicle, who has been identified as Mister Carl Harris. A crowd gathered, and when the crowd became unruly, Officer Patrick attempted to restore order. Mister Raymond Hayes, employed as a security guard at the local offices of OneCorporation International, was summoned to the scene by Mister Garth Wilson, a friend of Officer Patrick. He provided assistance to Officer Patrick. Officer Patrick and Mister Hayes, who is duly licensed to carry a firearm, found it necessary to draw their weapons as the incident escalated. Mister Wilson also had a licensed firearm with him and also assisted Officer Patrick." Kaheel picked up a plastic cup filled with water, sipped from it, and continued.

"A man later identified as George Bascomb, who lived nearby on Dock Street, reached into a nearby trash can about this time and produced a wooden stick. He then advanced toward Officer Patrick, attempting to sneak up behind him. He assaulted Officer Patrick, who fended off the blow and told Mr. Bascomb to drop his weapon. Mister Bascomb refused to do so, despite repeated warnings from Officer Patrick.

"Officer Patrick fired one shot that struck Mr. Bascomb in the chest and fatally wounded him. Mr. Bascomb was transported to City Hospital, where he was pronounced dead at 9:15 P.M.

"Carl Harris, and his son, Richard Harris, were arrested and charged with disorderly conduct, simple assault, conspiracy, and assault with a deadly weapon. They were released on $1,000 bail each."

Kaheel looked up, ramrod straight, swiveling his head slowly from left to right as if inspecting a line of troops. "Before we take questions, we'll hear from the district attorney."

Lynda Jacobs stepped to the microphone. Bespectacled, silver haired and pale, Jacobs favored pin-striped suits (with skirts—women were not permitted to wear slacks in her office) and high-necked white blouses. Slender but not thin, she was a tall woman, almost as tall as Kaheel, which always surprised people seeing her for the first time because of her deceptively soft-spoken manner. Although a lifelong teetotaler, she had ruddy cheeks. Detractors and political foes called her "The Silver Needle," both because of her stature, topped by its glorious mane of hair, and her fervent support of the death penalty. Friends and supporters called her "Lynda Nails," although never to her face, after a media pundit once said while campaigning on her behalf, "My friend is hard as nails when it comes to standing up for the law and prosecuting wrongdoers."

She looked out at the reporters with ice blue eyes and grabbed both sides of the podium. Andy imagined her actually chewing on nails between her thin lips. Jacobs cleared her throat.

"My office has examined all of the evidence presently available in this incident. We have questioned everyone who witnessed what happened on Dock Street," Jacobs said, her voice soft and melodic. "It's the conclusion of the office of the district attorney that the death of George Bascomb, while unfortunate and tragic, was justifiable homicide."

Twenty-two reporters tried to speak at the same time. Andy saw the video in his mind, saw George fall to the ground staring at Michael Patrick, his life fluid staining his T-shirt and the street's historic cobblestones.

Justifiable homicide. Damn. They're saying it was okay to kill George. They understand it as reasonable. The shouting voices became background babble; Andy realized he was surprised at his own surprise. Why was he shocked? The words "justifiable homicide" were familiar, a rote mantra when unarmed black people's lives were taken by the state. *Scabbard* readers saw the phrase regularly. Today, it might be a truck driver like George, next week a grandmother at a wrong address. It might be a security guard leaving work, or a retired professional athlete on his way to a meeting. It might be a young entrepreneur standing on his steps, minding his own business, but none that a cop was bound to respect. Their commonality would be their blackness. Driving while black, walking while black, standing while black.

Sometimes the circumstances raised questions that were reasonable to reasonable people. Gang bangers led two or three patrol cars on a high speed chase in a car they hijacked or stole; a dealer and two-time loser decides he doesn't want to go back to jail. Sometimes. Andy knew those stories, too. But more and more stories like George's appeared and rode the front pages through a wave of anger and "investigations" rife with euphemisms and discounted eyewitnesses. Then the anger faded into nothingness and obscurity like morning mist drifting out to sea. Until the next time.

Jacobs shouting into the microphone over the hubbub snapped Andy from his reverie. "Okay, okay. We'll try and take as many questions as we can, but we can't speak all at the same time." She pointed to a rotund radio reporter wearing headphones. "Tony?"

"Lynda, How'd you come to that conclusion? Neighbors say it was totally unjustified," Tony said. He made an adjustment to the tape recorder on his belt.

She placed a fist to her mouth, cleared her throat. "We have statements from the neighbors and, quite frankly, there's disagreement among them. We—"

"C'mon Lynda, you're talking little details. Not a single person in the neighborhood agrees with the scenario you just gave."

"Tony, we have statements. We looked at the consistencies and the inconsistencies. We know Mister Bascomb had a stick, or a club, and we know he tried to disarm Officer Patrick. We know that Officer Patrick repeatedly ordered the deceased to drop his weapon. These were important elements in our decision not to file charges." She pointed to another radio reporter. "Heshimu?"

"I'm told that Patrick said at one point, and I quote, 'I want to kill a nigger so goddamned bad I can taste it,' and that he was enraged and cursing at people," Heshimu Kenyatta said, adjusting his glasses on the bridge of his nose. "Can you confirm that, and did it factor into your decision?"

Jacobs pursed her lips for a moment before speaking. "A few witnesses said they heard the 'N' word; others didn't hear it. We have already said that words were exchanged in what all sides agree was a tense situation. I know I'm repeating myself but Officer Patrick was attacked while trying to perform his duties, although he was off-duty at the time."

"Follow-up," Heshimu said before anyone else could speak. "I understand that Patrick was the *source* of the tension and didn't identify himself as a police officer until after he shot Bascomb."

Jacobs turned to look at Kaheel. The commissioner leaned into the microphone. "We were told that Officer Patrick did say 'police officer' several times after he drew his weapon," Kaheel said, his eyes inscrutable. "It seems he may not have produced his badge until moments after firing his weapon. That's still under investigation. We're still trying to sort that out. Susan?"

"How come Patrick has a lawyer if he's not being charged?" Andy recognized the brown-haired woman, a reporter he knew back in his *Bugle* days. Not only was Susan one of the best print reporters in the city, she pressed many of his erotic buttons. A petite brunette with a sister's booty, she was a clotheshorse whose trademark was elegant and expensive footwear. Today, she wore gray suede high-heeled boots.

Kaheel waved his hand slightly as Jacobs moved in. "It's almost routine for the Police Officer's Benevolent Association to assist officers with legal counsel when a weapon is discharged and there's a fatality."

"But Isaac Erlickson?" Susan fired back. "He's one of the highest priced criminal attorneys in the city."

Kaheel's transparency usually served him well. It also made it hard for him to hide discomfort. "I believe Mister Erlickson may have some arrangement with the association where he's volunteering his services to any police officer, not just Officer Patrick. I knew Officer Patrick was talking to an attorney, and I knew he was talking to POBA. I don't know anything about Erlickson."

The questions droned into insipidity. Andy felt his anger simmering and connected it to his silence. This was all bullshit, he thought.

Minister Patrick Muhammad, editor of the Nation of Islam paper, the *Final Call*, had stood quietly against the wall, scribbling. When Jacobs said, "Two more questions," Muhammad shouted his before she completed the sentence.

"Ms. Jacobs, people in the black community are angry over this senseless shooting. They know it didn't happen as you've described it today. How are you going to justify your conclusions to the black community?"

Jacobs twisted her mouth slightly, and ritually cleared her throat. "Patrick, first of all, we have the weapon that Mister Bascomb attacked Officer Patrick with. He was being attacked in a hostile environment, and no one's mentioned that today. He was making an arrest and Bascomb just came at him."

"That's not true," Andy said. He spoke without thinking, spoke from the anger roiling in his stomach. "You're lying to us. You're taking the word of Patrick and that white rent-a-cop. You know it's not true. Why are you whitewashing this?"

As a buzz swept the room, Kaheel tightened, but Jacobs actually smiled. "I don't know who you are, but you're out of line," she said.

"I'm George's brother!" The words came out loud, etched with pain. He struggled, successfully, and didn't add, "bitch!"

Air seemed to be sucked out of the room. For a split second, Jacobs, rattled by the identification, lost her composure. She recovered quickly.

"I'm very sorry and understand why you're distraught," she said. "Now I know this business about the 'N' word and other accusations have been making the rounds of the rumor mills. But I have to tell you, and everyone, that it's my understanding that Officer Michael Patrick conducted himself in a professional manner the entire time. We have to understand that the whole affair is a sad situation. There are no winners here, but a man has a right to defend himself. Finally, we can't run our police department on the basis of what we have to justify because of rumors, now can we?"

Almost everyone in the room reacted, shouting new questions. Even Kaheel raised an eyebrow. He leaned over, whispered in her ear under the bombardment of questions.

"Thank you for coming, everybody. No more questions. Thank you!" Jacobs said, a tight smile on her face. She turned on her heel, Kaheel beside her, and followed her phalanx of aides to the elevator.

"It didn't happen that way!" Andy shouted after them, his voice loud now and full of heat.

Andy knew he would never hear a police news conference the same way. Some naïve part of him thought they would do right by George. Both Jacobs and Kaheel spoke with authority, as if they had been there. He hadn't been there, but seeing the tape was the next best thing.

"Commissioner, does this mean Patrick will be going back on the street?" someone shouted as the knot of suits and uniforms stepped into the elevator.

Andy fell in step with Heshimu as they walked toward the exit. They shook hands.

"Damn, you shook them up, brother," Heshimu said. "You're really Bascomb's brother?"

Andy nodded. "I remember you, although it's been a little while."

"Didn't you used to be at the *Bugle*?"

"Yeah. Andy Blackman. I just got back in the city. I remember your show. How are things at the station?"

Heshimu's broad ironic smile split his handsome chocolate face. "Same pile of feces, different day." He cocked his head. "Damn, you acted like you saw it."

Andy smiled but said nothing. "I shouldn't have lost my temper. But we have something pretty big."

"I'm on my way to the Covenant news conference now. It's about this 'something big?' You know something that proves this was a crock of shit?"

"You got that right. You didn't hear it from me, but you remember the Rodney King story about, what, eighteen years ago?"

Heshimu laughed. "Oh, baby." He paused for effect. "I know I'm changing the subject, but guess what?"

"What?"

"The word on the street is that OCI is gobbling up your old paper, the *Bugle*."

It was Andy's turn to laugh. "You're kidding, right? What's mighty OneCorporation International want with a po' cullud paper?"

"You just gave the reason." They were outside now, on the handicapped ramp leading to the triple thick glass doors. Heshimu stopped to light a cigarette. "It might be a cullud paper, but it's the biggest cullud paper we've got in the country, knowwhatI'msaying? OneCorporation wants its tentacles in our little ol' dark heads, too, because we spend money. If they could buy the *Scabbard*, they might. It's not about them being right wing or not, it's about money. And control."

They shook hands and parted. Andy thought about Heshimu's comment as he walked to his car. *They want their tentacles in our little ol' dark heads, too.*

When Andy arrived at the meetinghouse, the first person he saw was Glenn Greene. They greeted each other with an embrace and smiles.

Glenn was immaculate in a tailored navy blue single-breasted suit and patterned tie. Except for the earpiece with a coil that disappeared under his collar, he looked like a successful businessman. A two-inch scar above his right eye and his navy blue skullcap bore witness to his pre-Covenant days.

"What's up, stranger?" Andy said.

"You, my brother," Glenn replied. "When did you get back? Or are you back?"

"Just a few days ago. I'm full time with the *Scabbard* now. I didn't know you had a sister."

Glenn, never a demonstrative person, moved his lips slightly in what passed for a smile for him. "Yeah, Yahweh finally entered her heart, too," he said. "She told me if any god could do something with a rogue-head like me, something good must be going on. Sis is something."

"I'll say."

"Oh, it's like that, huh?"

"We just met, Glenn."

"Well, I'm glad. You're a good dude. She could do worse. Look, give me a hand. Claudia was supposed to be here, and Romeo is trying to ship out copies of the DVD so that most news outlets and meetinghouses will have it today. He hopes saturation might negate what he calls the OCI factor."

"What do you need?"

"You work with the press. That way I won't have to use a Sword to do it. Give them releases, do any hand-holding that's needed. You probably know the drill better than me."

Neighbors watched the television trucks and other news media vehicles park on the meetinghouse lot and on their street and wondered what old "Black Label" was up to now. They were sure it had something to do with that shooting.

The large crush of reporters made use of the main auditorium necessary. Still, most of the three hundred seats were vacant. Four television cameras were present, along with most of the still photographers and reporters who had been at the 'Shoe. Some who usually ignored Covenant news conferences sensed something big. They showed up despite their disdain for the organization's unorthodox religious views, political stance, and security procedures. When you came to the meetinghouse, you came through a gauntlet of security and walked through a metal detector after emptying your pockets or pocketbook. Period.

Minister David Walker, wearing a beige business suit and coordinated tie, walked into the sanctuary promptly at eleven o'clock. Four Swords, including Glenn, flanked him. Looking neither left nor right, he strode to a podium that had been set up in front of the pulpit.

The Sword built like a football tackle that Andy had met the night before replaced Glenn at the front of the auditorium beside Minister David. Glenn moved to the wall, overseeing everything and everyone.

"Good morning," Minister David said in his booming voice so well suited to his profession. "I'm Minister David Walker, the Teacher-Designate of Covenant of the New Commandment. Welcome to our humble meetinghouse.

"Many of you came directly here from a news conference at the

Horseshoe about an hour ago. There you were told a pack of lies about the horrible events that occurred on Dock Place six days ago that led to the murder of George Bascomb."

Several reporters rolled their eyes at the words, "pack of lies."

"I understand our reporter got testy after hearing the distortions of Commissioner Kaheel and District Attorney Lynda Jacobs," Minister David said. "Well, Andy Blackman had good reason to be upset. For one thing, George was his half brother. In addition, he saw the cover-up being put in place and couldn't contain himself." He looked toward the back of the sanctuary. "Brother Andy, raise your hand. And thank you for your fine investigative reporting regarding the announcement we're about to make."

Andy raised his hand. He knew his colleagues hated being scooped by the *Scabbard*.

Two more Swords materialized at the front of the sanctuary in addition to the security detail. One held a stack of newspapers, a special edition of the *Scabbard*. The other held a box with three dozen DVDs. Another Sword moved to the DVD player.

"Let's look at what really happened that night, when our lying law enforcement officials insist that Officer Michael Patrick's actions were justified." He looked at his watch. "I imagine they are cursing just about now, or will be shortly. My father is delivering a copy of what you're about to see to the Horseshoe for their perusal. It contradicts almost everything they told you this morning."

Two Swords moved the podium aside as the lights dimmed. George Bascomb's fatal encounter with Michael Patrick unfolded to a quiet room. As he watched, Andy knew that if he lived to be a hundred, he would never adjust to watching his brother get killed. When the DVD ended, the stillness was palpable for several seconds that felt like minutes. Finally, Minister David spoke.

"My father, on behalf of the Covenant of the New Commandment, said he will ask Commissioner Kaheel to fire Michael Patrick immediately," he said. "He will also ask the district attorney to file murder charges against him. We have reason to believe the decision to exonerate this despicable man was made in a matter of hours. We know Jacobs hates to prosecute cops, but we hope justice will be done. We doubt it, but we hope. We'll take a few questions."

Someone asked Minister David who had taped Bascomb's death. Andy knew he wouldn't reveal the source and didn't listen for an answer. The feelings that swept through him when he first saw how George was gunned down were back. He knew something else. Two something elses, really.

The second something else: this feeling had been there for years; he had tried to ignore it. He had pushed it down ever since that awful day in the bank with Romeo and Sonny. Patrick wasn't there that day, but he might as well have been. The nigger killer spirit in him had been there.

The first something else: he now acknowledged what he felt, and that allowed him to name it. It went against so much of who he thought he was.

Deep in his heart of hearts, in the very center of his being, he wanted to kill Michael Patrick.

SIXTEEN

As a boy, Cornbread the Third liked listening to Big Bread talk shit about what it was like back in the day. Coming up in the Fifties and Sixties was to have known a special time, to hear Big Bread tell it. He especially enjoyed hearing Big Bread recount the details of the humid August day in 1964 when the Avenue exploded in a frenzy of fires, snipers, overturned cars, and broken store windows. Repressed anger had also raged like an unruly infection that year in Harlem and Rochester, New York; in Paterson, New Jersey, and St. Augustine, Florida. In fact, an undercurrent of dis-ease ran through all of the trouble.

The incidents triggering the unrest were depressingly similar. A young black male incurred the wrath of law enforcement in a street confrontation of some sort. He was arrested, beaten, or shot. Word spread, and the stories usually gained embellishments as they danced in the streets. Those embellishments fueled already existing anger and acted as verbal gasoline for the uprisings.

Cornbread the Third wondered what it would feel like to start some shit like that. Some real, honest to God, throw down, major action, so that The System, as Big Bread called it, would stop fucking with black folks.

Big Bread had been about twenty when black folks tore up The Avenue. According to news accounts, two cops blackjacked a nineteen-year-old gang member who got loud and unruly after being pulled over. He had no driver's license or registration and became belligerent when placed under arrest. One embellishment had his pregnant girlfriend getting beat; another elaboration said she'd miscarried right there on the Avenue.

In Big Bread's version, there was a pregnant girlfriend on the scene who became hysterical. She wasn't beaten and didn't miscarry, he said, but raised a lot of hell by screaming.

"We tore that sucker up," Big Bread boasted each time he told the tale. "We ransacked window displays, burned a bunch of stores, turned over cars, and just generally raised hell."

City officials estimated the damage at well over a million dollars; three people, all black, died. Big Bread hadn't started it, and, truth be told, didn't do as much as he made it sound like even after it started. But he always told his grandson that something about the energy of people spilling out in the streets the way they did made something happen inside him. He always said it was the beginning of the end of his wine drinking and gang warring days.

Every chance he got, Cornbread the Third told his boys about the raps he had with his grandpops. What it was like when black folks stood up and started breaking shit when they had enough of what The System was doing to them.

He always glossed over the part where his grandfather said rioting—even when you called it rebellion—didn't make a lot of sense.

"Boy, those riots were usually disorganized and mostly just got black people killed, and disrupted goods and services that we still needed after we got over being pissed off," Big Bread said more than once. He usually mentioned something else his grandfather said: "Understand, young blood, some of these folks in the street was just out for themselves and looting anything they could carry that wasn't nailed down. Wasn't nothing revolutionary 'bout them, they were just plain stealing."

His homies always laughed, especially if they were high. They liked the exaggerations Cornbread the Third added each time he told a version of the story, a skill he inherited from the original Cornbread, Big Bread himself.

On the evening of the dueling news conferences, Cornbread the Third happened to come into the apartment he shared with his older sister while she ate and watched the evening news. He put together an unruly concoction of scrambled eggs loaded with ketchup that he then combined into a stew with some cheese hominy grits, two pork chops, and a Coke, and joined her.

First, Cornbread the Third listened to the district attorney say why Michael Patrick would not be prosecuted. "Then, in what has to be an embarrassment for both the district attorney and the police department, a second news conference took place with a bombshell announcement from the controversial organization, the Covenant of the New Commandment," the blonde newsreader said. "The black militant group distributed a videotape at the latter news conference that appears to show Officer Patrick shooting George Bascomb. Much of what is seen and heard seems to contradict the version of events provided just one hour earlier by District Attorney Lynda Jacobs and Police Commissioner Tim Kaheel. Let's take a look at the tape." She did a theatrical pivot in her seat as if to watch.

Cornbread the Third barely contained himself as he watched. "I knew

121

it! I knew it! I knew they was lying about killing that man," he grumbled to his older sister with a mouth full of pork chop.

"What you expect?" his sister said. "They always do that. Where have you been?"

"I know they always do it," an irritated Cornbread the Third said. "But this time they're busted with evidence."

"Jacobs and Kaheel both released almost identical statements that said they were studying the DVD for authenticity," the news reader said. "They said they will have more information in a day or two."

"Who's gonna fake a tape like that?" Cornbread the Third said. "What is wrong with those dumb ass people?"

When the reporter moved on to the increase in unemployment for the third straight month, Cornbread stopped eating.

The word on the street had been close to the tape he watched. Nobody he knew had believed the police version of events anyway. Whatever the truth, he realized that almost everybody he heard discussing it on his block was pissed off.

Later that night, while he and his boys smoked and passed a couple of blunts and discussed it, Cornbread the Third made a boast.

"We need to tear this motherfucker up," he said. "This ain't right, and I'm just the nigga who will fuck them up. I'm tired of them messing over our people, you know what I'm saying?"

His boys murmured agreement between tokes. They better send that racist to jail, they said. This shit ain't right, what he did.

The thing that had a lot of people upset was the word going around that nobody knew Patrick was a cop, that he was just a white dude starting shit. Although even being a cop didn't give him no right to act like everybody was saying he acted. *Everybody* was talking about it, saying what a damn shame it was that they just shoot us anytime they feel like it.

About a half dozen of his boys said they were down for doing something, anything, instead of just talking. "Why don't we just break some shit?" Cornbread the Third asked. "This needs to be a serious muthafucking uprising." He said he would throw the first brick.

Cornbread the Third's calmness was gone. He seethed because he didn't like cops anyway and, even though he didn't know this oldhead Bascomb, he knew that his grandfather was right. He wanted to be able to boast to Big Bread that he had started the shit. The sun had just tucked itself behind the high-rise projects that spanned Twenty-second Street. It was already cloudy; the sun seemed to transition quickly from a golden disk in daylight into a reddish orb dying on the other side of dusk.

They didn't choose the Avenue. The vibrant black businesses of Big Bread's era were gone. Most had been spared, but paradoxically never recovered, from the burning and looting on that August day in 1964.

Cornbread the Third and his boys moved to the intersection where the Avenue crossed University Boulevard. A chain drug store now occupied the corner where a black hotel had been. In back of the chain store was a smaller street where row houses had been converted to girls' dormitories for Church University. Administrative buildings sat opposite the store. The buildings served the continually expanding academic factory named for John Upton Church and created a traffic canyon from the center of the city through to the north for those preferring surface streets at rush hour.

Cornbread the Third and his posse moved boldly toward a ten-story concrete monolith bearing a black and gold marquee that announced the J.U.C. Offices of Liberal Arts and Sciences.

Cornbread the Third threw the first brick.

As the glass splintered, an incredulous security guard inside moved quickly for the telephone. Two other missiles shattered the façade completely.

Others in Cornbread's posse ran wildly on the east side of University, breaking windows on a nuclear science building and the administrative offices of Urban Studies.

"Fuck Michael Patrick! Fuck the motherfucker! Fuck Michael Patrick!" they shouted as onlookers stopped and stared in disbelief.

As the youthful rebels ran amok on University, darting in and out of traffic that slowed almost to a crawl, one of Cornbread's boys ran out of rocks. He grabbed a large metal trash can and flung it over his head at the front door of the chain drug store. The glass shattered but didn't break. Splintered lines zigzagged in every direction on its surface.

Then, just at the moment the mini-rebellion seemed about to sputter to a stillborn death, two things happened.

The first thing involved several men in their early thirties. Earlier that day, they had gone to an office a half-mile away looking for temporary day work and been unsuccessful. They walked back and stood shooting the shit on University just north of the Avenue when the first brick sang through the air. They liked what they saw happening, and added their own counterpoint.

As fate would have it, at that moment they were talking about what a goddamn shame it was that black people never got any justice. People like that cop that killed that black man should be shot, one of them said just as Cornbread the Third's rock broke the nearby window. They looked for anything they could get their hands on and started throwing whatever they had at the windshields of cars parked closest to them.

The second thing involved the driver of a blue Ford Custom sedan traveling south on University. The driver pulled to the curb as he crossed the Avenue. John Oliver, an African-American police officer, was en route to work at the 'Shoe. He assessed the situation, threw a lanyard with his badge on it around his neck, grabbed his radio with one hand, drew his service pistol with the other, then placed it in his waistband.

"Officer needs assistance," he barked into the radio. He placed a hand on his nine millimeter pistol, thought about holding it at his side. He needed a next move, quick, in the rapidly evolving situation. "An unruly crowd . . . Officer needs assistance in the seventeen hundred block of North University."

His next move was decided for him when two new participants in Cornbread the Third's rebellion saw him at the same time he spotted them. He held his badge high.

"You on that punk ass cop's side," one man yelled. He'd rummaged on the top of a trash can and found a discarded partial gallon of paint. He moved toward Oliver and hurled the can. It struck the hood of the blue Ford, splattering white paint along its right side. The thrower's friend, a skinny man with uncombed hair who had just drunk the better part of a pint of cheap blended whiskey, moved to provide moral support. He tore open the front of his jacket.

"What? You gonna shoot me? Shoot me like you shot that brother? Go ahead, I don't give a damn, shoot meeeee!" Wild-eyed, he started beating his chest with his fists. Spittle formed at the corners of his mouth.

Oliver kept his hand in place on his nine-millimeter. His pulse ratcheted up; his mind screamed, *hurry up!* The paint thrower grabbed a bent piece of metal about a yard long in the same trash can and advanced on Oliver again. Behind the thrower, new throwers hurled various missiles at the windows of a bookstore. The manager hurriedly locked its doors.

Oliver fired a shot into the air as the metal looped toward him. By now a crowd had started to form. Some watched; others gleefully joined Cornbread the Third's rebellion. Three people jumped into the broken window display of the bookstore grabbing compact discs and a few CD and DVD players. They looked a little disappointed there wasn't more to grab, except for plenty of books. Who wanted books?

Several other items were thrown in Oliver's direction as anxious sirens grew louder. Someone threw a portable DVD player they had just stolen. The object struck the right side of the officer's head, dazing him momentarily. He reflexively turned and fired.

The first fatality in Cornbread the Third's rebellion, a twenty-nine-year old homeless woman known as Sweetness Sally, looked stunned when the bullet pierced her chest near her collarbone. Addicted to crack cocaine, she had recently advanced—regressed, actually—to the new drug on the street called Sweetness. She acquired her nickname for a willingness to provide oral sex to anyone for money or Sweetness, preferably a few hits of Sweetness.

Sweetness Sally had done a couple of hits only an hour before Cornbread the Third threw his brick. She died high.

SEVENTEEN

To Andy, command posts meant boredom, drama, self-importance, and more boredom. Sometimes, paradoxically, even command post drama felt boring, although drama nonetheless. The self-importance came built in.

Command posts had personalities. Even before George's death, Andy liked police command posts the least. Even at non-antagonistic crisis events—a fire, or a rescue mission—he felt a disconnect, a distancing, a self-imposed wall.

This chaotic night on University Boulevard felt no different. In some ways, it was worse. The police department had not had a good day. First, a public relations embarrassment that originated with a critic as vocal as the Covenant. The timing couldn't have been worse. And now this.

Andy wanted to get into the streets. That's where the story was. But six-square blocks were sealed off tight. A police car or wagon blocked every intersection. Walking in or out without going through a checkpoint was grounds for arrest. The police detail at each barricade had the same message: First, go to the command post at Hayes Elementary School.

Romeo called just as Andy parked his rental car near the school. Andy explained his dilemma. "Minister David and Minister Johnnie are already on the streets," Romeo said when his friend finished. "They got in before the barricades went up. Glenn got in, too. They have some Swords with them who live in the area, and they're getting some people off the streets. Minister Johnnie says people are really pissed off. And the cops aren't helping much with their attitudes."

"Hey, we made them look bad today."

Romeo chuckled. "They made themselves look bad. Look, call me back if you get in and I'll tell you where to find them."

Rutherford B. Hayes Elementary School stood, dirty and decrepit, on the perimeter of the area under siege. Built in 1920, it was named for the nineteenth president of the United States, the man who gained the White House by ending Reconstruction. In its decay, the school seemed an extension of Hayes' betrayal of then-newly enfranchised black Americans. Originally a school for the children of middle- to upper-income whites, Hayes' last major renovations had come in the early 1950s. Under the terms of the mayor's declaration of emergency, classes were suspended there until order was restored.

Andy noticed two news helicopters whirring overhead as he entered Hayes. A grim officer directed him to the school's auditorium. A knot of police officials stood near an ancient podium at the front of the room. Reporters stood or sat around in several clusters, critiquing the events of the day.

The commandeered classroom smelled stale, filled with yesterday's air. Andy recognized Lieutenant Susan Sharpe, the police department's public information officer among those at the front.

Sharpe, a petite blonde, looked up as he approached. She frowned in recognition. "My goodness, where have you been, Blackman?" she asked.

"Hi, Lieutenant," Andy said. "Good to see you. I was living in L.A. for almost two years. Couldn't stay away from here, I guess."

She made a face. "You were in L.A. and you came back *here?*"

Andy and Susan Sharpe had hit it off professionally during his brief stint at a suburban weekly, the *Sentinel*, just before he left for Los Angeles. In some parallel universe, they might have become friends. He saw her look at the press credential dangling from his neck. A shadow flitted across her face.

"When did you go to the *Scabbard?*"

"A couple of days ago. But I've been in the Covenant for several years."

"So are you here to beat up on us some more? I saw your story."

He thought he heard grudging professional admiration. Sharpe knew the department sometimes had to take hits. He knew this wasn't the time to be combative. "Just trying to do what I do. In fact, I'm wondering if I can get clearance to go in to see what's going on."

"The short answer is no. Blackman, three people have died tonight already," Sharpe said. "We don't give clearance because even if you signed something, we'd be liable. You show your press card, they'll let you in, but you're on your own. I know some of your people are in there and, despite everything that's happened today, God bless them because I know they're trying to stop this."

He took out his pad and pen. "I heard about the first death. How'd the other two die?"

"They tried to be snipers with handguns. They fired from windows, and wouldn't give up their weapons. SWAT officers responded. No names released yet."

Andy got the locations of the shootings and Sharpe's cell phone number for updates. As he left Hayes, he wondered why Susan Sharpe had become a police officer in the first place. He walked to the first checkpoint he saw.

Jagged noises pierced the night air. Alarm systems sounded simultaneously frightened and urgent, their wailing warnings now useless protection against people who grabbed whatever merchandise they could. Occasional gunfire crackled. Overhead, two police helicopters had returned and joined the news helicopters, circling like satellites, sweeping rooftops with the artificial sun of high-intensity spotlights.

Minister Johnnie Walker stood amid an immense spray of broken glass talking with two teenagers. The conversation appeared intense. Five Swords of the Master stood in a semi-circle around their leader, their attention mostly focused on nearby police officers wearing riot gear. Other teens, in plain sight, piled all kinds of electronic gear from a RadioShack store into several boxes. Three other Swords moved among them with an adamant message the police had conveyed: despite the brief truce Minister Johnnie had negotiated, no one would be allowed to leave the site with a single item.

Across the street, police officers held rifles at the "ready arms" position. Walker and his paramilitary aides had arrived at the intersection just before the cops did. Lieutenant Carvel Thomas, who seemed to be everywhere and anywhere recently, gave Minister Johnnie fifteen minutes with them. He warned him that any rooftop sniping would immediately end the truce.

"Brothers, I'm not saying you shouldn't be pissed off." Minister Johnnie talked fast, aware of the time constraints. His animated hand movements punctuated his words, as if he were back on the block. He wore a waist-length brown leather jacket, a matching baseball cap, jeans, and black running shoes. "I'm pissed off, too. And, you're right, we do have to do something. I'm just saying this ain't it." He looked up and saw Andy approach. "Hey Andy, come help me with these brothers."

"Minister Johnnie, I have all the respect in the world for you," the tallest teen said. He wore sweat pants and had one hand in his pocket, pulling the pocket upward. The posture suggested he was either holding his pants up or fondling himself; it was the latest macho posturing rage on the street.

Andy's scribbling onto a small pad caught his attention. The teenager glared at him. "Whassup with the writing, oldhead?" he snarled. "You a reporter?"

"It's okay," Walker said. "He's a reporter but he's with our paper."

That satisfied both youngsters. "I mean, you're not like the rest of these preachers," the boy said. "But we are tired of being fucked—excuse me, I mean, messed over, and we got to do something."

Walker pointed. "See those cops over there? They are ready to bust a cap in your young ass if I can't get you to listen. They're not doing me any favors and they don't like me either. But my profile's high enough that shooting me now would cause them more trouble than it's worth. But not you, and not your boys, and it won't matter that I'm here. You need to get your boys off the street for *our* sake, not to please the cops. Why don't some of y'all come over to our headquarters? You want to talk about doing something to change things? I am down for that. We can talk all night and *plan* to do something. But this ain't it. They have more firepower than you; you can't win."

The two young men looked at each other. "I appreciate what you trying to do, Minister Johnnie," the shorter one said. "And we know you ain't no Tom." The taller youth turned to the others moving briskly up and down the aisles of the store's carcass. By now eighty-five percent of the shelves were naked.

"Hey y'all, Minister Johnnie made a deal," he yelled. "You got to leave that shit or we got to fight the cops. The minister wants us to go to his place."

"Fuck the cops, man," a stocky boy said. "I got my shit with me just like they got theirs. I'm not afraid of they punk asses."

"C'mon Lonnie, give it up," the tall boy said. "The minister's right, man. We wanna get that killer cop punished, you know?"

The stocky boy's eyes met Johnnie Walker's. He faltered.

"They'll kill you without even thinking about it," the minister said. "This is not the time. Y'all want to really mess with white folks, we can talk about how to do it and win."

After long seconds, the stocky boy put down his box.

"Is anybody else packing?" Minister Johnnie asked. "If they are, they *have* to give it up if we're searched. You tell them."

His truce negotiated, Minister Johnnie had the seven teens in a church van and out of the area in ten minutes. Incredibly, Minister Johnnie's orchestration of events prevented a search. As the van pulled away, Walker and Andy walked over to the ranking officer among the armed squad who had reluctantly watched the negotiations unfold. The officer, Carvel Thomas, had once attended Covenant lectures on Fifty-fourth. Andy remembered him from the crime scene of his brother's murder.

"I got lucky, you being here," Walker said. He looked at the sullen faces of the cops under Carvel's command. "I owe you one. I know what this took."

The lieutenant's eyes veiled his feelings. He glanced at Andy. "This has got to be off the record."

Walker nodded to the lieutenant, then gestured to Andy, who put his notebook and pen away.

"No, Minister Johnnie, I don't think you do know what it took," Thomas said. "We have orders to shoot when looters don't respond to our first command. I will have some explaining to do. Especially because it's you."

"But we saved some lives. And kept some property from being stolen."

Carvel Thomas walked him away from the others. "In other times, this would be a good thing," he said when they were out of earshot. "But these are not normal times, these are Bruder times. We both know that most cops are not bloodthirsty. But, I'm telling you, something's been changing in some of these guys' heads the last year or so. I will deny that I said this to you, but it's open season on black people. The mindset in Washington is trickling down to the local level, no doubt about it.

He stopped and faced Walker. "I'm a good cop, but I'm also a black man. I'm that first. If we had fired on those boys, I'd be praised to high hell when I got back. So I'm glad I saw you, too. I'm glad you showed that tape today, and I definitely can't let them hear me say that. We'll have to talk some other time; these cops with me are not real happy right now."

The two men looked at each other and shook hands. "I haven't been to a lecture in a while," Thomas said. "Maybe I'll get there Saturday. I need some spiritual food. I don't know how much longer I can do this."

"Be sure and say hello if you do," Walker said. "My son will probably speak. I'm getting ready to retire, you know."

A tight smile crossed Thomas' face. "You'll never retire, Minister Johnnie. And thank God for that."

They shook hands again and parted.

"Yahweh was surely with us tonight, I'd say," Andy said as he, Minister Johnnie and three Swords followed a police officer to a checkpoint.

Minister Johnnie smiled. "You know the old saw, Andy," he said. "Yahweh helps those who help themselves."

The officer walking with them looked at Minister Johnnie. His mouth was tight in a line; his blue eyes glittered. "I don't know who this Yahweh is you're talking about," he said, "but I do know that you're mighty lucky Lieutenant Thomas was in charge. Our men do follow orders. You may have thought you did something good, but I just saw you protecting some no good hoodlums, that's what I saw."

Minister Johnnie looked at Andy, saw the anger flare in his face, gave him a cautionary look. He looked at the officer's nameplate. "Thank you, Officer Carstairs, for your input," Minister Johnnie said. "We're glad the lieutenant was there, too, to protect us from the likes of you."

Carstairs' face reddened. He placed a hand on his sidearm. "We're in a war zone, so be real careful, okay?"

Andy moved toward him without even realizing it and ran into a wall of three Swords of the Master. "Are you threatening us, you racist asshole?" Andy yelled, consumed with anger. "Are you threatening us?"

One Sword placed hands firmly on Andy's chest as Minister Johnnie also blocked Carstairs' access to Andy. "Be cool, my brother," the Sword said. "This is not the time. Be cool."

Andy breathed heavily, struggled to regain his composure. Just like that, a flashback of emotions had engulfed his entire being. This is how Sonny felt that day, he thought. I know it is.

They were at the checkpoint. The officer there, unaware of what had triggered the drama just ending, looked at them oddly. The officer in charge recognized Walker, told his men to let him and his party through.

"We're going to have to work on that temper, man," Minister Johnnie said after they were several yards away. "I'm thinking of having you become the temporary press spokesman for the Covenant. You've got skills and I know you'll do a great job. But you will have to work on that temper. And there's something else I want you to do; someone I want you to meet."

"Thank you, minister, I'm honored," Andy said. He was still struggling with his feelings. "And I'm sorry, I could have gotten someone hurt."

He sat in his rental car without turning the engine on, feeling the turbulence of his interior life.

Is this what I was being interviewed for? Is this what he wants me to do? Andy's mind turned Minister Johnnie's request over. He sensed something more coming. He felt again that this past week of his life resembled a tributary moving into confluence with larger unseen forces.

Andy was not one who thought much about the cosmological importance of the ancestors—when Romeo used the phrase, it sounded like, "The Ancestors"—but now he remembered a belief his old friend had expressed his first night back. Romeo had grafted some of his cultural beliefs about Africa in with the religion he credited for saving his life.

They had sat in Romeo's living room and sipped herbal tea that first night back after leaving Dock Place. "When The Ancestors decide to move something or someone along, it feels almost miraculous as it manifests, if we flow with the events," Romeo said. "Sometimes we feel swept along; sometimes we resist and opportunities pass us by. You're back in the city for a reason."

In hindsight, it was clear that his brother's death was his date with destiny, one that everyone eventually had. Other forces in motion that George knew nothing about converged with his murder. Were it not for decisions made independently by Minister Johnnie and others, George would have been just one more wrongful death ignored by city officials. Andy knew that George's death was mixed up with his feelings, he just didn't know how.

Andy knew that Romeo remained unshakable in his conviction that divine guidance had moved him toward the Covenant of the New Commandment after Sonny's death. He had expressed his rage and bile for almost a year by kicking ass or getting his own kicked if anyone even looked at him funny. He seemed to be in a brawl every other week. When Romeo hospitalized a classmate with a vicious beating, even a compassionate principal sympathetic to his loss couldn't help. Expulsion from school was automatic, but a skillful attorney convinced the juvenile court judge that Covenant Academy would straighten his client out. Although the Butlers weren't Covenant members, they enrolled their son in Covenant Academy after hearing of the school's tough love reputation. Romeo joined the Covenant on his eighteenth birthday as a present to himself. "They could have sent me *anywhere* but they sent me to CA," he was fond of saying.

Maybe the ancestors were guiding him, too. His understanding of the Creator said that He/She guided everything, in fact, *was* every thing. How all that fit with ancestral intervention, or if it fit, he wasn't sure.

He pulled the rear view down and looked at himself. Haggard was the kindest description he could think of for what he saw in his eyes and the baggy weariness under them. A week ago, he and Debora were saying their goodbyes and having their let's-stay-in-touch conversation. Her daughters seemed happier than he'd seen them in months; they weren't even fighting with each other.

A week ago, George was still alive.

EIGHTEEN

"**N**O JUSTICE, NO PEACE! NO JUSTICE, NO PEACE! NO JUSTICE, NO PEACE!"

The picket signs carried three basic themes: "Police Protect PatricKKK." Others read: "We're Tired of Cover-ups – No More Cover-ups!" And still others read: "Justice For George Bascomb—Stop Killing Black People!"

Andy tried not to roll his eyes at the slogans. They were considered old when he was a college student. What we lack in originality, we make up for with volume, he thought to himself. Forty or so strong, the protesters trooped around the Horseshoe, voices loud and spirited.

He wondered what his half brother would say about the tensions and violence swirling through the city in the wake of his death. George is quiet and self-effacing. He's also a stand up guy, so he'd understand but might be flustered to be the center of attention. Andy winced. He was thinking of George in the present tense, as if he were still alive.

Andy didn't see a lot to write about. Minister David had quickly cobbled together three churches, two masjids, the local Nation of Islam mosque, and two grass roots organizations into an ad hoc coalition both interfaith and interracial. He'd grab a few quotes from David and a couple of the other congregation heads and whip something together.

They were coming back to the Horseshoe every day, Minister David Walker told an assemblage of reporters, until the district attorney reversed her horribly unjust decision.

"We are peaceful people, but we are people who must speak out against evil, and people who will always stand up for justice," Minister David said, resplendent in a midnight blue pin-striped double breasted suit and navy blue fedora broken down in front and back. "If Michael Patrick is innocent, then let the courts speak and say so, not a district attorney who apparently is as racist as Michael Patrick is. We demand that Patrick stand trial, and we won't let this city rest until he does so."

And with that, the minister, tall, imposing and dark, Africa strong in his face, rejoined the picket line.

"THE PEOPLE!... UNITED!... WILL NEVER BE DEFEATED! THE PEOPLE!... UNITED!... WILL NEVER BE DEFEATED! THE PEOPLE!..."

Andy walked to his car. He had time to stop at the near naked one-bedroom apartment he'd just rented. He felt fortunate to find a decent place midway between the meetinghouse and the *Scabbard* office. The neighborhood, like much of the city, showed signs of urban toughness: unemployed young men on the corners who might be just hanging out, or might be looking for customers; the ubiquitous corner stores knowingly selling legitimate products for illegitimate uses; homeless human beings, who now even populated the business district, looking like war refugees (which, in some ways, they were).

His furnishings at this point were a fold-up futon he had purchased the day before and a collapsible card table. He had yet to plug in the refrigerator that came with the apartment. He'd kept few furnishings from the West Coast, which might not arrive for another week: a plush leather chaise longue; a computer table and office chair; a bookcase; and a sofa that was little more than an oversized love seat.

On the card table sat a paperback copy of *Song of Solomon* and a nearly thirty-year-old hardback he'd found on sale called *Friendly Fascism: The New Face of Power in America*. Was it now *The Old Face of Power in America*? A John Upton Church professor had mentioned the book when he was in school; he'd borrowed it from the university library, read several chapters and then forgotten it until he saw the worn copy today.

Fatigue seeped through his body as if it had been injected. He hadn't really slowed down since getting off the plane. First, there was the trauma of George's murder. He and Rome had talked about the astronomical odds of lightning striking twice in the lives of friends in a way that was as similar as it was different. On top of *that,* place his conscious avoidance of calling Jhanae, which was like not seeing the eight-hundred-pound pink elephant in the room. She was with Wardell; he really needed to leave that alone. Somehow, he felt it a good sign that he thought of Claudia whenever he thought of Jhanae.

And beyond all his personal stuff rippled an undercurrent of . . . something. Something was going on in the Covenant. He felt it that night with Minister Johnnie. He felt it in Rome's presence. He remembered his initial thought, unbidden, when he heard about the deputy getting killed in California. *Is the Covenant involved?*

He looked at his watch. He had no deadlines. In fact, no one was at the office. He called and left a message that he'd check with Romeo later that day. He was due for an old-fashioned nap.

Less than two miles away from the Horseshoe, the rebellion inspired by Cornbread the Third's determination to impress his grandfather had lost steam. Police and OneCorporation International security guards, both in riot gear, lined both sides of University Boulevard and the Avenue two and three deep.

OCI guards arrested Cornbread the Third the first night. He and his posse ran amok for over an hour, elated at their success. Their numbers grew; at one point, two rival gangs temporarily became allies in the growing destruction. When they pressed toward the Church campus, though, dozens of OCI security guards seemed to materialize from nowhere, firing pepper spray projectiles. Cornbread slipped and fell as he tried to flee; the OCI guards pounced on him and led him away in handcuffs and wearing an ugly welt on his forehead.

Big Bread was not pleased to learn that mentoring his grandson was now costing him a thousand dollars as ten percent of the young man's bail. Big Bread knew the bail was too high; they were making examples of the ones they caught. Two more people had been killed while looting; the death toll now stood at five. Big Bread tried hard to convince himself that his grandson's behavior was not his fault.

An eager young intern from the district attorney's office, in his shirtsleeves despite the briskness of the weather, bounced down the steps of the Horseshoe with a sheath of papers that turned out to be a news release. He handed them out to reporters and a few aggressive demonstration participants who wanted to know what was going on.

A few scattered cheers went up as word circulated about the contents of the release. District Attorney Jacobs and Police Commissioner Kaheel were holding a news conference at 10 A.M. Thursday morning.

NINETEEN

The man, the lonely man, poured three fingers of bourbon, drank it quickly. He poured three fingers more.

Damn. He sighed again, regret thick in his exhalation. They would pay well but they meant him no good. The money mattered little to him. They had "their interests," and those interests now trumped his own. If there was a way out, he hadn't found it.

The weight of his schizophrenic position felt heavier than ever. The emotional discomfort grated his nerves like fingernails scratching a blackboard. Waiting for the phone calls was the worst part. Somehow, his decision to cooperate felt magnified in these moments of silence—sitting, waiting. When he tried playing music during one wait, the frivolity of sound seemed to mock him.

He drank the bourbon, poured another.

He felt himself unraveling. If he said something now, he might still salvage something, keep his life intact. Yahshua taught that it was never too late for atonement. But he knew, deep down, he feared his potential losses. That one, impulsive night in Vegas would disgrace him. There would be fallout because he had even considered doing what he was now doing. In the best of all worlds, nothing would happen, there would be nothing to tell, and it would all go away.

The ringing phone startled him. It always did. He picked it up as if it were a rattlesnake.

"The line is secure," said the man with the nasal, reedy voice. "You better have something for me."

"What do you mean, 'I better'?" The threatening tone irritated him, as did the nasal, reedy sounds that, for some reason, made him think of someone constipated.

"I mean, a deputy sheriff is dead out in California and we believe you people had something to do with it. We want to know what went down; we want to know what you can find out about this Unit 2236."

" 'You people'?"

"That's what I said. *You people.*" The nasal, reedy voice understood the condescension in the phrase, this polite, euphemistic way of saying "you niggers." "They

136

contacted 'you people.' They could have sent it straight to the Associated Press."

"If they had sent it to them, would you think AP had something to do with the Hubble shooting?"

"Don't be a smart ass. Listen, the Covenant of the new Commandment is involved. I know it. "

"That's preposterous."

"Why do you think the killers contacted you with their so-called communiqué?"

As he answered, the man tried to push certain thoughts away. "Listen, it's no secret how we feel about *you people* killing us, even when we're doing nothing criminal. We think it's criminal and we say so. Is there a federal law against that?"

"I'm not going to engage in a debate with you about the necessities of law enforcement in America." The voice dripped with privilege and authority now. "Our contact inside the Covenant will reveal himself to you in the next forty-eight hours. Between the two of you, we want some intelligence gathering before the week's out. We want the people who killed the deputy sheriff. As far as we're concerned, Unit 2236 is connected with your organization. Find out what that connection is."

"And if there's no connection, then what?"

"You'll need something solid to make me believe there's no connection. Just by contacting you, and only you, there's a connection."

"You're determined to make something out of nothing. Don't you think I, of all people, would know if they are connected?"

"Maybe, maybe not. Maybe you're holding back and think we won't find out. You get us something, and you get us something quick. I don't care who or what you have to betray to do it. Now look, you have a chance to both make some money and keep your indiscretions out of the public. If we have to move beyond just using the information we have on you to get what we want, we will. Am I clear?" The last two sentences came out in an unmistakably deadly hiss.

Betray. The word sliced through him like a razor. He felt only the separation of the cut at first; the emotional pain seeped in after, growing more intense each moment. He gulped the remainder of his drink and poured again. Just one more.

"You're clear."

He hung up, sat quietly in the stillness. He tried to push away a memory fighting its way to the surface. Was something going on that was hidden from him? There had been just the three of them in the room when the conversation

2236

took place. If there *was* something, then *he* was probably involved. Jealousy flared inside him like a toxin saturating his nervous system.

He sipped his bourbon, remembering feelings of being slighted yet again. Despite the importance of what he'd been given, he felt slighted still. What had been said in that meeting? . . .

. . . *"Everything is declining in the quality of life for black people. Everything! Surveys from our fifteen meetinghouses indicate much of the same everywhere. As bad as it's been for everybody, it's been worse for our people as always. And it's gotten far worse in the last ten years.*

"I know I'm supposed to be retiring, but the Covenant is my life. And where we see suffering, we must act. We can't do everything but we've got to do as much as we can . . ."

He looked away from me at that point. At him.

"Some things must be need-to-know from here on," he said. *"Two epidemics must be dealt with immediately. The drug thing and these indiscriminate cop shootings of innocents have both got to be responded to. These are literally life and death issues. And we know the shootings have bigger implications."*

Then he made a curious—and cryptic—comment. He asked us if we knew anything about Sinn Fein in Ireland. He knew about them; I didn't. I vaguely remembered hearing the phrase in some course when I was in college.

We would be legal, like Sinn Féin, he said. Others, he said, would heed Yahshua's directive to sell their cloak and buy a sword. When I asked what that meant, he said he'd said too much already. But I knew that he knew exactly what he meant. Sometimes he treated him more like a son than his own flesh and blood . . .

He shivered, despite the warmth of the whiskey in his belly. The hurt of not being trusted swam, mixed, and congealed with the pain of his dilemma. His dick had gotten him in trouble before, but nothing ever like this. By now he'd convinced himself that if he had been trusted more, this might never have happened.

This wasn't fair. Now that he was about to be first, he still felt second. Would he ever feel first?

He was in Vegas about a week after that meeting among the three of them.

It wasn't her whiteness. He'd been there, done that. Before he entered the ministry, an intense if brief relationship with an attractive white coed had developed and flamed out in college. Just before he met his wife, there was also a city councilwoman's married aide, ten years older than he, and insatiable. He had been spoken to harshly about the potential repercussions of that liaison.

No, it wasn't her skin. He was drawn to this woman in Vegas because she carried that high maintenance look to a whole new level. That facial and manicure and pedicure and massage twice a week because-I-don't-have-anything-else-to-do look. She wore five hundred dollar Manahlo Blahnik pumps, combined with a simple but elegant Donna Karan dress. Her coiffure was graceful, chic, understated. Her curvaceous body, and the way her clothes draped sensually over those curves, made him immediately think of a lush, voluptuous blonde sent by the government to corrupt a black undercover agent in an old, silly and hilarious comedy film rerun he had just seen on late night television. The irony was not lost on him when he received the pictures.

He'd stopped in the hotel's lounge just for a single bourbon on the rocks, and to feed his CNN news addiction. She was impossible to ignore, and the way she stared at him was shameless and unabashed. She smiled, transmitting heat, when he sent her a drink and ordered another for himself.

As it turned out, she wasn't white, or so she said. Her mother and grandmother, both Creoles, had married white men. Although she was often mistaken for white, she said she never denied her African ancestry when asked, or if it came up.

They didn't even pretend to make love. They fucked wildly half the night with an abandon he didn't even know existed. She did things his wife would never do. She said she would stay in touch.

The photographs that changed his life came via FedEx in a manila envelope two weeks later, with a name and phone number to call.

His mind kept trying to blame his decision on something other than lust and his own weakness. Like the resentment he felt at the time. His parents had warned him all his life about the negative power of resentments. They created even more pain if they were allowed to fester, he heard repeatedly as a child.

His whole life had seemed to be finishing second. Vice president of his high school class . . . an also ran in undergraduate school . . . associate editor of the school paper in divinity school. Even as a boy, it was the same. Second team basketball player in middle school instead of a starter.

He poured three more fingers of bourbon as he looked out at the bushes thick with shadows surrounding his home.

TWENTY

hen Andy entered the vestibule of Washington Memorial Episcopal Church with Claudia, he saw through the glass-paneled doors into the sanctuary. The burgundy-cushioned pews were still near empty. A line of mourners snaked out into the street along the front of the church, waiting to view his brother's body. Members of Swords of the Master and the Magdalene Society quietly went about their business of a security sweep of the building. Metal detectors framed the two entrances to the sanctuary.

"I'll see you after the service," Claudia said. "I know you have a lot to do. I'm sitting in the first row behind the family." She placed a gloved hand on his cheek. "Be strong."

Andy watched her enter the sanctuary. He called Marian and told her he was already at the church. "I'll line up with the family when you get here," he said. "I have work to do assisting the news media."

"Your mother asked about you and how you're doing," Marian said. There was gentleness in her voice.

Andy's visceral response, an internal tenseness, was an old friend, one he now expected when Mary Bascomb was described as "his mother." He preferred calling her "natural parent." More clinical, yes, but it was respectful. And the description of "mother" served as his ongoing tribute to Madeline Green, Mary's older sister. She had been his mother from his third week of life until she died.

"How is Mary doing?" Andy asked, his voice rigid with neutrality.

"She's taking it extremely hard. Please, try not to be hard on her, Andy. This is a terrible time for all of us."

"You're right. And this is not the time."

"We should be there a little before eight. Has the work you've been doing been hard?"

"I think it's helped even though, yes, it's been tough. I know George understands that, in my way, I'm honoring him."

"I know you are, too. God bless you, big brother."

"See you in a little while."

140

"Bye."

Andy walked back out the front door for some mind clearing air. He saw that police cars remained at least a block away. The police commissioner had created a discreet if formidable perimeter in each direction leading from the church. Wooden horses created a two-block barrier along the pavement that allowed mourners to line up in an orderly way.

It was the first night without a city curfew. An astute Community Relations officer's advice had been solicited and accepted. As a result, the curfew had been lifted, and only African-American police personnel were within one hundred yards of the church, doing what they could to convey an attitude of assistance and not one of intimidation. Two white conservative talk show hosts had bickered all day about the decision. "Are we back to the days of segregation?" one had asked his audience. "Are we saying that black people should only be policed by their own?"

Criticism notwithstanding, the CR officer's efforts were mostly successful. The undercurrent of hostility among the hundreds waiting to view George Bascomb's remains was palpable, mingled with an odd familial grief, although most had never met the deceased. Others watched the proceedings from the windows and steps of nearby homes, stone-faced.

Mourners who came only to view the deceased—a line of more than two hundred—still stretched out the front door. They had come all day, standing with dignified purpose in a light drizzle. They were the angry, the grieving, the curious, the morbid, the fascinated, the lonely. There were some renewing, too late, an acquaintance or passing friendship that dated back to middle school, high school, or a former job. Because of the long lines, those remaining for the service had been quietly asked to take their seats and view the body at the end.

As a boy, Andy, like many children, disliked funerals. The mysterious energy at the center of them made him uncomfortable. His child's mind didn't understand then that both the absence and presence of the honoree lying in the coffin were, on this singular occasion, essentially the same thing. Precisely because their life energy was forever gone, the guest of honor's presence filled the room in a way it almost never did when living, especially with ordinary folks like George Bascomb. As he grew older, viewing death became easier, so much so that when his mother died, he was able to kiss her still body although the cold rocklike hardness of her cheek immediately made him regret doing so, leaving a memory he didn't want.

When he stepped inside the sanctuary, he immediately saw something he had missed from the vestibule: the Covenant's floral tribute. Minister Johnnie had asked his son to supervise all arrangements. The Covenant of the New Commandment spray of flowers sat with regal prominence above the open casket of George Harry Bascomb, Jr., a monarch reigning over and dominating the other floral offerings. Minister David had commissioned the conspicuous display, a large bold oval of black, red, green and gold. Beneath the oval was a wide slash of silk ribbon. Across its face was emblazoned half of the New Commandment: LOVE ONE ANOTHER, AS I HAVE LOVED YOU.

By the time the first television truck arrived, Andy had a table ready at the front door with stacks of news releases and DVD copies.

An agreement had previously been reached with news agencies to create a pool that shared footage from the one camera permitted in the church. In his new position as press spokesman, Andy called Marian and got her to reconsider. Because he was asking, she agreed to the change. He assured her he wouldn't permit his brother's funeral service to become a circus. The church's MULT box was quickly placed into service at the rear of the sanctuary for those who needed it. Print reporters were crowded into a pew discreetly near the back of the church.

Andy walked up the aisle to the row where Claudia was seated. He leaned over and gestured with his head toward the front of the auditorium. "I wonder what that's about," he said. He wasn't someone close to David; he felt sure it had nothing to do with George being his half-brother. He wondered how Marian felt about it.

Claudia's eyes followed his nod. "The floral display?"

Andy nodded.

"Minister David's always been showy," Claudia said. "It's the way he's been for as long as I've known him. I often wonder if he's always trying to outdo his father." She fussed with the half-Windsor knot of Andy's tie, deliberately changing the subject. "I don't believe I told you that you look quite handsome today," she said, and then sobered immediately. "I know it's a sad occasion; I've just never seen you in a suit before."

"Thank you. I clean up pretty good when I have to," Andy said with a smile. He called it his "serious suit," a navy blue pinstripe single-breasted, accessorized with a pale blue madras shirt and patterned silk tie.

What was going on with their Teacher-designate, Andy wondered. It appeared the Covenant had come close to commandeering George's sunset services. But Marian had asked for their participation. She must be okay with it;

he needed to be okay with it.

Something about Minister David was bothersome. He felt it in conversation with other Covenant members. He felt the tension between Minister Johnnie and Minister David. And, as much as the younger Walker struggled to conceal it, his dislike of Romeo was noticeable.

Andy looked at his watch. The family had probably left Marian's. "Claudia, I'd like your perspective on something," he said. "Maybe we can talk later tonight. But sometime soon." He knew Marian's views about his coldness toward Mary Bascomb; his best friend in the world, Rome, had counseled forgiveness. He knew enough about himself to admit that Claudia, whom he knew the least, might have insights that could reach him where others couldn't.

She looked at the trouble on his face. "Just tell me when," she said.

An unseen organist segued from solemn hymn to solemn hymn . . . *Precious Lord . . . take my hand . . . Lead me on . . .*

Andy looked down at his program. George Harry Bascomb. Marian had selected a photograph taken the day of Andy's marriage to Jhanae. George had been his best man. The wedding was a small one; he and George wore identical dark suits and dark ties. His long, slender face was creased with his usual cool smile. Although cool, the smile was genuine, a man enjoying himself.

Now he was a life cut short at thirty-six years of age. George hadn't cringed and drawn back when he saw a neighbor and friend in danger. He died trying to do the right thing. *A greater love has no man than he lay it down for a friend.* Andy looked at the birth and death dates of his half brother and suddenly remembered a neighbor who lived in the same complex where Debora lived.

An old school brother, John Solomon always wore a fedora or wide-brimmed straw hat, tie, and serious demeanor. A homespun philosopher, John frequently, and unexpectedly, summarized the human condition in erudite sentences. "Most people tiptoe through life so they can arrive safely at death," he once told Andy while leaving a community meeting floundering in indecisiveness.

"I'm remembering a man I knew in California," Andy said to Claudia as they looked at the people waiting to view George. He spoke softly, something people seemed to instinctively do at funerals. "His name was John. John said he once went to the cemetery to remember a friend and stood there meditating. While looking at the headstone, he said, it occurred to him that most people saw the two dates, birth and death, the so-called 'sunrise' and 'sunset' on funeral service programs, as the important thing. But it wasn't, he said, it was the dash between the dates—while the sun was up, if you will—that was the most important. What the hyphen represented was what we should remember."

After the first overwhelming moments of disbelief and pain, he'd tried to tamp his grief and rage into a corner of his psyche to be dealt with later. He felt a lump in his throat. "George should still be walking his hyphen. Eight days ago, he was walking his hyphen." His voice cracked. He looked at Claudia, his eyes brimming with memories. "I'll miss him."

Claudia's mouth turned up slightly at the corners, although not in a smile. Quietly elegant, she wore a brocaded blazer with African motifs with a black silk button front dress and black pumps. She squeezed her new friend's hand gently with her gloved one. A gentle scarf with soft orchid tones lay artfully around her throat. "Thank you for John's remembrance," she said. "You need to let yourself feel your feelings."

He looked at her. "I have," he said. "Yesterday I realized I wanted to kill Michael Patrick."

Claudia's mouth did something funny but she said nothing at first. "Are you staying busy?" she asked after a moment.

"Very much so. Between moving here and working, I've got plenty to do. What I feel about George is a steady throbbing, whether I'm busy or not."

When the family arrived, viewers were still in line. George Bascomb, a private man in life, was a celebrity in death. The funeral director consulted with Minister David. They decided to pause the viewers, seat the family, and give these remaining visitors a choice of moving quickly past the bier, or waiting until the service ended.

Andy braced himself, touched Claudia's shoulder, and walked toward the vestibule. At the front of the assemblage stood Marian Bascomb and Mary Bascomb. An odd thought struck him: If his Mom was still living, she'd be here, and they'd be Marian, Mary and Madeline. Three Marys. His brother was not Yahshua, he was just another brother trying to make it. But what a strange, unplanned symbolism it was.

Mary Bascomb looked smaller than the image he kept in his mind. Her mouth was drawn together in a tight line, the only way he remembered ever seeing it. Since his mother's funeral nineteen years ago, he'd seen her only twice, each time unavoidably. Learning at the age of twenty that Madeline Green Blackman had adopted him had turned his world upside down. Whether it was his grief at the time or something else, he'd always blamed Mary Bascomb more than her sister for not telling him.

Mary clung to her husband, the Reverend Grady Bascomb, who Andy had met only once before. She looked as if she might collapse without the arm he had around her shoulder. Andy wished she had kept the old-fashioned veil on her tiny black hat down over her face. He felt guilty for the pettiness of his wish.

Andy looked at his sister-in-law and felt her eyes pleading with him. Marian Bascomb resembled nothing so much as stately African royalty. Without self-consciousness, she wore a dignity that more public women such as Myrlie Evers, Coretta Scott King and Betty Shabazz had worn when having to display their grief on a public stage. He returned her gaze and nodded; it was not asking too much to behave as a son should.

Andy embraced the woman he could not call mother. He felt the years of sorrow in her return of his embrace. They both wanted to speak but had no idea what to say.

They separated and Andy shook hands with her husband. "Reverend Bascomb," he managed to say, suddenly aware that this man had lost his only son. "They took my boy," the minister said, looking into Andy's eyes. "I know he's with Jesus, but . . ." He looked away as his voice trailed off.

They lined up in twos and entered the sanctuary. Marian stood beside Andy. After the Bascombs were Marian's parents, Minister Isaac Muhammad and his wife, Vera; Marian's two older sisters, Susan and Vera, and their husbands; Vera's three children; Susan's two sons.

In Marian's eyes, both the Covenant of the New Commandment and Washington Memorial had helped beyond the call of duty even though she and George were not churchgoers. Some voices whispered about the tragedy being exploited by "all those militant people"; for her part, Marian felt a measure of sincerity from both congregations. In these times, a measure was more than you got from most anything. She did not think about joining or not. It took all she had to think about anything at all that did not center on burying her husband. She knew George had seeming contradictions. He was interested in law enforcement and believed the U.S. was basically a decent country; he was also what used to be called a "race man." Because she had been raised as a Muslim, they had occasionally attended mosque. George had also flirted with the idea of joining the Covenant despite being a loner, not a joiner. She had been the gregarious one in the relationship. She found herself thinking that she and he would discuss it again after all this was over, and then caught herself. The habit of "we" would take sometime to break.

After she buried her man, she had to rest. He would want her to, would be fidgeting and fussing about her fatigue if he were still here. She bit her lower lip looking at his stillness in the gleaming silver coffin. She had to grieve but the stirring presence in her stomach reminded her that she must regroup, and soon.

Andy watched Minister Johnnie enter the pulpit from a side door. He noticed that he sat at stage right this time, behind the Sacred Desk. Apparently the eulogy qualified as real preaching. Although, knowing the minister, he would still score some political points.

Andy saw that the viewing line moved quickly now. The organ's plaintive voice moved seamlessly and unobtrusively from one hymn to the next. Despite the movement and bustle, the room retained a certain stillness peculiar to homegoings, as some church people called them. It was as if everyone took his or her cue from the honoree.

The service struggled, and mostly succeeded, for brevity. Father Thibideaux set the tone with a brief prayer. A childhood friend of Marian's followed with a dazzling solo. His moderately successful recording career was big enough to elicit several "ooohs" and "ahhs" when people saw his name on the program. At Marian's request, he sang "We're Going All the Way," a Jeffrey Osborne oldie that George and Marian had referred to during the sweet days of early courtship as "their song." Although there were dozens, only six cards of condolence were read. Then Minister Johnnie Walker stepped to the Sacred Desk and spoke passionately about this man he had never met. Minister Johnnie had expressed his philosophy about men like George Bascomb more than ten years earlier when nineteen of forty-one bullets ended the life of Amadou Diallo. "It could have been me," he told a reporter.

"Some folks are annoyed when a clergyman or woman eulogizes someone they didn't know, someone who wasn't in their congregation," Minister Johnnie began in slow, measured tones. "But I know this man. George Bascomb was, and is, every black man born in this strange, schizophrenic country known as the United States of America. I am reminded of a phrase used by the brilliant scholar, Professor Maulana Karenga. Doctor Karenga frequently notes that we are the descendants of uncounted millions of Africans who were 'snatched from their own history and possibilities.' George Bascomb is every single one of those millions. He, too, has been snatched from his possibilities by a vile, evil system of living that virtually always decrees that the killer or killers will go free. We pray that it will be different this time.

As Andy listened, he realized how different it was than listening to David. Listening to David was like listening to Jesse as the successor of Martin. He had all the skills, he puts in the work, puts in the time, but there's a certain indefinable spiritual center that was different, that didn't make him as dangerous. Malcolm and Louis, the same thing. True, Martin and Malcolm had come through more turbulent times, but they had done much to *create* the turbulence. Andy couldn't see David stirring up turbulence. He had never doubted that Minister Johnnie could, and would, at moments of his choosing.

An unearthly wail rose above the energy stirred by the Teacher. Andy knew before he looked that it was Mary Bascomb. Her pain sounded unquenchable, inconsolable. A uniformed nurse bustled over to assist the grief-stricken woman. Her husband embraced her. He let his shoulder absorb her loud sobs. He looked at Marian. She sat upright, stoic, but something else, too. Some intangible aura said, if Andy had to guess, that a part of her being knew she was a good woman who had been fortunate to love a good strong man.

Minister Johnnie had promised to be brief and kept his word. "I want to suggest how we should remember our fallen brother. If we are to survive as a people, we will need warriors. We speak of education and I say, yes. We speak of economic base building and, again, I say yes. We speak of electoral political clout and thrice I say yes. But we never speak of warriors because we have been taught—I should say, trained—not to fight. We will need warriors, too. We are losing them daily to professional sports, to misogynistic, self-hating music, and to the prison-industrial complex. No people will endure as a people without warriors. Brother Bascomb's life showed that we can be warriors wherever we are, whoever we are. George's *death* demonstrated the kind of *life* he led, the kind of man he was.

"Early in my ministry I decided I wanted two things said about me when it came time for me to lie where George lies now. They might say other stuff about me—and I'm sure they will"—chuckles murmured through the sanctuary —"but I hoped then, and still do, that people will say I wasn't greedy and that I wasn't a coward.

"George's selflessness suggests he wasn't greedy and it surely demonstrates that our brother wasn't a coward. What went on that night on Dock Place wasn't his beef. He could have let it go and said, 'I hope Mister Harris gets out of this the best way he can.' But George didn't ask the question that Cain asked. He didn't ask, 'Am I my brother's keeper?' George said what we try and teach at the Covenant: Yes! Yes! Yes!" Booming, fevered feelings flavored each affirmation as he struck the podium three times with a hand. "*I am my brother's keeper!*"

Minister Johnnie took a deep breath and composed himself. "A greater love hath no man than he lay down his life for a friend." He paused. "I promise you, Brother George, your death will not be in vain. While we are here in this vale of tears, our enemies will not stop killing us until we make them stop. We must find a way. Sleep well, my brother. The struggle continues." He asked everyone to bow his or her head in prayer.

Andy stopped beside the bier and looked down at the remains of his brother in the natty black pinstripe that he would now wear into eternity. George had jokingly called it his "styling and profiling Sunday-go-to-meeting" suit. His face was relaxed now, and not twisted with surprise and pain, as it had been when Andy had seen him writhing on the ground in the video. Marian had placed a single red rose between his hands resting a bit awkwardly on the top of his thighs. He'd brought her a single red rose on their first date after the cookout.

"George, my baby, George, my baby . . ." Mary Bascomb's thin voice, keening the words over and over, touched a place inside Andy. One son wasn't coming back, ever. One son could try.

They've started something with you, something they didn't know, something they couldn't have imagined, Andy thought looking at the stillness of this man who, perhaps foolishly, wanted to do the right thing. *I can't see into the future so I don't know where this is going. Like Minister Johnnie said, your death will not be in vain. There's an African proverb that says, until the lion tells the story the hunter will always win. In their telling, you are a nigger someone wanted to kill so bad he could taste it. Those telling the story will fiercely defend the nigger killer; I know they will. But we will tell your story, too, we will write about you, and we will tell what happened that night on Dock Place, and what happened afterwards. Sleep in peace.*

As he turned from the bier, he looked up and saw Claudia looking at him. He looked into her eyes for a long moment and saw a mixture of feelings looking back at him. Later, on her porch, they kissed for the first time. It was gentle, it was restrained and yet it wasn't, and it was good.

The next morning, six Swords of the Master carried George Bascomb's silver casket to the canopy at graveside and placed it on the thick straps over the gaping hole in the ground awaiting him. Just as they did so, the skies opened and the drizzle turned into a downpour. Six other Swords held crossed silver swords, used only for ceremonial occasions, over the open cavity that awaited dust to return to dust. After acquiescing to a public funeral, Marian requested that the burial be private for the family. Other Swords stood at the cemetery entrance and strategically but discreetly near the graveside to ensure that the news media honored the request.

Although a veteran, George's casket was covered with a red, black and green flag instead of the stars and stripes he had served with distinction. Minister Johnnie Walker presented the flag to Marian, and then he and Andy escorted her from graveside to the waiting limousine as three Swords held large black umbrellas over their heads.

TWENTY-ONE

ello, Bulldog. Yes, I heard; my office called just before you did, said they're holding a news conference shortly. Hold on a minute, will you?" Ike Erlickson held his cell phone aside and signaled the Federal Club masseuse with his other hand. "Darling, I know I'm already late but I need five minutes. This is important."

Her smile of agreement indicated that Mister Erlickson could have as much time as he needed. The attorney picked up his ever present cigar, then put the phone back to his ear.

"I understand Lynda's under a lot of pressure to reverse her position since that videotape became available."

"A lot of pressure is right," Hudson said. "They're going to charge him with murder two. Bill Kaheel called me personally. He said the fucking DVD leaves them no choice. I took the liberty of telling him you'd bring Mike in later today. Hope you don't mind."

"Of course not. I don't have anything on my calendar except a massage. I wasn't going to the news conference anyway. How's Mike taking it?"

"So-so, I'd say. I'm taking him and Kathy out later to cheer them up."

"Listen, my friend, I'm going to let this lady work her magic on these tired old muscles." Erlickson looked at his cold cigar, thought about lighting up, decided against it. "Getting this kid off is a hell of a challenge, and I love challenges. I've decided this is my last hurrah, and I want to go out a winner. You still think I'm the Michelangelo of the courtroom?"

One corner of Hudson's mouth turned up. "I've never regretted giving you the nickname. If anybody can win this, you can."

Erlickson pursed his lips. "I may have to go some places I've never gone. But I'll do what I have to do."

Kathy felt the tightness in Mike's shoulders as she massaged close to his neck, trying to push his fears away with her fingers. Mike sat with his shoulders hunched forward, making it difficult to reach him.

"Can you sit back, honey?" she asked. "It's a tough break, but you're going to be okay, I know it."

Mike hardly heard her. He inhaled deeply and let out as a sigh as she made an effort to make him sit back. He shook her effort away.

"C'mon babe, not now," he said. "I know you're trying to make me feel better." He stood up. "I've got to go meet Mister Erlickson."

"Do you want me to go with you?"

"No, you'd just be bored. It's just some procedure stuff. Some paperwork, they take my picture, fingerprint me, and I sign myself out."

Hearing what he said touched some place in his gut and, without warning, he picked up a large ashtray and flung it across his girlfriend's living room. It shattered against the far wall, next to a picture of a smiling Kathy and her taciturn godfather, Bulldog Hudson.

"Goddammit, it's not fair!" he shrieked. "I'm not a criminal! That fucker attacked me!"

Kathy stepped back, her eyes wide. "Mike, please, it's going to be all right, I just know it. Honey, let me go with you. I want to be there for you."

"I said no," Mike said. He inhaled deeply, ran his hands through his hair. "I'm sorry. I shouldn't have thrown that like that. Look, I've got to go and meet Mister Erlickson." He picked up his windbreaker and kissed his fiancée quickly on the lips. Her body rigid, Kathy said nothing.

"Look, I'm really sorry." Mike placed a hand under her chin, tilted her head up to look at him. "I didn't mean to frighten you. I'll come back down after I take care of this, okay?"

"Sure, okay," she said, then turned her head. One hand played with a strand of her long blonde hair, a habit that Mike knew meant she was nervous.

"Mike, have you thought about getting some counseling since this thing happened?"

Mike looked at the woman he wanted to marry. Didn't she understand anything about him? "Counseling? What do I need counseling for? I'm a cop, I had to shoot a guy who attacked me. I need counseling for that? First, my commander wanted to know if I needed to talk to the psychologist downtown. Now, you want to know if I want to talk to somebody. About what?" He paced as he talked. "Tell him I'm sorry? You know what I'm sorry about? I'm sorry I didn't pull my badge out, that's what I'm really sorry about. And I'm sorry I'm losing my job, because I'm a good cop and it's all I want to do. All I want to do is protect people against the bad guys. Now, I might end up in jail." Realizing what he had said, his face twisted and he looked away. "Can you believe that?"

Kathy's voice was quiet and small. "Mike, I thought you might be able to talk about your drinking."

Mike glared at her. "Oh Jesus fucking Christ, Kathy! Yes, I'd had a few drinks that day, but we've been down this road before. I do not drink that often and I don't drink that much."

"I know I know I know," she said, her words tumbling over each other. "But you change so whenever you do, and I just thought you should think about it and maybe talk to somebody, that's all."

She was always bugging him about that, about how he changed after he had a few nips. Mike wanted to hit her. Instead, he pulled her to him, embraced her. Her body was still rigid. He buried his head in her tousled blonde hair, closed his eyes shut, trying to make the world go away.

Why is this fucking happening to me?

TWENTY-TWO

At precisely ten o'clock, Commissioner Kaheel and two aides exited the elevator in the lobby of the Horseshoe and walked to the bank of microphones in the precise spot where they had previously announced that Michael Patrick had properly used his firearm to mortally wound the late George Bascomb and thus committed a justifiable homicide.

"Where's the district attorney?" Andy said loudly as the police commissioner fiddled with some papers on the podium.

Kaheel shot him a dirty look. "Ms. Jacobs was called away with an unforeseen personal emergency," he said.

"She was here this morning," said a television reporter standing next to Andy.

"Like I said, she was called away suddenly." Kaheel's look indicated he didn't want to discuss it anymore.

The reporter leaned over to Andy and spoke *sotto voce* from the side of his mouth. "He's lying. I just left her office less than ten minutes ago. They said she was on the way down."

Those opening questions established a contentious tone that lasted throughout the news conference. Kaheel didn't hide feelings well, and the consensus in the room was that he looked pissed.

"Last week we told you that it was the conclusion of the district attorney's office, based on what we then knew, that insufficient evidence existed to press charges against Officer Michael Patrick in the incident that led to the death of George Bascomb," he read from a statement. "Since that time, additional information, which I'm sure most of you are familiar with, has surfaced. Therefore, we are announcing the imminent arrest of Michael Patrick on charges of second-degree murder."

An audible *whoosh* of surprise swept through the large foyer. Camera flashes sparkled.

"Mister Patrick has been suspended from the police force for thirty days, with intent to dismiss. Mister Patrick's attorney, Isaac Erlickson, has informed us that he will be surrendering his client later today." Kaheel looked up, wearing his discomfort on his figurative sleeve, and braced himself. "We'll take a few questions."

Andy fired first, shouting over everyone else. "Why second degree? Why not first degree?"

"First degree murder charges are only appropriate when we believe we can prove that a homicide was premeditated," Kaheel replied.

Andy had anticipated the answer. "Follow up," he said on the heels of the commissioner's answer. "District Attorney Jacobs has said and demonstrated in several cases, primarily with African-American suspects, her belief that state law permits first degree if a suspect has even a few seconds to think before taking action. I can name two cases where police officers were shot apparently in the heat of passion, and she's claimed premeditation and won. The tape shows that Patrick had at least a minute, maybe more. He had time to back off."

Heads that swung to listen to Andy swiveled back. Kaheel looked as if he had eaten three lemons, one after the other.

"You'll have to ask Lynda about that," he said. "I can't comment."

And so it went. No, they had not felt any pressure because of the street disturbances. Absolutely not. No, they were not responding to the pressure of community groups. No, Patrick would not be held without bail; it was his understanding that Patrick would be released on his own recognizance. Patrick was not a flight risk. Yes, there was a precedent for a murder suspect being released on OR. No, he could not comment on the Police Officers Benevolent Association's decision to hire high-ticket defense attorney Isaac Erlickson. He had heard, but could not confirm, that Mister Erlickson was providing *pro bono* services.

Andy thought about the non-answer answer the commissioner had given. Kaheel was a decent man but they both knew his answer about murder one and murder two was bullshit.

In one of the biggest cases ever to hit the city a decade earlier, an African-American activist, Malik Al-Amin, had happened upon a fracas between a police officer and the activist's cousin. The melee left the officer fatally wounded. In that case, several faulty factors—temporary amnesia by police officers and security guards; an absence (or withholding) of tests on the activist's hands and licensed weapon found at the scene; shaky prosecution witnesses; a racist judge with membership in POBA who helped obfuscate details; all of this, coupled with a defendant who refused to go quietly into the night the judicial system had prepared for him somehow coalesced into a first-degree murder conviction. Even leaving aside the rather important question of whether Al-Amin had even pulled the trigger, his presence had, by all accounts, been unplanned and spontaneous. The shooting hadn't occurred on Jacob's watch, but she used questionable methods to defeat his appeal, and she continued to use the precedent established in the *State v. Al-Amin*, which said a decision made within seconds could legally constitute premeditation.

Kaheel knew, and knew that Andy knew, Lynda Jacobs never used the principle in police shootings. A few months after Al-Amin was convicted and sent to death row, several officers trained their weapons on an unarmed twenty-year-old African-American sitting dazed in his car for eight minutes. When the young man moved without warning, one officer blasted the top of his skull off from fifteen feet away. After a community uproar, Jacobs filed manslaughter charges that were dismissed at the cop's preliminary hearing. A local black attorney in a prominent law firm said the wrong charges had been filed and tried to get murder three instituted. Jacobs fought the effort with a fierceness absent in prosecuting the case, claiming she couldn't win third-degree murder if the courts wouldn't uphold manslaughter.

When the press conference ended, Andy called the district attorney's office, fully expecting a second non-answer answer. He got it.

"We feel that after careful review the charge of second degree is appropriate and cannot comment further because the case will be going to trial. We will vigorously pursue a conviction of Mister Michael Patrick on these charges," Jacobs' director of communications said in response to Andy's query.

TWENTY-THREE

ilford "Mel" Sales couldn't remember ever feeling so tired. The trial had drained him. And he still faced six months, maybe a bit more, in jail. A raw and empty ache had been with him since the jury had said: guilty of murder in the second degree. Thank God for Judge Hoffman, he thought. Hoffman said he'd suffered enough, that the shooting was clearly involuntary manslaughter. The ache had lessened, but it wasn't gone.

He had replayed that night in his head at least a hundred times. He was sorry about her baby, he really was, but he would go to his grave convinced that the bitch was selling drugs from her home. It was a stroke of bad luck, picking the wrong night, a night when nothing was there. If he had it to do again, he would get a warrant instead of calling in a disturbance at her place.

When he saw the weapon in her hand, his training kicked in without him even thinking about it.

He leaned back on his sofa, closed his eyes. He was so glad the news crews had finally called it a night. They should have known he wouldn't be making any kind of statement. Good to know that LAPD would roll a black and white by every hour or so to see that things were okay. Since those niggers had killed Steve Hubble, there was no need taking chances. Play it safe, wait a couple of days before you bring your family home, his lawyer said.

As he stood, he saw the blinking red police light reflecting off the closed Venetian blinds on the front windows. Puzzled, he walked to the window and peeked. Two plainclothes officers, their shields on lanyards around their neck, walked toward his front door. One black, the other—he wasn't sure. In the darkness, Sales couldn't tell if he was Hispanic, or maybe Italian.

He opened the door just as the swarthy one reached for his doorbell.

"What's going on?" Sales said. "You guys LAPD? Something wrong?"

"No, nothing's wrong," the swarthy one said. "I'm Detective Webb. This is Detective Smith." He extended his hand. "We heard the judge cut you some slack."

Sales held the door as they entered, then closed it behind them. "Yeah, thank God for Judge Hoffman," he said. "I thought the patrols were just going to

156

drive past. LAPD didn't say anything about them stopping."

"We're part of a different squad," the man called Webb said.

"I don't understand," Sales said.

The man called Smith smiled. "You might say we gained entry like you did, under false pretenses."

Sales frowned. "What?"

"Your sentence for murdering an unborn child has been overturned," the man called Webb said.

At that moment, Sales noticed something peculiar. Both detectives wore the same badge number: 2236.

Andy enjoyed watching Claudia work. Focus infused every phone call she made, every web search she did, and every directive on Romeo's behalf to meetinghouses in other cities. With Romeo away, her workload seemed to double.

It was their second full day together in the office. She had a routine; he needed one so he could stop behaving like an infatuated high school sophomore.

He signed in on his terminal, logged onto the wire service. It was a slow news day. He scrolled through the first two dozen stories available. Nothing worthwhile turned up. On a hunch, he scrolled through the day before and the day before that.

One story, from the day before, puzzled him as much as it puzzled Los Angeles police. A street level drug dealer and his apparent supervisor had been found writhing in pain on a South Central street in the City of Angels. The street dealer had the fingers of one hand broken; the supervisor had both hands broken. Police found a quantity of the cocaine-heroin derivative known as Sweetness spilled on them and around them in the street. Elsewhere the same night, in nearby affluent Baldwin Hills, police found "Freeway Frank" Richardson shot in the head execution-style outside the luxury condominium where he lived. Although never arrested or convicted, Richardson reputedly oversaw a seven-figure drug empire. The three men, all African-Americans, had the numbers "2236" scrawled on their foreheads with a marker pen. The injured men told police their attackers wore ski masks and black clothing. The wire story said authorities were exploring the connection, if any, between the men and the death of deputy sheriff Steven Hubble, allegedly killed by a group called Unit 2236.

The story nagged at something in Andy's memory. He made a note to call the L. A. meetinghouse and get their correspondent there to write a piece.

He scrolled again until he saw the name "Delores Olds" in the slug column. He opened the story.

"Fuck!" he yelled as he finished reading.

Claudia looked up with a frown. "Excuse me?" she said.

Andy slumped back in his seat. "You remember the Delores Olds shooting?"

"Sure I do. She lost her baby when that depraved deputy shot her. They charged him with second-degree murder." Now Andy's expletive registered; her face changed. "Oh, don't tell me. He got off."

"In a way it's worse, Claudia. The all-white jury found Milford Sales guilty of second-degree murder. When he came in for sentencing yesterday, the judge said he had reviewed the case and thought the jury's decision too harsh. By law, he can't throw the guilty verdict out but he's reduced it to involuntary manslaughter. Sales was sentenced to one lousy year; the wire story says he should be on the street in six months."

Neither said anything for several seconds. "When does Rome get back?" Andy asked.

"I believe day after tomorrow. I don't know why he doesn't want any calls, but that's what he told me."

"Sure. Look, when we leave tonight, would dinner and maybe a silly movie be in order?"

Claudia smiled. "We both need it, don't we? Let's."

Andy made the call to Los Angeles. They were already on it. He took notes and told the correspondent to e-mail anything new that broke.

"Rob, listen, does anything about the drug story seem odd to you? Or familiar? Okay, I just wondered."

Thirty minutes later, a story came in from Detroit. Seeing the name of the city jogged his memory on the drug story.

He and Jhanae were dating at the time. He had attended a few Covenant meetings and was considering joining. Although devoted to non-violent action as a problem solver, he remembered having grudging approval when he heard about what became known in the Covenant as "The Detroit Incident."

As an outsider then, Andy viewed the paramilitary Swords of the Master as theater as much as he viewed them as security. But as theatrical as they might be in protecting their leadership, he knew, as did most of the black community, that they were the real deal if forced to defend themselves.

Andy did a search in *Scabbard* archives and found the story. The Detroit Incident had occurred in 2001:

A drug-ridden Detroit neighborhood had asked the local Covenant meetinghouse for help in getting rid of the dealers. The police weren't able to keep them away; when they did make arrests, people were afraid to testify and the dealers came back after being released. When a neighborhood family was threatened for their persistent vigilance, the block association appealed to the Covenant. Detroit placed calls to Minister Johnnie. After consulting with his Detroit minister, the Teacher agreed to put a team on the street for thirty days. If the Swords were successful, the block organization requesting help would provide a voluntary donation of their choosing to Covenant Academy, the organization's educational arm. If for some reason they weren't successful, the block association owed nothing.

The Swords set up round-the-clock patrols. Drug dealing declined immediately. Some said their mystique was enough: brothers clean as they could be, patrolling in *business suits* no less, with attitudes on their face that said clearly, come with it if you think you can.

On their third night in the street, three reckless young gangsters tried to do a deal within eyesight of a Swords patrol. The unarmed patrol approached them; two Swords spoke quietly with the leader while six others stood point. One of the petty dealers went for his pocket. He received three broken fingers for his effort and was sent on his way without the .25 automatic he reached for. His partners considered their options and didn't draw. They were disarmed, too. The customer moved away in a brisk walk without any urging.

A brief public uproar ensued when the Swords involved were charged with aggravated assault and possession of stolen property. Aroused from their apathy, the association had their block captain's back as she raised hell on talk radio, television, and in the newspapers. Critics called the Swords "vigilante hoodlums." Other block clubs offered support. Covenant membership temporarily, but dramatically, increased. The besieged district attorney dropped the charges.

No drugs had been dealt in that area since.

The unarmed Swords had a high rate of success where and when they chose to patrol. They had not proven to be a panacea, in Detroit or anywhere else. Because of limited human resources, and, more often than not, hostility from the authorities, the young warriors of Yahshua selected their battles carefully, and took as many jobs as they could. However, after two Swords were shot and seriously wounded in Newark, and a Swords captain was shot to death in Chicago the following year, Minister Johnnie declared a moratorium on the work. He tried, unsuccessfully, to obtain permission for armed patrols in several cities where residents requested their services. Every municipality had turned them down.

It was a coincidence, Andy said to himself. It had to be. He knew what Swords could do. Swords and Magdalenes received a minimum eight-week course in self-defense. Minister Johnnie considered self-defense an inalienable right.

"I admire our great ancestor, Doctor King," the Minister was fond of saying, "and I subscribe to non-violent action—the operative word there is *action* —for political reasons." Congregants liked the way he said "action," and laughed and applauded for what he said next. "But as a way of life, if you don't have sense enough to defend yourself when attacked, then shame on your sorry . . ." He'd pause and smile. ". . . self. Fooled you, didn't I?"

Was the Minister sending Swords after drug dealers? It would explain, besides their militant politics, why this Unit 2236 was contacting the Covenant.

Andy found it difficult to embrace the logical conclusion that surfaced next. Unit 2236 had said they were going after drug dealers. But their larger message was claiming responsibility for killing Hubble.

"Are you okay?"

Andy looked up. Claudia was looking at him with concern on her face.

"You looked . . . scared," she said. "Maybe that's not it, but you looked as if something was definitely wrong."

He looked at this woman who had captured so much of his attention in such a short time. Maybe she could shed some insight. "I was just thinking about something that may be a coincidence," he said.

The phone rang. Claudia answered it, then motioned to him to pick up at his desk.

"Hey Andy, it's Romeo. I don't have much time. I just had a statement dictated to me, and you'll have to work late tonight. I'll ask Claudia to stay and help you."

"No problem."

"This will be your first official act, and probably your last, as spokesman," Romeo said. "It's too late for you to call a news conference for the evening news. So send out an advisory that you're holding one in the morning. Start putting a story together for tomorrow's deadline. But don't call anybody for comments until morning; we don't want to give this away."

"What's the story? And what's this about 'my last official act'?"

When Romeo told him about the story, Andy wasn't totally surprised. A giant jigsaw puzzle seemed to be clicking into place. "As far as the other, we can't talk about it now. When you get off, give Minister Johnnie a call. He wants to see you."

"When you get back, we need to talk," Andy said.

"I've been thinking the same thing, my man," Romeo replied. "I should get back late tomorrow. Let me speak to Claudia."

Andy stared out the window as his oldest friend and one of his newest friends talked. He thought about his brother, he thought about his feelings, and he thought about what Romeo had just told him. Clearly, a new chapter was opening in his life.

TWENTY-FOUR

Thick pillows of overcast clouds fostered crispness in the air, making the day feel colder than it actually was. Andy's news conference, scheduled for the marble steps of the meetinghouse, was changed at the last minute after a stiff wind joined the chill. Glenn Greene and several Swords signaled the press corps and brought them into the lobby area just outside the main auditorium.

A pantheon of black heroic personalities, all painted in oil, circled the lobby, looking impassively down on visitors. Minister Johnnie had added one during each anniversary celebration in the Covenant's forty-one years of existence. The first and largest, a rendering of Yahshua with hair like lamb's wool and bronze skin, presided over the room in a solid gold frame from its place directly above the entrance to the auditorium. General Toussaint l'Ouverture's portrait hung on one side of the Great Teacher; the Reverend Richard Allen on the other. The minister allowed two exceptions in his portraiture of African heroes and heroines. Fidel Castro had been the honoree in 1979 to honor the twentieth anniversary of the Cuban Revolution. The Cuban president had sent a personal message of thanks to the Covenant leader. A portrait of the warrior from Argentina, Ernesto "Che" Guevara, went up the next year, hanging between the Reverend Nathaniel Turner and the Reverend Dr. Martin Luther King, Jr. It was clear to visitors that the Covenant held political and military achievements on behalf of black people and the dispossessed as much in high esteem as they did religious greatness. Minister Johnnie drummed it into Covenant members: eating, shelter, producing, education, employment, ownership of land—*everything* about their daily life was religious and it was political. Religion was not to be separate from their daily needs. Why would any god not want to help people with their daily needs? As far as politics were concerned, Minister Johnnie unabashedly subscribed to Chairman Mao's axiom that politics is war without bloodshed while war is politics with bloodshed.

While talking with his second-in-command on the security detail, Glenn noticed two dark-skinned men in dark suits, conspicuously trying to be inconspicuous, standing at the edge of the assemblage. Both hung back, talking to each other as the television crews moved their equipment inside. Both carried reporter-style notebooks. Their neat, button-down not-quite-in-fashion look screamed law enforcement. Federal probably, rather than local. The taller bespectacled man smiled self-consciously when he saw Glenn staring at him.

Glenn intercepted Andy outside of David Walker's office, where the temporary press spokesman had been making last minute notes.

"We have two FBI types out there," Glenn said. "They may be local but I don't think so. Does that change anything?"

"Not really," Andy said. "You know how the minister always quotes Malcolm: always assume that law enforcement is present in any gathering. Ask them their media affiliation when the news releases are handed out, just to see what they say. Other than that, leave it alone. Minister Johnnie said they would probably make their presence felt. They probably know that we know. They *want* us to know."

Andy and Glenn walked toward the lobby. Claudia and two women he didn't know were waiting for them. Claudia held a stack of news releases.

"Hi, Glenn." She kissed her brother on the cheek, and then looked at Andy. "I took the liberty of recruiting these sisters to help me help you," she said. "Is that okay?"

Andy nodded. "Thanks."

"You look great, by the way." She tugged at the lapels of his black suede sports coat, pretending to straighten them.

"Thank you," Andy said. "You knew we'd have a big crowd here today, didn't you?"

"Of course. Sales' death has been leading the news all morning. They want to know if we've heard from Unit 2236. The story's getting legs."

"Your brother said there are two feds in the audience," Andy said. Claudia didn't seem surprised. "Well, here we go. It's show time."

Camera flashes winked as Andy stepped to the podium. The room quieted but still managed to feel noisy. Glenn and another Sword flanked him. He and Romeo had rehearsed what they called "the party line" for an hour. "Don't deviate, regardless of what direction the questions come from. We need some breathing room. And, like I said, you and I need to talk as soon as I get back."

"Good morning. My name's Andrew Blackman. I'm Minister Johnnie Walker's temporary press spokesman. It's good to see so many of you here, and I'm sure you all want to ask the same question." He picked up one of the sheets of paper in front of him on the podium.

"We learned about the same time you did that Los Angeles County Deputy Sheriff Milford Sales was shot to death yesterday near his home. Mister Sales had just been found guilty and sentenced in the homicide of Ms. Delores Olds' nine-month-old fetus.

"Shortly after his death, officials of the Covenant of the New Commandment received another communiqué from the people who claimed responsibility for the death of another sheriff's deputy last week." Andy felt the poised tension in the room. "I will read the statement but, before I do, I have a statement from our Teacher, Minister Johnnie Walker. 'On behalf of the Covenant, the Walkers are saddened by the death of the two officers even as they understand the dynamics that seem to have led to those deaths. We are re-evaluating whether we can any longer act as spokespersons for the people who call themselves Unit 2236. They have said in their communiqués that they would honor and respect our wishes. For decades now, the Covenant has deplored the plethora of innocent black people killed by law enforcement, and we have been alarmed at the marked increase in such deaths in recent years. But we must also ask ourselves if our people will be scrutinized and persecuted for something they are not doing.' Minister Johnnie Walker says he will have another statement for you in the near future." Andy picked up another paper from the podium. Although no one said anything, the room seemed noisier.

"This is the statement from the people who call themselves Unit 2236." He read: "With the sentencing of Milford Sales, the forces of injustice have spoken once again. Even when an all-white jury saw fit to do the right thing and convict Mister Sales properly, a judge, displaying his apparent racism, saw fit to simply slap this outlaw deputy on the wrists. If the second-degree murder charge had stood, supplemented by an appropriate sentence, Mister Sales would still be alive. We serve notice once again that we will allow the judicial system to perform correctly. If it fails to do so, Unit 2236 will administer justice. Law enforcement will no longer be permitted to murder black people with impunity. Delores Olds' child deserved a chance at life. Milford Sales' criminal behavior and wanton disregard of life, along with the ludicrous sentence, has brought about the forfeit of his own life to the December 4th Brigade of Unit 2236."

When Andy looked up, everyone tried to speak at once. He waited with a hand up until everyone stopped shouting. "We know a nationwide manhunt is underway for the people who have claimed responsibility for these two shootings. Although Minister Johnnie Walker has indicated willingness to talk with the authorities if they ask, he emphasizes that he has no additional information to provide them."

The questions came, rapid fire. How do they contact you? Do you approve of what they are doing? Would they contact you if you didn't approve? Why won't you condemn them? Are your leaders afraid of going to jail?

Andy stayed with the agreed script. The Covenant leadership was evaluating whether or not it would be productive to continue receiving these communiqués. They would have a statement soon. They offered their condolences to the Hubble and Sales families, as they had to the Morris, Olds, and Bascomb families. They found it regrettable that the media showed less interest in the loss of life to the Morris, Olds, and Bascomb families, a negligence that appeared to have racist undertones.

Their "party line" had an answer to a certain question if anyone asked, but it was not to be volunteered. Romeo told Andy he had done the research and double-checked with Minister Johnnie. Their answer was crafted from his answer.

When the question came, it was from Heshimu Kenyatta, the reporter Andy had met the week before (He told Andy later that he asked because he was old enough to have a suspicion of the name's meaning): did they give any indication why they called themselves the December 4th Brigade?

"They give no indication at all," Andy said. "We were curious about it, too, and did some web searching to see what we might come up with. We found nothing at first. I mentioned the date to an older relative whose politics are progressive. He directed us to add the year '1969' to the search.

"We stress that this is only an educated guess. On December 4, 1969, Fred Hampton and Mark Clark, two leaders of the Black Panther Party in Chicago, Illinois, were murdered by the authorities in an early morning raid. Hampton was literally executed in his bed. If you think 'murdered' and 'executed' are hyperbole, do the research yourself. No one was convicted or even tried for the deaths. A grand jury paradoxically found wrongdoing but indicted no one. It's an educated guess on our part that this group, Unit 2236, may take the name of their brigade from the tragedy that occurred on that date in 1969."

Andy was not surprised when no one wanted to know more about Hampton and Clark. He saw it on the faces of most of the reporters. The news conference was suddenly over.

Andy saw the two suits moving toward him as he tried to head down the hallway to David's office. He faked not seeing them. The tall bespectacled one stepped in front of him to block his path. He held up his open wallet to show identity card and badge.

"Good morning, Mister Blackman, I'm T. Orenthal Middleton, FBI," he said. "We'd like a few minutes of your time."

Andy pursed his lips. "I guess Brother Simpson was a hero to your parents. You two must be the only ones in the country—in the world—named Orenthal. How can I help you?" He felt satisfaction at seeing Middleton try to hide his reaction at the sly way Andy had just played the dozens. Glenn and another Sword materialized on either side of Andy. Still not used to security being directed his way, Andy kept a smile off his face as he read clear annoyance on the face of Middleton and his partner.

"I'm Justin Cheatham." The other agent extended his hand with the greeting. "We wanted to speak with you alone."

Andy returned the handshake. "They go where I go." He made a show of looking at his watch. Middleton was already pissed; might as well keep messing with him. " You asked for a few minutes."

"We're collecting whatever information we can about Unit 2236," Middleton said, glaring at Andy. "An obvious place to start was with Covenant of the New Commandment."

"I can only tell you what we all know, which is not very much," Andy said. "Minister Johnnie said he received a note in an envelope the first time, and a phone call the second time. He wrote the second message down and sent it to me. I read what he sent. That's it."

"You said he received a phone call with the last message?"

"That's what the Minister said." He looked Middleton directly in the eyes; a light reflection kept him from seeing what he was looking for. *Make them ask*, Minister Johnnie had told him. *I want to know if they're tapping our lines. I'm sure they are.*

"Did he say where he got the phone call?"

You're good. "Nope. I assume he took it at his office or at home, or on his cell phone. Well, his cell phone's not listed, so probably one of the other two."

"Anything else?"

"Minister Johnnie is meeting with our board to discuss whether we should continue to receive these communiqués. As you know, Unit 2236 has given the Covenant this option."

"Have they indicated what they would do then?" Cheatham asked.

"Minister Johnnie said they haven't said anything other than what I've told you. He was thorough when he briefed me."

"Sounds like he was expecting us."

"We were expecting law enforcement," Andy said. "A high schooler could figure that out. You, local police, the CIA, the army, we were expecting somebody." He smiled. "Maybe they'll start sending the communiqués directly to you."

Middleton extended his hand. "Tell Reverend Walker we may want to interview him, too."

"I wish we could be more helpful," Andy said with insincerity.

"Knowing your politics, I'm sure you do," Cheatham shot back.

Andy winked. "Touché," he said with a grin.

TWENTY-FIVE

They knew him as Mister Matthew, a respected elder and board member at the meetinghouse. A retiree, the part-time security guard had joined the Covenant in the late Seventies. Mister Matthew's faith in Yahweh, the Great Teacher Yahshua, and, by extension, Minister Johnnie, was indeed larger than a mustard seed. Anything he could ever do for the Teacher to help his work, he did without asking questions.

So when Minister Johnnie wanted to know if two people could talk quietly and be secure where he worked, Mister Matthew said yes. As it happened, he had just watched a late night rerun of *All the President's Men*.

"The garage in the office building where I work is practically empty and closed after about seven P.M. every night," Mister Matthew said. "Why don't we do what Deep Throat and Woodward did? No need re-inventing the wheel."

Minister Johnnie smiled. "It sure works for me," he said. "Thank you, Matt. One of them will always call when they want to meet. Telephones would be so much simpler, but they're dealing with extremely sensitive information and we thought somewhere where electronic devices were unlikely would be best."

"Minister, I'm just glad I can be helpful."

Minister Johnnie described his police source to Mister Matthew, but said nothing about the kind of work he did. It wasn't a matter of trust; it was a matter of need-to-know. He also described Andy Blackman. Although he had just returned from Los Angeles, Matthew remembered him instantly. "He's that boy writes for the *Scabbard*." They would never stay more than an hour, Minister Johnnie said. He gave Mister Matthew Andy's cell phone number should a problem arise while the men were there. Mister Matthew said it would be relatively easy for them to hide in the cavernous three-level underground structure; he would work that out for them.

The two men met for the first time on a messy Thursday night. The cold, insistent downpour reminded Andy of a *film noir* setting as he dashed, shoulders hunched, across River Arbor Boulevard for his clandestine meeting. The parking structure was locked; under no circumstances should either of them drive their unauthorized vehicles into the garage, the minister said.

Andy recognized Mister Matthew as a Covenant board member as soon as he entered the lobby of the twenty-story River Arbor Offices building at the edge of the center city district. Apparently there was little traffic into the building on Mister Matthew's shift. The diminutive gray-haired man was doing T'ai Chi movements behind his guard station at the rear of the deserted lobby. He moved through the slow, circular postures with a fluidity and balance that belied his fifty-eight years. Andy wondered if he would look as graceful as Mister Matthew when he was his age. The guard stopped when he saw Andy.

"Good evening, young man," Mister Matthew said. "How are you this wonderful evening?"

"I'm fine, Mister Matthew," Andy said. "I didn't know you did T'ai Chi."

"Been in the class since Minister Johnnie started it about fifteen years ago," the older man said. "Helps me keep up with you young fellows. My instructor calls it the fountain of youth, and it sure feels like it."

"Is that right? You might look up and see me in class one of these Sundays."

"I'll look for you." He nodded toward the elevator. "You can go down. Your friend's already here."

As the elevator descended to the second parking level, Andy wondered what kind of brother would be taking this kind of chance inside the police department. He thought of Carvel Thomas. He was cool. There had to be other brothers like him. Well, he was about to meet his "friend."

It had been a whirlwind two weeks since he'd returned to the city, Andy thought. He'd buried his brother; he'd met a lady who so far was keeping his mind off his heartache; George's murder had sparked a riot; someone was shooting cops and had adopted the Covenant to get their message out; and now he was having covert meetings with a police department source who wanted to help Minister Johnnie's cause. All in two weeks. Damn.

The man stood at the other end of the deserted garage next to a utility closet. If you didn't know otherwise, he didn't look like a cop. He wore a funky pair of cargo pants, sneakers, an oversized sweatshirt, and tinted rimless glasses. As Andy walked toward him and his eyes adjusted to the light, he frowned at what he saw.

The man smiled at Andy's surprise. His name, which Andy would not learn for several months, was Danis Burton; he was a police captain. He was a prematurely balding white man with a fringe of blond hair still circling the lower part of his scalp. His bald look belied his age, athleticism and quick mind.

"You thought I was black," the police officer said.

"Yes, I did." Andy said. "The Covenant has some white friends, but not many, and almost all are leftist types. It never occurred to me a white police officer would take the kind of risk you're taking."

The man managed a slight smile. "Someone took a risk for me once. I'll tell you about it one of these days. If the department ever suspects there's a double agent inside, they will probably think he's black, too. Johnnie and I think my color works to our advantage." He told Andy the pseudonym he would be using if he ever found a need to write about any of this privately or as a reporter: "Miss Jones." "There's no reason for you to know my name," he said. "I'm a faceless bureaucrat at the Horseshoe, and I like it that way."

"Why not 'Mister Jones'?"

"I picked it as a private joke with a friend. If I ever think you're going to meet him, you can ask him. It may be the only time you'll see him smile. It has nothing to do with gender; I'm a raging heterosexual. I just have a sense of humor, and when Johnnie said why re-invent the wheel, I said, 'Why, indeed?' That's all." He looked at his watch. "Okay, I have a little something for you. It's difficult knowing how many snitches are in the Covenant, but I don't think there are too many. Yet. They may start to plant some more now with this Unit 2236 business going on. Where I've been assigned in the past two years gives me more access to knowing about the undercovers we place. I'm close on one now, but he's on loan from the feds so I haven't been able to get to his dossier yet. I think he's been with you a while and may be close to Minister Johnnie. I say 'he,' but with the difficulty I'm having, I'm even considering the possibility it's a woman.

"It will probably be best for me to give Minister Johnnie hard copies of anything you need when I can. He can destroy them as he sees fit." He took out an envelope and held it out to Andy. "Like this. It's a list of low-level informants. None that I sensed were really sharp. Mostly people trying to beat a case and stay out of jail. I suggest you don't let them know you know. Watch them and see if you can turn any of them into double agents. I think these bozos on the list are only dangerous when you don't know who they are. But by definition, I'm pretty sure the fed I'm trying to pull covers off of, man or woman, is quite dangerous."

"Is that it?"

"For now." His dark eyes bored into Andy's. "I'm very sorry about what happened to your half brother. You have my condolences. I've been a cop since the Reagan years. It's never felt as bad as it feels now, including under Reagan.

When I started, I thought the kind of thing that happened to George was an aberration. A part of me still wants to believe that, except so many are happening recently. Down at the Horseshoe these days I feel a sense of, like, 'what's anybody going to do about it?'

"When the thing happened with Rodney King. I'd been around five or six years by that time and had absorbed some of the culture. And as I watched the beating that man took, and the attitude behind it, something inside of me shifted. I saw him trying to protect himself from the awful ass whipping he was getting. When I heard the cops who did it say they felt threatened, I understood what I had been trying to shut out." He paused, frowned. "It's a lot worse now." He looked back at Andy. "I'm glad I can help. I hope you get to meet my friend one of these days. I'll leave first. You wait five minutes. Next time, you leave first."

He turned, walked through the exit door, and took the steps.

TWENTY-SIX

The night vibed with absolute delight right up until 10:57 P.M. First, they went to a movie in a theater with only one screen. They both laughingly agreed afterward that "stupid" was meant as a compliment to describe the film they saw. Then dinner in a small New York-ish kind of restaurant where the tables, tablecloths and chairs didn't match and real cream was used in the exceptionally strong coffee. The small tables featured eccentric, creative candles; their candle brought a smile to both their faces: lovers kissing in a standing position with their legs entwined in erotic embrace. Animated conversation, some serious, some flirtatious, some like the movie, allowed the walls screening and protecting the scar tissue on their emotions to lower ever so slightly. Wondrous sautéed salmon filets were followed by more coffee. Then came decadent double chocolate mousse desserts, followed by more animated conversation, all saturated with a plenteous supply of giggles the movie had put them in the mood for.

At 10:56 p.m., less than five minutes from Claudia's apartment building, the driver of an unmarked black Chevrolet Explorer plopped a whirling red light on its roof and signaled Andy to pull over. Both he and Claudia liked oldies stations; Claudia was making like Patti, wailing along with Michael McDonald on the classic, "On My Own," when the pulsing light the color of blood sliced into her melodic reverie.

"Did you make a bad turn?" she asked, tilting her head to look first behind them, then at him.

"Not that I'm aware of," Andy said, shutting the six-year-old Corolla off. Maybe something was wrong with the temporary sticker; he'd had the car less than twenty-four hours. A creature of habit, he'd tried to find a car to match the one he'd sold before leaving Los Angeles. He clicked the unlock button and opened the door.

"Please remain inside the vehicle," a disembodied deep voice said through a speaker on the Explorer. The tone was flat and unemotional but it was clearly an order. Andy closed the door. He started to get his wallet and immediately realized it would be a mistake. He placed both hands on the steering wheel. Patti and Michael wove their contrapuntal riffs back and forth in the stillness.

One cop stopped behind Claudia on the passenger side, but where he knew she saw him with peripheral vision. The other one, tall and built like a redwood, walked up to Andy's window. Andy had cracked it to allow brisk autumn air in.

"May I see your driver's license and registration, Mister Blackman?" he said, bending to look into the vehicle. He was young, maybe in his mid-twenties, with the clean cut, apple-cheeked look Madison Avenue used in Marine recruiting ads. His right hand rested lightly on the butt of his nine-millimeter. Andy recognized the tight wheel hat with the strap across the top as a symbol of the elite police unit called STOP: the Select Tactical Operations Patrol.

Mister Blackman. So it's like that, is it? With exaggerated movements that he hoped displayed a non-threatening demeanor, Andy retrieved his wallet from his left hip pocket. He never took his eyes away from the black eyes looking at him and registering no discernible feelings. "My registration is in the glove compartment," he said. The STOP cop nodded once.

"Can you tell me why I'm being stopped? I'm not aware of any traffic violation I committed." He looked up again. He recognized a mixture of something he sometimes saw in the eyes of white strangers. It took him a long time to figure out they were surprised, especially in settings like the one he was in, that his demeanor and use of language didn't fit their stereotype of African-Americans. Andy was acting as if he knew his rights.

"There's been an increase in both assaults and robberies in this area," Marine Advertisement said mechanically, as if reading from a card. "The Select Tactical Operations Patrol has received orders to make random stops of vehicles in the area." He knew Andy didn't believe him; Andy knew he didn't care if he was believed or not.

"When's the last time you were arrested?" the STOP cop asked.

When? What the fuck does that mean? Andy thought he heard a quick inhalation from Claudia. He took a deep breath, struggled to control the flare-up welling inside him. His street upbringing wanted to call the cop a bunch of motherfuckers. In that moment, he understood the purpose of the question. He could like it or not, but if he acted on "not," at the very least they would throw disorderly conduct on him. If it escalated, his wounds, fatal or otherwise, would stem from resisting arrest.

"I have never been arrested, *Officer*, " Andy said when he trusted himself to speak. He clenched his teeth.

"You're a reporter?" He knew it was a question that didn't have to be answered because the man was looking at his new press card with his photograph on it. Not to mention already knowing who he was.

The STOP officer leaned over and handed Andy his wallet and registration. He squinted as he looked at Andy. "Yeah, okay. You look different on television. Have a good evening," he said. "And be careful."

They remained silent as Andy drove the remaining four blocks to her home. The joyousness of Tavares clapping and stomping their way through "Heaven Must be Missing An Angel" didn't fit their mood. Before the stop, Andy would have flirted and said something corny. Now, the tune sounded brittle; he reached to turn it off as he pulled into a parking space. Claudia stopped him, covering his hand with her own. She felt soft, warm and somewhat electric because they had avoided touching each other all evening, until now.

"They're trained to say things like that, Andy," she said. "You should know that. Not officially, but training officers give them 'tips' on how to press people's buttons."

He exhaled. "We're all criminals," he said.

She took her hand away. He started to reach for it, changed his mind. Easy does it.

"He knew my name. I think the word is out to lean on us because of the Unit 2236 business. They think we know more than we know."

Claudia looked at him with a calmness that surprised him. Inside, he fumed. "We have to be careful," she said.

They stood on her porch and kissed good night after she had taken her key from her purse. It was both warm and restrained. Andy relished her full breasts flattening against his chest, the sweetness of her scent, the light in her eyes, and the slight smile full of promise and hope when they pulled apart.

TWENTY-SEVEN

ndy's eyelids felt like sandpaper each time he blinked. He looked at the clock perched on his temporary nightstand—actually a plastic milk crate. The digital clock read 4:30 A.M. The red colon between four and three winked dispassionately.

At first he didn't notice the blinking light on his answering machine. When had he gotten a call? He lifted the handset to check the message and saw the ringer button parked on silent.

It was Claudia. "Andy, I wanted to tell you again that Friday night was great, despite that STOP cop trying to rain on our parade. It's almost midnight on Saturday night; maybe you're asleep. I have to take a flight to California first thing in the morning to see my daughter. It's last minute and costing a fortune but something urgent has come up. I know we have tickets for the *Raisin* revival next Saturday. I should be back on Wednesday, Thursday at the latest. You know I hate cell phones, but if you have to reach me, Romeo has the number at the school in Ojai. Looking to see you as soon as I get back." Her voice clicked off.

Andy frowned. She didn't sound stressed, so apparently there was no accident. No need to worry, although he was sorry he'd missed her call. He smiled, remembering what he'd said the first time he saw her. Mean, mean Claudia Greene. He laughed suddenly. What was that song Uncle Sherman used to sing along with? *Lawdy lawdy lawdy, Miss Clawdy, Lawd, you sure look good to me . . . .* When his uncle felt like cutting the fool, he'd bend low and do an old dance up on his toes that he called The Slop. "Y'all don't know how to dance today," he'd say as he zigzagged across the floor. He'd have to tell Uncle Sherman about "Miss Clawdy" next time he saw him.

Reality check time, Andy thought. What was going on was none of his business. Yes, they were attracted. But he'd known the woman less than three weeks. She has to go see her daughter. Case closed.

He rolled over, turned the paperback book in his hand over, still open, and laid it on his stomach. Although he wasn't finished, he knew why his homie had asked him to read *Song of Solomon*. A part of him didn't want to know. He rubbed

175

at the grainy feeling in his eyes. Finally he placed the book next to the clock.

Rome wanted him to read about the Seven Days. And, intuitively, he knew Rome's reason had something to do with whoever was killing these killer cops.

One group—fictional—replicated any wrongful killing of black people with a near-identical killing of white people. When white people killed four little black girls in Birmingham, Alabama, the Seven Days found four little white girls—*any* four little white girls—and killed them. They sought symmetry and anonymity.

The other group—actual—tracked down the law enforcement perpetrator of a killing and executed the killer if the courts let him off—if he was even tried at all. He now wondered why only one of Tanya Morris' killers had died. He hadn't thought about it before. This was a different philosophy, one that would draw more attention than the fictional Seven Days would and have profound repercussions.

Romeo hadn't asked him to read this book in a vacuum.

As long as they'd known each other, Rome was always the one who exercised leadership and seemed to be a step ahead. Romeo had been elected "most likely to succeed" in his senior year at Covenant Academy while Andy muddled through Germanville High. Romeo was class president and captained Covenant's track team. Rome was always ready to throw down if a rumble jumped off. At sixteen, Rome was the brother in their crowd listening to Wynton Marsalis while he and the others were playing Run DMC.

Was Unit 2236 a part of the Covenant? His mind couldn't wrap around an image of the Swords actually assassinating anyone, their paramilitary bearing and fierceness notwithstanding. He felt certain the police department—or the feds, or both—had informants inside the Swords. Wouldn't they know about the kind of activity Rome was suggesting, if he was suggesting anything? According to his Uncle Sherman, agent provocateurs had ravaged the ranks of the Black Panther Party, the Fruit of Islam, the Us Organization, and others during the Sixties. Even groups pledged to nonviolent action were infiltrated. In the Illinois Panther chapter, the man responsible for the chapter's security had actually been on the FBI payroll, Uncle Sherman said.

Of course, Minister Johnnie was thorough enough to make intelligence a two-way street. He had some idea of what they knew, even if he didn't have anywhere near the size network that law enforcement had.

If something was happening, why was Rome telling him? They were best friends, but there had to be more than that. Did Rome actually think he was competent material for such an undertaking, if such an undertaking existed?

Unit 2236 used guns. It seemed a safe assumption that they knew other ways to kill. He was out of shape, and had limited experience firing a weapon. He and Uncle Sherman had visited firing ranges several times when he was about twenty, and that was the extent of his experience.

He thought about the STOP cop trying to provoke him earlier. Being pissed off is not the same as hating someone. Did you have to hate somebody to kill them? Hadn't someone said revolutions were fought, not from hate, but from feelings of love for one's people? Was this a revolution? An insurrection? Andy answered his own question. At the very least, it was resistance. If the system intended to keep its foot on the neck of black people, Unit 2236 had a machete and was making a determined effort to cut that sucker off. It might make them bleed all over us; still, never again would there be a foot on the neck. If they tried, a crippled opponent's second foot would be much easier.

Andy looked at his copy of *Song of Solomon*. A part of Andy said he was hallucinating; another part felt that forces were in motion, and that the Covenant had something to do with it.

He rubbed his eyes again and looked at the clock. Four forty-eight. He was really tired. Nigga, go to bed. Ain't nobody planning nothing.

TWENTY-EIGHT

Andy bent over with his hands on his ashy knees. His breath came in dry heaves—large, desperate gulps of air. His ancient gray sweatshirt, bearing a likeness of Queen Latifah on the front, had a large sweat stain starting at the neckline and partially covering the actress-singer's gorgeous face. His running shorts clung to him like wet tissue paper. His thigh muscles ached and trembled with exhaustion.

Romeo, about ten yards away, held the football like a quarterback looking for a receiver. He, too, looked as if someone had poured a bucket of water over him but his breathing came much easier.

It was an Indian summer Sunday with a hint of coolness. A sunny and cloudless blue sky combined with a gentle wind had bicyclists, joggers, and just folks greedily taking advantage of Johnson Square. Most surmised it was a last gasp of autumn before the almighty "Hawk" settled in for the winter months.

"You only *look* like you in halfway decent shape," Romeo said with a laugh. "You getting old, brotherman. C'mon, we better stop. I don't want you dying on my watch."

They walked along one of the curving footpaths until they saw a vacant bench far enough from other visitors to talk undisturbed.

Andrew Johnson Square, one of several in the center of the city, had been a landmark almost since the city's inception in the seventeenth century. On its north side, about eighty yards from where the men sat, had once stood a raised wooden block, six foot high, large enough to hold nine average sized human beings abreast. Twice-weekly auctions of African captives had taken place at noontime. An obscure word-of-mouth legend, one not taught in schools, said that on a sunny October afternoon much like the one Andy and Romeo enjoyed, three Africans rebelled. Given the months of unholy forced travel already endured, the uncertainty of life ahead felt worse than death to them. The three, on a prearranged signal, took their chains and quickly strangled the auctioneer and broke his neck before being shot to death. From then on, all male adult captives were sold one at a time. Although slavery was outlawed in 1831—the same year

Nat Turner rebelled and was hung—the block remained in use until the late 1840s. A civic organization (coincidentally led by Minister Johnnie's personal attorney) had been pressuring the city for six years to erect a commemorative plaque on the site memorializing the insurrectionary act. City officials refused to acknowledge the legend. The attorney's organization, and others, referred to the square block of greenery, benches, and squirrels (and, unofficially, rats) as Congo Square instead of using the slaveholding president's name the city had named it for. Although President Andrew Johnson was a southerner without connections to the city, a wealthy nineteenth-century robber baron who admired Johnson leveraged a six-figure donation to the municipality into naming rights for the square. After renovating the park, he named it for the seventeenth president.

"Is everything okay with Claudia?" He no longer gulped air the way a starving man gobbled food. "She called me last night but I missed it. She said something about flying out to see her daughter."

"What did she say?"

"Just that something had come up suddenly. She didn't sound stressed or anything, but I was just wondering. Being nosy, I guess."

"She's fine," Romeo said. "She told me she'd be back Wednesday, and that she needed to spend some time—see—F.L."

Andy knew his friend well enough to sense that, as her boss, he knew more. He decided to change the subject and leave it alone for now. "I haven't finished the book, but I read far enough to know about the Seven Days," he said. "That's why you wanted me to read the book, isn't it?"

Romeo looked him directly in the eyes. They had been friends for nearly thirty of their thirty-nine years. They'd been through a lot together; both had improbably watched a loved one shot down by ostensible protectors.

Truth time.

"Yeah, I was sure you'd figure it out," Romeo said. "Let's get something to drink. You need it." They walked to a nearby cart vendor. Romeo said no more until they walked away with two icy bottles of water beaded with perspiration.

"What did you feel about the Seven Days?" he asked.

"I think that's some wild shit is what I think." Andy took a large gulp of water, then another, turning the bottle up.

Romeo smiled. "Wild shit," he repeated. "Yeah, I guess you could say that. Did you agree with their philosophy, their actions?"

Andy looked at his friend, took another swallow. "You're still beating around the bush."

179

"Yes, I am. I will come straight in a few minutes, I promise. I need to know what you felt."

Andy looked straight ahead as they walked. His thoughts and feelings bumped into each other. Someone had claimed their bench; they kept walking.

"Even though I believe nonviolent actions work better, I understand the feelings of revenge," he said finally. "I have felt some of that, you know that." He emptied his bottle, wishing he had bought two. "I felt it again after George was murdered. But, you know, when I feel it, there's always some fear mixed all up in it. It's a feeling like, like I could never be normal again."

"Quite a word, normal is," Romeo said, "How about the randomness, the balancing of things that the character Guitar talks about?"

"Morrison's a great writer," Andy said. "My skin crawled when I thought of them doing that. And, even though it was fiction, I could see them doing it and it didn't feel right. The Seven Days saying all white people are guilty is like saying all black people are inferior. Picking people at random for assassination didn't feel like my idea of justice."

They stopped and sat on the edge of an immense empty fountain. No one was within fifteen yards in either direction except scampering squirrels.

"You want to finish this?" Romeo thrust the bottle toward him. Except for speckles of sweat on his shirt, there was no indication he had been exercising. A grateful Andy took the bottle.

"But there is a school of thought that says all white people, even well-meaning white people, allow the few to do what they do, along with the support of some traitorous blacks," Romeo continued. "Just as some say that, as a group, black people allow this madness to be heaped on us, our economic success stories notwithstanding.

"We try to personalize it, blame it on somebody like, say, President Bruder," Romeo said, his hands gesturing as if he were speaking to an audience seated before him. "And Bruder's definitely sending signals out that allow these shootings to continue because, more and more, all of us are seen as criminal. But over fifty million people voted, including more black people than I care to admit, and said they want a man like Bruder. So they're culpable, too, aren't they?"

"But, Rome, that's my point," Andy said. "How would someone like the Seven Days know if the white person or persons they kill wasn't someone vehemently opposed to Bruder and what he stands for? There's always a small group going against the stream. There are always some black people trying to fight back, even when most are going along to get along, or too busy with the daily struggle of getting over to be bothered. And wasn't there a white group out front, going against the grain back in the Sixties?"

"The Weather Underground?"

"Yeah, that sounds right. I'm just saying randomly killing people didn't seem right. I don't know how the book turns out yet. I did like what Guitar had to say about it not being about hating white folks, but about loving black folks."

The look Romeo gave him, and the small smile, was clearly one of approval. Still, it answered nothing for Andy.

"You've been dancing around something, man, and that's not like you, not with me," Andy finally said. "What's going on?"

Romeo caught his friend's look. "I said straight talk, didn't I?" he said. "I've been working on something for most of the last three years that will rise or fall on trust." His voice was quiet and even. "Trust, love, commitment. They've become synonymous for me, but only within the fold of the Covenant. You are my best friend in the world still. With the exception of my family, I feel closer to you than anyone in the Covenant, or in life. But having said that, there are still things you must cross over to if I'm to share certain things with you. I know you'll understand if you make the decision to cross. If you don't, you'll still be my man. Even if I have to deal with you down the road, it won't be personal."

"Deal with me? What's that supposed to mean?" Andy felt annoyed and wasn't sure he had a right to be. "What the fuck does that mean, *deal with me?*"

Romeo placed a firm hand on his friend's forearm. "Time is tight," he said. "I need to see something in you, or not, as the case may be.

"Have you ever heard of Sinn Fein, the nationalist Irish political organization?" Romeo asked. Andy had, but vaguely. "But you are familiar with the Irish Republican Army?"

Andy nodded.

"Sinn Fein was founded in 1905, is legal, and participated in the systemic political process," Romeo continued. "Everybody knew they were the above ground voice for the underground IRA. Well, the Covenant is about to take on the role of an organization like Sinn Fein. But what I'm about to share with you must be more secretive than even the IRA. If I go on, and you decide to pass, I have one request that's actually a demand. You must never mention this conversation to anyone either way. As my friend, I trust you to do that. If you do walk away, I have permission to let you. Only a limited amount of people will know what I'm about to tell you. If you betray this conversation and we trace a leak to you, people will come to see you and there will be nothing I can do about it, even though you are my best friend in the world. Am I clear?"

Andy's head seemed to be buzzing but it didn't hurt. A chasm loomed ahead. He could step over, or he could stand here, petrified. He smiled tightly as he remembered a phrase that was now embedded in pop culture: Are you going to take the red pill or the blue bill?

"Talk to me," he said.

Andy tried hard to digest it all. Romeo gave him a history and sociology lesson, spiced with a dose of resistance theory. He was both right and wrong about the Swords of the Master being involved. As the visible self-defense arm and sworn protection of the Covenant of the New Commandment, they would remain so. They would remain unarmed, except when receiving contracts as a professional agency to provide security and carry licensed weapons. Firearms would be used only in those circumstances. They were law abiding and would remain so, even when the law wasn't law abiding. Their reasoning was really rather simple. If they armed themselves, federal, state and local authorities would use the opportunity to wipe them out. Essentially, the Swords would remain a part of the "Sinn Fein" structure, so to speak.

Covenant leadership had exhaustively studied and analyzed the fate of the Robert F. Williams self-defense units in Monroe, North Carolina, more than a half-century earlier, Romeo said. The Black Panther Party's theory and practice had likewise been combed through thoroughly.

This was the first time Andy heard any mention of the Four Stars of leadership in the Swords of the Master. As Teacher of the Covenant, Minister Johnnie was the official leader of the Swords and had always worn a silver eagle, the military rank of colonel. About a year ago, without fanfare, he began wearing a triangle. Everyone thought it referred to the golden triangle in the sanctuary's meetinghouse.

The Four Stars were determined to learn from history and thus not be condemned to repeat it. Of the Four Stars, the rank and file Swords knew only of the Third Star. Those selected for Unit 2236 got to meet the First Star. Romeo, the Second Star, never wore rank publicly. Only Minister Johnnie, the Third Star, wore rank in public. And only he knew the identity of the Fourth Star.

The "cut off the head" theory had been used against Robert Williams and the Panthers, and against others. Against Williams, the law and the Klan were all wrapped up together. The message was overt and clear: black people could not, and would not, be permitted to organize and defend themselves.

The Panthers received the same message, but with an added layer of hypocrisy. At the time of the group's founding in 1966, the law allowed Californians to carry loaded firearms publicly in the state as long as the weapons were not concealed. Then Huey P. Newton, Bobby Seale, and a couple dozen of leather jacketed, beret-wearing black men and women seized the time. They grabbed law books, shotguns, rifles, and pistols and patrolled the police to ensure correct performance of their duties. Within months, the law was changed. It had never been meant for black people—especially a disciplined, organized group of black people—in the first place.

"I learned in a graduate sociology class that the very first thing a government must do to be a government is lay claim to the legitimate use of violence and coercion, both within and without," Romeo said. They walked as they talked, returning to the vendor for more bottles of water.

"If you can't protect a people, you're not the government. If you can't police a people, you are not the government. And no one, without exception, must be permitted to 'police the police' or the army, as the case may be. The people must be utterly convinced that anyone else who uses violence is criminal, crazy, or both. As a journalist, surely you've noticed in news accounts that violence becomes 'force' in the hands of the State. The U.S. government and its agencies are never 'violent.' They use 'force.' Only the bad guys, whoever they may be, are 'violent' or 'terrorists.'" He said all this using techniques he'd perfected in public speaking, using small vocal inflections to make verbal quotation marks.

"In news reporting, the state of Israel uses force; the Palestinian community commits acts of violence or terror. The nation's enemies are now all terrorists, using cars, trucks, hijacked airplanes, whatever they can get their hands on, to kill people. But a state dropping one-thousand-pound bombs from fast moving jets and killing civilian populations by the thousands upon thousands are not terrorizing anyone in the very same reporting." He adopted an exaggerated newscaster voice. "They are conducting military missions where the use of force sometimes produces collateral damage," he said.

"I'm telling you this for a reason, my friend," Romeo said. "Targets we select for executive action—" he stopped and laughed. "See, we use euphemisms, too, because it makes you sound right." His smile disappeared. "The people we kill will probably be given heroes' funerals and be applauded for their lives of service. Our actions, on the other hand, will almost certainly be vilified as criminal, evil, and obviously not Christian or spiritual. It will be most important for them to turn people against us, especially black people. The majority of whites will instinctively condemn what we do."

Romeo placed a hand on his friend's shoulder. "The Morrison book is a technique we use to start a conversation as we recruit. Unlike the fictional Seven Days, our targets will always be guilty of a crime for which they are not punished. They will usually be military, meaning police or other agencies acting on behalf of a government that has, in fact, failed to enforce the law. We have a strict prohibition against random or innocent executions, so much so that we will abandon a mission if at all possible before taking the life of innocent people. Security assigned to protect targets will not be considered innocents. Executive actions will only be taken after the law fails to act, or acquits someone who is obviously guilty."

"But the Swords won't be doing this?" Andy felt light-headed.

"Yes and no. We've created the shadow cadre that people now know as Unit 2236," Romeo said. "The overwhelming majority of Swords won't know the connection to 2236 because they don't need to know. I am the liaison between above ground and underground. Need to know will be strict. You must understand, here and now, that betrayal of the work of Unit 2236 is a capital offense."

"Who decides?"

"The Fourth Star. He or she is very rich, very public, very moderate appearing, and in no visible way connected to the Covenant. If his or her identity ever becomes known and connected to us, or if 2236 becomes connected to the Covenant, it will probably be the beginning of the end for the Covenant, because we will be hunted down by 'the murderous, cowardly pack.' Remember that line from Mister Blackshear's class?"

Andy nodded. Blackshear had been a fierce Garveyite tenth-grade English teacher who had somehow slipped under the radar and into the public school system. He had made the entire class memorize Claude McKay's "If We Must Die."

"There will be no known association of Unit 2236 with either the Swords or the Covenant, except the sending of communiqués. The decision on accepting future communiqués is a charade we're playing out. Except in the presence of unit members, you will never even mention the existence of the Fourth Star. In this way, we must be different from organizations like Sinn Fein for now.

"Andy, I've understood your view that King was right about nonviolent action," Romeo said. "I think you see now it should be a tactic, though, and not a way of life. The Covenant will surely use nonviolent direct action when it takes us where we want to go and gets us what we want." He inhaled. "I took this chance because I felt something shift inside you when George was killed. It's how I felt when Sonny died. Are you in, or do we forget this conversation ever occurred?"

Andy knew his answer before he voiced it. And yet, only a few days ago, despite Sonny, despite George, he might have hesitated. With his Uncle Sherman, it had been a small thing that moved him to action and eventually throwing in with the Panthers, a small thing that still remained in his soul more than forty years later. A desire for a cold beer was a small thing, wasn't it?

"I Want You!" they told Uncle Sherman. Wear our uniform and pay obeisance to our golden calf even as the calf pisses on you and tells you it's raining. But Uncle Sherman, a uniformed soldier, couldn't buy a beer in a segregated Kentucky bar in 1963, in the land of the free and the home of the brave, and it radicalized him.

With him, it was a small thing, too. A summary of how it was, a routine police stop in a way of life that criminalized him simply because he was alive, and would therefore always be guilty. Like Rodney King or Tyesha Miller or Amadou Diallo or Patrick Dorismond, he was guilty of the American felony of driving while black, walking while black, or even standing while black. *When's the last time you were arrested? When, nigger?* The STOP cop was just doing his job. Some things were just too American to change.

Andy looked his friend in the eye and stepped across the chasm. His next words sounded far off to him.

"I'm a pretty unlikely assassin," he said.

Romeo's face softened. "We'll provide the skills and training you need, and you'll be surprised," he said. "But Unit 2236 will succeed or fail on trust, commitment and love, and you'll understand why when we get you ready. You trust me with your life; I trust you with mine. We have thought this thing through and we understand our limitations, believe me. At this stage, and possibly for years to come, we can only win by not losing. We have three West Coast teams, but we've only heard from the December 4th Brigade. We are now recruiting three East Coast teams. You will be with the August 21st Brigade, named for the day in 1971 that Soledad Brother George Jackson was assassinated. But this is for the long haul, and Che was right. In revolution, one wins or one dies. Most of us may not see the victory." He paused, his eyes reflective. "This is where Sonny has brought me."

The two men stood up. They shook hands and embraced simultaneously. Andy knew that he would be very sore in the morning. His leg muscles were tightening already.

2236

"Are you allowed to say why the group is called Unit 2236?" Andy asked. "Yes, I can tell you, but see it for yourself. Look in the Book of Luke."

TWENTY-NINE

ndy looked at himself... he couldn't see his face ... only a blank oval
... He looked around ... a long corridor loomed before him ... Where
was he? Sonny, tall and military looking, walked toward him ...
George was with him... they came toward him, walking down a gleaming metallic
corridor... Where was he? George, styled in his Sunday-go-to-meeting navy blue
pinstripe ... Sonny, Army sharp in class "A" greens ... they walked past him, one
on each side... They motioned; he followed ... He watched himself follow... the
trio moved past several doors... Sonny opened one... they entered a bar... Andy
watched himself squinting... A figure stood at the bar... Uncle Sherman... But
when he turned, Uncle Sherman was Sonny again... several guns lay on the long,
narrow bar... Sonny smiled... he gulped down a mug of beer... The blonde bartender reached for a pistol on a ledge behind him... George grabbed a stick... the
bartender shot him... Sonny threw beer at the laughing bartender, who turned and
walked away... Andy watched himself take a gun from the bar... He shot at the
bartender... shot again... and again... and again... Andy walked away ...
Sonny walked away ... George was gone... where was George? The gleaming corridor was gone, too... An ocean stretched before them... dark, silvery... a lunar
reflection... dark... no land... none at the horizon... no land anywhere, except
where they stood... A wall of Africans—men, women, children—for as far as he
could see... faced him... they wore rags... wore royal robes... ceremonial clothing
... Western dress... from past present future... they faced the ocean now... they
stretched as far as he could see... there was music somewhere... Where was this
place? Music every where, no where... now here... omnipresent... Romeo and
Sonny and George and Andy without a face... Africans everywhere... were they
making the music? The lament of a choir... a choir of millions... bells... tolling
... mournfully tolling... Africans... walking across the water... sun reflected
across the water... Andy and Sonny and George and Romeo stepped on the water
... they moved toward the sun... Sonny wore tattered bloody rags now... George
too... Romeo too... Andy too ... bells... mournful... as they walked... into
the sun... bells... as they walked ... into the sun... bells... they walked... into

187

the sun . . . walked . . .

He felt disoriented. Where was he? Nothing looked familiar. Or felt familiar. He rubbed his eyes, looked around. Slowly, his memory joined the rest of him. He'd have to tell Claudia that her sofa worked like a sleeping pill.

Dream fragments replayed, receded, slipped away, disappeared into his wakefulness. What he remembered was indeed intense. He flopped back on the sofa. His body hurt. The soreness in his out-of-shape muscles had lessened, but was far from gone.

He and Claudia had gone to a revival of *Raisin in the Sun.* Afterward, she invited him in for tea. Without a word spoken, they knew they wanted each other. They knew it was too soon. He wondered: what was it like to love a woman first, and then make love? He didn't know. Physical intimacy always came first for him. Feelings followed, sometimes. He had loved Jhanae, but dazzling, mind-bending sexual couplings highlighted with her jeweled pelvic movements came first. Debora, too. Not dazzling or mind-bending, but potent. As a young man in his late teens and twenties, sex first was a given. Desire masqueraded as love until it didn't. Now he was almost forty, and had never loved a woman when he and she first made love. Had anyone ever loved him first? What would it feel like to love someone first? The only way to it was to do it.

Claudia, always slow to warm to physical intimacy in a relationship, liked their silent, unspoken agreement. She knew that when she gave, she held nothing back. She felt odd knowing that if he wanted to make love, she would not stop him even though she wasn't ready. But a part of her knew that he knew that she wanted to feel something far deeper. They had only scratched the surface.

They both knew they were having a trust test. Her comments about her trip bordered on enigmatic. Her demeanor gave him reason not to push. Andy's trust in her gave her hope, although she suspected it might get worse before it got better.

"I wanted to tell my daughter I love her. I needed to spend some time with her," she said when she had returned to the *Scabbard* office on Thursday. Her face had gone suddenly reflective. "You know, it's funny. I told F.L. that Mommy's working to build a better world for her. But with an IQ of 160 and her precocious toughness, F.L. is going to do well whether the world gets better or not. She's really a remarkable daughter." The phone rang at that moment and Claudia answered it.

Andy started in on his own work, making calls for the story he was working. Increased federal subsidies had been announced for the prison-industrial complex in the state, complemented by stark cuts in public school funding. It was as if the Bruder administration didn't even feel a need for subtlety. But as he made his first call, he couldn't help but wonder: you flew all the way to California to tell your daughter you love her? Was something wrong with that picture? His gut told him no, not wrong. Maybe the picture was just incomplete.

Now, two days later they sat in her living room, still enjoying the newness of their friendship. They talked for hours, exchanging histories and how their lives had brought them to this night. She'd grown up in Detroit; he was a native of the city. Both had been married and divorced, both had degrees.

Her dad had been a member of the Student Non-Violent Coordinating Committee, and her folks still lived in Detroit. F.L. was an absolute delight, an adventurous sort who thrived on her school's experiments with new ways of learning; he had no children and had moved back home because of a failed relationship with a good person that just didn't work.

Working at the *Bugle* had been trying, as well as low paying. He wasn't making much more with the *Scabbard* but it meant more. They both agreed that combining their spiritual and professional lives might be as good as it got.

His birth father had doo-wopped with moderate success as the lead singer of a quintet called the Continentals. Missing in action in Andy's life, he still worked the oldies circuit, capitalizing on three hit records the group had in the late Sixties. Andy hadn't seen him since his *real* mother, Madeline, died. Madeline Blackman had adopted him when he was just twenty-one days of age; her death came swiftly and unexpected from a brain aneurysm at forty-three. Only then did he learn that her younger sister, Mary, was his birth parent. Until then, he thought Madeline's estranged husband, Sherman Blackman, was his father. Since the revelation, he'd grown to have a good relationship with the ex-Panther he called Uncle "Bad Cat."

"Will you ever forgive her?" She said it softly, trying to keep it non-judgmental.

The question caught him off guard. "You're perceptive," he finally said when he realized he didn't know the answer to her question.

"It's how you're saying what you're saying." She said. "Your anger feels like it's way down inside you, Andy. What is it, that she kept it from you? Madeline —your mother—took part in that, too."

"No. I wish they'd told me but, no." He felt the tightness in his face. "I've wanted to ask her why she gave me away, and I'm afraid to hear the answer." He was quiet for a long moment. "I know she was an actress and went to Hollywood

189

trying to do her thing, and I guess it's tied up in that. I've thought I shouldn't feel like this because she did give me to Mom, for which I'm forever grateful. She could have put me anywhere."

"I don't know Mary Bascomb, Andy," Claudia said. She reached over, placed her hand on his. "I've only seen her once, at the funeral, and at Marian's afterward. Although she's grieving the loss of George, a painful, painful loss in itself, I can tell you this because I'm a woman. I saw her look at you at one point, and I could see the price she paid for doing what she did. And I didn't know this at that point. I just saw a woman in great pain. Whatever her reason or reasons, which of course I don't know, I saw in her look a woman who has probably hurt every day of her life since she did it."

They were quiet. Andy remembered something in his mind's eye: Mary Green Bascomb visiting him as "Aunt Mary." He'd been five the first time, about eight the second time. He had avoided her as much as possible at his mother's funeral and hadn't seen her again until they buried a cousin named Isabel ten years later. The last time was at George and Marian's wedding.

Andy realized now that he'd never seen her happy. As a child, it hadn't meant anything, and he couldn't even say he "knew" it then. Even at George's wedding, she smiled and did all the right things, but there was an ever-present aura of sadness underlying and surrounding her being.

Andy looked at Claudia and she saw the thanks. He wasn't over it but he heard her. She patted his hand as if to say, you're welcome.

They saw it was almost three A.M. Claudia had gotten a blanket and promised him a healthy breakfast in the morning. They hugged but, without even discussing it, thought it best not to try even the most restrained of kisses.

Then he'd fallen asleep and dreamed of death and ancestors.

THIRTY

For Andy, strangeness aptly described the entire day. It began as an unseasonably cold October Saturday, even for the end of the month.

Minister Johnnie had spoken from the Old Testament, something he almost never did. (Although, being Minister Johnnie, he quoted the Prophet Joel, who implored his people to prepare for war by beating their ploughshares into swords and their pruning hooks into spears.) Claudia had been both withdrawn, and then so passionate that he knew the conflict was major.

It wasn't just the physicality of the kiss, which had been overwhelming and had left them both almost breathless. Open, yielding, abandoned.

It had been the look in her dark brown eyes. Fear? No. It had seemed like more of a big question mark.

After Saturday meeting, the four of them—Romeo and Malikah had joined them—had gone to pig out on the oversized breakfast platters served at Bobby Crenshaw's Soul Food on University.

When Claudia hardly touched her scrambled eggs, grits and turkey bacon, he'd asked what was wrong. "Nothing," she said although she was clearly distracted.

Romeo, too, had been unusually quiet.

"I can't believe we've known each other such a short time," she said on the drive back to the meetinghouse parking lot where they had left her car. "You feel so familiar. In a good way, not the 'breeding contempt' way."

"Claudia, you have something on your mind."

"Yes."

"Can we talk?"

"I can't. One day you'll understand, but you just have to trust me on that."

Because the conversation had been so heavy with awkwardness, he said no more.

"Do you want me to follow you to your place? Maybe you can find a way to talk through whatever it is," he asked. They had been the only ones on the now empty parking lot.

191

"No, I've got a lot to do to get ready for tomorrow." She looked down as she said it. Get ready? Was something going on at work tomorrow that he didn't know about?

She threw her arms around him and kissed him. Gently at first, then open-mouthed, and finally, with desperation, a hunger that surprised, delighted, and confused him.

Now, he sat in front of his own building, wondering what it all meant. Later, before he got in bed, he called her. There was no answer.

She wasn't at work on Monday and didn't call in. Romeo was out of town and didn't seem concerned about it when he called in for messages.

When Andy arrived at his apartment that night, he found the note under his door.

THIRTY-ONE

ndy and Miss Jones picked another rainy night for a rendezvous. A penetrating chill permeated the garage, the kind of cold that made Andy wonder why the rain had not turned to snow. It was a week before Thanksgiving, the holiday Minister Johnnie caustically referred to as "Genocide Day."

Miss Jones was there when he arrived, again looking younger than his age in baggy slate grey corduroys, wool knit cap, combat boots, and a heavy leather bombardier's jacket glistening with rain.

"Andy, are you familiar with COINTELPRO?" Miss Jones asked as a way of saying hello.

"I've heard Minister Johnnie refer to it," Andy said. "I believe it was a government program designed to attack and destroy the black power movement back in the Sixties." Even speaking low, their voices reverberated in the empty cavernous second level of the parking structure. It annoyed Andy, made the conversation seem less private.

"You're partially right," Miss Jones said. "The acronym stands for 'counter intelligence program.' It was originally designed around the McCarthy era when they were going after communists. In COINTELPRO, J. Edgar Hoover allowed the FBI and other law agencies do all manner of illegal and vile things, even by their own standards. They used murder, lies, misinformation, and who knows what else to disrupt any groups Hoover didn't like. And Hoover definitely did not like black people. I believe he made his FBI bones by going after Marcus Garvey. Generally speaking, he was not a nice man, and COINTELPRO was the tool he used for retribution against almost anyone seeking progressive change. In the 1970s, Congress dismantled it and told the FBI to start obeying the law. But you're right. Hoover specifically ordered, in writing, that it be used to prevent, at all costs, the rise of what he called a black messiah.

"Well, the bad news is, it was never dismantled. In fact, a little known office called CP2 has been a tiny subset of the FBI's covert ops division almost since they supposedly shut it down. Sort of the son of COINTELPRO, you know?

It's was quietly placed there during the Reagan administration. I guess those who knew wink-winked and looked the other way. Yes, CP2 stands for COINTEL-PRO 2. It got a few strong teeth when the PATRIOT Act was passed. Now it has a full set of dentures. With little or no fanfare, they're being given a budget and told to find Unit 2236 and destroy them. You might find it as a brief on page thirty in some newspapers, but don't count on it. They're hiding the request in a bill giving tax exemptions to corporations that want to expand their overseas operations. CP2 probably wants to flex its muscle in a disinformation and terror campaign against the Covenant, the only connection they can make with Unit 2236. By the beginning of the year, spring at the latest, they'll be kicking asses and taking names."

"But except for the communiqués, there's been no connection made between the Covenant and Unit 2236." Andy thought his protest sounded convincing.

Miss Jones' eyes twinkled; Andy thought he suppressed a smile. *Did he know?*

"Do you think that matters? Haven't you been listening? Andy, they don't need a link, they'll invent one.

"One last bit of info. Something connected to what I'm about to say may lead to a story for you, but you must find another source, preferably two," Miss Jones said. "OneCorporation International is getting ready to do a shit load of hiring. Shouldn't be hard given the unemployment levels right now. My understanding is that eight out of ten jobs will be security guards, but not your usual rent-a-cops. What they're building at OCI amounts to a private corporate army. I think they already have between three and seven thousand in their current rent-a-cop division. They're going to upgrade their training and hire more. I'd bet the farm it's connected to putting fire to the Covenant's ass."

"Why don't they just use the Guard against us?"

"The profit motive, for one thing. Bruder wants to throw some money to OCI. You forget he was their former CEO. And for another, it creates jobs for both poor whites and poor blacks in doing something Bruder finds useful— getting rid of some uppity opposition that's growing an increasingly higher profile. Tyrants need scapegoats, my friend." He looked at his watch. "Gotta go. You leave first this time. Oh, I almost forgot. You're going away shortly, right?"

He does know. "It's possible," Andy said.

Miss Jones smiled. "Tell Robert that Miss Jones said hello."

"That's a common name."

Miss Jones' smile widened. "You'll have no doubt who I'm talking about."

Minister David hoped Wardell would make it quick. He and his wife hadn't gone out in months and she'd reminded him of that fact. He'd promised her a four star restaurant and a show. He had agreed with Ward's suggestion that security stay with other leadership other than his father more than they had. Placing him with Romeo was his way of showing him that he appreciated his security background and expertise.

"So, Brother Ward, how can I help you today?" David looked at his watch. "We've got about twenty minutes."

"Yes, sir," Wardell said. "I know you stay busy, Minister David, so I'll get right to the point. But you're going to have to block out some time soon where we can talk through some important matters."

David stared at the man. Keyes' assuredness bordered on arrogance. David knew it was an asset for the kind of work he did, both for the Covenant, and in his own security consulting business. But sometimes it got on his nerves. "Well, that depends on what it is you have to talk about."

"May I use your scratch pad?" Keyes asked. David nodded. Keyes took it and jotted something down. He tore the page off and slid it across the desk.

"You ever talk to a dude with a funny-sounding voice at that phone number?" Keyes said. "He told me you and I were birds of a feather, so to speak, even if for different reasons."

We have someone inside the Covenant who will make himself known to you. He'll identify himself by letting you know that he knows this phone number.

David struggled to make his face a mask that would not betray his feelings. Fear sat in his stomach like undigested food, but he didn't want this man to know it. "I certainly wouldn't have thought it was you," he said.

Keyes took the paper back, tore it up, put the scraps in his pocket. "You said you don't have much time. Our contact, whose name neither of us knows, said we should use the code name 'John Edgar' for him when we discuss work we have to do. John Edgar has given me an assignment in Memphis, so you're going to have to arrange some time away from Romeo's detail for me. If anyone asks, say I went to San Diego."

"What will you be doing?"

"It's a need to know situation. When it happens, it won't be hard to figure out."

"Will it hurt my father?"

Keyes stared at him for several seconds, then leaned forward. "Probably," he said. "What do you expect? Look, I don't know why you're doing what you're doing and I don't want to know. I was surprised as hell when he said you were my informant. I mean, damn. But it sounds now as if you're trying to serve two masters, and you know what the Bible says about that." He smiled his cool smile. "John Edgar says you insist there's no connection between the Covenant and Unit 2236."

David felt as if he might throw up. "That's right, there isn't."

Keyes leaned back, crossed his long legs. "I told him the same thing, that I haven't found anything. He believes me, but he doesn't believe you." The cool smile again. "Well, with us working together, if something's there, we're going to find it, ain't that right?" He looked at his watch and stood. "We didn't even need twenty minutes."

THIRTY-TWO

alf of the Checkers Gang was playing chess. Jake pummeled Otis the way he usually did, storming his positions like Hannibal crossing the Alps.

An early morning telephone call had taken Big Larry away. Thirty-five years sober, Big Larry left immediately to accompany a distraught mother and her strung out nineteen-year-old son to a rehabilitation clinic twenty miles northwest of the city. Big Larry didn't play chess anyway, although he'd vowed years ago to learn. But if he wasn't reading something or the other, he enjoyed watching his mentors battle even though he didn't thoroughly understand what they were doing.

Varnell was working. Varnell played but couldn't play. Jake and Otis usually took turns beating up on him when they sometimes took a "checkers break." "Only way you gonna learn," Jake would say after checkmating Varnell in eight moves. "A man sixty-some years old ought to know how to play by now."

The center's television set droned the world's latest troubles on an all-news station as Otis took his whipping. The district attorney and police commissioner were locked in a high-level meeting about the Bascomb matter with the mayor, who was running for re-election, a newsreader said.

Jake took Otis' queen. Otis groaned. "Aw, how did I miss that? That's just bad playing," he said. He moved his black bishop out of harm's way.

"You got that right," Jake said. He moved his own queen. "Mate," he said with a grin. "Mind's pretty sharp for an eighty-year-old, huh?" He liked to remind them at every turn that he was not ready for a retirement home.

They started setting up a new game. "I'll let you play white," Jake said. "Don't know when you'll win a chance." Jake treated trash talking like psychological warfare.

"I ain't studyin' you, Jake," Otis said. "What you think is going to happen to that cop that killed the brother down near Dock Street a few weeks back? I knew that sooner or later it was going to happen here. You think they will convict him?"

Jake removed his thick glasses and started wiping them. He peered at his longtime friend like an owl. "Convict him? I tell you every chance I get that white folks ain't gonna treat us right, regardless. As long as you worked for the fire department, I would think that you would know that. You say they didn't brainwash you, but when you start thinking they're going to convict that cop of murder, I wonder."

"Well, they have charged him."

"Charging him and convicting him are two different things. You saw what happened out there in California. The *jury* found the cop guilty of murder, but the judge said, nah, you can't do that." Mister Jake chuckled as he lit a cigarette. "Unit 2236 took care of his ass, though."

Otis moved a pawn. "I knew his daddy," he said. "Grady Bascomb. Didn't know him well, but he came to work for the fire department not too long after I started. Sometime in the Seventies he was there. Nice man. Understand he got religion and became a preacher."

"Some of the cops that work in black neighborhoods think they licensed to kill, like James Bond. I always said they never should have made those damn double-oh-seven movies. Licensed to kill." Jake snorted, then moved a knight out.

"Now there you go, getting on my man James Bond. What's he got to do with this?"

"Nothing. But that whole thing of being licensed to kill just sounds messed up."

"Bond didn't kill no black folks," Otis said. "They hardly hired any black folks to be in James Bond movies."

"I ain't talking about Bond, I'm talking about having a license to kill."

"Oh. Well, you should have said so." Otis took one of Jake's bishops with a sly smile. "You better pay attention."

"You just take care of your business and leave mine alone," Jake said. "Shame about that boy almost killing himself with that damn new drug, too. Big Larry called and said he was lucky his mother found him when she did."

"I heard that Sweetness is a mess. Heard it's worse than that crack cocaine." Otis moved one of his own bishops. "They ought to shoot those damn dealers who sell that mess."

"Maybe, maybe not," Jake said. "How about the folks bringing it here? Who owns them planes bringing it here, tell me that? I don't know too many black folks own their own planes, how about you? They the ones need shooting."

"Now, Jake, you know as well as I do that nobody will shoot those rich white folks. You know that as well as I do."

"But you talking about shooting the dealers. And that's all right, too. I'm just saying wipe out everybody connected with the mess, that's all. And, soon as I said it, you backed up off it right away. Check."

Otis cursed under his breath. Withdrawing his king to what he thought was safety, he looked up at the television set as he heard the words ". . . South Africa . . ."

"My, my, my," Jake said, feigning weariness as he moved. "Mate."

Big Larry strolled in at the exact moment of Otis' humiliation. "All right, put that mess away, Otis ain't going to win anyway. Let's get the real game set up."

"Hush, Larry, I want to hear this. Hold up a minute, Jake."

The senior Checkers Gang member set up the board as all three watched the news.

". . . escaped injury. The six Afrikaner rebels died in a hail of bullets from Lumemele's elite security unit. He immediately blamed the United States for the assassination attempt on his life and accused President Bruder of covertly funding the white rebel faction. In a rambling tirade, Lumemele described Bruder as a 'murderous white supremacist dog who longs for the good old days' when apartheid was law in South Africa."

The South African president's image replaced the anchorwoman's image on screen. "If Mister Bruder wants to invade our peaceful nation to try and take *our* gold and diamond mines from us, he's welcome to try," the bespectacled Lumemele said. "Our army will greet U.S. forces in the proper way. We do not bow to the American empire or anyone else."

"Damn! That's what I'm talking about," Big Larry said.

Mister Jake grinned his nicotine-stained grin. "We get a brother like that over here, we might get some stuff changed, you know what I'm saying?"

Within minutes, half of Big Larry's red checkers sat like prisoners of war in front of Mister Jake.

"I just might stop playing," Mister Jake said. "I'm getting tired of beating y'all all the time."

"Mister Jake, stop your lying," Big Larry said. "You ain't going nowhere and you know it." He saw that another whipping was a foregone conclusion.

"You don't know that." Mister Jake took Big Larry's last two pieces. He started setting up the board. He looked at Otis. "C'mon, sucker, you're next."

Mister Jake's voice got quiet. "I've been wanting to do some traveling.

2236

Jake Junior wants me to come down to Atlanta for a while. Wants me to move down there, actually, but that's sure not going to happen. Haven't seen my grandson in a year, though, and he's almost ready for college. We've always talked about the three of us going on a vacation together. I ain't getting no younger."

Otis put down the *Ebony* magazine he had been reading and moved to the table. "That's the truth," he said. "But I'm with Big Larry. You don't even know how to stop playing checkers."

"But I can cut y'all a break," Mister Jake said with a sly smile. "Y'all got to be tired of taking an ass whipping *all* the time."

Big Larry produced a mock scowl. "Sometimes I wish you was younger so I could smack some of the black off you. Don't you feel that way sometime, Otis?"

"My name's Bennett and I ain't in it," Otis replied, quoting an ancient children's rhyme. "I'm not getting Mister Jake mad at me."

"Look, Mister Big-ass Larry, just 'cause I'm an old man don't mean I can't kick your butt," Mister Jake said. All of them laughed, even Big Larry. The image of eighty-year-old Jacobin Robinson duking it out with sixty-four-year-old Larry George Palmer was a funny one. "I'll do to you what them Negroes did to the Avenue," he added, raising a gnarled fist and growling. "Tear you up."

"That uprising was something else, wasn't it?" Big Larry said. "Folks get tired of being messed over all the time. I've got a theory about these uprisings, though. We never called them riots when I was in the Black Panther Party."

"Oh Lord, here we go with 'all power to the people,'" Otis said. "The people don't want power, Big. People want to be told what to do."

"Well, my theory is that it takes twenty to twenty-five years for steam to build up, and then people have to let it out. It's like in the poem, when Langston says, 'Or does it explode?' Well, it explodes in cycles. In between cycles, the system just kicks our ass day in and day out. We let off the steam and then we're okay for another twenty, twenty-five years."

"In your so-called theory, when was the last one?" Otis wanted to know.

"Just like I said, it's been almost twenty years since L.A. blew up over the Rodney King mess. See, that's another thing in my theory. When there's an uprising, they do a report and promise black folks stuff. Then we calm down, and after we're calm, they stick the report on the shelf and that's it until the next time. They had the Kerner Commission Report and some other reports promising all kinds of changes after the Watts uprisings in '65, and Detroit and Newark, and all the rest. Folks quieted down and they forgot all about them reports until those cops got off for trying to kill Rodney. Then they wrote another report saying the

200

problem was they hadn't done the stuff from the earlier reports. Then we calmed down again. Now here we are, and they're going to do the same thing all over again. And we'll probably go for it."

"Well, you see, Negroes keep thinking that white folks are going to change," Mister Jake said. "That's the problem. I keep telling y'all, white folks ain't going to treat you right, regardless. And with Bruder in the White House, you might not even get one of those jive reports this time. You might just get Bruder's foot up your butt."

The checkers game, as frequently happened, paused for political commentary.

"You got that right," Big Larry said. "But some new stuff may be going down. I know you heard about these people calling themselves Unit 2236."

"They sound like the real deal, don't they?" said Mister Jake.

Big Larry held up a copy of the *Scabbard*. "They been sending communiqués to the *Scabbard*." Big Larry's eyes were bright, the way they looked when he talked about his days as a Panther. "They say they offed that deputy who killed Tanya Morris. And now they've shot that fucker who killed the woman's baby last year out there. The judge decreased his sentence, and it looks like Unit 2236 overruled the judge's decision." Big Larry chuckled at his joke. "They are some bad dudes, ain't they?"

"Tell the truth," Otis said.

Big Larry gestured at the tabloid. " 'Claimed responsibility' is the way the *Scabbard* put it, like when freedom fighters kill people overseas." He opened the paper. "Listen to this. 'If any people in the United States have suffered what the Declaration of Independence refers to as "a long train of abuses," black Americans have. Until and unless law enforcement begins obeying and enforcing the law and protecting black Americans, until and unless courts prosecute the lawless, Unit 2236 will undertake the protection of black Americans. Executive action will be taken against any so-called law enforcement officers who murder black Americans. Unit 2236 also serves notice on drug dealers everywhere that they will no longer be tolerated in our communities. Selling drugs is a capital offense. We will get rid of the violence in our neighborhoods by cleansing them of drugs.' It goes on to say, let me find it, 'we regard corporate media, especially OneCorporation International, Inc. and its holdings, as an adversary, and will send all future communiqués to the *Scabbard* unless the newspaper asks us not to do so.' Minister Johnnie Walker, the leader of the Covenant for the New Commandment, said the newspaper has an obligation to provide information to the public and will publish the communiqués verbatim, without editorial comment. And, get this. Walker refused to denounce Unit 2236. 'Expecting me to denounce this organization is insulting,' he said. 'I denounce the conditions that make some individuals believe they must take the step that this Unit 2236 is taking.' Authorities in San Bernardino condemned the group and said they will do everything they can, quote, to bring these terrorists to justice, unquote." Big Larry looked up. "Ain't that something?"

"Damn," Mister Jake said.

"What does Unit 2236 stand for?" Otis asked.

Big Larry held the newspaper out; Otis took it. "It doesn't say," Big Larry said. "Sounds like some brothers out there are as serious as a heart attack, like we used to say."

"How do you know they are brothers?" Otis said.

"Oh, c'mon Otis, that's common sense," Big Larry said. "Do you think there are some white men out there seeking vengeance for the murders of black people? Get real."

"Maybe it's some black women avenging their sisters." Otis grinned. "I'm just messing with you."

"No, you right, black women don't play," Big Larry said. "We had sisters in the Party who were more righteous than some of the jiving brothers, you know? But, hey, when we hear about military stuff, we always think it's men doing it."

"When they catch them, I bet they treat them worse than they treated the Panthers, and they tried to wipe them out," Mister Jake said. "I never heard of the Panthers doing nothing like this 2236 group is doing. This 2236 is something if it's true. I almost find it hard to believe."

"You right, Mister Jake," Big Larry said. "Before Huey Newton went to jail, the Party was facing down cops in the street and all, but I never heard of their underground taking nobody out like this. And I was there in the Party for almost two years. Well, I'm glad they shot that old racist cop myself, I'm not going to lie. I'm tired of us being treated like dogs."

"Did you see the hero's funeral the sucker got who shot the young girl?" Mister Otis said. "One hundred forty cars in the procession, a twenty-one gun salute, the whole nine yards. And I bet they do the same for the one who shot the pregnant lady. Cocksuckers."

"But what does it mean?" Mister Jake said finally. "They sound too good to be true. And, like I always say, white folks ain't going to do right, regardless."

"What does it mean? It's like Brother Malcolm used to say, Mister Jake,"

Big Larry said, re-reading the story for the third time. " 'Time will tell,' Malcolm always said. So I guess time will tell."

Three

We hold these truths to be self-evident, that all men are created equal, that they are endowed by their Creator with certain unalienable Rights, that among these are Life, Liberty and the pursuit of Happiness. --That to secure these rights, Governments are instituted among Men, deriving their just powers from the consent of the governed, --That whenever any Form of Government becomes destructive of these ends, it is the Right of the People to alter or to abolish it, and to institute new Government, laying its foundation on such principles and organizing its powers in such form, as to them shall seem most likely to effect their Safety and Happiness. Prudence, indeed, will dictate that Governments long established should not be changed for light and transient causes; and accordingly all experience hath shewn, that mankind are more disposed to suffer

. . . while evils are sufferable . . .

than to right themselves by abolishing the forms to which they are accustomed. But when a long train of abuses and usurpations, pursuing invariably the same Object evinces a design to reduce them under absolute Despotism, it is their right, it is their duty, to throw off such Government, and to provide new Guards for their future security.

THIRTY-THREE

It was hard to surprise Mister Jake, but the triple jump did, capping one of his occasional losses.

"Uh-huh, I got you!" Varnell's loud raucous laugh boomed through the room. "You slipping, old man, you are slipping!"

Mister Jake stared at the board. "When a man's been off a month, it's bound to affect his game," he said, scowling. "You better enjoy it while you can."

"I gotta give it to you, Jake, you talk trash even when you lose," Mister Otis said. "Varnell put a serious hurting on you. I thought you were going to play while you was in Atlanta."

"Didn't I tell you? Ben's dead." Mister Jake started setting up the board automatically.

"Hold up, Mister Jake," Varnell said, relishing the moment. "You have to get up, you just got whupped. You are so used to setting up, you forgot it's rise and shine."

Mister Jake rolled his eyes at Varnell behind his thick glasses. He moved and Big Larry sat down.

Mister Jake looked around and saw no center employees. He decided to sneak a cigarette. The new director had them fussing at him about his smoking. "Died last fall, about the same time all that mess got started up here," he said. "Nobody bothered to tell me."

"How old was he?"

"Seventy-eight. He'd been sick for a while, they tell me. Said his heart just gave out."

"Sorry to hear it. Y'all went way back, didn't you?"

"Fifty years. I met Ben at the National Memorial African Bookstore on 125th Street, near where I grew up. We were both looking for Paul Robeson's book, 'We Charge Genocide!' That caused us to strike up a conversation."

"Y'all used to call yourself 'race men' then, didn't you?" Big Larry said as he made his first move.

"You better keep your mind on the game," Varnell warned. "Don't play me cheap."

"Varnell, I'll whip you with one hand while I'm playing with myself with the other," Big Larry shot back. "I ain't studyin' you."

"Oh, that's cold, Varnell," Mister Otis said, looking up from his magazine.

"I still call myself a race man," Mister Jake said, drawing on his cigarette and exhaling. "I don't see what's changed all that much. White man still is not going to do right, regardless. We've got ourselves a few more middle class Negroes now and we think we're doing something."

"Preach, Mister Jake," Big Larry said just as Varnell double jumped him. "Damn," he said.

"Told you, you better keep your mind on the game."

"Y'all can mark my word or let it go," Mister Jake said as he spotted a staff member and put out his cigarette. "President Bruder is getting something ready for our ass, you hear me? I predict he'll have troops in South Africa before summer, and that he'll be helping the white minority, them Afrikaners, fight against Lumemele, who is a sure enough righteous brother. And, believe me, our Negro soldiers will have to be killing their brothers and sisters over there or else. When Bruder does that, they are going to barricade Negroes here and put us in camps and give us loyalty cards or some such mess, you mark my word."

"They been putting us in camps for the last thirty years, haven't you noticed?" Mister Otis said, putting down his magazine. "They call them jails but it's the same difference. Three million niggers in jail is the same as being in concentration camps. And we're so dumb, we're helping them."

Mister Jake played with his cigarette stump, looking for an opportunity to light back up. "Yeah, that Bruder's been making a lot of noise about 'our national interests' and the 'economic well-being of the world.'"

"Meaning OneCorporation's interests and OneCorporation's economic well-being," said Big Larry.

"And meaning he wants to steal the gold and diamond mines back," Mister Jake said. "I hope Lumemele nukes his flabby ass."

"Wait a minute now." Mister Otis rolled up his magazine and pointed it. "They nuke his flabby ass, that means they would be nuking us, too. I mean, Lumemele's my man and all, but I don't want to take a nuke for him. And anyway, they dismantled the nuke program back when Mandela took over."

"I'm with you on that one, Mister Otis," Varnell said. "Y'all need to quiet down though, so I can beat up on no-playing Big Larry."

"Yeah, it was okay for those Afrikaner bastards to have nukes, but they weren't going to let Negroes have their hands on no nukes," Mister Jake said. "I got to pee." He got up and ambled off to the bathroom.

When he returned, Varnell possessed a two-game winning streak and the conversation had shifted to Michael Patrick's trial.

"I'm telling you, they don't send cops, black or white, to jail for killing black folks." Big Larry accented each word, punching the air with a pointed finger as he spoke.

"Now, see, that's where you're wrong," said Mister Jake as if he'd been there all along.

"Mister Jake, how you just going to jump in the conversation all of a sudden?" Big Larry said in mock exasperation.

"Because, as always, I know what I'm talking about and you don't," Mister Jake said. "If a brother had been drinking, like I heard this white boy was, and didn't identify himself, he would be an embarrassment and they'd make him do about eighteen months, maybe a couple of years. As long as his victim was black. A black cop shoot a white person like Patrick did, his butt would be going away for a while. This white cop is *white*. And the word on the street is he's connected somehow to that cracker who used to be an inspector, Bulldog Hudson. *And* he used to work for OCI. Now if you'd done your homework like I have, you'd understand something."

"But I said they weren't going to send him to jail!"

"But you said whether he was black or white. In these circumstances, it's because he's white that he's not going to jail. Now I hope you've learned something."

Otis laughed. "You need to stop with your mess, Jake. But I hear you."

"I know what I'm talking about," Mister Jake said. "You all are not even taking into account something else. These Unit 2236 people have shot one of those other two deputies who were in on killing that girl, Tanya Morris, out in California, plus they killed the police security team they had supposedly protecting him. That's five cops right there, plus the first two they shot, that's seven. Now when I said they are getting something ready for our ass, I meant it. They are not going to have Negroes going around this country killing cops. People might start realizing that thing they call the thin blue line is vulnerable, and they won't allow nobody, white, black, brown, whatever, to think like that. Vietnam and Iraq were bad enough overseas, they can't have no mess like that here, people protecting their 'hoods. And remember now, these Negroes in Unit 2236 taking the drug dealers out, too. They have maimed I don't know how many street dealers right here in this city. In Los Angeles, they've killed four high level dealers that I know about. These Negroes in Unit 2236 are some bad mammy-jammers, you hear me? If they reaching the upper echelons of drug traffic, they are ruining some major profit for somebody real big. The feds have to crush this mess and soon. This is some Nat Turner mess. And you remember how fiercely they hunted him down."

"I disagree with y'all," said Varnell. He did another double jump to extend his run of wins to three. "Whooooo!" He jumped up and did a strutting swagger around his chair. "I am just too bad! C'mon Mister Jake, sit down so I can beat up on you again."

"You talking too much trash, Varnell. I'm going to have to bring you back down to size." Mister Jake took off his kufi, blew inside the crown, and placed it back atop his thick silver hair.

He sat and studied the board with exaggerated mannerisms. "Now, before I put this young man in his place, let me tell you this. When I was a young man, I used to say if you could find a small, committed group of race men who kept their mouths shut, first, and didn't try and get their pictures in the paper and on television, second, and traveled around blending in, looking like typical bourgeois Negroes, third, they could do a bunch of damage. This was back when they were attacking our leaders: Martin, Malcolm, Medgar, Fannie Lou Hamer, James Meredith, George Jackson, all of them. I said then if they knew there were consequences for moving on our leaders, you'd have a different ball game. This Unit 2236 group, I don't how they're doing what they're doing, but they sure seem to be on the right track."

"I didn't know nobody ever attacked Fannie Lou Hamer," Varnell said.

"Beat her within an inch of her life when she tried to vote," Mister Jake replied. "Left her lying in her own blood. And got two scared Negroes to do the deed. Like I say, white folks just ain't going to do right no how."

In the law offices of Erlickson Strauss Nixon, a press conference announced that a change of venue petition had been granted in the case of the *State v. Patrick*. The trial would be held in neighboring Antelope County instead of Liberty County, where the shooting occurred.

"Our research shows that media coverage has tainted this case to such a degree my client could not possibly get a fair trial in Liberty County," said Isaac Erlickson. As always, his white mane of hair gleamed under the television lights. "The court apparently agreed. We therefore thank the court for this change of venue, and we believe that Michael Patrick can receive justice from a jury of his peers. From the outset, this has clearly been a case that is taking place only because of political pressure."

In response to a reporter's question, Erlickson acknowledged that nearby Antelope County's demographics "could be perceived as favorable to my client."

Ninety-six per cent of its residents were white; the median income was $68,000; they had voted by a wide margin for President Bruder. Although happy about the selection, Erlickson said, almost anywhere in the state was preferable to Liberty County. (His research showed the population was fifty-eight percent African-American. Liberty County's median income was $31,000 [and falling], and only nine percent had voted for Bruder in the previous election.)

THIRTY-FOUR

ide-awake, Andy stared out the window of the 727, looking inward at the new life facing him. As he looked at the night sky, loving and losing and killing all felt entwined in a way that felt foreign and, truth be told, uncomfortable. All knotted up together in such a way that he didn't know how to separate them. Had it been only three plus months ago that he'd flown home from California, his mind in turmoil about events that now seemed half a lifetime ago? On that flight, the past had indeed been prologue to life-altering moments. But today, George's death, meeting Claudia, and now a new commitment—Unit 2236—all momentous on their own, seemed to be foothills of a metaphorical mountain looming ahead.

The plane bumped through a wave of turbulence. Andy glanced out at the enormous cumulus beneath the jet winging toward Memphis. He liked the illusion of the plane seeming to be an enormous bus or train gliding across a snowy expanse.

Claudia. Moving along on cloud ninety-nine, and then . . . what? He remembered a cryptic conversation with Rome that explained everything and nothing. He had approached his friend a day or two after making a decision to join Unit 2236, and just before Claudia disappeared. If they got much closer, he wondered how he could keep what he was doing from her.

"When you have a minute, I want to talk with you about all this and Claudia," he said. They were standing on the meetinghouse parking lot, which was still damp from a torrential downpour the evening before. "It's only been a couple of weeks, but we seem to be getting close."

Romeo placed a hand on his friend's shoulder. "People who need to know know about you two. Until further notice, things are what they are. You must not say a word. But I feel you, and it's something we've—the leadership—discussed in a general way. This was before y'all started making goo-goo eyes at each other. You're both good people, and we wouldn't want to lose either of you." His eyes became serious. "I need to warn you. You may be tested in a way that you don't expect."

After they parted, Andy had thought about his friend's parting remark. *Tested? What am I doing? What have I got myself into? Romeo Butler is my main man, but damn!*

He remembered standing in the parking lot that day, staring at a shallow puddle of rainwater. Even the trivial became so vivid that he still remembered it. Several sparrows moved in and out of the little pool as if it were a Jacuzzi. As they exited, each one stopped to shimmy and furiously shake the water from its tiny body. He almost imagined them grinning as they frolicked. Some went back for seconds. Andy had watched them for several moments.

His eye is on the sparrow, he remembered thinking. Enthralled for the moment by their fun, he wondered how much he believed that.

"Tested" took on new meaning when, five days later Claudia abruptly disappeared without explanation. Except for the note. Romeo grumbled and said he'd have to find a replacement for her. His calmness was unnerving. In truth, Romeo let little disturb him these days, at least on the surface.

"Andy, our lives are moving to a new level is all I can say," he said when confronted about Claudia. "How close are we, man? If you really listen to me, deeply, you'll be fine. If you're feeling fear, well, you're not feeling faith is all I can tell you. I told you before, we care about both of you."

Things are all right, even if they don't seem to be, Rome was telling him. So far, it had kept him going.

Keeping busy had helped. Working a conditioning regimen with Romeo had definitely helped. An hour of aerobic conditioning and thirty minutes of weightlifting had gone from painful to helpful.

His spiritual father figures, Uncle Sherman and Minister Johnnie, had been there, doing what Harry Robingham, his natural parent, had not been there doing. It bothered him that, as a grown man, he still felt a roiling in his stomach when he thought of Harry's name.

He and Uncle Sherman had talked before he left. All Andy could tell him was that he'd be "out of town on business for a while." The wily old man knew something was up. He also understood the importance of not needing to know exactly what.

"Y'all in that Covenant better watch out," Uncle Sherman had said. The look on Sherman Blackman's face commingled fear, sternness, and pride when he said it. "Boy, you looked good on television, though. My nephew," he said; you could almost see him puffing his chest out.

Suddenly Sherman stood up and went to a box on top of his chest of drawers. He took out something, looked at it for a long moment, returned to his lived-in easy chair and sat down slowly. He took off his tinted glasses and looked at his nephew with clear, steady eyes.

"When I was in the Black Panther Party, and it wasn't for very long, I never saw a gun the entire time," he said finally. "I knew they were there, but I didn't need to know where they were. I knew if the defense captain wanted me to know, and found a need for me to know, he would tell me. I knew, too, that I was a little older and kind of petite bourgeois, compared to some of the street brothers and sisters. I knew there might well be a trust factor, and that was okay, because *I* knew I wasn't a pig."

He paused. At sixty-six, he had never gotten used to exposing himself emotionally. "I'm saying that, whatever's going on, I'm proud of what you're doing. You're the closest I've ever had to a son, and I know I'm acting like you're getting ready to go to college or some shit, instead of being forty and an important part of something with people who are about the business of black folks, but indulge an old man, okay?"

He opened his hand. In his palm was a small, quietly expensive, onyx symbol. Each of its sides was scythe-like; one pointed up, the other down. Each was connected to horizontal ovals connected to each other. It was on a thin gold chain.

"This is called a Gye Nyame," Sherman said. "It comes from West Africa, where most of us probably came from. I've seen in a book somewhere that it means, 'Except God.' Nothing was at the beginning of creation and nothing will be at the end of existence, except God. "

He looked over his nephew's shoulder, eyes unfocused. "Arlene, my first wife, I called her Lena, gave this to me on our first wedding anniversary. We were at a Black Power Conference in Washington, and I asked the lady who sold it what it meant. Lena was always more spiritual than me, and she felt like it might connect me to some things, so she snuck back and bought it and surprised me. She didn't civilize me the way she hoped. I lied my way right out of that marriage." His attention remained inward, viewing the past. Andy heard a residue of regret, smudged with loneliness.

"Here, take this," he said, handing the pendant to Andy. "Think of it as an amulet for your journey with the Covenant people, wherever it leads you. Wear it, or if you want, just keep it around like I did. I expect you'll be plenty busy in the coming days. I want you to know Uncle Sherman's running with you, doing whatever you doing."

Andy took the pendant. He welled up inside but said nothing at first.

He and Uncle Bad Cat were tight, but he had never seen him quite like this.

"Thanks, Uncle Sherman," Andy said, looking at the onyx ornament, wondering what mysteries had lurked in the consciousness of the creaters of the ancient symbol.

"You're welcome," Sherman said. Andy thought he heard a catch in the older man's voice. "You be careful, you hear?"

Andy smiled as he remembered the talk with his uncle. He touched the African amulet resting on his chest, the black onyx almost invisible against his ribbed black sweater.

He looked out the window of the 727. He was en route to some unnamed destination near Memphis (he assumed it was near Memphis) to learn how to kill people.

The flight attendant approached with her stainless steel cart of peanuts and soda, wearing her pro forma smile. A thought Andy tried to keep buried kept coming back, a thought he didn't even want to share with Romeo. First of all, it was thin, and even he felt it was shaky. He felt like he'd been punched in the stomach the first time it surfaced.

What was it Miss Jones had said? He was having difficulty uncovering the fed inside the Covenant. *I'm even considering the possibility it's a woman.* Andy reached for his briefcase and took out Claudia's note. He'd looked at the note at least once a day since he'd found it on the floor just inside his apartment door. It helped him beat the ugly thought back.

In the brief three weeks they had known each other before she disappeared, intensity seeped into the relationship imperceptibly but insistently, the way real ginger root flavors steaming water and slowly transforms it into a lively, exciting, and spicy brew. They explored the different facets of friendship as they arose.

When kissing her goodnight after an evening of working late together, one kiss turned into three; his hands moved over the fullness of her hips. His ardor tried to overrule the patience they had talked about and agreed upon. She resisted his insistence gently at first, and then pushed him away with anger.

"I am not a woman who wants to be pawed in her hallway," she said with steel in her voice. "And I am not ready to take it where you were trying to go."

Another time, she indirectly expressed doubts about his interest in her when he said he was on deadline with some freelance work and wanted to re-schedule plans they made. He had exploded. "Hey listen, I told you what I'm doing, I don't know why you are coming at me like that, and I'm really not going to say anymore. Bye." He had hung up without waiting for an answer.

Each apologized to the other for their anger before a day had passed, and each time they talked their way to understanding. But there had been no talk about commitment, and definitely no use of the "L" word.

But there had been that last kiss.

He opened the note yet again.

"I love you in a special way," Claudia had written in immaculate script. "Please, trust me."

People were going to train him to kill people.

The thought belonged in some parallel universe, not inside of him. Like anyone, Andy knew how it felt when you wanted to hurt people. He had never been a boy to have many fights. He didn't enjoy fighting and probably lost more times than he won. It was in high school that he first noticed that some boys enjoyed, not just fighting, but hurting people. Once, while winning one of his few fights, he felt a rush that might be considered enjoyment while throwing fists at his opponent. Now, as he flew toward Memphis, he wasn't petrified, but his apprehension level was high as he thought about the days ahead.

When he'd expressed these feelings to Romeo, his friend called them "an asset." He wasn't sure he knew what that meant. Rome replied that Unit 2236 wasn't interested in recruiting sadists or sociopaths. The Four Star command had done their level best to get a reading about the tendencies of those who were chosen. It sounded like a paradox, but they wanted people with relatively strong spiritual centers.

"You'd be strange if you didn't feel some fear," Rome said at the time.

Andy looked at his watch and reviewed his mental checklist of instructions. A car—actually a limousine, Rome said—would pick him up at the Memphis airport.

"There will be a blindfold on the back seat," Rome had told him less than twenty-four hours before. "You can meditate, sleep, listen to music or an audio book on a CD player. Anything you want to do and are able to do with the mask on is permissible. You cannot chat with the driver. You'll be riding for a while, so make it easy on yourself."

Romeo had said something else as they sipped Vietnamese coffee at the Burgundy Moon, a downtown coffee shop patronized by a potpourri of artists, students, musicians, black nationalists, armchair revolutionaries, and literary types.

"I think this journey began for us way back when, in the bank," he said. "I know it did for me."

Until now, Andy thought that frightening day had pushed him toward a way of living that solved problems without weapons. Even Minister Johnnie called violence "the lowest form of communication."

"But it is communication nevertheless," the Minister said during one of the walks they took after Andy signed on to Unit 2236. "Malcolm taught that if a man speaks French, you don't try and communicate with him in Russian. You communicate in a language he understands. If he communicates with you forcefully, you may think he's going to understand non-violence but he won't. If he's in the business of oppression, he'll choose nonviolence for you but not for himself. Nonviolence does have its place as a tactic, especially in civil disobedience and even, or *especially* against violence. King understood that nonviolence was most effective against violent opponents like those in the racist South. It's useful when you're communicating with other people who are watching and you're trying to expose your adversary, as Doctor King was."

"But King said we should love the enemy, as Yahshua taught," Andy said.

Minister Johnnie had smiled. He, Andy and Romeo stood looking over the muddy river rolling along beside King Drive. "You notice I avoid that phrase as much as possible in my sermons. But I always answer when I'm asked, and I say to the asker that they have to find their own answer, that this is *my* answer. And you will hear this again, Andy.

"In the late Sixties, I stood looking in a record store window one day with a buddy from SNCC. There was a new record album by Jimmy Smith, the great jazz organist, called "Respect." Brother Smith was wearing a martial arts *gi,* and posing in six square photographs on the cover. In the first picture, he had his hands in prayer position and he was bowing. In the others, he was moving through a karate *kata,* showing striking and kicking postures. I knew little about the martial arts, except they were for fighting. I asked my friend why he thought he was praying and fighting. I still remember his answer. 'The martial arts, taught correctly, are very spiritual disciplines. Those moves where he's fighting, they're also prayer positions, designed to keep evil away from the person who uses them.' I've never forgotten that." He paused. "You don't have to hate a person to knock them down if they're trying to harm you. If you're fighting someone who is always hurting other people, maybe you can do enough damage to that person that they'll rethink their ways. If that happens to happen, you've actually done a loving thing for them—and the world." He pursed his lips. "If you kill them and they've been a danger to society, you've provided a service. Yahshua wasn't a wimp, as some churchgoing people have made him.

"I admit, too, that I have trouble loving my enemies. I don't have trouble not hating them, but I have trouble loving them. They attack us in so many ways, day in and day out, and they've been doing it ever since we've been here, unceasingly. Jobs, schools, hospitals, the jails, anything and everything, we're under constant attack. And they have convinced us, especially us middle-class folks, that we shouldn't defend ourselves, we should count on us all living together and trusting them to do the right thing. It's like my daddy used to say, our enemies piss in our faces and want us to believe it's raining. Well, I know piss when I see it."

So here he was, on his way to train and learn a new "language," a new way of "communicating."

Rome was right about that day at the bank. It was a defining moment, and Romeo had seen the obvious sooner than he had. If the Teacher were a violent man, surely he would have manifested it sooner than this. A forty-plus year ministry without force, except in self-defense, spoke volumes. Even with Unit 2236, Minister Johnnie was simply saying the reign of terror, the shooting of innocents, the rationalizing of rogue behavior from people like Michael Patrick, and the massive influx of drugs, all of it had to stop. Now.

The plane began its descent toward Memphis International. Andy remembered how, after Sonny's death, Romeo gradually withdrew into himself. They remained inseparable, but different. Sometimes they sat for hours in the living room of his friend's new home, saying nothing. Romeo would read, his eyes fierce, trying to find an answer for utilizing his all-consuming rage.

Sonny had enlisted intent on a twenty-year career but become disillusioned in the wake of President Reagan's invasion of Grenada in 1983. He mentored his baby brother with suggestions about his reading habits. "Read people who care about folks like us," Sonny had told him. He did just that over the next several years, voraciously absorbing the writings of Fanon, Nkrumah, Giap, Stokely Carmichael, Che, George Jackson, Huey P. Newton, books about Ho Chi Minh, and others.

Romeo's dream of emulating Sonny's track stardom didn't happen. The following year, he was expelled from Northwest for fighting and hospitalizing a fellow student. A family friend told the Butlers about Covenant Academy. Crispus Butler, Sr., admired the work of Johnnie Walker from a distance; he convinced his wife to give the private school a try. Two years later, Romeo won a full Covenant of the New Commandment scholarship to Howard University, Johnnie Walker's alma mater.

When Romeo went away to college, they drifted apart for a few years. One would always be there for the other, they said at the time. So far, that had been the case. Now everything about their friendship was at a whole new level.

People were going to train him to kill people.

THIRTY-FIVE

ndy's redeye flight touched down in Memphis just before four in the morning. Bleary-eyed, he made his way to the luggage room.

As he walked toward the glass sliding exit doors, Andy did a double take. A tall, well-built black man walking on the pavement across the departure terminal looked exactly like Wardell Keyes, Romeo's security man. Incongruously, he was smoking a cigarette, a no-no for Swords of the Master, and discouraged among Covenant members. He wore a dark green woolen crew cap and black raincoat that Andy had seen Wardell wearing; he moved with the rolling athletic gait Wardell used. Andy blinked. It was Wardell.

Andy started to move through the exit doors to call out to his colleague. A memory stopped him; he felt what he called his intuitive "warning antennae" shoot up.

The day before, leaving the meetinghouse, he had bumped into Jhanae. They couldn't avoid each other. She was coming down the walk toward the entrance as he came out of the building. She stopped when she saw him, as if she wanted to turn and flee, then pushed both hands into her pockets and looked at him.

"Hey," she said. "Long time no see."

"Hello there," Andy said.

"How're you doing?"

"How am I doing? I'm doing fine. You?"

"I'm good, Andy. I haven't been getting to the meetinghouse much lately."

"I know I haven't seen you here much since I got back. How's Wardell?"

He was surprised at the discomfort the question appeared to cause. His ex-wife's chocolate skin actually seemed to blanch. "Ward's fine. He left for San Diego about an hour ago. The Covenant keeps him busy these days." She forced a smile. "Is Minister Johnnie here?"

"No, he's gone. Is there anything I can help you with?"

At that moment, he saw the strain on Jhanae's face. Her small, dark wide-set eyes looked almost . . . afraid. She avoided his gaze.

"No, thanks. Look, I've got to go now. I'll see you around, okay?"

"Sure, Jhanae. See you around."

She took a step, stopped, looked at him. "Andy, be careful, okay?" She turned and moved away with the long, lithe strides Andy still enjoyed watching. She was a woman born to walk in high heels.

Andy remembered frowning then as he frowned now. San Diego was a ways from Memphis. What was the brother up to? He knew Wardell hadn't seen him. He watched Jhanae's new love stamp out his cigarette, flag a taxi and get in. Whatever Wardell was doing might be none of his business, but Rome needed to know.

A black Lincoln limousine waited exactly where Romeo said it would be. The driver, a fiftyish man the color of plantains with a smidgen of brown added, was reading a book. He wore blue tinted glasses and seemed taciturn even before he said anything, Andy thought. If he didn't get the right answer from the man, he was to say "thank you" and keep walking.

"I'm 121," Andy said, striving for a noncommittal look on his face.

The driver's face did not change expression. "Welcome to Saint Luke's," he said in a deep baritone voice. "May I please have your watch and your cell phone?"

Andy did as he was asked, then got in the limousine. Except for the driver, the luxury vehicle was empty. The leather seats felt and smelled new and expensive. The windows were so opaque Andy couldn't see a thing outside. As Rome had said, there was a black mask without eyeholes on the seat. If he sat precisely in the center of the seat, water, a soft drink he didn't recognize, and several sandwiches were available simply by leaning forward. He took a compact disk player and earphones from his travel bag, placed the earphones around his neck, placed the player on the seat, and put the mask on.

"You can meditate, sleep, listen to music or a story on a CD player, anything you want to do and are able to do with the mask on," Romeo had said. "You cannot chat with the driver. You'll be riding for a while, so make it easy on yourself."

The limousine slid noiselessly away from the curb and into traffic. With the mask in place, Andy remembered the sensory deprivation flotation tanks he had used several times while living in California. The dark tanks held eight hundred pounds of salt water that allowed a person to float for one hour without sight, sound (unless one requested some New Age-style music), or touch. The result came close to a feeling of weightlessness. The lid was not locked on the tanks; raising a hand and opening the tank door alleviated any claustrophobic feelings, which he never had. Inside the device the first time, Andy remembered being startled when he opened his eyes and it was so dark that nothing changed. He lost his temporal and spatial sense. When it ended, he felt the kind of relaxation that comes from a week's vacation of doing nothing.

Now, only his sight and sense of location were affected. As the drive continued, his sense of time melted. He understood why the driver had asked for his watch, even if he couldn't see it.

He would be wherever he was going for a minimum of thirty days. Probably longer. He had eased into a low profile after surrendering the one-time temporary press spokesman position. He probably wouldn't be missed. He made sure at least two people on his block knew his cover story: he was working on an in-depth story for the *Scabbard*.

How long they stayed would depend, in part, on how well and quickly they responded to firearms training. Romeo said the people coming to Unit 2236 had various levels of ability. The common denominator among them was that they all could be trusted.

As in any military situation, the Rules of Conduct and the operation itself were not up for back and forth debate. There was no room for deviation.

Their commander used the code name "Robert." ("Tell Robert that Miss Jones said hello.") He would cover some things on the first day that were meant to be unnerving. It would be the last time anyone could leave without repercussions. They would be blindfolded, returned to the airport, and that would be that. Even then, they would not be free to divulge the existence of Unit 2236 unless they wanted "a visit."

There was at least one other difference in this military arrangement. "You don't receive a discharge," Romeo said. "This is new. We don't know what the future holds. Maybe, if you live to be an old man, we will find some way to retire you. Otherwise, we're all in for the duration. You may go a year or two, or more, without any orders for assignment. They used to manage to kill an innocent black person, somewhere in this country, every few years. Lately, it's been once a month. But you're with us for life." Rome had looked at him with what could only be called a look of love for a dear friend. " 'One wins or one dies.' Our challenge to what exists is small but tenacious, small but without surrender. We win by not losing. Robert will speak on this at some length that first day."

The two men had embraced. Rome said he would make at least one visit during his training.

Because the limousine was not stopping for traffic lights or stop signs, Andy sensed they must be on an interstate or a freeway. Not that it made any difference to him. He knew nothing about Tennessee, if they were still in Tennessee.

He fell asleep during the second chapter of an audio book mystery novel.

The rooms were Spartan but expensive. There was a single bed, a nightstand with a digital alarm clock that was unplugged, a desk with a lamp and a telephone, an office chair, a chest of drawers, a chaise longue, and a closet.

The driver had awakened him through an intercom. "To your immediate left is an elevator," the driver said. "Take it to the second floor. You are in room 121. You will receive further instructions by phone, which, by the way, can only be used internally. Tonight and tomorrow only, you are confined to quarters. Meals will be brought to the door of your room. It will be your only day of rest until you leave. The following morning, you will receive a wake-up call at six o'clock; breakfast will be brought to your room about six twenty. Take the elevator to 'B.'" We will start promptly at seven o'clock.

"One last thing. On the first day of training only, as a security measure you will be required to wear a head covering that fits like a ski mask. It's in the top drawer of your chest. Your fatigues are in your closet." He paused. "That's it for now." There was a click. As Andy got out of the car, he saw the limousine trunk open. He retrieved his luggage and walked to the elevator.

He was in a garage. He suspected it was underground but couldn't be sure. A rush of fatigue swept over him. He'd been traveling for a lot of hours. He had no idea how long. This place belonged to the Fourth Star, Rome said. They were taking all precautions to conceal its location.

As Andy took off his watch and unhooked his cell phone from his belt, he realized he hadn't turned it back on. When he did, he saw an e-mail text message waiting for him. It had been sent from a free library. He opened it: im thinking of adopting a ward of the state. hes not only nice my life feels as if I have found the keys to the kingdom, if u know what I mean. If u think its a good idea, write back and tell me u understand what im doing. have fun on your vacation. Also, WE are visiting his Teacher on the Sabbath. More details are available. All the best, Miss Justine Jones.

Ward Keyes was a cop. Well, all righty, then. Andy remembered his conversation with Jhanae. She was trying to warn him and felt bad about diming out her man. So whatever he was doing in Memphis, Andy thought, he's up to no good. I'll have to tell Robert as soon as I can.

The revelation would have started adrenaline pumping at some other time, some other place. Even the nap did nothing to change being up for almost forty-eight hours with less than four hours sleep.

What would Jhanae think if she knew what he was doing? An ache welled inside wondering what Claudia would say. He knew she would understand and be supportive. Without question, Debora would have freaked.

He fell asleep dreaming about Claudia.

THIRTY-SIX

Nearly twenty-four hours after being seen at Memphis International Airport, Ward Keyes sat smoking a cigarette in a black Lexus rental car on the parking lot of the 24-Hour Titan Rest and Fuel Stop on the outskirts of Memphis. A tiny earplug was connected to his wireless transmitter-receiver which was, in turn, connected to identical gear wore by one of four men walking toward the large combination restaurant-convenience store-rest room stop about fifty yards from Keyes' vehicle.

The men stopped. The one with the transmitting device spoke in hushed tones to Keyes. Keyes opened his cell phone and made a call.

Two Memphis police patrol cars sat at the entrance to the Titan rest stop. Inside the building, a plainclothes cop was taking a leak when his pocket radio flashed.

In view of subsequent events, Memphis police officers would later puzzle over the APB transmitted at 3:27 A.M. that morning, but knew their job was to follow orders, and they did. They didn't know what Keyes knew: if well-meaning police officers hurt anyone, there would be hell to pay.

"All officers, stay clear of the Titan Rest Stop until further notice. Say again, stay clear of Titan Rest and Fuel Stop until further notice." The police department's chief information officer personally deleted the APB from the computerized log of outgoing messages within three hours of its broadcast.

The four men, all wearing black clothing, donned black ski masks, and then walked with assured movements into the brightly lit building. They produced fully automatic firearms from under their black flak jackets as they passed through the automatic doors. None wore gloves; anyone who looked saw they were dark-skinned, and probably African-Americans.

"This is a holdup in the name of the people! Nobody move! Nobody move!" Keyes listened to the voice crackle through his radio. A brief burst of gunfire, as ordered, followed. Keyes knew that it went either into the ceiling or was aimed at some dead zone area without civilians.

The robbery took less than five minutes. People in the rest stop complied with orders and lay face down on the floor with their hands on the backs of their heads. As an added precaution, three men and women stationed in the bathroom areas who seemed to be civilians cautioned the few people seeking relief in those areas to stay inside to keep from getting hurt.

The four masked men stopped at the front entrance before they left. Two of them fired brief bursts again.

"The Covenant of the New Commandment will avenge black people!" one man screamed. "We are Unit 2236, their instrument of vengeance! Vengeance is mine, sayeth Yahweh!"

One of the others fired a burst. "The Covenant of the New Commandment!" he shouted.

The fourth man did the same. "Unit 2236!" he yelled.

They fled.

Outside in the Lexus, Keyes smiled and lit a cigarette.

THIRTY-SEVEN

A ndy felt as if he was slipping on a new identity as he dressed in the military fatigues that he found in the closet. He wondered if the other men felt the same way.

The common denominator among them was that they could all be trusted.

That was a good start for seven men who had never met each other. Someone—the Four Star command structure, in all probability—trusted them all. Andy wondered if he trusted himself as he prepared to leave his room and step into the unknown.

Life-and-death as a way of living was foreign to what was familiar to him. His life, even in the Covenant, had been about finding some form of security, or what passed for security. College had been more about getting a decent job than it had been about knowledge. Getting married had been more about companion comfort than about love.

Love. Until now, Andy realized, the word had been an abstraction, an idea. Nothing had ever required *all* of him. Not his relationships, not his family, not even the Covenant, where it was the watchword. This work would require total commitment, Romeo had warned.

He pulled the black ski mask over his head and stood up. His entire being felt tingly, alive, awakened with energy he almost didn't recognize. Well, here we go.

When he entered the training room, he smiled beneath his mask. So much for assumptions, he thought. What was it his first journalism teacher had said: when reporting and writing a story, assumption is the mother of all fuck-ups. While waiting to join Unit 2236, he had assumed and conjured images of military barracks, dusty roads, and living close to the land.

Their meeting space resembled a corporate boardroom where overpaid executives met and made decisions about the fate of the planet far more than it did, say, a barracks classroom where underpaid soldiers were trained to kill anyone the overpaid executives saw as inimical to their interests and profits. From what Andy had seen thus far, the building they were in felt like a palatial mansion. One difference: this plush, penthouse-like room was in the basement instead of atop a skyscraper. An elevated basement, apparently, since an expanse of lawn, spotted with clumps of snow, was visible at window level. A cloudless blue sky and some naked trees in the distance were also visible through the room's sole window. The window prevented claustrophobia but provided no clues about their location. The seven men in the room, all wearing black ski masks, couldn't see a hint of highway, street or road. No telephone poles or other landmarks were visible. *Nada.*

The meeting room table was blonde mahogany. Rich wood-paneled walls and the furnishings—lamps, rugs, and hardwood floors, all of it—reeked of luxury. They sat in seven of nine expensive brown leather high-backed swivel chairs. There were four on each side, and one at the end of the table that faced the rear of the room. Behind that chair, a long table sat against the wall, made of the same expensive blonde mahogany as the conference table.

A sturdy gold frame on the wall above the table enclosed the work of an anonymous master calligrapher. The inscription was the Biblical injunction Andy had read the day he decided to cast his lot with Unit 2236:

Then said He unto them, But now, he that hath a purse, let him take it, and likewise his scrip: and he that hath no sword, let him sell his garment, and buy one. Luke 22:36

Romeo had explained that the selling of a garment was ceremonial; Unit 2236 didn't care how much they received. Andy sold a two hundred dollar London Fog double-breasted black trench coat to a pawnshop on the Avenue as his "garment." The twenty-two dollars he received didn't come close to covering the cost of the two brand new automatic pistols sitting next to his number/nameplate on the table. One side of the nameplate had his code number: 121. On the other side was a name: Bryon. Two sixteen-bullet clips, a legal pad, two high quality pens, a small pitcher of water, and a water glass were placed at each setting with the two pistols. (Romeo had noted that Luke 22:38 went on to say, "And they said, Rabbi, behold here are two swords. And he said unto them, they are enough, arise, let us go." Romeo had grinned. "If they were packing two pieces, we pack two pieces," he said.)

A blackboard covered the entire front wall. Above it was a cylinder containing a pull-down screen. On the dark mahogany desk at the front of the room was a laptop computer and PowerPoint projector.

On the wall directly across from Andy was a poster with the face of an unsmiling man he didn't recognize. He would learn about Ruchell Magee and his forty year-plus incarceration in California prisons through a Google search. The quote beneath Magee's picture would be the battle cry of Unit 2236 members:

"As long as I keep fighting, nobody know how the fight gonna turn out. There's a possibility I *might* win. If I stop fighting, I can't win. I also believe that one man—one man—can make a difference, if he's sincere. "

Andy could tell little about his ski-masked classmates. He wondered if they felt like him: exhilarated, apprehensive, wondering what they had gotten into.

Andy heard a faint whirring noise; seven heads turned and looked toward the door as it opened automatically. Andy's limousine chauffeur came through the door in a motorized wheelchair. There was a barely audible intake of breath in the room. Apparently, he had been everyone's "driver." He came to a stop at the end of the table and turned his chair to face them.

"Good morning," he said, his deep baritone resonating through the room. "I am Robert." He paused, obviously for dramatic effect, to let his presence sink in. "I am also the First Star.

"The work you are about to embark on is not fun, or pretty, or courageous, or to be enjoyed. Those who lead the Swords of the Master believe a philosophical underpinning is essential to this very special work in Unit 2236. Therefore, we will spend one hour daily, sometimes two, being grounded in very specific principles that we hope will keep you sane, and will prevent you from becoming monsters. We cannot guarantee an exemption from either possibility. We pray that you will be spared from both."

As he adjusted to the shock of meeting the man Miss Jones wanted him to say hello to, Andy knew, without knowing how he knew, that Miss Jones was somehow connected to whatever winds of fate had placed Robert in the wheelchair.

"We have some housekeeping information to give you before we get down to serious business," Robert said. "However, we must inform you of an unforeseen development. At 7 A.M. this morning, the entire Covenant of the New Commandment went on alert. The Swords of the Master and Unit 2236 are on full alert until further notice. If things swerve out of control too quickly, you may be asked to do things you aren't even trained to do yet.

"Such is life in the big city," he said. There was dryness in his voice, a quality they would come to know well in the weeks ahead. "I direct your attention to the television monitor." He wheeled over, inserted a disk, and used a remote to start the recording.

A frozen image of an earnest looking young black male talking head appeared. Below the man's image, which managed to be toothy without smiling, stretched an electronic banner with a stylized blue eyeball graphic and the words,

"OC EYE Exclusive!" "This was video recorded earlier from a local news station," Robert said. He pressed the "play" button.

"Four armed men escaped with thousands of dollars during a daring pre-dawn holdup at a rest stop on the interstate just outside of Memphis this morning," the brown-skinned newsreader said. "The men, wearing black ski masks, appeared to be African-Americans. They fired several bursts from their weapons, but no one was injured. The robbers shouted slogans that indicated they belong to the controversial religious organization, Covenant of the New Commandment. In a startling development, authorities say the bandits may be the first definite link between the Covenant and Unit 2236, a band of cop killers who have terrorized the nation with the murders of at least eight police officers.

"Security cameras captured these dramatic images," the young newsreader said. Behind him, the events at the rest stop played out on a screen. After the damning slogans were shouted, Robert pressed the "stop" button and then "off."

"What you have just seen is bullshit," Robert said. His eyes, impassive behind the rimless eyeglasses, scanned the room. "I can assure you that it's exceptionally coincidental that these assholes wore black ski masks similar to the ones you wear now. We don't know yet who is responsible, or why. I can only assure you that when we do find out, they will be severely dealt with. We need to let you know as things develop. So far, we've learned that Minister Merrone Wilkinson-Workman, the woman who leads the Memphis meetinghouse, and her husband, Allan Workman, have been arrested, as have the commanding officer of the Swords and the commanding officer of the Magdalene Society in that meetinghouse. Later today, I expect to hear from the Second Star, the Third Star, or both, with orders for all of us. Are there questions?"

There were none. Stunned, Andy raised his hand almost without realizing it.

"Yes, what is it?" Robert asked.

"Sir, I have something I'd like to share with you privately," Andy said. "If you want to tell the others afterward, I have no problem with that. I'm pretty sure it's relevant, but I don't want to make false accusations."

Robert stared at him. Andy felt a peculiar and powerful physical presence from the older man. *He acts like he could kick my ass even from the wheelchair,* Andy thought. *Which is probably not far from the truth.*

"We'll talk when we take our first break," Robert said. "Is there anyone else?" The room was still. The video had unnerved everyone, it seemed, except

Robert. Something unplanned had happened, and no one knew what it meant. "Then let's get back to why we're here.

"We hope to minimize misunderstandings. Although I was opposed to the decision, you may still back out if something today in any way causes doubt." He spoke now as if he were returning to a script.

"In our work, doubt may very well be the only sin. In its etymology, sin originally meant 'missing the mark.' When you leave here, missing the mark will be impermissible." He picked up the automatic pistol on the dark mahogany desk next to him, lest anyone miss his meaning.

"We will tell you, with a different meaning than our Great Teacher Yahshua did, 'Go and sin no more.'" Robert smiled a smile they would get to know well, a slight showing of teeth, a smile with absolutely no mirth in it. He placed the pistol in his lap.

They would hear Robert's acerbic wit many times during their stay at the place they eventually nicknamed "WiTHWA": "Wherever The Hell We Are."

"Although I walk the Path of Yahshua, I am also a military man," Robert said. It was hard to read his eyes behind the blue tinted eyeglasses, a result Andy was sure was deliberate. "I have asked no one's permission, except Yahweh's, for how I walk that Path. I suggest you do the same. I talk like a military man, despite the spiritual dimensions of my life, because I find it effective."

No one saw his hand move. One moment he was talking to his recruits, and in the next, 123—whose code name was "Clarence"—cried out in pain.

Robert kept a drawer full of tiny hard red rubber balls where he sat. As he demonstrated with 123/Clarence, his aim was unerring. ("I lobbed my shots the first day; I can kill you with one of these if I so choose," he told them on the third day. "I was afraid you all would leave if I told you that the first day.")

"You cannot afford to let your attention wander," Robert said. There was no animus in his voice. "It's one of the best ways to get you or your partner killed." He removed his eyeglasses, revealing hazel eyes the color of a marble "shooter" Andy had favored as a boy. His gaze traveled from one recruit to the next, finishing with Andy. He replaced his glasses and moved his legal pad directly in front of him.

"We have rules and we have Rules of Conduct," Robert said. "All of the Rules of Conduct are created by the tribunal that governs Unit 2236, the three Stars from whom I take orders. You will memorize the Rules of Conduct and burn them into your brain. The rules, small 'r,' are mine and designed to help you internalize certain things. My rules are few."

"Rule one. Do what I say. In a way, this is the only rule and encompasses all the others, the Rules of Conduct included. My daddy used to tell me, 'Boy, there's one rule in this house. Do what I tell you to do.'"

Andy saw now he had misread a certain hardness that was Robert for a taciturn style. Robert loved to talk, but everything had a point. He tried not to waste words. He certainly didn't mince any. Andy glanced around at his colleagues to see how they were taking this.

Stars exploded suddenly inside his head. The pain followed, just behind his temple, where the hard rubber ball had caromed off his head.

"If you want headaches, fine." Robert held up a ball. "I have lots of these." He turned to Andy. "Go pick the ball up, 121. And pick up 123's ball, too."

Heart and head pounding from the surprise, Andy did as he was told. When he had settled back in his seat, Robert continued.

"Rule two. Don't fuck with me. And a corollary to this rule: Don't let this wheelchair fool you. Rule three. Lateness is not permitted. The first time you will run a mile for the lateness. The second time you will run a mile for each minute you are late, and a minimum of two miles, regardless. If you are late a third time, you are violating both rules one and two." He smiled the mirthless smile.

"You are the seventh cadre in Unit 2236. When you complete your training, you will be known as the August 21st Brigade. This is the day in 1971 that Soledad Brother George Jackson was assassinated at San Quentin prison. If you don't know who he is, I assure you that you will know everything about him there is to know by the time we complete your training. While here, you will read *Soledad Brother* and *Blood in Your Eye* to learn about the man you honor. Jackson was a teenager who didn't deserve twelve years in prison for the petty crime he was convicted of, a man who transformed himself into a field marshal for the Black Panther Party. He asked no quarter and gave none, which is why he had to die. Our brigades all honor freedom fighters who became martyrs in the fight for the liberation of black people. We will honor Brother Jackson with our work, as the December 4th Brigade honors Fred Hampton and Mark Clark, and the new November 11th Brigade honors the martyrdom of the Reverend Nat Turner. Hampton was a deputy chairman in the Illinois chapter of the Black Panther Party. People who called themselves law enforcement assassinated him in his bed. Clark died in the same murderous attack.

"We also have the September 9th Brigade, which honors the men who died during an uprising by prisoners at Attica Penitentiary on that date in 1971; the April 6th Brigade, honoring Bobby Hutton, the first Black Panther Party member to die, killed in 1968; the February 21ˢᵗ Brigade, an elite unit that honors El Hajj Malik El-Shabazz—Malcolm X—murdered in 1965; and the April 4ᵗʰ Brigade in honor of Doctor King. Although Doctor King was an apostle of nonviolence, he was unquestionably a freedom fighter who was martyred, and we feel obligated to recognize that."

Robert took a glass of water from the desk and sipped. "In terms of the military aspects of the Covenant for the New Commandment, we are the esoteric, if you will; the Swords of the Master are the exoteric. . In addition, 125—Ronald—will teach some fundamental martial arts training. I might add that we don't expect Bruce Lees to emerge in the brief time you are here. In fact, pray that you don't have to use what you learn. If you do, fall back on what you know from the streets until you have internalized, through continued practice, what you learn here." He paused. "Of course, if you pay attention and follow instructions" —He looked at Andy and "Clarence"—"you should have no need for hand-to-hand combat. We will place enormous emphasis on how to kill silently and quickly, be it with silencers, piano wire, knives, poison darts, or other means."

His face, already serious, somehow became more so. "The most important Rule of Conduct is simple and fundamental: For now, there is one acceptable circumstance in which you are permitted to take executive action against any innocent person, be they bystander, friend or relative of the defendant, or an eyewitness. If your own life is in danger, the Four Stars will consider that an exception. If your life is not in danger, all cadres are directed to abandon a mission rather than kill an innocent person. Any security personnel assigned to protect a defendant are not innocent persons; they are regarded as soldiers on the field of battle." He took another sip of water. "Because we are at war, and because of the times in which we live, civilian casualties will become unavoidable in the future. The Covenant will delay that future as long as we can.

"Drug dealers are a different breed," Robert said. He turned his glass up and emptied it. He reached into a desk drawer, produced a large bag of peppermint balls, and held it up. "I have a sweet tooth; this is how I assuage it. Help yourself." He passed the bag around. Andy noticed the mints were exceptionally strong.

"Once we have incontrovertible evidence someone is a drug dealer, we look at where they are in the food chain. The higher they are, the more likely we will order you to kill them. Sometimes they're armed and protected better than the police, and we may order an entire brigade into action with a well-choreographed battle plan. Street dealers may be allowed to live if they give up a name higher on the food chain. Breaking a hand, arm, foot, sometimes more than one, will usually bring cooperation. Of course, if a street dealer draws on you, take him out."

Robert picked up the pistol on his lap. "The Four Star command's response for killing innocents is capital punishment to any member of Unit 2236 who violates this standing order. Do I make myself clear?"

The silence affirmed Robert's clarity.

Andy sat opposite the First Star. He faced a ceiling-to-floor picture window overlooking a garden sparse and naked, waiting for the greening of spring.

He told Robert about seeing Wardell Keyes at the airport. He also recounted his conversation with his ex-wife, Jhanae, and his perceptions of her that day.

"I didn't think it appropriate to voice these suspicions in front of people I don't know when he might very well have legitimate business I knew nothing about," Andy said after completing his debriefing. "Except there's more. I received a text message last night from a source in the police department who knows you. He told me to tell you hello. I don't know his real name, but his code name is Miss Jones."

It was the only full smile Andy would see on their instructor's face during the weeks he was with him. It split his face; glee filled his eyes. "Miss Jones!" He snorted an odd noise. "Tell that crazy fucker hello back when you see him." He slapped a hand on one of his inoperable legs, and then became serious. "What was the message?"

Andy read it; Robert nodded. "There's been some discomfort with Keyes for a couple of years, but nothing we could put our finger on. Given what transpired this morning, and this message, it seems like we've got his sorry ass. Miss Jones is very thorough; he wouldn't make a mistake on this. You were right in not approaching Keyes or letting him know you saw him."

"May I ask about the joke with your friend's name?" Andy asked.

Robert's eyes twinkled but this time he didn't smile. "Miss Jones and I go back a lot of years. In my pre-Covenant days, I guess you could say I was a bit of a pornophile, and my friend knows that. He picked the name to kid me because he knew I'd get the reference. You've read about the Watergate scandal? It happened around the time you were born."

Andy nodded.

"Well, you may remember that the *Washington Post* had two piss and vinegar reporters working the story. One of them met in a garage with a source who was only known to the world as 'Deep Throat.' That was also the name of the first porno film to go mainstream. Porno chic, they called it at the time. The second big film, and arguably a better movie, by the way, was called *The Devil in Miss Jones.* When he said why reinvent the wheel, he was talking about both the garage and the code name. He knew I'd get it." He looked at Andy. "He's a good man. Anything he can do for us, he will." Andy thought Robert's eyes seemed to be looking at memories.

"I will inform the Third Star on our secure line," Robert said. "He needs to know about this conversation we had. Tell the others we will reassemble in twenty minutes."

He turned and whirred down the hardwood-floored hallway.

Andy rubbed the sore spot on his head as he watched Robert disappear into the elevator. Any second thoughts he had about adding assassin to his résumé were dissolving as he assessed the events of the last forty-eight hours. Before George's death, before Unit 2236, Andy saw now how much he loved the Covenant of the New Commandment. He had joined partially to please a woman, but stayed because he liked how he felt about himself, and because he saw work being done that he wanted to become a part of, work that made him feel worthwhile.

Ward Keyes was on loan from the feds. Clearly, he was intent on doing what he could to destroy the Covenant. Even without Unit 2236, the Covenant was considered dangerous, so Keyes had fabricated a link when he couldn't find one. A wave of sadness passed through him as he realized Jhanae was unwittingly caught up in something she probably hadn't bargained for.

Andy took a deep breath, exhaled. He was at war; he damn well better embrace it.

THIRTY-EIGHT

he police convoy snaked along the winding, sloping curves of King Drive. Only one local STOP cop and one federal officer in the eight vehicles trailing his black sedan knew the name of the man with the nasal, reedy voice, and the name they knew—John Edgar—was a pseudonym. But everyone knew he was in charge.

His presence gave feds the final say. The locals weren't crazy about the idea, public relations-wise, but the feds wanted it to go down after midnight, and before dawn, that night. That's the way it was. The man with the nasal and reedy voice had flown in from Washington to personally oversee the operation. When he saw they would have a new moon, he thought it a fortuitous omen. Being darker could only help them, he felt.

His smooth cinnamon-colored skin, combined with an unlined and hairless face, made him look younger than his forty-nine years. So did his bearing. He walked erect, as if he belonged to the U.S. Army's Third Infantry Old Guard Battalion at the Tomb of the Unknown Soldier, and he had, in fact, been a member. Until selected to lead the top-secret bureau section CP2, John Edgar had viewed his time at the Tomb of the Unknown Soldier as the high point of his government service. He knew then that his country offered him a chance to be anything he wanted. And what he wanted, what he was good at, was employment in defense of his country.

He went to work for the FBI immediately after leaving the Army. Superiors noted his quiet zealousness and "excellent" annual performance ratings; within five years he served as a Special Assistant to the Director. He heard about CP2 almost by accident. When reviewing an appropriations document for his boss, someone had scribbled "CP2" in the margin next to a generic line item in the Covert Ops section.

In the 1970s, Congress had ordered the original Director's Counterintelligence Program (COINTELPRO) dismantled after sordid revelations of illegal activities—murders; provocateur-led illegal activities that discredited activist organizations critical of the government; infiltrations of a

236

wide range of organizations, including churches and pacifist groups; and a host of other "destabilization techniques." However, J. Edgar Hoover, long a law unto himself, refused to eliminate the program. He didn't tell the legislators no, he simply renamed the unit and kept it on very low profile. Quietly and slowly, it returned to do identical, but lower key, work as CP2: Counterintelligence Program 2.

A police car blocked each cross street that fed into King for a half mile above and below Roosevelt Lane. Few people were inconvenienced during those early morning hours.

The STOP commander argued for a quartet of rooftop snipers but was overruled. A police helicopter was deemed too noisy for the initial phase, but was on standby on the Horseshoe helipad.

The Memphis operation the morning before had worked like a well-oiled machine. Nailing this America-hating Johnnie Walker was long overdue. He was not only a terrible example for young people, he made things so much worse for African-Americans, the cinnamon-colored man thought to himself.

In the garage attached to the house directly behind Minister Johnnie's home, the black suburban utility vehicle and other security vehicles were gone because the Swords needed the space.

The couple who lived in the house, and shared the high shrubbery surrounding the minister's home, had been Covenant members for thirty-one years. They were sweet middle-aged nice folks, so low key and quiet that other people on the block knew them and didn't know them. They had invisibility about them when they chose to use it.

At this moment, to put it mildly, the couple was tired. They had used special telephones provided by Minister Johnnie, telephones provided by the Fourth Star (who they knew nothing about) for close to eighteen hours, doing what Minister Johnnie told them they might have to do one day. They sat on their aging sofa, held hands, and prayed.

The cinnamon-colored man with the nasal and reedy voice scowled when his cell phone vibrated. He ignored it. It stopped briefly, and vibrated again. He opened it.

"Yes?" he said, stifling the irritation he felt.

"The STOP commander just got a call from a detective named Carvel Thomas. He wants to patch him through to you." It was the aide who had traveled with him, a woman whose demure, soft-spoken demeanor belied her ruthlessness.

"Can't it wait?"

"Sir, he thinks you should take the call. If you prefer, the commander said he could relay the information to you."

A sensation of foreboding germinated somewhere inside the cinnamon-colored man with the nasal and reedy voice. "Put the commander through." He didn't want to be bothered with a detective who was trying to impress his superiors.

There was a click. "Go ahead, Inspector."

"Hi, this is Inspector Hampton," the voice on the other end said in a faded black Southern accent.

Oh my Jesus, a jig, the cinnamon-colored black man thought. "Make it quick," he said.

"One of my best detectives got a call from Johnnie Walker with an urgent message for the person in charge here. I'm quoting Detective Thomas now. 'To avoid a senseless loss of lives, you should call the following number.' " He read the number. John Edgar wrote it down. The foreboding grew.

Just then, exactly ten minutes after a sleepy Carvel Thomas had called the STOP commander, a battery of high-powered floodlights lit up the perimeter of Minister Johnnie Walker's Roosevelt Lane home.

"What the fuck?" the cinnamon-colored man with the nasal, reedy voice sputtered as he saw spillage of the light over the rooftops less than a block away. He radioed the convoy behind him to stop. "Get out and see what the hell's going on," he said to an FBI agent in the second car.

The agent walked to the corner. He noticed lights going on in windows as he walked. His eyes widened as he looked at the tableau thirty-five yards away, admiring it in spite of himself. Windows along the block were slowly awakening, too.

"Sir, you'd better come and see for yourself," the agent said when he returned to the lead vehicle.

"Will you cut the shit and tell me what the hell is going on?" His voice was high, angry enough that it was no longer nasal and far less reedy.

"Yes, sir," the man said, his face reddening. "There are at least two hundred African-American men standing in formation in front of the target residence."

Sputtering expletives, the supervisory agent leaped from his car and strode quickly, almost jogging, to the corner. "Jesus fucking Christ!" he seethed. "He knew! He fucking knew!"

Sleepy neighbors, annoyed at first by a disturbance they didn't understand, smiled at the awesome sight. Two hundred and ten, to be exact, members of the Swords of the Master stood at parade rest in front of Minister Johnnie's home, both on his small lawn and on the porch. To a man, they wore business suits, ties, and spit-shined shoes. Dressed or not, their demeanor expressed a clear intent that said they might as well be wearing military fatigues. Glenn Greene stood centered in front of them, also posed in a perfect parade rest.

John Edgar found himself speechless, wondering how many more of them there might be, and where they were. There was a leak, probably in the police department. An unmarked police car down the street from Walker's house in the twelve hours preceding the raid had reported no unusual activity. As he refocused through his anger, he remembered the notebook in his hand with the telephone number in it.

"Hello, who is this?" The voice that answered the phone was a deep, articulate baritone.

His voice nasal and reedy again, the cinnamon-colored supervisor gave his pseudonym and said he was in charge of the task force with a search warrant and arrest warrant for one Johnnie (the actual spelling on his birth certificate) Nathaniel Walker.

"I'm M. Raphael Roper, Minister Johnnie Walker's attorney," the deep baritone voice said. "I've advised him against speaking with you. This is an outrage. You didn't have to come here like thieves in the night. Nor did you have to come on a Saturday morning, which they celebrate as the Sabbath. If my client were a white corporate executive, I would have been called and I would have been permitted to surrender him for arrest at a more convenient time of day.

"I am prepared to surrender him now for arrest to avoid any bloodshed from your bloodthirsty task force. He does not want his men to die. But for the record, and this is being recorded, the Swords of the Master outside are unarmed down to the last man, although a majority own legally licensed weapons. If your goons attack physically, the Swords came prepared to fight, to let the world see them die defending the man they regard as their Teacher. They will *not*, I repeat, they will *not* respond to an arrest order, understanding clearly that they are resisting the law. It's called civil disobedience, sir. I suggest you allow us to come outside and negotiate a dignified surrender at a reasonable time later today. And you need to know that litigation is being considered for this terrible police state display."

The cinnamon-colored agent agreed because Walker had outfoxed him. The admission made him grind his teeth in frustration. He had thought of embedding a news team with the operation and decided against it. He saw a news helicopter approaching from the southeast. Reporters were probably clamoring at the barricaded streets. He couldn't possibly order his task force in now.

Like the FBI agent who first saw them, John Edgar grudgingly admired the fierce discipline of the men who stood outside Walker's residence, and their apparent willingness to die for what they believed.

Covenant leaders had guessed correctly that the authorities would not want the spectacle of unarmed men being cut down in an American city splashed on television internationally, even if all two hundred plus of them were resisting arrest. They knew better than to bring their guns, although the cinnamon-colored man was sure they would have done so, and used them, if ordered. But this Johnnie Walker was too smart for that.

Neighbors standing in bathrobes in their doorways along Roosevelt Lane watched with admiration as Minister Johnnie and his rail-thin, sartorially immaculate attorney stepped onto the walkway outside the Walker home. (Ila Walker had been taken to an undisclosed location the day before.) The neighbors didn't know exactly what was going on with Black Label, although most figured it had something to do with that mess down in Memphis. Robbing a rest stop didn't sound like Black Label, but you never knew about somebody, did you? He was a good man, others said, and the police probably had it wrong.

Fuming, John Edgar lit the tobacco in the bowl of his meerschaum pipe. He hadn't smoked one all day and he needed it. They had to plug the fucking leak.

One man shouldn't have this much power, he thought, as he walked toward Walker and Roper. He took a large drag on the pipe and felt a little better.

Robert's phone calls had rousted them from bed and ordered them to the training room. They had passed the deadline for withdrawing; their masks were gone. All of them seemed to be about the same age, Andy noted. Ronald/125, the one Robert had designated the martial arts instructor, looked a bit older.

When they were seated, Robert, without comment, placed a disk in the televisions set that had been recorded only an hour earlier. What Andy saw jolted him even more awake: a floodlit shot of Minister Johnnie's home.

"A nationwide manhunt remains on for the four men who robbed the Titan Rest and Fuel Stop outside of Memphis early yesterday. But this latest development with Johnnie Walker, the leader of the controversial Covenant for the New Commandment, has the nation wondering what's next in this bloody and still unfolding saga."

The rotund, dreadlocked reporter, looking as earnest as she possibly could, stood across the street from the Walker domicile, her dark face grave. The phalanx of Swords of the Master remained in place on Walker's lawn, a dramatic visual backdrop for her camera operator. She appeared to have dressed in a hurry in her full-length skirt with a hideous print and wrinkled grey blazer.

"To summarize, authorities have given Walker until three P.M. today to surrender to police. Walker's attorney said that Walker would conduct services before surrendering. The Covenant of the New Commandment observes the Sabbath on Saturday. Walker will be charged with conspiracy to commit armed robbery, and also with several new domestic terrorism statutes that deem him a potential threat to national security. His attorney has made arrangements to have the controversial religious figure released on $200,000 bail. Authorities were stunned early this morning when a pre-dawn raid stalled after more than two hundred of Walker's paramilitary arm, the Swords of the Master, blocked the entrance to his North Germanville home. In a related development, a Walker aide, Merrone Wilkinson-Workman and her husband, Allan Workman, were arrested late yesterday in Memphis and held on $50,000 bail each. Two other Covenant officials are being held on $25,000 bail. All have been charged with conspiracy to commit armed robbery and with the same domestic terrorism statutes placed against Walker. A federal official, speaking on condition of anonymity, said they have evidence connecting the religious cult to Unit 2236, the cop killers who have terrorized the nation for more than four months. But no charges have been filed yet. This is Cecilia Cravens reporting for Channel OneCorp, the OCI mega-station, where our business and your news are the same thing."

Robert clicked the television set off. His wheelchair whirred briefly as he turned toward his new trainees. "We know the government uses the cut-off-the-head theory," Robert said. Light reflected from his glasses for a moment. "We anticipated it, although we didn't know when or where. We believe this was the first attempt on the Minister's life, and that there will be others.

"His subordinates argued unsuccessfully for keeping Minister Johnnie thoroughly separated from this operation, but he wouldn't hear it. We cannot guarantee they won't kill him while he's in custody. We can only guarantee it will be costly. If they had proceeded with their assault this morning, I can tell you this: it's true that many of the unarmed Swords would have died, but mechanisms were in place, and I can't say what they were, to destroy at least half of that convoy, more if possible."

Andy felt light-headed. The stillness of the room was soaked with gravitas. Without warning, he felt his brother's presence around him, and in him.

He felt George talking to him . . . *Hey, Andy. Whassup, partner? I see you're still playing all fly balls to the wall, aren't you? You are sure enough getting ready to start some shit, huh? You know what they're saying, don't you? They're saying they want to kill you niggers so bad they can taste it.*

THIRTY-NINE

The early evening chill along King Drive touched the Teacher's shaved head like a caress. He liked it. Still, he wanted some hair back on his head. If he grew it back, he thought, enough remained to wear a style popular when he was a young man. They called it "the Hustler" back in the day. Close cropped, shaped with a razor all the way around. If he could no longer wear a 'fro, a salt and pepper Hustler was more like him than a shaved head. He smiled, happy to be distracting himself with trivial thoughts during this time of trials.

He and his son walked on the gravel pathway paralleling the river next to the Drive. A dozen Swords walked with them, keeping a discreet distance. Only Glenn carried his licensed weapon. If the feds or cops vamped on the Teacher, the Swords were ordered not to resist until the authorities were close enough for hand-to-hand combat. Glenn didn't kid himself about the license meaning anything in court if he somehow survived shooting as many as he could.

The Minister felt complete; he felt Holy Breath suffuse his being this night as it usually did at the quiet place he loved by the ocean fifty miles from the city. Maybe it was the water that did it. He looked over at his son. David was deep in thought, too.

His son looked good, better than he had in months, maybe a year or more. His skin and eyes were clear. He looked rested.

"How do you feel?"

"You know I always hate admitting you're right, but you were. I do feel better. I was in denial. I didn't think I was drinking that much."

" I know. That bourbon was kicking your ass."

"Father knows best."

"That sounds bitter."

They walked without words for several strides, silhouetted against the pinkness of sunset, pinkness divided by bluish peninsula and island-shaped clouds.

"It's been hard walking in your shadow. I have never seemed to get it right enough for you."

Minister Johnnie chose his words carefully. This wasn't about hurting David, although truth did that sometimes. "We had a conversation once way back when, after you didn't get a Covenant scholarship for college. You thought you should get one because you're my son. I told you then that you had the skills, the intellect, to do at least as much as I've done, and more. But you didn't have the passion. You still don't."

"I've told you, you saw things I didn't see, did things I didn't do. Our generation is different."

"David, I've tried different ways to tell you this, and you don't seem to hear it. I'll try again. You say it's generational, but there are people your age who do have the passion. They see we're locked in a life and death struggle that seems to get worse instead of better. Yes, you've been middle-class all your life, and yes, you've had some advantages, and yes, there are more in this generation like you. But black people collectively are under siege, and it's gotten progressively worse under the last several administrations. I'm hoping that you will start to see a little more clearly now that you've completed rehab. I believe you will find the passion within you. Many lives will depend on it, which I'll explain in a minute."

Whatever else he hadn't inherited, he had his father's stubbornness. He didn't like the assessment but he said nothing. The two proud men walked a little ways more in silence.

"I know you've thought I didn't trust you, and you're partially right. I didn't trust your liquor. I was about ready to ask the board to reconsider having named you the Teacher-Designate. But now that you've been to Wissahickon Hill and gotten yourself sober, there are some things you need to know. The events of the last few days tell me I don't know how much time I have. And there's also something that's troubling me." He paused. "Let's start back," he said, turning his collar up against the breeze off the river.

"When you assume the role of Teacher, you will also assume leadership of Unit 2236." He let the words sink in, and thought he sensed tenseness envelop David.

The Teacher explained the four star hierarchy to his son even as he felt, and listened to, an intuitive hesitancy inside himself. He heeded the internal discomfort by not identifying the Fourth Star by name. "If something happens to me, the Fourth Star will contact you," he said.

"If this happens, you will replace me as both Teacher and the Third Star. You will select a new Teacher-Designate. You may have to go underground to keep Unit 2236 alive if you're unable to continue the dual responsibility. Do you have any questions?"

David said nothing; his father continued. "I know you've been angry, and I know you feel others, especially Romeo Butler, have had access you don't, even as my son. I'll say it again. We are defending ourselves in a life and death war. If you feel you're not up to it—for any reason—say so and vow to keep this conversation secret, as if it never happened."

They walked. "Have you sent Wardell Keyes anywhere recently?" Minister Johnnie asked suddenly.

The pause that followed was longer than it should have been and the older man noted it. "He asked me about going to San Diego for a few days because he has family there, and I said okay."

"How well do you know Keyes?"

"The relationship has been more professional than personal, but I'm getting to know him." David's heart pounded.

"I want Keyes assigned to my security detail when he returns. Get someone new for Romeo, or should I ask Glenn to do it?"

"I'll find someone for Romeo."

"When you were in Wissahickon Hill, you probably heard the expression, 'You're only as sick as your secrets.'"

"Just about every day."

"Were you honest? Did you tell them everything?"

"Why do you ask?"

"Son, we've done alcohol and drug counseling at Covenant for nearly thirty years. We host twelve-step groups. I understand the process. Every addict I've talked to who's gone through it says that an honest, fearless inventory is liberating. I have no reason to believe you didn't tell them everything; I'm only asking if you did. Sometimes folks think they have, and stuff they've honestly forgotten comes up later, and they deal with it then."

"I did as good as I can do. I'm glad to be back home. And I appreciate your newfound trust in me."

"Maybe you should tell Judith that you will need to stay at our place for a few days. We have a lot to go over. Unit 2236 is a complex operation and there's much to learn. I could have died yesterday. And the irony is, they were coming after me because of that bogus government operation in Memphis.

"One more thing. You cannot tell Judith now about what we're doing with Unit 2236. If I am killed or incapacitated and you assume the Third Star, it's different. Then it's not fair if you don't tell her. I've told your mother. But you're not on active duty yet, so to speak, so she doesn't have to know yet. Understood?"

2236

"Understood."

Later, in his office at home, the Teacher felt something in his stomach he rarely felt. He hated it when he did feel it.

Uncertainty. His only son.

Keyes had never felt right. Now, Burton has uncovered him, and my own son may be lying to me. David says he sent him to San Diego, and I know he was in Memphis when the impersonators robbed the store. It's not just his drinking that's a problem. Why hadn't the feds arrested him, too?

Minister Johnnie closed his eyes. He felt suddenly old. Judas was his only son. He knew Ila's heart would be as broken as his was.

They were fighting a big war with a small army. They couldn't afford any mistakes until they had more people in the field. Even then, they wouldn't be permitted many mistakes.

He must become certain.

Later, in his office at home, the Teacher-Designate stared at his telephone as if it were a rattlesnake. He couldn't call John Edgar just yet. He wanted a drink really bad. What had Keyes said?

John Edgar has given me an assignment in Memphis . . . If anyone asks, say I went to San Diego . . . It's a need-to-know situation. When it happens, it won't be hard to figure out . . .

He wanted to pound his head on something to stop the noise inside him. His father had always been intuitive. It felt like he knew something when he asked about telling all his secrets. He couldn't possibly know what they were making him do. And what did he know about Keyes? If he told him about Keyes and John Edgar, and what he knew about Memphis, he was disgraced and finished. But he couldn't tell John Edgar about his father's leadership of Unit 2236 either. He had to find a way out of this mess.

He had told the people at Wissahickon Hill about his one-night stand with the woman in Las Vegas. He found himself unable to tell them about the pictures, because then he would have had to tell about the blackmail, and John Edgar. He hadn't had a drink in fifty-six days, including his four weeks at the clinic.

He didn't know if he could call John Edgar at all.

FORTY

The Director's eyes were cobalt blue and had a piercing effect that made many people uncomfortable. He had used this physical feature to his advantage throughout a twenty-three year career in the Bureau. He combined the piercing stare with a folksy manner that he thought emulated former President Ronald Reagan, whose presidential tenure had inspired him during his first years as an FBI agent. The Director's eyes made John Edgar uncomfortable, a phenomenon that didn't happen easily or frequently in his social or professional intercourse with people.

"You screwed up," the Director said.

John Edgar sat erect, his back ramrod straight and not against the back of the leather chair. Paradoxically, his military bearing projected an attitude of submission. "Yes, sir," he said.

The Director picked up a manila folder on his desk, waved it. "You haven't had a vacation since you've been with the Bureau," he said. "Do you like it here?"

"Yes, sir."

"Good. Take a month off. Go somewhere nice, have some fun. When you come back, put something together that works. Don't rush. Get it right. If this Unit 2236 commits any crimes during that time, we'll monitor it with whatever locals who have jurisdiction. But when you get back, I want CP2 to come up with something good, something debilitating, something that knocks them on their ass. Understood?"

"Yes, sir. With your permission, sir, I'd like to forego the vacation."

The cobalt blue eyes bored into him. "The vacation is an order. When you return, you have ninety days to produce something beneficial and productive. Understood?"

"Yes, sir."

When the phone rang, Minister David had made his mind up. There was no bourbon to still the roiling sensations in his stomach.

"Yes?" he said into the handset.

247

The hiss added to John Edgar's voice made him sound almost inhuman. "Do you have anything for me?"

"No," David said, his eyes closed, hoping the man wouldn't threaten to send the pictures out.

"You had better get something quick," John Edgar said.

"I'm doing the best I can," David said.

"Your best is not good enough." There was a pause. "I'm going to be away on business for a month. You should consider it a reprieve. When I return, if you don't have anything, I will give you just thirty days to invent something that we can act on. If you get anything in the meantime, I will send you a number or e-mail where you can let me know. I don't want you to wait until my vaca_ my business trip is over. Am I understood?"

David felt perspiration trickling down the middle of his back. "Understood," he said.

The line went dead.

FORTY-ONE

ornbread the Third and two of his boys shivered in the frigid February morning air. They stared at the neat two-story brick structure on Fifty-fourth Street, and the mostly well-dressed women, children, and men crossing the parking lot and entering the building. He and his crew wore tight jeans, black fatigue jackets over black shirts, and oversized Apple caps broke down low over one eye. Momentary second thoughts kept them from walking in.

They looked at each other, wondering if it was such a good idea after all. They had known about Black Label Walker for years. Now, with this Unit 2236 action jumping off, they wanted to see what he was saying that Unit 2236 found attractive. The mystery of their name and what they were doing had gotten Cornbread's attention.

In most places, he and Bugeye and Drugbucket were intimidating, not intimidated. But not here. There was something about the brothers in Swords of the Master. And for Cornbread the Third, as far as that goes, it was true of the Magdalene Society sisters, too. The half dozen Swords on each side of a freestanding metal archway inside the door reminded him there would be no cutting up or talking shit. The building felt like a church even if it didn't look like a church. Toking a couple of joints back on the block had felt like the thing to do. But now his high was wearing off.

"Y'all still want to do this?" Cornbread the Third asked. "God might strike us down dead and shit 'cause we high."

Bugeye and Drugbucket laughed. "I still wanna do it," Bugeye said. "I hear this old head can really throw some words. Can you imagine, a preacher with the nickname 'Black Label?' That's my kind of nigga, a man of God who drinks good Scotch." They all laughed again.

"He don't drink no more, I don't think. That's what he used to do when he was as old as us," Cornbread the Third said. He looked around. "Blacks folks living well over here, ain't they?"

"No shit," said Drugbucket. "C'mon, let's go on in, we over here now."

The three young men walked into the Covenant lobby, bravado informing their steps.

"Good morning, brothers," the well-dressed Sword closest to the door said, a broad smile on his round face. He held out a round tray to each man. "Please place all metal items that you have in your pockets in this tray, young sirs. And remove your hats, please." All three heard the demand in the request.

The first surprise was the search. The second surprise was that it wasn't just about them, as it often was with the cops; *everybody* walking in was being searched. The third surprise was the crisp efficiency. It reinforced the quiet understanding they all had that these brothers did not play.

The Swords acted like Minister Johnnie Walker was the president of the United States. *Damn.* They had only seen this kind of power exhibited by the police and the Secret Service on television. And, despite their firmness, the Swords of the Master acted different toward them. The Swords respected them in a way they didn't get in too many places. Cornbread the Third had never in his life been called "sir" anywhere by anyone.

"Yes, sir, I know you understand this is very necessary," the Sword said, sweeping his hands along Cornbread the Third's body without wasting a movement. "You do know that they arrested our beloved Minister last week, right?"

"Yeah, I heard about it," Cornbread the Third said. "That was some cold shi — that wasn't right at all."

The Sword smiled at the younger man's *faux pas.* "Yes, sir, you got it right. It was cold. Coming like thieves in the night, they did. We believe in protecting our leader with our very lives. Just like you would go down with your crew here if something jumped off, right?"

"Yeah, I guess so." Cornbread the Third took his change, keys, and the silver chain he wore around his neck back. The Sword held his small pocketknife.

"You'll have to get this back on your way out, brother." The Sword looked Cornbread the Third in the eye with the unspoken message: Either that, or turn around and leave. "It will be over there." He pointed to two Swords. Cornbread nodded and joined Drugbucket and Bugeye, who had also parted with pocketknives.

Both men were staring at the gold-framed black faces lining the entire vestibule. "Man, Jesus is black!" Bugeye said, his protruding eyes bigger than usual.

Drugbucket had never seen so many pictures of black people in one place before. He didn't know who most of them were. He did recognize Castro. And King. Malcolm X. That was about it for him.

They sat near the back. "Hey y'all, there ain't no crosses here nowhere," Drugbucket said as he looked around the sanctuary. "I thought they was Christians."

"They are, I think," Cornbread the Third said. "There's a reason we don't know about, I guess. My grandpops says Minister Johnnie is real deep." He stroked his chin, trying to imitate his elder's gesture and voice for his friends. "Old 'Black Label' is a deep brother. He thinks about things more than most of us.' Grandpops was surprised when I told him we were thinking about coming over here."

"He know why you wanted to come?" Bugeye asked.

"Yeah. He said we ain't gonna get nothing. He said they already said they don't know who Unit 2236 is, or where they are."

"Plus, they won't be hanging up no recruiting signs either, knowwhatI'msaying?"

"Yeah, well, we here now. Y'all want to get with the Swords of the Master instead?"

"I don't know," Bugeye said. "They ain't taking down no Blues like the brothers in Unit 2236 is, knowwhatI'msaying?"

The main auditorium was larger than the school auditorium at the high school they had sporadically attended before dropping out. It had a capacity of three hundred, which it now did on a regular basis. When the Covenant anticipated larger gatherings, television monitors were used in basement classrooms, or a larger auditorium was rented.

Cornbread the Third was puzzled but kept it to himself. The Bible verses in front of him didn't fit with what little he knew of Minister Johnnie's people. He saw strength in Covenant members that he saw on the street, the sistas included. When he and his boys saw a sista wearing a red, black, and green headband, or a tricolor beret, they didn't talk trash to them as they passed. It wasn't something they thought about or decided, it was just the way it was.

As often as not, the sista would look at them, smile a greeting *first*, and keep stepping about her business. They usually returned the greeting with "Hello, sista," or a nod. Plus, the sistas were usually *fine*.

Cornbread couldn't figure out the connection between his perception of strength and all the talk about love on the wall in front of him.

Across the front wall of the auditorium, spanning almost its entire width, was a long bar of gold with sides that tapered in slightly at the top. Engraved on it were the words, "THIS IS MY COMMANDMENT: LOVE ONE ANOTHER, AS I HAVE LOVED YOU." In smaller letters that followed,

"John 15:12."

Above it was a smaller gold bar, also with tapered sides, that read, "LOVE YOUR NEIGHBOR AS YOURSELF. Matthew 22:39."

Above that was an equilateral triangle of gold. Its base was such that the three golden parts formed one large equilateral triangle. Inscribed on the triangle were the words, "LOVE YAHWEH YOUR ELOHIM WITH ALL YOUR HEART, AND WITH ALL YOUR SOUL, AND WITH ALL YOUR MIND. Matthew 22:37."

None of the three young men had a clue who or what "Yahweh" or "Elohim" were or meant. "Let's ask on the way out," Cornbread the Third suggested as he continued to ponder the imagery in front of him. It was deep, he knew that much.

Seven crystal stars stood in a line in the large composite equilateral triangle from the base to the upper point, bisecting it into two isosceles triangles. The fourth star, the central one, was much larger than the others. Two spotlights from each side of the room focused on it and remained on at all times. They made the largest crystal gleam like a miniature sun.

The three young men did not understand most of what they saw. That would come later for Cornbread the Third and Bugeye. As they tried to absorb what they could, Minister Johnnie Walker, surrounded by four Swords, entered the auditorium, to ringing applause. David Walker, already seated, stood and embraced his father.

By now, Swords and Magdalene sisters ringed the room. "He got as much protection as the president," Bugeye whispered.

"Yeah, I was thinking that earlier," Cornbread the Third said, watching the brothers scan the audience.

"Good morning, brothers and sisters," Minister Johnnie said. In recent weeks, the Teacher had regularly worn black leather sport coats during public speaking. He did so now. Those in the Covenant said the minister was in "combat mode."

"I greet you with peace, blessings, love, and power." He looked around the room, filled to capacity, and smiled. "I include the enemies among us, the informants, and the agent provocateurs in that blessing, although they may not include themselves." It was a standard Walker line that rippled low chuckles across the room.

"I thank you for your calls, e-mails, and other offerings of support during the events of the past week. I am humbled, as always, by that support.

"I'm going to get right to it this morning," Minister Johnnie boomed. "No preliminaries, anecdotes, or jokes. I'm sure you will agree we have some serious, and almost certainly dangerous, times ahead. For that reason, I am taking John, the fifteenth chapter and thirteenth verse, as the basis for this morning's message. 'Greater love has no man than this, that he lay down his life for his friends.' It comes right after part of our new commandment from the Great Teacher, when he has told his disciples to love one another as he has loved them. I want to use this verse to talk about last week, to talk about the Covenant, to address—*publicly* —my personal, as well as our official position on Unit 2236, and to provide some advice for the coming days, advice that you may accept or reject."

There it was again, that word "love," Cornbread the Third thought. He felt uncomfortable and didn't know why.

Hundreds of miles away in WiTHWA, the seven members of Unit 2236's August 21st Brigade sat in the Boardroom watching the Teacher's weekly talk. Andy thought almost the same thoughts as the young visitor to the Covenant. Only they didn't make him feel uncomfortable.

Here we are again with the word "love," Andy thought. He knew he needed to read the Bible more. He knew about the ultimate test of love as taught by Yahshua, but had forgotten that it was right next to the injunction to love one another.

"Before I get too far into it, I do want to let you know that all of our people in Memphis have been released on bail and are fine.

"Now." It was a signature Walker technique that said: let's get serious.

"We are under attack by our government, both federal and local—and probably state, too—because they say we have something to do with some people who are speaking forcefully on behalf of black people. Unit 2236 has communicated with the Covenant of the New Commandment and asked us to release communiqués on their behalf, and we have done so.

"We've done so because we've been asked to, and because people have a right to know what's happening. We've done so because there's nothing illegal about doing so. And for the informants in the audience, I'm gonna say it: we're doing it because I, for one, am glad that someone has decided that the authorities can no longer murder innocent black people with impunity! Go back and tell the person holding your leash that I said so, and that I really don't give a damn how they feel about me!"

The auditorium exploded in applause and loud cheers. People stood and shouted. Cornbread the Third and Bugeye and Drugbucket applauded too and looked at each other. *Damn!*

"A brother with a stick trying to disarm a crazy white man is not a criminal," Minister Johnnie said. He had the microphone in his hand and moved back and forth across the stage in a slow, deliberate walk. "They trying to get you to believe he was attacking a cop. All George knew was that he was trying to disarm a crazy white man!

"I'm not going through the other twenty-five or so of us who were cut down in the last two years for the crime of being somewhere and being black —you know, like driving while black," Minister Johnnie said. "But I do want it known that I will never, ever, denounce the people who call themselves Unit 2236 for deeming the deaths of these people crimes and then acting accordingly. The Great Teacher said render to Caesar that which is Caesar's and render to Yahweh that which belongs to Yahweh. I answer to no one but Yahweh, I will never answer to anyone but Yahweh, and if my life is on the line for that, if this racist government wants to put me in jail for that, well, come and get me!" He held his arms out in front of him in a gesture of surrendering to handcuffs. As his audience hollered and screamed, he shouted over them, "If you can get past the Swords who will be defending me!" That brought more whooping and hollering.

Minister Johnnie went on to explain that he had surrendered for arrest to prevent bloodshed in the particular instance of the raid on his home three weeks earlier. It was the wrong time to take a stand, he said.

"But one thing must be clear: If I must die in defense of the rights of black people, I will! I recently heard some sisters quote our brother, Claude McKay, who got it right in his poem back during the bloody Red Summer of 1919, and not a damn thing's changed since then, except they kill us with more sophistication now! If Winston Churchill can quote McKay while fighting the Nazis, I know we can quote him because he wrote the poem for us!" As his congregation screamed approval, Minister Johnnie segued into McKay's poem without missing a beat.

Although familiar with old school gangsta rap and some real oldhead political stuff by people like Arrested Development and Public Enemy and Chuck D, Cornbread the Third didn't know that what he thought of as "poetry" sounded anything like the words Minister Johnnie fired at his audience.

"Though far outnumbered let us show us brave," the Teacher thundered, "and for their thousand blows deal one deathblow!"

"Yes! Yes!"

"Tell it!"

"Teach!"

Without realizing they had done so, the three teenagers were on their feet, too, clenched fists punching the air. (Forty years after its heyday, the Teacher still insisted that his congregants use the Black Power salute. "I'll never retire it or let it go out of fashion in the Covenant," he insisted.)

"What though before us lies the open grave? Like men we'll face the murderous, cowardly pack, pressed to the wall, dying, but fighting back! Fighting back! Fighting back! Fighting back!"

The audience chanted the words over and over with their Teacher, fists raised. His words reverberated, playing in different ways in different minds.

Cornbread the Third had never thought about fighting anyone except people who disrespected him or his crew. It might be another crew, or it might be an individual thing. He didn't tolerate disrespect.

Now here was an oldhead, and a deep oldhead at that, talking about black people fighting back the way Big Bread said it used to be.

At WiTHWA, Andy wondered if the Third Star was signing his death warrant with his words. Maybe he had done so long ago, simply by being who he was. The U.S. had no use for men like Minister Johnnie unless they served the stars and stripes.

Ward Keyes was one of the Swords onstage. His eyes dutifully scanned the ecstatic audience. His thoughts, though, remained with his employer. Keyes was surprised, but pleased, that he had been transferred to the elite detail around Johnnie Walker. *Nigger, you know way more than you're telling,* he thought to himself as he listened to the lecture.

The joyful exuberance wore itself down. Minister Johnnie stood at the Sacred Desk waiting for the precise moment to speak over the decrescendo of excitement.

"A very great man once told us that we have some difficult days ahead," Minister Johnnie said as if he were talking one-on-one with each of them. "He was murdered less than twenty-four hours after he said it. I believe that Doctor King was prescient, but I wonder if he saw how difficult those days would become as one decade rolled into the next, and into the next. When he said it, the winds of change still blew. Now we smell the stench of almost full-blown repression and the acrid effluvium of increasingly indiscriminate death among our people.

"We live in a nation that has a document called the Declaration of Independence. As citizens, so-called, we have to assume the document applies to black people and brown people and red people and any people who were born here, if it's to have any meaning. Unlike many Americans, I've read it. *All* of it. It says to the citizenry, in explaining their rebellion against Great Britain, that when a government becomes destructive of the rights of life, liberty, and the pursuit of happiness, people have the *right* to alter or abolish it. It goes on to say that you don't do this for 'light or transient reasons.' There's a sentence in it that goes like this: '. . . and all experience has shown that mankind are more disposed to suffer *while evils are sufferable*, than to right themselves by abolishing forms to which they are accustomed.' I'm telling you, these were some smart white folks who wrote this. Prudence and experience say people are patient, and should exercise patience, *while evils are sufferable*.

"But! But! But! When a long train of abuses, designed to do the same ol' same ol'—that's what they meant—continue, these white folks said you not only have a *right*, you have a *duty*, to throw off that government and create a new one. Now, I can't read the minds of the folks in Unit 2236, but it looks like they are doing something like these white folks back in the day said they should do. If you ask me, they're saying they will match the train of abuses suffered by black folks for over 390 years against the piddling train of abuses suffered by the land-owning hypocritical enslavers known as the founding fathers. If they had reason to fight, Unit 2236 seems to say they damn well have a right to fight, too! So when President Hugh Bruder denounces what his white folks said and did in the Declaration of Independence, then I *may* think about denouncing what Unit 2236 is doing, but not before."

For ever so brief a moment, as people applauded loud and long, Ward Keyes let a cloud of disgust move across his face. His Swords commander, Glenn Greene, saw it. And, because the closed circuit camera happened to be panning past him at that moment, Andy and his colleagues saw it, too. Everyone but Robert and Andy found it curious and strange. Because of their previous conversation, the two men knew he was revealing his true self.

"I don't know how long Yahweh wants me to walk among you and with you," Minister Johnnie continued when his congregation quieted. "I'm ready to go when the Elohim of the worlds calls me. But I will close with this. The Covenant of the New Commandment will transmit the communiqués of Unit 2236 as long as they ask us to do so, regardless of who doesn't like it. We will be their Sinn Fein. And because of recent events, and because evils no longer seem sufferable, I will go deeply in prayer and ask myself if I can in good conscience ask the Swords of the Master to remain unarmed."

The last words danced through the room like an electric shock. No one said it but everyone knew it.

It amounted to a declaration of war.

Cornbread the Third hung back after he and his crew retrieved their knives. He was glad none of them had decided to pack their pieces that day. Because they were leaving their 'hood, they had discussed it and decided it wouldn't be right.

"Y'all hold up," Cornbread the Third said as Bugeye and Drugbucket started through the door. He turned to the young man who had returned their knives. "Uh, can I ask you a question?"

"Oh, yes sir," the Sword said. "What can I do for you?"

"Uh, I know the Minister has said he don't know where Unit 2236 is and all," Cornbread the Third said. "I'd sure like to get with them. But, what I was wondering, how does a brother get hooked up with y'all? Y'all seem like the next best thing."

The young Sword smiled. He knew "next best thing" was meant as a compliment, not an insult. "Sir, stay right here. I'll get someone to talk with you about that."

Bugeye and Drugbucket looked at each other when they heard Cornbread the Third's request. Well, it wouldn't hurt to see what they told him.

Glenn Greene came out of the auditorium and approached the trio. "Which one of you wants information about the Swords of the Master?"

"Uh, yes sir, it's me," said Cornbread the Third.

"I'm Glenn Greene." He extended his hand and they shook.

"I'm Corn – Willis Richardson."

"Come with me, there's a conference room where we can talk," Glenn said. "Your friends can wait here if they like."

"All right if we listen, too?" Bugeye asked.

Glenn nodded. "Of course you can, my brother. I'll get one of the brothers to get us some iced tea and something to snack on."

They talked for an hour. When they finished, all three decided they would return the following Saturday for lecture.

FORTY-TWO

ndy and the six other bleary-eyed trainees shivered as they stood at attention in the pre-dawn darkness. All seven wore military fatigues, boots, and navy blue watch caps. They stood in a natural clearing in a dense grove of trees, facing Robert and a tall, muscular man. He was light brown-skinned and wore a thin pencil moustache. Robert sat to the man's right. Several small balls lay in his lap on the blanket covering his legs.

"While we are in training, my code name is Nat Turner, " the muscular man said. "I am second-in-command to Robert; I am his legs and I will help supervise the regimen of preparing you to defend our people with your very lives. I will demand excellence in all areas of our work, and will accept nothing less." He glanced toward the other end of the line.

"You all may stand at ease," he said. He walked in quick strides to the tallest trainee. "I saw you smirk. Is something funny?"

"The code name seems rather dramatic," the tall man said.

The trainer grabbed the man by both lapels of his fatigue jacket. With his face inches away from the trainee, Nat Turner spoke in quiet tones; his words held no emotion. "The code name is deadly serious," he said. "We have no humor in what we're about to do," he said. "I have disciplinary measures that may also seem dramatic, but they will clearly demonstrate my seriousness. You cannot leave here, so you have no alternatives. Don't make me tell you again. Do we understand each other?"

"Yes," the tall man said. Nat Turner released him.

The quietness of the command made Andy shiver, and not from the cold. *You have no alternatives.* Damn.

"Right now, you are poorly conditioned recruits," Nat Turner continued. "When I finish with you, all of you will be warriors. Failure is not an option." He looked at Robert, who nodded. "Let's move out in single file., shortest to tallest."

Andy—at five foot, ten inches, he was the shortest—fell in step behind their trainer as they threaded their way through the trees until they reached an unpaved, narrow road. Nat Turner started jogging; his new recruits struggled to keep up.

They ran for a quarter mile, the fog from their breath punctuating the run like miniature smoke signals. "Now you can fan out and run abreast of each other," Robert shouted as he rolled alongside.

"Repeat after me," Nat Turner shouted. "Eight twenty-one!"

"Eight twenty-one!" the seven men gasped.

"Louder!" Robert's gravelly voice shouted.

"Eight twenty-one!"

Andy thought about Claudia as he placed one foot in front of the other and struggled to keep up on the dusty dirt road. He only thought about her every day, several times a day. It occurred to him that she would have been just as mystified at his sudden disappearance. His cover story for his neighbors being on a writing assignment wouldn't have washed with Claudia once he said he had to be incommunicado. He wondered about his six colleagues. Some of them had to be married. Did they say, "Listen, sugar, I have to drop out of sight for an indefinite amount of time. I can't tell you where I'm going or what I'm doing."

He pushed the thoughts away. But the hollow ache in his chest, the one that came every day, several times a day, lingered.

"Eight twenty-one!" Nat Turner roared. He sounded as fresh as he had at the beginning.

"Eight twenty-one!"

"Eight!"

"Eight!" Their little motley crew sounded stronger, too, Andy thought.

"Twenty!"

"Twenty!"

"ONE!"

"ONE!"

The sky had segued into a spreading band of blue at the horizon when they huffed and puffed to a finish two miles later. Andy felt as if flames were searing his lungs as he gasped for air. Most of his colleagues looked the way he felt.

"You may lean against a tree for a moment, but you may not sit," Robert said. "In a few minutes, Nat Turner will lead you in a cool down walk."

"Move out!" Nat Turner's voice rang across the clearing too soon.

As they walked, the journalist in Andy studied his comrades as if he were preparing a magazine story about them.

Their identity numbers ran from 121 to 127, but Robert had also assigned them code names. "Calling each other by numbers daily will grow tedious," Robert had said. "We have another layer of pseudonyms which will remain with you, in addition to your numbers, throughout your service in Unit 2236. You will know personnel from other brigades only by number unless you meet one on an assignment. At that time, you may share these false identities with each other. Under no circumstances will you, or anyone else, make your actual identity available to other personnel. This is the Second Rule of Conduct. There may be rare exceptions but the Third Star or the Fourth Star will decide them."

In the weeks that followed, Andy discovered traits that distinguished his team members from each other. "Melvin" was about his own height and color but athletically built. He wore a bushy moustache and sunny demeanor that belied a seriousness Andy heard during class discussions. "Clarence," the most unlikely looking assassin-in-training among them, wore close-cropped hair, thick glasses on his clean-shaven face, and had a tendency toward quietness that accentuated a professorial manner. "Bill," with an IQ of 167, turned out to be the class clown among them. Gregarious to a fault, they learned that his two loves were quantum physics and doo-wop classics older than he was. The more obscure the songs were, the better. Bill, Bryon/Andy, and Melvin spent several nights before lights out crooning songs from long-forgotten groups. "Ronald," at the age of forty-three, still ran the one hundred meters dash in less than ten and a half seconds. Clearly the jock among them, he also had a black belt in hapkido. "John" was mysterious. He said little and observed a lot. "Richard," unknown to Andy and his fellow trainees, worked for the Covenant as its certified public accountant and had written three books, including the best-seller, *The Case for Reparations for Descendants of African Captives: A Moral and Economic Imperative.*

The code names for the men were a personal joke, Robert said.

They walked another half mile, rested for fifteen minutes, and then did calisthenics. Straining his way through thirty sit-ups, Andy silently thanked Romeo for getting him started on physical training. They were told all breakfasts would be eaten in silence unless otherwise stipulated.

After the morning run, nine breakfast trays always awaited them in a room adjacent to their basement meeting room. They never saw who prepared the food. During their stay, their breakfast meal usually would consist of fruit, cereal, yogurt, toast and coffee or tea. Occasionally, eggs, home-fried potatoes or grits, and a variety of breakfast meats would be served. After the second week, Andy became aware of his mild addiction to breakfast scrapple, a regional food of pork scraps and corn meal prepared in a brick and fried to a crisp brown. He had disciplined himself to eat it only once a week. At WiTHWA, he missed it the same way he did when he first moved to Los Angeles.

Afterwards, they filed into the mahogany boardroom where Robert waited.

"As efficient as we will make you at killing, the fifty-minutes you spend with me each morning will help you become better thinkers," Robert said. "When you leave here, you will primarily be executioners replacing a failed judicial and political system. Within a year, two at the most, you will almost certainly be urban guerilla fighters." He smiled his mirthless smile. "Among other things, you will become almost as good as I am with the use of rubber balls."

Killing. Andy still felt distance when he heard the word. No, distance from the act. The word was not the thing. What was it Robert had said? *You will be grounded in very specific principles that we hope will keep you sane, and will prevent you from becoming monsters. We cannot guarantee an exemption from either possibility. We pray that you will be spared from both."*

On the fourth day, a one hour martial arts workout was added to their exhausting routine. The small, perfectly square room that served as a *dojo* was Spartan. The ancient symbol that represented yin and yang adorned one wall. The floor was divided in half. One side was polished mahogany wood; exercise mats covered the other half. As Andy changed into his spanking new martial arts *gi,* he noticed that a few of the others, Clarence and Richard in particular, needed physical conditioning as much as he did. He remembered Romeo's comment that they had been selected because they could be trusted. It was a trait far more important than their athleticism.

"It will take more time than we have here to make you proficient," Nat Turner told them. "You will continue to train after we finish here. I will provide some techniques that you can absorb quickly. Always think of three immediate targets: the eyes, the throat, and the groin. A strong and precise blow to any one of these areas should incapacitate your opponent and give you an immediate advantage."

During some rest breaks, Nat Turner dispensed martial arts philosophy as well as moves and postures. "The Swords teach that martial arts postures are "prayer positions" designed to keep evil—an attack by anyone intent on hurting you—away," he said. Andy remembered Minister Johnnie's reference to the same definition. As he spoke, Nat Turner executed some blocking and parrying postures and made transitions to several striking moves.

As a young man, Andy had never fought much. And he recognized early in life that some boys and men enjoyed the sheer physical contact of combat; he wasn't one of them. As he watched their training supervisor, though, he committed to give his all in Unit 2236. In remembrance of his brother and Sonny, he had placed himself in a life and death situation.

"You, Bryon," Nat Turner said, pointing at Andy. "On your feet."

Andy stood. Not knowing what to expect, he felt his pulse quicken.

"I picked Bryon because he is smaller than I am," Nat Turner said. When they were close, Nat Turner grabbed Andy's wrist with a large hand. He showed Andy how to relax his arm and, in turn, grab his wrist. "Step forward and place your right foot behind my right," he instructed. "Now push."

Nat Turner went down, then quickly regained his feet. "We will show you several techniques like this, where your size or strength isn't the deciding factor." He glanced at Andy. "Thank you."

They warmed up and practiced their first *kata*—a sequence of fighting movements. Andy imitated Nat Turner' movements as best he could. During the strenuous workout, he found a few muscles he didn't know he had.

Talking, permissible at lunchtime, felt awkward and forced for Andy during their entire stay at WiTHWA. They were seven strangers. Nine, including Robert and Nat Turner. He couldn't ask some of the questions new acquaintances normally exchanged: Where do you live? What do you do? Where did you grow up? What school did you go to? By any chance, do you know so-and-so at your meetinghouse?

They all belonged to the Covenant. That was a given. If they didn't have the religious and spiritual underpinnings of the Covenant, Robert said, the Third Star didn't want them in Unit 2236. After leaving WiTHWA, they knew they might run into each other during visits to meetinghouses. If this happened, they were instructed to behave as if WiTHWA didn't exist and act as if they were meeting for the first time, even if no one else was close by.

Conversations inevitably gravitated to the work they were doing. After their first day of training, they talked about martial arts. "I studied judo in college," Bill said. "I thought that was strenuous. Man, these hapkido workouts are more than a handful."

"You're older, too," Robert interjected. Even in their "free" time together, Robert or Nat Turner, if not both, were present. "You're all over thirty. Although, when Nat Turner finishes with you, your bodies will perform like those of twenty-five-year-olds."

There was silence for a few moments. A collective mental groan seemed to fill the room.

"Robert, how long will we be here?" It was Richard. "My recruiter was a little vague about that." Andy thought Richard's eyes were guarded, distrustful. Wary, maybe.

"Until you're ready," Robert said. The way he said "ready" closed off further inquiry into the matter.

In his room that night, it occurred to Andy that these men seemed a lot like him. Maybe he'd seen too many movies. He had fantasized they would be steely-eyed silent types. Cinema killers. But he wasn't like that himself. They were brothers he might sit next to at meetinghouse on Saturday mornings. They were men he might interview when covering a story. He'd known brothers a lot like them when he was at Church University. Now, here they were, seven John Everymen as potential killers.

They drilled daily in the techniques Robert had developed with the balls. Andy discovered that he had an aptitude for throwing them. He'd made it a point to stay focused since being popped by Robert. He absorbed the First Star's technique faster than the others. Robert's moves were relaxed, and he appeared to point at his target as he threw. The team began repetitive drills the first day that eventually developed quickness and control. Robert showed them life-sized targets they would use in the weeks ahead. "I will throw with you," Robert said. "Your goal will be to hit the target with me or ahead of me." He showed his teeth in the smileless smile. "No one has reached the goal yet."

Both Ron and Mel demonstrated either experience or innate skills during the early days on the firing range, a sub-basement soundproofed rectangular room further underground beneath the basement mahogany boardroom. On the first day at the range, all of Ron's sixteen shots hit the bull's eye; Mel missed two. The Fourth Star had spared no expense on their training camp, or on his teachers. Nat Turner not only executed everything he did in an exemplary manner, he was a top notch communicator of information. Andy could hardly believe he was doing almost eighty percent in pistol target practice. They had been there less than a week. His rifle skills were another matter.

"Bryon and John, stop closing your eyes as you fire," Nat Turner said as the team loaded fresh clips. Andy nodded and shouldered the carbine. The subcommander insisted on rifle proficiency before he turned them loose with automatic weapons.

"Trust me," he said, "when you gain some mastery here, you won't just spray an area with your automatic weapons and hope to hit something. You'll focus."

Within two weeks, Andy and his comrades could break down, clean, and reassemble a handgun, a sawed off shotgun, and an old M-16 carbine within minutes. They learned to attach silencers within seconds.

"In early assignments, a weapon and silencer will be provided shortly before you make contact with the convicted defendant," Robert said. He took target practice with them "to stay sharp." During training, the First Star fired more than five dozen rounds and never missed a bulls eye.

"You will always have instructions on where and how to dispose of the executive weapon so we can be assured it will never be found. The Fourth Star's pockets are deep enough to keep firepower coming, as assignments require, well into the future.

"When entire teams are sent into the field, weapons will be waiting for you in the vehicle where you rendezvous. You will leave them there and they will be disposed of as we see fit."

Andy sat straight up in bed, terrified. He exhaled after he realized he had been dreaming. About Claudia.

In the dream, she was an agent provocateur, talking to Commissioner Kaheel, talking to District Attorney Jacobs, being chased by masked members of Unit 2236 who fired at her. He woke up as he looked down at her bullet-riddled bloody body.

He remembered her note. *Please. Trust me.*

"Eight twenty-one!"
"Eight twenty-one!"
Through the gray of early morning, Andy saw the steep, almost vertical, verdant hill ahead. From a distance, the density of trees and foliage obscured the severity of the incline. He pushed the negativity away that immediately crowded his mind. He leaned the way Romeo had showed him and pumped his legs.

Clarence fell to his knees, panting, halfway up the hill. Ron and Richard grabbed him, threw his arms around their neck and jogged alongside him, providing verbal encouragement. He half walked, half stumbled, jogged when he could, and made it to the top without falling again.

Andy's legs felt twice their usual weight as they neared the crest. For a moment, he thought he might join Clarence. He gritted his teeth and kept on keeping on. *I can do this!*

Robert sat at the crest of the hill waiting for them. When he looked at the trio of Ron, Richard, and Clarence, Andy thought he saw a look of approval flit across his expressionless face.

"Behind you!" Nat Turner's voice boomed with urgency. Andy whirled and fired twice at the crouching figure aiming at him from behind the unmade bed. The figure cried out—the voice harsh, tinny, and in pain—then slumped over.

"You just shot a ten-year-old," Nat Turner said as he came out of the engineer's booth. Robert looked out from the booth, his face expressionless. Andy winced.

The video display made a quick whooshing sound as it disappeared. The trainer stood close to Andy and spoke softly. His six fellow trainees sat on a backless wooden bench, watching from behind a glass partition next to the engineer's booth.

"You know, unlike the others, the situation that this simulation is modeled after," Nat Turner said. "A police officer killed a boy in similar circumstances. He had a disadvantage you didn't, namely dim lighting." Using a remote device, the trainer brought the images back. The boy's toy weapon was bright orange.

"The color doesn't necessarily mean the weapon's not real," Nat Turner said. "But the boy and an orange-colored weapon together make it unlikely. The flip side: it's hard to see the boy's face and the split second might have cost you your life."

He placed his gloved hand on Andy's shoulder. "It's the toughest simulation we have and it's a tough call. Almost no one passes it. You can sit down."

Andy felt a queasiness in his stomach as he headed to the door into the booth. His was a simulation. He tried to imagine the horror of it happening for real but he couldn't.

"It's an ugly simulation," Nat Turner said after Andy was seated. "Almost everyone who draws this makes the mistake that Bryon made. It's a visceral way of saying to you that we must not make mistakes. Are there any questions?"

Andy raised his hand. He still felt as if he might throw up. "Robert said that we're killed if that happens with an innocent civilian. Would I be shot if that really happened?" He knew his six comrades were thinking the same thing.

"It would be a close call." Robert's gravelly voice crackled through the intercom from the booth. "We told you that if your own life is in danger, the four

Stars would consider that an exception. The four men who killed Amadou Diallo said they thought their lives were in danger when he reached for his wallet; most black people don't believe them and think Diallo was killed because he was black and therefore already criminalized. I would vote leniency, both because of the precedent of the little boy in California, and because this weapon, albeit a toy, was pointed at you. I cannot speak for the other three Stars."

Andy understood the answer but did not feel comforted.

More than once, as he rested his sore muscles, Andy found himself musing over a conundrum that had baffled him most of his adult years: why more black people didn't actively resist the insanity of their lives. Virtually all of the rebelliousness that existed among young people seemed turned inward against each other, not outward. Even as a proponent of non-violent direct action, Andy always knew that resistance was needed to bring change. Armed resistance had seemed like extreme folly until tragedy struck close to home. *At* home.

His weeks at WiTHWA showed him that resistance was not hopeless, it was hard work. Only concerted action would bring change. Many, if not most, had been duped into thinking the electoral process would bring progress, despite a dearth of evidence. What had Frederick Douglass said: Power concedes nothing without a demand. Nonviolent civil disobedience, armed struggle, or both, as long as there was struggle.

Finally, Andy had concluded, the life and death aspect of engaging in struggle was just too much for most folks, black, white, brown, or anyone else. So many black folks were just trying to survive, trying to find ways to get through the day, the week, the month. Plus, centuries of conditioning had convinced almost everyone that resistance was futile, a phrase he remembered hearing in reruns of an old science fiction television show.

FORTY-THREE

n the case of *State v. Patrick,* murder charges helped, in one instance, to make strange bedfellows. The odd coupling presented itself at one of two news conferences on the first day of jury selection. The media briefings occurred on the front lawn of the august Ionic-columned Antelope County Courthouse. The premature spring day, almost two weeks before the vernal equinox, mingled warmth and sun with the lightest of breezes. The day was so nice that strangers said hello to each other.

The case's racial tension—something the president of the United States said no longer existed—attracted more attention than the administration and other race-neutral policy makers desired. The *Scabbard,* as the news conduit for communiqués from Unit 2236, witnessed something previously unheard of: mainstream media agencies picking up information from a black newspaper. As a result, the nation now knew that twenty-seven African-Americans had been slain in questionable police shootings in thirty-three months. With the pending trial, another statistic became a corollary to the story: coincidentally or otherwise, there had been no questionable shootings since George Bascomb's death and the emergence of Unit 2236.

For somewhat sleepy Antelope County, and Levyville in particular, the trial was a humongous event. To Antelope County residents, Dock Place was almost an abstraction, light years away from their idyllic town of Levyville on this March morning.

The first press conference, the strange bedfellows one, involved the Reverend Doctor R. Aloysius "Al" Scott, III, president of the Alliance of African-American Ministers, Incorporated, and the Covenant of the New Commandment's Minister David Walker.

Al Scott had never liked Walker *pére* or *fils,* and back in the day opposed their membership in the AAAM on grounds that the Covenant for the New Commandment was not a church—they said so themselves, he noted—and therefore not eligible. Privately, he bad-mouthed what he described as "disturbing theology that spoke so little to the death and resurrection of our Lord and Savior,

Jesus Christ." Other clerical voices prevailed, however. The AAAM accepted the Covenant into membership about five years into Black Label's ministry after it became clear to many that his rapidly growing organization would be a force to be reckoned with in the city, whether they liked it or not.

Al Scott's self-image was that of a mover and shaker in city politics who had patiently paid his dues, scrambling through and around AAAM politics into the presidency. He belonged to the Mayor's Council on Diversity (COD); he also was signed on with President Bruder's local Faith Based Initiatives Commission (FBI). It was only to gain access to federal grants, he assured his parishioners, aware of the black community's disdain for Bruderian ideology and politics.

In the past, Scott had characterized the Covenant as impulsive, angry, and not well-grounded in scripture. Shuttling (some said shuffling) between COD and the FBI, Scott constantly met with people that the Ministers Walker criticized for tossing crumbs to black folks if they bothered to toss anything at all. The incessant barbs kept a level of tension between the Walkers and Scott.

When George Bascomb was shot to death, AAAM officials remained mute at first. As the story quickly grew, Scott scuffled (some said shuffled) to get coverage.

"Speaking on behalf of the Alliance of African-American Ministers, Incorporated, I think we should not, in the throes of emotion, rush to judgment. The Alliance, speaking on behalf of 320 churches, asks all African-Americans in this great city to allow the authorities who represent us to conduct a thorough investigation and present all the facts about what happened on Dock Place," he said at the time. "The mayor has assured me that he personally will see that the investigation is exhaustive, that it will be immediate, and that it will be fair. This is truly a tragic situation. The Alliance extends its deepest sympathy to the Bascomb family."

At the time, the Walkers told reporters who called for comments that there was little hope for justice "in a city with a racist mayor who never stands up for black people and a district with different standards of justice: one for cops, another for white citizens, and still another for disenfranchised black people. On top of this unholy trinity sits a racist judicial system that never convicts cops for killing African-American citizens."

The joint news conference was actually the mayor's idea. He suggested to Scott that he, Scott, suggest the idea to the Covenant. The case had polarized the city, the mayor said, which was to be expected. The mayor supported Patrick, albeit covertly. He needed "an Afro-American there to speak to how well the system works; someone to address the traditional values: truth, justice, and the

American Way." He needed someone there looking after the city's interests, whatever they may be.

David surprised Scott by agreeing to the news conference after consulting with his father, who wanted nothing to do with the man he derisively referred to as "Subservient Scotty." They both knew Scott was trying to play them, but you had to be good to play a player, Minister Johnnie said. They wanted Scott, in Minister Johnnie's words, "to come off looking like the Uncle Tom asshole that he is."

The second news conference was solely Isaac Erlickson's show but conducted with full support from the Police Officer's Benevolent Association. No one in attendance at the Levyville trial could remember when the attorney with hair like a politician or television newscaster had last lost a case. Erlickson loved a challenge. He vowed after his last loss that under no circumstances would he lose another case before ambling off this mortal coil.

At WiTHWA, bemusement swept across Andy's face, and the faces of his colleagues, when the Covenant Teacher-Designate and Scott strolled to the microphones together.

Both Minister David and Scott were dressed to the nines. Walker was attired in a brown three-piece three-button Hickey Freeman suit, dark brown shirt and tie, dark brown suede tasseled shoes, and a dark brown wide-brimmed Stetson broke down front and back. Scott was decked out in an Armani double-breasted grey sharkskin suit, black boots, a light blue shirt with white collar, a yellow and blue silk tie, and wide-brimmed grey fedora.

"Think they're gonna do Point Counterpoint?" William/124 asked with his crooked grin.

"Talk about the 'Odd Couple,'" said Richard/127.

"Good morning," Scott boomed into the microphones after reporters settled in and settled down. "I know some of you are from out of town, so I'd like to introduce myself. I'm the Reverend Doctor Robert Aloysius Scott, III, pastor of The Rock of St. Peter Baptist Church. On my right is my colleague, Minister David Walker, leader of the Covenant for the New Commandment."

He enunciated his words carefully, in a self-conscious manner that sounded forced, as if he wanted to erase any ethnic or geographical shading from "each an-duh ev-e-ree word-uh."

"I want to say on behalf of the Alliance of African-American Ministers, Incorporated, that this trial taking place today is an overwhelming victory for an aroused and unified black community," Scott said. "It also vindicates the democratic process and shows that Americans of color can seek redress through judicial channels and achieve success."

Andy smiled as Heshimu Kenyatta jumped in. "Doctor Scott, some voices in the black community are saying Patrick will never be convicted, that white policemen are never convicted when a black person is the victim. Would you comment?"

"I think that kind of talk is premature," Scott said. "I will admit that I was disappointed when the charges were downgraded from second degree murder to manslaughter. But justice must be given a chance. I feel confident that evidence presented at the trial will determine Patrick's guilt or innocence."

"Do you believe Patrick's guilty?" a reporter yelled.

"I believe it would be prejudicial to make that kind of determination," Scott said. "There were eyewitnesses and their testimony will come out at the trial. One more question and then my colleague will have some comments."

Heshimu tried again but someone shouted louder. "Haven't the police tried to discredit witnesses? For instance, the entire Harris family was arrested for disorderly conduct and interfering with an officer. What effect do you think that will have on a jury?"

"I thought those charges were dropped. I'll have to check on that." Scott stood erect and jabbed his finger in the air. "Let me say that, while our judicial system is less than perfect, the Alliance believes that justice and fair play is finally coming to Americans of color as part of the surge we have made toward first- class citizenship. I know we've had setbacks as a people but we must press on. I believe strongly in the anthem of my youth from the Civil Rights Movement, that we shall overcome some day. We're watching this trial carefully, and we feel that Michael Patrick will have his day in court and that the proceedings will be impartial.

"I believe that Minister David Walker wants to make a few remarks." Scott turned to Walker with a smile that showed a lot of teeth. He shook Walker's hand. Flash attachments twinkled like fireflies.

"I'm here today as an observer for the Covenant *of* the New Commandment, and I wish I could be as optimistic as my brother here," Walker said. "I am in fact surprised that a trial is being held at all. I can count on one hand the times that I'm aware of when a white police officer has been tried for killing an unarmed African-American, male or female. I am unaware of any convictions."

"How about Abner Louima's attacker? He's been in jail for a while and I think he was sentenced to twenty or thirty years," a reporter shouted.

Watching on WiTHWA's large television screen, Andy smiled because he knew Minister David's answer.

"That case proves my point," Walker retorted. "The cop who sodomized Louima with the broomstick several years ago went to jail because he embarrassed his police department and all of law enforcement," Walker said. "If he'd shot and killed Louima during the arrest, he might still be on the streets. A shooting like that of George Bascomb is a nuisance, it's bothersome, but it's not an embarrassment. Even though George was defending his community, the court will always take the side of an officer who says he was protecting himself. Let's be clear: Evidence shows that Michael Patrick is a racist who violated the law."

He looked sideways at Scott, who had become increasingly distressed as Walker spoke. Now he looked constipated. "Like I said, I wish I could be as optimistic as my good brother, Al Scott, is, but I'm not. If there's a way to free this racist cop, they'll find it."

Robert placed the set on mute. "If the white lawyer comes on before lunch ends, we'll watch," he said. "If not, we have to get back to work."

The seven members of the August 21st Brigade were wolfing down large bowls of fruit cocktail when Isaac Erlickson, resplendent in a silver gray Armani sharkskin suit, white shirt, wine-colored silk tie and pocket square, and gleaming black loafers, walked to the battery of microphones. He radiated success, money, and an air of intimidation.

"My statement's brief, gentlemen, and I'll answer a few questions," Erlickson said, looking down his nose over a pair of bifocals at pages that were mere props. "My client's getting his day in court, although he shouldn't even have to be here, being tried for what was clearly self defense. A jury of his peers is trying him, and we're going to prove that the very idea of a trial has been a tragic mistake. I hate to say it, but there have actually been two victims in this unfortunate incident. Questions?"

"I've seen the tape. You really think you can beat it?" a reporter in front of Kenyatta shouted.

"Yes, we're going to beat it," Erlickson said. "The pendulum's swung the other way in this country, and thank God for that. People are tired of being afraid to walk the streets. People respect policemen again, which is the way it's supposed to be. And Officer Michael Patrick is a fine policeman, a fine man, one of the best, who will get his job back when this is over, mark my word."

"Follow up," the same reporter said quickly. "Public opinion polls show that a majority think Patrick's guilty of at least manslaughter."

"I don't put much faith in polls," Erlickson said, peering over his bifocals.

"You notice that very little is being said now in the black communities. I believe that outsiders caused all that uproar and rioting when this tragedy occurred. Most fair-minded Afro-Americans know this will be an honest and impartial trial."

"Are you satisfied with the jury?"

Erlickson smiled. "We got the best jury we could get. The people in Antelope County are good people."

Andy realized the reporters were lobbing Erlickson softballs. Kenyatta's voice rose above the din. "Isaac, I talked to someone who was there and saw it all, even before the images on the DVD," he shouted over other reporters trying to speak. "This person said it's indisputable that Patrick didn't have to shoot him. I don't know where you get your information because the people I talk to in the black community are angry about the case."

The crowd on the lawn quieted. Momentarily taken aback, Erlickson recovered quickly. "I don't know if your friend's on the witness list or not," he said. "If not, the district attorney must not put much stock in what he or she says they saw. If they are, I'll hear their story when this person gets to testify." He waved and turned in the same motion. "See you all in court. Thank you."

Robert clicked the remote and the screen went dark. "Okay, you've had your entertainment for the day. Let's get back to work."

FORTY-FOUR

Ergency filled three knocks on Andy's door. He sat up, struggling to shake sleep and weariness away, then stumbled to the door in his bare feet. Robert sat in the hall, a pistol pointed at him.

"Always ask who's at your door," the First Star said. "Yes, this is a secure facility, but always ask, with your weapon at the ready. Especially in the middle of the night like this." He holstered his pistol and whirred into the room without asking permission. A small black suitcase sat in his lap.

"We have a situation," Robert said. "Sit."

A "situation?" The residue of sleep disappeared quickly from Andy's mind. Although he felt considerably stronger than he had a month ago, fatigue was a constant companion. He sat.

"A small-town police official—he's a lieutenant—near here has just learned we're here and that our activities are, shall we say, questionable and clandestine," Robert said. "Never mind how we know. We *know*. For security reasons, I can't name the location, or you might realize where this camp is located. We're trying to find out how it happened. Fortunately, we don't think he knows we're Unit 2236. Thus, he doesn't know our *raison d'être*. When we called him, we hinted that we might start taking out narcotics dealers. We think he believes us. But as noble as that may be, it's still illegal. If he knew what we really do, I'm not sure we could have offered him an arrangement. At least he thinks it's an arrangement.

"When we told him we knew that he knew, we offered him a mid-five figure sum to keep quiet. He's accepted. But if it doesn't go down in the next three hours, he might turn on us."

As Andy listened, uneasiness crept into his stomach. Robert snapped the clasps on the suitcase, opened it. Andy had never seen so much money in one place in his life. Neat stacks of one hundred dollar bills sat stuffed side by side in the small suitcase.

"We don't have any other choice that we see at present," Robert said, closing the suitcase. "We're sending you to deliver the money. Instead, you'll

273

shoot him."

Andy's mind became absolutely still as he got inside what had just been said. Ready or not, it's here, he said to himself. Here now.

Robert would drive and be Andy's backup in case something went wrong. Andy would wear a blindfold until they were almost at the drop point. The weapon would have a silencer. The police official would be sitting in a car, alone. Robert would drive up, signal with his lights, Andy would get out, go to the car on the passenger side, open the door, and place the suitcase on the seat. When the cop reached for it, Andy would kill him.

"Any questions?" Robert asked.

"No, sir," Andy said.

Robert smiled his mirthless smile, a clue that Andy missed.

Andy's emotions tumbled and jarred each other as the First Star drove him toward a milestone in his life that had jarringly moved up in time. He was going to kill another human being. Unlike before, he now sat next to Robert. This time he felt grateful for the mask covering his eyes.

Get out. Briefcase in left hand . . . pistol in waistband . . . open passenger door with right hand, place the suitcase on the seat . . . take out the pistol . . . .

Despite the night chill, he was sweating.

"Take the mask off."

They were on a deserted pier. Several boats stood quietly like oversized sleeping sea mammals. Twenty-five yards away, a dark automobile sat, headlights off, facing the water. Robert slowed the limousine almost to a crawl. Andy pulled his gloves on. Robert handed him the pistol. Andy unzipped his black windbreaker and stuck the weapon in his waistband.

"The safety is already off. Just aim and fire."

The limousine headlights flashed, dimmed, flashed again, and then remained on dimmers. The limo stopped.

Briefcase in left hand. . . . open the door with your right hand . . . .

"You've done well in training. One shot should do it. Two if you must."

Andy took a deep breath and closed the limousine door. So this is how much fifty thousand dollars weighs, he thought.

The car was a late model Pontiac Grand Am. Andy slowed as he approached the vehicle and then stopped. There were two people inside! Robert said he would be alone.

If your own life is in danger . . . we consider it an exception . . . If your life is not in danger . . . abandon a mission rather than kill an innocent person . . . security personnel . . . are not innocent persons, they are regarded as soldiers on the field of battle . . . .

The driver's door and passenger door opened simultaneously. It all seemed to happen in slow motion. There was no thought, only reflex. Andy reached for his pistol, aimed and fired as the man came out of the car on the passenger side, gun in hand. The man fired a second after he did. Andy fired again at the man sighting on him over the car. Andy heard a plopping noise, felt a plop, and saw a white plop.

Glenn Greene removed a riot helmet and looked at him, impassive, white paint splattered on his chest. He looked down at his own paint-splattered windbreaker. The driver, also wearing a riot helmet, had two paint blobs on the helmet's shield. He walked around the Pontiac and removed the helmet.

"My man, Any," Romeo said, smiling at his friend. "Except that you'd be dead, you did a good job. Get in."

FORTY-FIVE

ndy listened to his oldest friend as a welter of feeling surged through him. He was pissed; he understood. He was relieved; he was afraid of this new knowledge of himself. He was glad and sorry that he had passed, sort of. There was more twisting around inside him, he knew, even if he didn't know what.

And, as Rome told him, "Except that you'd be dead, you did a good job." As promised, Robert had his back and "shot" Romeo, too. Of course, with the foreknowledge that it was a crucial training exercise. He hadn't known Glenn was in Unit 2236, but he wasn't surprised.

"You didn't ask Robert any questions and you should have," Romeo said. "There are no bad questions. With what you've learned over the past few months, I'd think you'd wonder about a man coming to pick up fifty thou without any backup. Would *you* go alone? I don't think so. If you had asked, Robert would have said kill them both, under the edict the security for a target is fair game. I suspect your confusion made you hesitate."

"Yeah, it did."

"The order was absolute; *everyone* must be tested," Romeo said. "We feel certain that anyone working with a law enforcement agency won't kill a police officer. We also need to know the chances of someone freezing, which could be fatal for them and us."

"Why you?"

"Why not? First of all, you're my main man. I wanted to see you, see what you think. I want to find out how the training's going from your viewpoint. We have an evaluation of you. And I have some information for you."

"Oh?" Andy thought he saw something flicker in Romeo's eyes with the last comment. "What kind of information?"

"We'll get to it. What's your assessment so far?"

Andy was silent. Wherever the hell they were, a person could see the magnificence of a breathtaking starry sky on a cloudless night. He couldn't remember when he saw this many stars in the city. Finally, he spoke.

"I imagine this is what the army is like, except we live in better surroundings," he said. "I don't have anything to measure him against, but Robert's an impressive man. How'd he get in a chair?"

"He did two tours in 'Nam. Took a bullet in his back during the second tour."

Romeo listened as Andy talked about the six people on his team. They forged camaraderie out of necessity, Andy said. Each had faltered at some point in the training, and the others had picked up the slack for their comrade.

"Good," Romeo said with a smile. "How's your writing coming?"

"I'm almost finished researching some police shootings. Man, it's painful to see such a disregard for black life. Although, you know, when I was looking into one of the cases, I saw how much our youngsters have increased their killing of each other."

Romeo nodded. "Yeah, Swords are out there every day trying to reach some of the young brothers, especially brothers in the streets. But we're all taught the same thing, Any—that black life is not valuable in this country. Mix in a little self-hate, and you've got young gangsters acting out their socially directed roles as poorly educated fodder for prison, blowing each other away whenever they feel like it."

Behind them, Robert flashed his lights quickly.

"You said you had something to tell me." Somehow he knew it was about Claudia, and somehow it felt like it would be good. Still, fear knotted behind his navel.

"It's not really information, but it's something from the heart." He paused. "I told you the general staff was aware of your . . . situation with Claudia. Unit 2236 is life or death and has little room for deviation. As your best friend in the world, I'm telling you her note to you was the real deal. If you had any ambivalence, don't." He looked at his friend, searching for a reaction.

"You knew about the note?"

"Man, I wish I had more to tell you."

Andy stared at the stars, thinking about the first day he saw Claudia. The first moment he sensed some interest on her part. The first time they'd held each other. He thought about how well they knew each other, how little they knew each other. He thought about the ache inside that was a constant companion. He hadn't felt like this since his marriage had crashed and burned, even with Debora. He thought about how he had to stay focused, how he had to push through this.

In fact, he thought about every possibility except a rather obvious one.

Robert flashed his lights again. He and Glenn nodded to each other, smiled acknowledgment of their comradeship, but said nothing as they switched vehicles.

FORTY-SIX

onths earlier, a stroke of luck had provided the Star command with information about Stan East, a realtor and decorated military hero. Because a Compton street dealer/supervisor named Rahsaan was a good listener and had a good memory, he heard more than he was supposed to hear one night. Rahsaan made a mental note of the information, hoping that it might help him make some money down the road.

As it happened, a member of Unit 2236's first class had just received permission days earlier to "talk" with Rahsaan after several nights of surveillance as he peddled his wares.

Rahsaan smiled as he walked up Long Beach Boulevard to his parked black Infiniti. It had been a good night and he had more than fifteen hundred in his pocket to prove it. His team was netting more than five thousand a week since he had locked down control of Sweetness in Compton.

A nondescript Hyundai slowed down next to his Infiniti just as he reached for his car keys. "Whassup, Rahsaan?" a voice said.

"Do I know you?" Rahsaan said as he turned. He frowned as he saw the two men wearing black ski masks. A pistol with a silencer was leveled at him. "What the fuck?" he said. The silencer, more than the gun, told him something serious was going down.

"Get in," the man in the passenger seat said. "Keep your hands visible. We know you're carrying." The driver kept his gun trained on Rahsaan while his passenger got out, looked around, and then quickly disarmed and frisked him.

After placing Rahsaan in the back seat, the man joined him. They drove to a desolate area and parked behind an empty warehouse. Rahsaan didn't know who they were, but somebody was going to pay for this shit. He did as instructed, seething the entire time. They ordered him out of the car.

"Y'all ain't jacking me up for my cash," Rahsaan said. "You could have taken that back there. I hope you know who you're fucking with."

"That's what we want to know, Rahsaan." The man who had sat in the passenger seat did all the talking. "We're from Unit 2236. And we want whoever we're fucking with to know that drugs can no longer be sold in Compton."

Rahsaan snorted, bravado in his voice. "Y'all must be fucking crazy. I don't know what this 2236 shit is about, but I can tell you that drugs ain't leaving Compton."

The ski-masked spokesman was about Rahsaan's size. He handed his pistol to his colleague, who trained both guns on the drug dealer. "This is how it's going to work, Rahsaan," he said. "Give us the name of your supplier and you can leave. Lie, and we'll come back, which you really don't want. Refuse, and we will break one of your fingers at a time until you comply. If you have a high tolerance for pain, we will then start on your toes. We have lots of time."

"Why don't y'all just take my money and be done with it?" Rahsaan knew he could rumble with the best, but these ninja-like niggers felt scary.

"We don't want your money, we want a name."

Rahsaan's face remained sullen. He couldn't give Skinny up; they went way back. His partner had been breaking him off a piece of action for too long. Plus, Skinny was more ruthless than he was. He tried to resist and found himself bent over the hood of the Hyundai in an excruciatingly painful arm lock. The driver forced his mouth open and stuffed it with a large cloth.

The forefinger of his left hand made a surprisingly loud cracking sound. Even in his pain, he knew there was no way he could explain to Skinny, because Skinny would have to explain to his supplier, who would have to tell that guy he was talking about that day. He screamed so loud into the cloth he didn't hear the cracking of his middle finger.

When he could think again, he was frantic. He had been in the living room. Skinny had left the bedroom door open. "Look, I can do a better deal with Stan East, the real estate dude, okay?" his supplier told somebody. "I don't give a damn if you do know, nigga, you don't want to mess with East, that's far worse than getting in my face . . . Yeah, whatever . . ." He didn't know who East was, but it was the only way to save his man, Skinny.

When they grabbed the ring finger of his throbbing hand, he made frantic noises and tried to show willingness in his wide, frightened eyes.

"I got a big name for you," he blubbered, spit running from his mouth. "Much bigger than my contact. I got two names for you, just, please, no more."

The ski-masked men looked at each other and nodded. "If the names are good, you won't hear from us again," the spokesman said.

He told them what he had heard about Stan East and his profession. He also told them who supplied Skinny. The hooded men used a portable scanner to copy his driver's license, then drove him back within a half mile of his car.

Rahsaan called Skinny and told him what he had done to keep from giving up his name.

"Skinny, man, I don't know who they are, but I had to do something!" he said, his voice hoarse with pain. Skinny listened intently, trying to absorb this information and connect it with other information.

Skinny knew who Unit 2236 was, or at least had heard about them. They had killed that cop named Hubble. Had to be some bad motherfuckers. Plus, they knew where he bought his shit, and where *he* bought his. He definitely didn't want that connected to him in anyway. Plus, him and Rahsaan did go way back.

Skinny said he knew a nurse who could set Rahsaan's fingers and give him something for the pain. Maybe it was a good time to vacation indefinitely with a relative he had down near Raleigh.

Six women—and the First Star—knew her as 111. She also had a code name. Of course, the First Star knew her real name.

Stan Oliver East, a former career military officer and now a successful multimillionaire real estate tycoon, knew her as Callie House, a foxy player who said she was a Detroit native, had been living in Belize for five years and gotten bored. She had just moved to the Los Angeles area. He had never sampled dark meat before; she gave the impression they might be able to play after they did some business. Money, honey, first; then, she might give up some honey, honey.

Six men—and the First Star—knew him as 102, and also by a code name. Of course, the First Star knew his real name. After transferring from the Los Angeles Covenant meetinghouse to Memphis with his wife and advancing rather quickly into leadership, 102 had staged a very public falling out with the religious group after what came to be called "the Memphis mess."

Stan East knew him as Isaiah "Ike" Dickerson, a dude studying accounting and business at Los Angeles Community College and trying to both help Cousin Callie out and make a little "somethin'-somethin'" on the side.

Four weeks of surveillance on East and the man who supplied Rahsaan's supervisor gave the 12/4 Brigade what they needed. Shortly after that, "Callie House" started looking to purchase "something nice in Malibu, or even further north." When she first met East, she remained mysterious about how she made her money as she looked at properties.

She started hinting that she was a player who had no time for chump change and only did serious money deals when she found discreet people. When they started negotiating, East steered her to the man who supplied Rahsaan's supervisor. Even though he'd found the deal, it was worth breaking off a twenty thou commission to a top lieutenant to keep his hands off the product.

Before Callie could arrange a meeting, the supplier, a would-be music producer of three gangsta hip-hop acts, was found with piano wire around his neck that permanently affected his breathing. Police were investigating, but not very hard, and there were no clues. At that point, Callie insisted that if a deal was going down, she would only deal with East. By now she noticed that his eyes always swept over her voluptuousness before he looked her in the eye. If they could close the deal, she said, they should be able to "get to know each other better." But she didn't like to play before she got paid.

Now, they lunched at a chic hotel on Sunset near La Cienega, eager to finalize this deal for $750,000 worth of undiluted Sweetness. East stood to clear about $300,000 for about two hours work because he knew where to buy, got a good price, and was trusted.

The real estate executive had been captivated with the buxom black woman across the table from him from the first time she walked into his Brentwood office. In his fifties, with expensively coiffed gray hair and a salon tan, East prided himself on being at the same weight and having only a slightly softer body than he had thirty years earlier on active duty. Married with three teen children, he saw himself as irresistible to any woman he decided he wanted.

"Callie, what an unusual name," East said when he first met her.

"My grandmother named me," the woman replied, flashing a brilliant smile. "It's short for Caledonia. She told me a popular song in her day was named for a woman named Caledonia." She knew he'd prefer that kind of story instead of being told about the real Callie House, the mother of the black reparations movement.

She and Dickerson indicated they were cousins and business partners. East understood that Dickerson was also an unofficial bodyguard if she wanted him to be. She had panache. Her clothes always combined elegance with the slightest touch of eroticism. Like now. Her black silk button-front dress provided a mere hint of décolletage. With breasts as full as hers, she knew that was enough. He had all the women he wanted, whenever he wanted; he had never had a black woman, or even wanted one, before now . . .

"You understand that my involvement in this kind of work usually consists of simply moving money around for my clients," East said. "I've preferred not to get involved directly with product."

"Stan, baby, we've gone over that," Callie smiled. "Let's get this done so we can move on to . . . other things." The suggestiveness in her tone was unmistakable.

East looked around. The four of them sat by a window. The fourth person was clearly East's backup. He was squat, with a thick neck and a quiet manner. He said nothing the entire time the four of them were together. They were having an early lunch; the room was nearly deserted. A key and a business card seemed to materialize in East's hand.

"The bank is on La Cienega," he said as he handed the key to Dickerson. There was something about this self-assured spade he didn't like. "This is the address; the briefcase combination is on the other side. I called. They're expecting you."

The man he knew as Dickerson stroked his chin and took the key. "I'll call when I have it," he said.

"Now may I see the money?"

The woman sat with her back to the room. She picked up the leather briefcase beside her on the floor, placed it on her lap, and opened it. East smiled at the sea of green as she riffled several piles at random that showed it was all money. "Un-sequenced centuries, as you requested, darling." She closed the briefcase.

"So we'll have another drink and wait for our call from Isaiah." She held up the drink before her. "Shall we toast to a profitable day for everyone?"

They clinked glasses. East's partner held his glass of Pellegrino up and sipped.

"Ike Dickerson" called forty minutes later. She knew East was getting restless. Whether it was to get this deal closed, or to jump on top of her, or both, she didn't know. Now she smiled a smile of promise.

"Shall we?"

"Let's."

She extended the briefcase toward him. "This is yours now," she said and immediately cursed herself. Now she had to keep him interested in getting some pussy. If he changed his mind for any reason, they would have to think fast.

East took the briefcase, left a one hundred dollar bill on the table. Together they walked to the elevator. She saw him look at his watch. As he started to speak, she leaned against him, letting him feel her fullness and inhale her perfume.

"I hope you're not in a hurry," she purred.

"Oh, it's going to be like that, huh?" He leaned over and kissed her full mouth.

She licked her lips. "It's definitely going to be like that."

East unlocked the room and entered it. The quiet one took up a position outside. He heard Callie close the door behind them. Then she said a curious thing.

2236

"Unit 2236."

East frowned and turned to face her. "What?"

"Dealers die," she said. There was a muffled whoosh; the shot hit him smack between the eyebrows. She quickly posted by the door, pistol ready.

"Mister East? You okay?" his aide said through the door. He came in reaching for his piece and saw "Callie" too late with his peripheral vision just before her shot tore into his throat.

She checked their pulses, then disassembled the pistol and removed the silencer. She called Jay.

"We've closed the deal," 111 said. "Do you have the product?"

"I do. I'm on my way up. I waited to call you until I was almost back."

They sprinkled about a kilo of Sweetness on East, then left the rest on the floor next to the bodies with their signature notice on an eight-by-eleven card on East's chest: DEALERS DIE. UNIT 2236. The card also claimed responsibility for the respiratory problems of East's late lieutenant.

He took the barrel and trigger housing/handle; she took the slide, spring, rod and spent shells. That evening he drove to Ventura, had dinner, and quietly walked to the beach, where he dropped the parts into the water. She dropped her components into a pre-designated trashcan that was emptied moments later by 106, who took them to a junkyard where they could be incinerated.

The man, 102, called the police; the woman, 111, called the *Los Angeles Sentinel* and the *Los Angeles Times* and told them what they would find at the chic hotel on Sunset near La Cienega.

Two hours later, she sighed as she drove the rented silver Lexus into traffic on Fairfax Avenue. She headed north and took the eastbound ramp onto the Santa Monica Freeway. She didn't look forward to the three- or four-day drive home. But taking $750,000 through airport security was a major no-no. When the Fourth Star had loaned the money for the operation, orders to the Third Star were explicit: you hand it to the operative, and it never leaves her sight until she returns it to you. She sighed again as tension drained from her shoulders. It would be so good to be home.

She missed him.

FORTY-SEVEN

They were leaving.

An odd closeness had grown between them. The relationships were different from any Andy had known. Relationships, such as they were, where each man had virtually no information about the lives of the other six. But no one now sitting in WiTHWA's "corporate boardroom" doubted that anyone else in the room would come to the other's defense with his own life if it became necessary.

The figurative girding of their loins for the days ahead began and ended with Robert, the First Star, and his aide-de-camp, "Nat Turner." Looking back, Andy saw that Robert's taciturnity and relentless, unforgiving quest for excellence forced a cohesion they were now grateful for. For his part, Nat Turner was as good an assistant as any man or woman could want.

"Although I honor the precept in John 15:13, that the greatest love is in laying down our lives for our friends, I cannot always be your friend," Robert told them more than once. "I will not hesitate to kill you if I have to, although, as Yahshua asks, I won't hesitate to give my life to protect you if I have to. You must accept this duality about me in what has transpired here."

The seven presented him with a mock red ball they had secretly made, autographed with the code names used in camp. It was larger than the ones they got zapped with and had no bounce. Since the names were fictitious, they saw no harm.

In spite of himself, Robert allowed about ten degrees of mirth to invade his smile when they presented the gift to him.

"'Thanks for being a tough motherfucker,'" he said, reading the inscription on the ball. He looked up. "We may be the only religious organization on the planet using that kind of language in praise of our mission," he snorted as they laughed. "Even if it is the last day, don't think I won't ball zap you just because you gave me this."

"That's probably as close as he can come to telling us he loves us," Melvin whispered. "Ow!"

Compared to other zappings, they all knew Robert had practically lobbed the ball. "I warned you," he said. "I won't ask what you said; it might embarrass me."

Andy/Bryon and Melvin had become close, as had John and Richard. Andy sensed that a familiarity between Melvin and Bill meant they knew each other before coming to WiTHWA. (In fact, both came from the Cleveland meetinghouse.)

"Some last minute housekeeping, and then I'm going to play a message from the Third Star," Robert said. "Afterward, you will depart at different times in one group of three and one of four, wearing blindfolds as you did when you arrived.

"You will have no contact with each other. If, by chance, regular Covenant business brings you in contact, you should act as if you're meeting for the first time, as we've said before. Minimize contact so that others don't inadvertently reveal your identities. It's best for all concerned that you remain unknown to each other.

"You need to know that the November 11th Brigade is comprised of women because some of you may draw assignments to work with one of them.

"Sisters are an integral part of Unit 2236 because we've learned from studying other liberation struggles that they can draw less suspicion and sometimes go where men can't as this thing intensifies. Also, both the Third and Fourth Stars were adamant about women warriors being a part of this.

"You will follow orders absolutely. But, as some of you found out in training, you must ask questions. Of course, on real missions we won't withhold crucial information as we did in training."

Robert picked up a DVD from the desk. "The Third Star wishes to salute and address you." He placed the disk in the player. The entire address was as a talking head. Minister Johnnie spoke to them as if they were all sitting on his porch.

"My brother warriors, although using words is a way of life for me, my vocation, I do not have adequate ones to thank you for what you have done, and will do.

"We have said what the Great Teacher said in Matthew 10:34 many times in defense of the right to defend ourselves. We move now to a time of action. 'Do not think that I come to bring peace. I do not come to bring peace but a sword.'

"We are tiny by choice. A mentor of mine in the Sixties once said that a dozen or so brothers who kept their mouths shut and were committed to their people could let our government know they cannot kill us with impunity. At the time Martin, Malcolm, Medgar, and others less known like Jimmie Lee Jackson and James Chaney, were being murdered. Some of our white brethren, like Viola

Liuzzo, Mickey Schwerner and Andy Goodman were being cut down, too. My mentor said that when one of ours fell, a couple brothers should have quietly boarded a plane, gone to where it happened, without fanfare, and executed the people who did it when we could. This was at a time when virtually no white person, cop or otherwise, especially in the South, was convicted or even tried for killing us. If they got one of our leaders, she said, we should get one of their leaders. I guess Unit 2236 was born then, almost a half century ago, talking with that particular mentor.

"I have never believed that Yahweh is on one side or the other when we human beings battle each other. It's like asking which side was he on, Cain's or Abel's, which is how long the madness has been going on. But I'm just as certain the god I have given my life to serve does not want my people to be forever bearing the brunt of injustice.

"The Fourth Star has paid for immaculate false identities for each member of Unit 2236: a driver's license, a passport, two credit cards, and a safe deposit box with $10,000 in it. After a mission, the safe deposit balance will always be returned to $10,000.

"One last point. We have informants and agent provocateurs in our midst." The Teacher's eyes narrowed. "We've probably had them for most of the Covenant's existence. Because of the government's frustrations, we expect them to try and disrupt the Covenant, whether they can connect Unit 2236 to the Covenant or not. Memphis was an example. We want to keep the Covenant aboveground, teaching those who want it, for as long as we can. But as the Roman Empire went after the early Christians and drove them underground, we, too, must expect them to come after us." The corners of his mouth turned up, but it wasn't exactly a smile. "We're quietly ordering all Covenant members to arm themselves if they haven't already, in order to protect their homes and their loved ones.

"We must be mindful of what the Great Teacher warned us of as we move into this phase of our lives. Near the end of the twelfth chapter of Luke, he warns his followers in this way: 'I have come to set fire to the earth,' he tells them, 'and how I wish it were already kindled!' He speaks of being under restraint until he undergoes his baptism, which I have always taken to be his crucifixion.

"Then he asks his disciples, 'Do you suppose I came to establish peace on the earth? No indeed, I have come to bring dissension. . . a family of five will be divided, three against two, and two against three; father against son, and son against father, mother against daughter and daughter against mother, mother-in-law against daughter-in-law and daughter-in-law against mother-in-law.'"

"I would add to this black man against nigger and nigger against black man. Michael Patrick's words have burned into me since I saw the taping of the murder he committed. 'I want to kill a nigger so goddamned bad I can taste it,' he said. But instead, he killed a black man."

Andy welled up at the Teacher's compliment to his brother. During his toughest days at WiTHWA, remembering George always renewed him.

"Nigger's never been a pretty word. Still, as a people we've always used it, but differently from those who hate us when they use it. The media, the purveyors and controllers of information, especially since the rise of OneCorporation International, have elevated or lowered it, depending on your point of view, to a profanity: the 'N' word, they say, or an N followed by five dashes. I've never believed they do it for the ugliness in the word. They do it because the entire history of this nation is contained in that word. The pioneers and founders stole the land from indigenous people they saw as niggers and then stole people to build the land, people who they then named niggers.

"When I was young, I saw a cartoon of a strong, black brother. And you know the kind of suits that sports team mascots zip themselves into? Well, this strong brother was unzipping a suit like that he had been wearing. The face on the suit represented a buffoonish type of black man. A dumb, clownish, trifling nigger, if you will.

"So, as we used to say, I've flipped the script. The Four Stars are figuratively killing niggers too, and out of those 'deaths' we're resurrecting black men. All of you were black men and women before you ever started training, but you know what I mean.

"In the literal sense, we will have to kill some niggers: informants and agent provocateurs. Drug dealers. And black government officials who carry out anti-black policies, to name a few. Instruments of harm directed at our people don't just come wearing law enforcement uniforms.

"When the word is given, Unit 2236 will be the instrument of justice to deal with anyone working for the government as an informant or agent provocateur. Two people are already under suspicion who may be extremely dangerous to us. The word will be given soon.

"You are already hunted men and women. We will train cadres as fast as we find good people. If our people support what we do, they will help us survive. If they don't, we may not survive the year. Most of us probably won't live to see the victory. But remember, we win by not losing. As long as we keep fighting, no one knows how the fight will turn out. My prayers and all of my love go with you." The screen went dark.

Robert removed the DVD, placed it in a metal trash can, set it afire, and then doused the flaming disk with a quart of water.

Two people are already under suspicion who may be extremely dangerous to us. Andy, and his six colleagues, knew the Covenant was probably infested with informants by now. They had always been under surveillance; the Unit 2236 actions had almost certainly intensified that scrutiny. But Minister Johnnie had referred to two people "extremely dangerous to us." Andy felt certain that one of them was Ward Keyes, who was rather high in the security apparatus. Keyes had something to do with the mess in Memphis, he was sure of that.

His faith in Claudia's note, and his friend's reaffirmation of that note, had beaten back irrational connections his mind tried to make between her disappearance and the Teacher's suspicions.

He couldn't imagine who the other person was.

FORTY-EIGHT

ke Erlickson got the kind of jury he knew he could get in Levyville, the kind he needed to prevail in *State v. Patrick*.

Levyville materialized in Antelope County during the boom years following World War II. U.S.-led Allied Forces had just made the world safe for what they called democracy three years before Levyville broke ground. Young men who fought and survived the war came home to create families and find decent places to live. Fortified by the GI Bill, they had money to spend, and were ready to work hard as the country transitioned from war to peace (or at least took a deep breath before sending troops wading onto the Korean peninsula).

All returning veterans were not welcome in Levyville, though. Some soldiers couldn't buy the new suburban tracts going up regardless of how much cash the GI Bill gave them. Where development occurred, the federal government drew red lines on maps to clarify the exclusion of Negroes in places like Levyville.

Now, Negro veterans needed homes, too, and the government knew that. Policymakers reasoned that properties would open up in urban areas as families living there moved into spanking new real estate like Levyville.

At Levyville's week-long sixtieth anniversary celebration two years before Mike Patrick's trial, the town's progress in diversity was noted. By then, one point seven percent of the population in this suburban prototype was African-American, another one percent was Latino, and about six percent were Asian-American. For the most part, newcomers of all hues saw the bright side. "Levyville: the Town That Thinks Like A City" had come a long way. Some unpleasantness existed in the country's history. Everyone knew that.

But times had changed.

Veteran courtroom observers in the area talked about the *State v. Patrick* trial for years afterward. Many were simply awed at watching the legendary Ike Erlickson in action. Others spoke in hushed tones of the strategy the diminutive legal giant unfolded as he defended his client in the Bruderian climate of Levyville.

Economically, it was a booming times for the area; Levyville was fast gaining a reputation as the "Simi Valley of the East." The computer industry readied a third generation of HoloScreens for consumers in the cookie cutter technology parks surrounding the big town that thought of itself as a little city.

Despite years in the Covenant and being fresh out of Unit 2236 boot camp, a residue of lifelong conditioning still insisted somewhere in Andy's psyche that the courtroom was a neutral place where justice was doled out evenly and without favor.

As he waited in line outside the courtroom to be scanned and x-rayed, Andy remembered research he'd done for a story on death row inmate Malik Al-Amin. Al-Amin, a harsh critic of the system for half his young life at the time of his conviction, admitted in an interview that he went into his trial believing fair play and truth would acquit him. To his surprise, he learned the prosecution was not in search of justice, as he'd been taught; they wanted to *win*, and pulled out all stops to do so.

Andy remembered Al-Amin's words: "Our young minds are fed the information and we absorb it and internalize it: A judge is not political; he's impartial. A person is innocent until proven guilty. And so on."

He now felt irrational feeling that people would be reasonable enough to see and hear the evidence of what had happened to his brother that horrible night. If they didn't see the evidence, he, or one of his comrades would be duty bound to create an equally horrible night for relatives and friends of Michael Patrick, or die trying.

City officials had selected the largest courtroom in the building. It had two jury boxes, one on each side of the bench. Print reporters like Andy sat in the box to the judge's left. Heshimu Kenyatta was the only other black reporter in the box, Andy noted.

It had taken a week to select a jury. The jury foreman was a retired insurance executive; three others were also retired: an electrical engineer, a truck driver, and a Southern Baptist minister. Two forty-something housewives were picked. A linguistics associate professor from Levyville Community College, and a first-year male elementary school teacher were picked. A tobacco company district sales manager (the only African-American on the jury), an administrator for a public relations firm, a computer programmer, and a legal secretary rounded out Michael Patrick's peers. All but the retired minister and the tobacco company executive belonged to families that had been in Levyville since its founding.

When they filed in, Andy looked at their faces. He sensed that they saw themselves as "typical," whatever typical meant. And they were right. He looked at them as ordinary people. Now they were going to decide if a man—definitely one of their peers—had shot his brother to death with malice and intent. Would they—could they—see George as one of their peers, too? When they heard the facts, would they look inside themselves and see that George Bascomb had the same aspirations they had, lived an urban life much like their suburban life, and died because a man employed as an enforcer of the law became irrational and a law unto himself? Or would they say Michael Patrick had a legal right to shoot his brother? A "right" codified into law for him a century and a half earlier when the courts ruled that no black man, free or slave, *nor any of his descendants*, had any rights a white man was bound to respect. Andy remembered how startled he'd been at what the Teacher had said when lecturing on the Dred Scott Decision:

"Unlike *Plessy v. Ferguson,* the so-called "separate but equal" edict, which was judicially reversed by *Brown v. Board of Education,*" the Teacher said, "the 1857 ruling of Chief Justice Taney in the Dred Scott Decision has never been judicially overturned; it's still the law of the land."

FORTY-NINE

You look tired, Rome."

"I am, Any. I am."

It was their first time together since the night on the pier near WiTHWA. They stood on the courthouse steps apart from the lunchtime clumps of officials, administrators, media, law enforcement, observers, and the curious. State police ringed the courthouse, brought in at the request of the Levyville Police Department. Andy saw at least two uniformed rooftop snipers. He had the distinct impression they didn't want to be inconspicuous. They wanted to be seen.

"I'm putting in full days at the *Scabbard*, and then after that my work day starts," Romeo said with a tight smile. He looked around. "I thought you said Keyes was here."

"He was. He took a call, or made one, while I was talking to you, and left suddenly."

"Well, we don't think he knows that we know."

"It's gotten bad, hasn't it?" Andy asked. Romeo's answer was worse than he expected.

Romeo exhaled his tension. "Things are moving out of control. The Covenant, as we know it, may have to disband. Minister Johnnie thinks they're going to move to kill him. He thinks something's coming to justify a national crackdown on the Covenant. We're pretty sure Unit 2236 is still informant free; the Covenant isn't, and we don't know who all of them are." He looked around. "Let's walk."

Andy looked at the cloudless sky, marveling at its immensity, feeling the insignificance of man's daily struggles, including his own. They had to fight; when did it end? Everyone, everywhere, was fighting. When did it end?

"We've come such a long way in a short time, Rome," he said as they turned onto a shady tree-lined street with several faux rustic shops. "Since George was murdered, time seems to have accelerated."

Romeo looked wistful. "It didn't start with George. Or Sonny. It's not our police department, or the one in L.A. It's a way of life, Andy, that says you and

I don't matter much. Things are moving faster because you're involved. They've been moving fast for me for years.

"I don't have much time, man. But Minister Johnnie wants you at his house as soon as the trial recesses today. There's something we have to find out and we don't know any other way. And I'm warning you now: what you hear will sound very weird. Go with it, okay? All this may change very suddenly for all of us."

Johnson/Congo Square was nearly empty. A few revelers decked out in jaunty shamrock green derbies praised the Emerald Isle in song as they passed through.

Andy had never heard their particular St. Patrick's Day ditty before. He, Minister Johnnie and Minister David sat where he and Romeo had five months earlier. This square holds a lot of secrets, he mused.

Minister Johnnie, his puzzled son, and Andy had said little during the walk to the park. Minister David talked much more now with his father and, ironically, wished he didn't. His FBI handler had been back three weeks and was getting impatient. His father had also become impatient with him. How could he lead Unit 2236 without going through the training, his father had asked.

David was trying not to know more. He didn't want to betray his father's work, and he didn't want the pictures destroying his life. What was it his father liked to say? "If push comes to shove, then I'll . . ." Then he'd say whatever action he'd decided to take. Well, push was coming to shove for him and he felt his life twisting into a knot he couldn't undo. And what was Andy doing here?

David had risked not telling John Edgar anything since returning from rehab. He certainly couldn't say, "If something happens to my father, I'll be the new head of Unit 2236." Now he had a week to give him something or invent something that could damage the Covenant. If he refused, the Covenant's moral underpinning would be severely damaged by pictures of the number two official screwing an expensive bimbo in Las Vegas. It felt like a lose-lose situation.

Glenn Greene's Ford Taurus, with three of his top Swords, sat at the curb about fifteen yards away.

"We may have a serious problem with Romeo," Johnnie Walker said. They stood by the empty fountain where Andy and Romeo had talked. Minister Johnnie propped one large foot up on the fountain's concrete lip and leaned his forearms on his thigh. Except for an occasional jogger, and the watchful eyes of the Swords, they were alone. "A very serious problem. All the work we've done all these years could go up in smoke if he's not stopped. And the craziness is, he thinks he's doing something good."

What you hear will sound very weird. Indeed, Andy thought.

"I would confront him, but I'm only seventy percent sure of my intelligence. It's about Unit 2236. If I confront him prematurely, it could jeopardize my source's life. If my source is wrong, it's best it be done this way. I can then deal with the source personally, and not jeopardize my relationship with Romeo."

David nodded, almost not wanting to know what his father was going to tell him. If he didn't know anything, he didn't have to tell them anything. His dinner felt queasy in his stomach. He looked at Andy with unspoken questions in his eyes.

"That's how serious this mess is," Minister Johnnie said. "If Romeo has to be disciplined, Andy will replace him, just as you will replace me if something happened. We've all sworn loyalty to something bigger than any of us as individuals.

"I've learned that, for some reason, he's planning an operation he hasn't cleared with me. I don't know if he's an agent and wants to discredit us or not. I really don't think so, but you never know." He looked David directly in his eyes. "I've placed more trust in him than I have in you, and I apologize, because it's looking like I'm wrong.

"I have reason to believe that Romeo has a cache of weapons stored at his home and has something going down in the next ninety-six hours. Five days, at the most. The source believes it's a near suicidal attack on the security up at Levyville Courthouse. It sounds insane, although the rationale to the team he's using is that the initiative's daring is supposed to impress me."

"Why would he jeopardize his wife and daughter like that?"

"That's one of the things that makes me believe my source. Romeo's sent his wife and daughter on vacation for two weeks. If something goes wrong, apparently he doesn't want them here."

Andy's head felt like it was spinning as he tried to figure out what was going on. Romeo knew that a strange conversation was going to occur, which meant he knew it was about him. If he knew . . . as understanding dawned, Andy hoped that his face remained immobile. Minister Johnnie didn't trust his son and was lying to him! Why? To test him?

"Dad, I think you should just ask him straight out." David knew he would have to call John Edgar about this.

Minister Johnnie shook his head. "I can't explain it, but my intuition says that doesn't feel right, and I always trust my intuition. If this thing is true, he might suspect my source. I want you to approach him. Ask him if there's anything significant about the next two weeks. I think he may confide in you because, although you two haven't been close, he knows you're in line to be the Third Star, and he has to respect that. Unless he's an agent. If he says no, drop it but have a couple of Swords watch him for the next couple of weeks. Don't tell them why.

"If he admits it, lie and tell him someone on his team brought it to you and you have to tell your father, but you'll try and convince me that the operation is needed. Then let me know right away so I can stop it."

They stood quietly for almost a minute. "I'll do what I can," David said finally.

Andy, who hadn't said a word, felt the wisdom of this man who had already taught him so much. He was giving his son false information and wanted someone who knew it was false to witness.

David wondered if he could bargain ahead to get the original disks and negatives from his tormentors for this powerful information. It all felt so out of control now, as if a firestorm were raging all around him.

David blinked. The only person in the tiny cafe wearing a jacket from the honor society named after Justice Clarence Thomas was cinnamon-colored and wearing rimless glasses. The U.S. Supreme Court jurist's likeness stared at him from the back of the man's blue suede jacket with his famous impassive bespectacled visage. The cinnamon-colored man sat by the window reading the *Wall Street Journal*.

David walked with hesitance to the table. "I was told to ask for John Edgar," he said.

"Sit," the man said without looking up. It was definitely the nasal, reedy voice David had come to dislike so much.

"I thought you were white," David said.

The man folded his newspaper and stared at the Covenant's second-in-command for several seconds before he spoke.

"That's because you believe color's important," the cinnamon-colored man said in quiet tones. "You've lived in that Covenant group all your life. They've convinced you whitey's out to get you, and that only a white man would head an operation as important as mine. Well, be clear. I'm a young man, and I may yet become director of the Bureau one day because I know that color doesn't matter in this country. I can go as high as my talent takes me. And be very clear about this: I believe as much as our revered first Director did that we must, at all costs, prevent the rise of a black messiah who thinks he must save the race." He saturated the word "race" with contempt, as if he were discussing a virulent germ. "Which brings us to the order of business today."

The man took out a stack of a baker's dozen of manila eight-by-eleven envelopes. He slid one to David, who appeared ready to vomit.

"Your memory needs to be refreshed. I think you need to look at the pictures again." He held up one of the envelopes so David could see that it was addressed. "There's a set for each OneCorporation newspaper in twelve major cities. I have several more in my office for the networks and OC Eye."

He leaned forward as he spoke to David. "What the fuck is wrong with you?" he hissed. "I don't give a shit about your personal problems, how much you drank before or don't drink now. You said you have something, and I am telling you that you better have something for me, now, today! This is your last chance to come up with something. I am ready to feed your ass to the dogs."

David tried to stall. "When I called you, I said I'm working on something. I thought you were giving me another week."

"If you don't have anything now, you won't have anything next week."

The cinnamon-colored man looked around and signaled the waiter. "Before we order food, I'm going to have a vodka martini, straight up, with two olives. Shaken, not stirred. My friend will have bourbon on the rocks. Make it a double." His eyes bored into David's, challenging him to rescind the order.

When the drinks arrived, David let his sit. John Edgar sipped his martini. "You and your black militant friends are in some shit over your head, my friend," he said. "I'm going to give you some information that I hope you'll take back because you can't do a damn thing about it. Then, I want some information from you.

"President Bruder's getting ready to send support troops into South Africa to get rid of that asshole Lumemele, who has become a major nuisance to our interests there. The Afrikaner freedom fighters are doing the best they can, but they need help. We haven't been able to justify money for them, and we've had to be creative.

"The president has supporters raising money to help this effort, which is important to him, and he's very, very pissed because one of his supporters and friends, a real estate man named Stan East, was murdered a few days ago. Unit 2236 claimed responsibility."

David's heart seemed to fall into his solar plexus. His mind raced. The Covenant was finished, regardless of what he did. They had bitten off way more than they could chew.

"We don't know how this ragtag Unit 2236 learned about East, but the president will not tolerate losing any other people close to him. I've been ordered to destroy Unit 2236 and anything close to it. The president will announce in the next day or two that he's asking Congress for funding to deputize OneCorporation's Security Division for domestic security. He believes that the private sector can keep the country safe and is the way to go in terms of cost effectiveness. They will swat make-believe terrorists like these cop killers and murderers of patriots like East and free up the National Guard to help the military in South Africa. So, in addition to my current counterintelligence work, I'll have thousands of OCI employees at my disposal for my cleanup operation." John Edgar looked pleased with himself about this expansion of his authority. "I'm telling you all this because somebody—I suspect it's your father—has started something they can't finish and can't possibly win. Operation Big Bug will get their ass."

David winced. "Operation Big Bug?"

"I named it myself," John Edgar said. "It's a little crude, but what the hell. Last year, I saw a revival of an old Sixties play called 'Slow Dance on the Killing Ground.' The protagonist had a theory that humanity was made up of big bugs and little bugs. Little bugs, he said, spent their entire existence doing a slow dance to keep from being squashed by the big bugs who run the world." He smiled, enjoying David's discomfort. "I've always wanted to be a big bug, and now I am."

The cinnamon-colored man leaned in very close to David and removed his rimless glasses. "Now, you can sink with the little bugs, or you can swim with us. Either way, I don't really give a shit. Do you want to talk to me?"

He was trapped. Damn Romeo for confirming that he had an operation in progress. Still, he pushed for a little breathing space. "Are you forgetting that you didn't call me, I called you, and I said I was working on something important for you?"

"Give it up."

David talked; John Edgar listened. During the conversation David gave him two names: Romeo Butler and Andy Blackman. "So you see, my father didn't even know about the weapons cache and is vehemently opposed to it. Although I was told Butler's flying solo, Andrew Blackman's got to know; they go way back." David realized he felt giddy about what he'd just done.

"So, you see, I really didn't know anything before," he lied. "This is the first major confidence my father's taken in me."

John Edgar looked impatient and not totally satisfied. "So is Johnnie Walker in charge of Unit 2236 or not?"

David decided that, despite the impatient look from his nemesis, he had given up enough. He knew about Butler's impending raid; he knew that Andy Blackman knew about it. He wouldn't tell him about the Four Stars, or the seven brigades. Maybe he could still save his father.

"I get the feeling it's Butler who conceived and runs Unit 2236," David said. "This is the first that my father has really gotten wind of. He's getting older, and hasn't been as hands-on with everything. What seemed to bother him most is how an attack like the one Butler's planning may impact the Covenant negatively if Butler's name comes out. If I get more, I'll tell you."

The CP2 chief reached into his briefcase and produced a white business envelope. Inside were thirty $1,000 bills.

"This can be lucrative, my friend," the man said.

"Are there plans to kill my father?"

The cinnamon-colored man's smile was enigmatic. "Government agency assassinations are illegal," he said. "My program has no plans to neutralize Johnnie Walker. If we get Unit 2236, we would have no reason to harm him or even harass the Covenant. Incidentally, have you found out what Unit 2236 means?"

"No, I haven't. You've infiltrated us for decades, why stop now?"

The man's smile was genuine. "David, infiltration isn't harassment, it's just keeping an eye on things. That's our job, to protect freedom and make sure certain ones of you don't threaten our liberty." He looked down at David's untouched glass.

"My friend, you haven't touched your drink," he said with a smile. "I was just going to order another for us both."

The look on his handler's face told David it wasn't a suggestion but a command. He sighed and reached for the glass.

FIFTY

The first witness, Elizabeth Harris, was nervous. She didn't like officialdom, an aversion born growing up in Selma, Alabama, during the turbulence of the 1960s.

Her birthplace was actually a little hamlet several miles from Selma. She remembered well an early encounter with authority. She was little Elizabeth Johnson then, standing next to her sharecropping father in the fall of her thirteenth year. Joshua Johnson, a proud quiet man, tallied the season's tobacco crop with the landowner, who also happened to be a deputy for the local sheriff. Because she was good at arithmetic, little Elizabeth had kept a running tally with her daddy to see how much they earned. They hadn't earned a lot, but every dollar mattered. The landowner, a burly man with a sunburned face who never smiled, presented her father with numbers very different from hers, numbers that said her father owed him a little more than his crops accounted for. When she started to object, her father's strong hand squeezed her arm so hard he hurt her, a hurt she still felt all these many years later. She knew something was wrong with the way things were when she looked up at the rock of a man who was her father and saw him facing the white landowner with his head lowered, his eyes staring at the ground.

"Do you swear to tell the truth, the whole truth, and nothing but the truth, so help you God?"

"I do."

"State your name."

"Elizabeth Harris."

"You may be seated."

"Mrs. Harris, were you in the unit block of Dock Place last September twenty-ninth at about 7 P.M. on the night that George Bascomb, the deceased, was killed?" The prosecutor, Hugh Fuego, a UCLA Law School graduate, already had a reputation in the district attorney's office, one that stamped him as ambitious. He was anxious to look good in his first homicide trial.

"Yes, I was."

"You live there, is that correct?"

"Yes. My address faces Dock Street. My backyard faces Dock Place. "

"I see. I believe your husband became involved in a verbal altercation with the defendant, Michael Patrick, at about that time. Is that correct?"

"Yes."

"Will you tell the court what you saw that night?"

Memories. She closed her eyes. Anger washed through her, suffocating the nervousness. She pointed at Michael Patrick sitting at the defense table with Isaac Erlickson and three assistants, startling him.

"I saw that man, Michael Patrick, deliberately murder George Bascomb."

"Objection!" Erlickson said without looking up from notes he appeared to study. "My client is on trial for manslaughter, not for murder."

"Sustained," Judge Bass said. "The witness will refrain from using the word 'murder' in her testimony."

"Well, then, I saw him slaughter George Bascomb," Elizabeth Harris said. Ice coated her voice.

A titter sprinkled through the room, causing Judge Bass to strike his gavel once. Andy smiled and scribbled.

Elizabeth Harris recounted what she remembered of the dialogue between Patrick and her husband. She told of her surprise when Michael Patrick drew a weapon. She spoke of Patrick's anger, his racial epithets, and how he kicked her dying neighbor.

"Did the defendant ever identify himself as a police officer?"

"No, he didn't, not until after he had shot George."

"Did it appear the defendant was acting in self defense when he shot the deceased?"

"Mister Patrick was the only one on Dock Street pointing a gun." She thought about her comment. "Well, him and that security guard."

"Your witness," Fuego said, returning to the prosecution table.

Erlickson stood, pulling at his monogrammed shirt cuffs. "Mrs. Harris, you said that my client, Michael Patrick, kicked the deceased as he lay on the ground. For the record, this is a lie, isn't it?"

Fuego's partner, Arlene Morehouse, was on her feet before he was. "Objection, your honor! Defense is leading the witness!"

"Overruled. Proceed."

The pattern is established, Andy wrote among his notes.

"It is a lie, isn't it?"

"No, it isn't. I saw him kick George."

301

"What kind of shoes did Officer Patrick have on?"

"Sneakers, I think."

"Then he couldn't have hurt Mister Bascomb much if he kicked him, could he?"

Elizabeth Harris looked at the defense attorney as if he'd lost his mind. "I have no idea," she replied. "I have never been shot and then kicked."

"The witness may step down," Erlickson said without looking at her.

Carl Harris followed his wife to the witness stand. Then his son Richard testified. Lorraine Saunders testified. Andy started on a second notebook.

They told the same story and didn't waver under Isaac Erlickson's attempts to needle them: Carl Harris and Michael Patrick argued. Patrick was angry; Harris was solicitous. Patrick used the word "nigger" on at least two occasions. After drawing his gun, Patrick said, "I want to kill a nigger. I want to kill a nigger so goddamned bad I can taste it." No one knew Patrick was a cop. George backed away from Patrick when he saw the gun. Michael Patrick was in no danger from anyone when he shot George.

Finally, Marian Bascomb testified. Arlene Morehouse, also African-American, stood close to the witness stand and gently led her through the interrogation.

Marian held up well until her final moments. Belly swollen with her first child, she looked paradoxically beatific throughout her painful testimony.

Toward the end she looked at Michael Patrick, who returned her stare with what could gently be called arrogance.

"You did not behave like an officer of the law," she said. "You behaved like an unrestrained animal."

Erlickson started to object, thought better of it, and sat back.

No need gaining the grieving widow any more sympathy, he thought.

"You know, and God knows, that you did not have to shoot my husband that night. Whatever happens in this courtroom, you will be judged by the Creator one day." She paused. "You murdered my husband."

This time, the word "murder" remained in the record.

FIFTY-ONE

The next day, Hugh Fuego offered into evidence a copy of Jonathan Gardiner's DVD that had captured the events on Dock Place the evening of the twenty-ninth of September of the previous year. Those events by now carried myriad descriptions, among them murder (George Bascomb's family), a terrible tragedy (a mainstream newspaper), alleged manslaughter (the judicial system), an unfortunate conflict (Ike Erlickson), justifiable homicide (a white nationalist newspaper), a racist lynching (a black nationalist newspaper), a wanton loss (an African-American mainstream newspaper), a nigger killing (President Bruder's inner circle, minus his Black Brigade, and *never* for attribution), business as usual (everyday black folks), a spook erasing (a riffraff white nationalist newspaper), and so on.

Andy looked at the jury in the dimmed courtroom as the videotape ran the first time uninterrupted. For the most part, the twelve faces remained blank. Andy thought he saw a miniscule smirk on the elementary school teacher's face as Patrick drew his weapon. One of the housewives winced slightly each time the word "nigger" was heard; the retired minister made a face when Patrick said, "I want to kill a nigger. I want to kill a nigger so goddamned bad I can taste it." The black sales manager frowned when Andy's brother moved behind Patrick with the stick and swung it.

Fuego ran the DVD a second time. Andy got up. He didn't know how many times he could watch George get killed. He resisted an irrational urge to walk over to the defense table and beat the shit out of Michael Patrick.

He walked out of the courtroom. It was almost lunchtime but he wasn't hungry. He glanced down the corridor. The brown-skinned woman talking to Romeo made him freeze. She wore a brocaded blazer with African motifs. Claudia smiled broadly at him, although her eyes appeared to well up with tears.

He walked briskly toward her as she moved quickly toward him. Without saying anything, they hugged each other for a long time.

"We must have looked like a television commercial running toward each other," she said, giggling into his shoulder. Romeo remained at a discreet

303

distance with a grin on his face.

"I know you'll explain when it's time," Andy said. "I'm glad you're back."

She kissed him gently on the mouth. "It's good to be back," she said. "Thank you for trusting my brief letter."

He whispered in her ear. Her eyes filled with surprise and joy, her mouth opened but said nothing. She nodded. Andy made a little gesture with his head and Romeo walked over.

"Will you be my best man?" Andy said.

"Oh, hell yes," his friend replied with a clap on his shoulder. He embraced them both as passersby glanced at the giddy couple.

When they finally released each other, the three of them walked outside. About a block from the courthouse, Romeo placed himself in the middle and put an arm around the shoulders of each friend with a firm embrace.

"You both are all I thought you would be and more," he said. "You both know and have displayed well the meaning of love, trust, and faith.

"I know Claudia said she'd explain," Romeo said to his oldest friend. "*I'll* explain. From this point on, in secure surroundings, you may talk to each other about things you couldn't before." He stopped and had them face him.

"Then said He unto them, But now, he that hath a purse, let him take it, and likewise his scrip: and he that hath no sword, let him sell his garment, and buy one." Andy's mouth opened, closed.

Claudia seemed less surprised. "I didn't know, but I thought so," she said. "I hoped so."

"I guess it never occurred to me that you could . . . you know," Andy said.

She tapped him playfully on the chin with her fist. "I'm a tough broad," she said, and kissed him again.

FIFTY-TWO

A ndy and Claudia sat overlooking the water on King Drive, hands entwined, watching the sun relinquish its dominance to nightfall.

They had come in separate cars; now they sat quietly in Andy's, thinking of words so far unsaid, words that would bring them closer, that would change everything in so many ways, and in so many directions. Words...

In the beginning was the Word...

"We're getting married," Claudia said. "What do we feel for each other? I know what I feel, but what do *we* feel?" Her brown eyes were open and vulnerable to all answers.

"I want to be with you," Andy said. "Permanently. And for all the right reasons."

"We haven't known each other very long." Andy realized it wasn't an objection. He heard joy in her voice as she said it.

"We'll have to spend each day getting to know each other better. And we've never made love."

"We'll have to practice a lot," she said. They both giggled, squeezed the other's hands.

Andy was suddenly serious again. "Once, when we were talking at your place, I realized that I've never been in love with someone first before being sexual." Feeling full almost to overflowing, he paused. "I had no idea it would feel like this."

They were quiet again, their thoughts alive with the magic of discovery.

"Let's get out," Andy said.

They walked to the front of the car. He placed his arm around her; she rested her head on his shoulder. They stood side by side, looking over the water. The sun, hanging just above the horizon, was a large rose ball, painting an uneven streak of red in both directions beneath immense blue-gray clouds suffused with a dwindling tint of purple.

"You've read about the $3 billion contract the government just awarded to OneCorporation's Security Division?" Andy asked.

"Yes. It amounts to activating a private army with federal money. And it creates jobs for some white folks who are angry that cops are getting shot. Probably some black folks, too, who want to prove their patriotism."

"Or who desperately need a job. I'm not sure how far our Teacher thought ahead; I wonder if he saw this coming. Obviously when you go to war, the other side will go to war, too."

"Baby, they've always been at war with us. What you're seeing is just a heightened, more overt phase. A hundred years ago, they allowed the Ku Klux Klan to be re-activated. This time they're turning a corporation loose on us. And they'll probably come after the Covenant first is what you're thinking, because we're organized and we've been an outspoken advocate for black folks."

Andy nodded. He took out his reporter's notebook and turned to some notes he had jotted in the back in his own private code. "We're on the same page alright. Claudia, what scares me is this. The Swords will want to fight, and there's no way they can win. We've all given our lives to the Covenant, and they're ready to go down. It will be a bloodbath."

"I suspect Minister Johnnie will order our Covenant underground."

"And I suspect they know where most Covenant members live, which is real different than knowing what some of us like you and I are doing. Underground may not help the Covenant the way it helps us, because there are too many to go too deep underground. Anyway, I have an idea I want to run past Minister Johnnie and probably the Four Star command. I want to try it out on you and have you play devil's advocate to see if it's our best possible way to fight."

They got back in his car and talked.

"I think they may see it—Minister Johnnie, anyway—mainly because it's you suggesting it," Claudia said after he finished.

"Let's go for it," he said.

Claudia's face clouded. She looked away, then back. "I'm sorry," she said. "It happens more now that I've actually been in the field." She rubbed Andy's arm, placed her hand back on it. "I'm thinking about us and the heartbreak that can come so suddenly and quickly in what we're doing. And I find myself thinking about my daughter, who I've tried to prepare without really being able to tell her anything. A part of me knows I'm doing this for her, and another part asks why, since I may not be here for her."

"Claudia, all of us are in danger. It probably felt like this for Yahshua's early followers back in the first and second century. I'm sure the Roman empire was just as relentless as this one is."

They were both silent for what seemed a long time. "Is it John 15:13?"

Andy finally asked.

They said it softly together: "Greater love hath no man than this, that a man lay down his life for his friends."

They kissed deeply, holding nothing back. Claudia shivered against him. The sun surrendered, fell below the horizon, letting the chill of evening embrace them both.

FIFTY-THREE

lthough Fuego and Morehouse both knew why Lynda Jacobs had selected them, they tried not to know. They never talked directly about it to each other.

Morehouse had been more candid with her older sister: "Girl, Jacobs picked us for our enthusiasm, color, and inexperience. I will probably leave and go into private practice when this case is over. She can't possibly look like she doesn't want to convict a cop. That's where our energy and hustle come in. But this is Hugh's first homicide case, and my second. Brown and black prosecutors show off the office's diversity." When her sister rolled her eyes, Morehouse had shrugged. "In fairness, we would have still been the ADAs if they tried the case in the city," she said. "Without the change of venue, it would have played different. Everyone tries to pretend race doesn't matter. In this case, it matters big time."

Andy sat on a bench in the hallway pounding at the keys of his laptop. Romeo had ordered/begged him for a thirty-inch story outlining the pattern Ike Erlickson, aided and abetted by Judge Albert O. Bass, was establishing. With each African-American witness so far, the defense attorney had insinuated into his questioning phrases like, "But that isn't true, is it?" Or, "We both know it didn't happen that way, did it?" Generally, he called black witnesses by their first name. With each white witness called by the prosecution—police officers, the police Internal Affairs Division commander, crime scene specialists, forensics specialists, the city's medical examiner, and so on—he was deferential even as he worked to bend their testimony to benefit his client. Erlickson's signals resonated through the courtroom: black witnesses lie; white witnesses are truthful.

"Hi, Mister Blackman."

Andy looked up. "Hey Jonathan, how are you? Is this your first day at the trial?" He moved his briefcase so the young man could sit down.

"Yes, sir," Jonathan Gardiner said. "I've been called to testify. May I take a picture of you?" He held up a little tube about the size of a cigar. Andy smiled his assent and Jonathan clicked off two shots.

"How do you feel? Are you nervous? You're a big part of why we're even

308

here having a trial, you know," Andy said.

"That's what Miss Morehouse and my mom said. Hey, I did what I had to do, and I'm glad I could. But listen, I've been meaning to call you but my schoolwork is up to here." He placed a large hand parallel to his nose. "Do you have a minute?"

"Sure. What's up?"

Jonathan looked around, lowered his voice. "I've been following what's been going on and all, and I'm wondering how does somebody find out how to join up with Unit 2236. I've read about how the Covenant's not connected with them and all, but nobody else knows anything."

Andy looked into the eyes of young Gardiner; a clear, steady gaze looked back. "I don't know, son," he said. "What makes you want to join up with Unit 2236?"

"I told you before, I don't like cops. I *know* I don't look or act like no banger, but still they hassle me anyway. They hassle my friends, too, and it looks like it's because we're black."

Andy thought about the road he was on, where it was leading, and what they had to do to get there. This decent young man, who was the future, wanted to kill cops. Because he didn't like them. Andy Blackman knew he was prepared, when ordered, to kill cops because his leader had declared war, and for the self-defense of black people. It made as much sense as killing people could make.

"You have a few minutes, Jon?" Andy asked. The portly young man nodded; Andy motioned for him to sit.

"Jon, do you love black people?"

Jonathan shrugged. "I don't know, it's hard sometimes," he said with an embarrassed smile. "You know how some of us are. I know what Minister Johnnie teaches but I just don't know."

"Suppose Unit 2236 was fighting with non-violent direct action. Or without weapons, like the Swords of the Master. Would you still be interested?"

"You mean like King and them did back in my grandmom's time? Nah, I doubt it. I don't believe in letting anybody hit on me like that. I don't know how they did it. And the Swords are alright but they're not doing what Unit 2236 is."

"Jon, I can't speak for Unit 2236, but I don't think they're doing what they're doing because they hate cops," Andy said. "I think they may hate a way of life that has never valued our people. And there is a difference."

Andy looked at his watch. "Look, I'm on deadline, but let's talk a minute. And if you want to talk some more, call me and let's have lunch one day next week." Andy put his computer on sleep mode and closed the lid.

"Jon, from what the Covenant knows about Unit 2236 so far, people don't go to them, they manage to find the people they want. We get communiqués and we release them.

"I know I'm going to sound preachy, brother, but I hope you find a way to stop hating on cops. And I hope you can find a way to love your folks more, as lost as so many of us seem to be." Andy was surprised, and pleased, at Jonathan's attentiveness. "Listen, if you've got to hate something, hate a way of living that says cops must be protected at all costs, even when they're wrong. Not just wrong when they embarrass their blue brotherhood by stealing or taking bribes, but when they take innocent black lives. This guy on trial, Patrick, murdered my brother, but, Jon, he's just a cog in a big wheel. He gets paid a good salary to protect the wheel. As a people, we're not even on the wheel. If we forget how the wheel has rolled over us for hundreds of years, and say that's all past and done with, a few of us are allowed on the wheel. But then, we must always understand that the wheel is more important than we are. Any talk of a new wheel more suited to everybody and not rolling over anybody is out of the question."

"But if Patrick's acquitted, won't Unit 2236 kill him, little cog or not?"

"Well, at least you're really listening," Andy said with a smile. "I don't know if they'll kill him. It seems likely, given what they've done so far. One of the unfair things about the wheel now is the judicial system. This Unit 2236 seems to be building a new judicial wheel if they won't seriously fix the old one."

"It's an interesting metaphor, Mister Blackman," Jonathan said. "You think they can build an entire wheel from where they're starting?"

"Jon, I don't know. But you've posed an interesting question. If enough people abandon the old wheel, and start working on the new one, it can be built. All empires fall, Jon, it's just a matter of when. It seems like a real long shot from where we sit. But you and I know the old wheel doesn't work."

"Mister Gardiner, what made you decide to videotape what happened on Dock Place last September twenty-ninth?" Arlene Morehouse, elegant in a basic black business suit, black blouse, pearl necklace and conservative low-heeled black pumps, stood near her witness.

"I heard arguing and went to the window," Jonathan Gardiner said. "I saw this white man"—he glanced toward Michael Patrick—"arguing with Mister Harris."

"Objection!" Erlickson barked from the defense table. "We object to the characterization of my client as 'arguing.' My client was holding a discussion about his property."

"He was arguing," Jonathan Gardiner said. "I know an argument when I see one."

"Young Jonathan, I think you hate white people and took your pictures for that reason," Erlickson shot back.

"Objection sustained," Judge Bass said, punctuating his comment with his gavel. "Strike the answer from the record."

Andy sighed. He couldn't remember a single instance when Bass had overruled an Erlickson objection thus far in the trial. Watching a legend operate in concert with a deferential jurist was instructive. A morbid place in his mind wondered why folks like Erlickson and Bass shouldn't be recipients of executive action from Unit 2236, too. In looking at technique and considering rationality, Andy and Erlickson's critics overlooked the reason he became a legend: he got results.

Erlickson knew the police officer versus attacker issue was crucial. He decided this youngster was as good a place as any to draw a line in the sand. He wasn't a hoodlum but he had just enough anger.

"When did my client, Officer Patrick, display his badge?" Erlickson asked on cross-examination.

"It's on the DVD," Jonathan Gardiner said. "It was after he shot Mister Bascomb."

"How do you know he didn't display if before you started shooting your pictures?"

"Objection, your honor." Arlene Morehouse tried to stifle her annoyance. "Counsel wants to raise questions irrelevant to the witness' frame of reference and wants him to speculate."

"Overruled. Continue, counselor."

Andy imagined sighting through a scope at Bass and squeezing.

"I have no idea what he did before," Jonathan Gardiner said. "I know what I saw him do."

"Did you edit your pictures before you gave them to the Covenant of the New Commandment?"

"No, and I resent you saying that I might."

Jonathan, be cool. Andy understood the young man's anger but he suspected it wasn't playing well.

Erlickson whirled theatrically. "You resent it?" His voice got louder, intense. "You resent it? Why? Because you've been caught in a lie!"

"Your honor, please!" Fuego said, as Morehouse said, "This is reprehensible!" Both prosecutors, agitated, sprang to their feet and started toward the bench.

"Counselors, approach the bench," Bass said, even though they were already doing so.

Andy watched the four officers of the court discuss whether or not the defense attorney's behavior was egregious. He glanced around the jury box at his fourth estate colleagues. If he was reading faces correctly, most of them seemed stunned by the one-sidedness they were witnessing.

He looked at Jonathan. His frown seemed to indicate that he felt the verbal equivalent of being sucker punched.

"I have no more questions," Erlickson said as the legal huddle broke. "The witness may step down."

The prosecution rested.

Except for experts on forensics and the like, Isaac Erlickson called only a handful of witnesses. Only two, besides Michael Patrick, were on Dock Place the night of September 29. Both were white.

(Patrick's double date friend, a disillusioned Garth Wilson, had moved back to Montana. When Erlickson and Morehead depositioned him via videoconference, Wilson, remembering he had drawn a weapon that night, invoked the Fifth Amendment on the grounds that he might incriminate himself.)

Raymond Hayes took the stand as the first of those witnesses. He wore a navy blue two-button suit, a starched white shirt, a red tie with blue patterns, and highly polished black military-style shoes.

"What kind of work do you do?" Ike Erlickson asked. He stood close to the witness stand, talking to Hayes as if he were an old friend.

"I'm a police officer," Hayes said. He brushed his thinning hair across the dome of his head in a futile effort to conceal hair loss.

"You're a member of the police department?"

Hayes' face pinked slightly. "Well, no, I'm employed by OneCorporation International. But I wear a uniform." He had suggested wearing his uniform to court; the defense attorney had counseled against it.

"Good, good," Erlickson said with a smile. He looked toward the jury box as if to confirm Hayes' integrity. It was a small gesture, one perfected over decades before dozens of juries. "Now I want you to tell me what you saw the night George Bascomb met his death."

"Uh, I wasn't there when it started, but when I arrived this black fellow, Bascomb, was beating Officer Patrick on the head and___"

"*You* were aware that my client was a police officer." Erlickson said it as a declarative statement, looking at the jury as he did so.

"Objection," Morehouse shouted. "Leading the witness."

"Overruled. Continue, Mister Hayes."

Hayes frowned, thinking. "Wellll, I sort of sensed it, I guess," he said. "I mean, he was the only white man there and he *did* have a gun so, instinctively, I felt___"

Morehouse leapt to her feet, furious. "Objection! Your honor, the witness is not being factual, he's relying on personal opinions. After all___"

"Overruled," Bass said, looking over his bifocals at the prosecutor as if she were a science exhibit. "Continue, Mister Hayes."

Andy rolled his eyes. Most of his familiarity with the courtroom came from television and cinematic drama. *State v. Patrick* seemed to fit right in, he mused.

"Yes, well, Officer Patrick stumbled backward, kind of shaking his head. Bascomb was preparing to strike him again when the gun discharged. It appeared that Officer Patrick was tensing up, trying to regain his balance and backpedaling, sort of, leaning backward with his gun hand straight out in his hand, when it went off."

Andy watched Erlickson watching the jury as Hayes recited; he seemed to like what he saw. "Thank you, *Officer* Hayes." He turned to the prosecution bench. "Your witness."

Morehouse stood, but remained at the prosecution table. She took several moments to compose herself before speaking. "Mister Hayes, you are aware that the shooting of George Bascomb was captured by a video camera?"

"Yes, I am."

"It shows the events occurring differently than you described."

"I saw what I saw. Maybe what I saw happened before the fellow started videotaping, I don't know. But I saw what I saw."

"Thank you, Mister Hayes. You may step down."

Erlickson then called David Sanders, a John Upton Church graduate student and the only white person living on Dock Street at the time. Sanders, a slight, clean-shaven man in his mid-twenties, wore a tweed sport coat, a crew shirt, blue jeans and brown leather sneakers.

Andy vaguely remembered the young man. Romeo had wanted to

interview him but he had disappeared.

"I've been trying to reach you for some time, Mister Sanders. Are you still a resident of Dock Street?"

"Well, yes and no. I had to drop out of school for personal reasons. I'll be going back this summer. I'll be living on Dock Street again."

"So you haven't been in the city for several months."

"That's correct."

"But you were living on Dock Street last year when this incident occurred?"

"Yes, I was on my roof listening to some rock CDs when I heard a commotion."

"Will you tell us what you saw?"

"Well, I looked down and I saw three men, three black men, spread-eagled against the wall and there was a white man—in fact, it was Mister Patrick." Sanders gestured toward the defense table. "Another black man—who, I know now, was George Bascomb—picked up a stick or a board, I'd say a stick, and swung at Patrick. He hit him, either on the left side or on the elbow, then started backing away."

Andy saw that Erlickson didn't like where this was going. Apparently he hadn't interviewed him beforehand. He wondered if Erlickson had grabbed Sanders before the prosecution did because he was white. Andy smiled and scribbled.

"The black man backed away in a crouch, sort of, and Patrick shot him," Sanders said. "Deliberately."

"Objection!" Erlickson shouted reflexively. A hubbub of confusion swept the courtroom.

As it died down, Bass gestured for Erlickson to move toward him. "But it's your witness," he said quietly.

Andy scribbled. Erlickson seemed to be ad libbing. He got Sanders to admit his politics were somewhat liberal. In one of those moments the defense attorney was famous for, he asked the young man about his studies. Sanders said he was a graduate student in English with a creative writing major. The prosecutors looked at each other. Bass appeared bemused.

What was his thesis about?

As fate would have it, Sanders was writing a nonfiction historical account of the Weather Underground. All over the courtroom, people saw the light of combat gleam in Erlickson's eyes.

Andy wrote "surreal" and underlined it in his description of what followed. It would be outdone only in summation. When he read other accounts of the trial later, some, but by no means all, confirmed that it wasn't just Andy's biases at work. Erlickson's work seemed like something out of antebellum days.

"I thought you communist types disappeared with the Sixties," Erlickson announced to the courtroom.

Both Morehouse and Fuego were up, speaking almost at the same time. "Your honor, this is ridiculous!" Fuego said. "Your honor, I don't see___" Morehouse began.

Erlickson's voice grew louder as he turned against his own witness. "Your honor, I am trying to show that this witness is biased. He probably thinks every white policeman is a pig." He whirled toward Sanders. "If there is feeling between white man and black man, you are standing against the white man, is that right?"

"Your honor, please___"

Bass struck his gaveled twice. "Objection overruled. I find this line of questioning very interesting. You may answer the question."

"Isn't it true that you're a friend of Richard White, and isn't it true that Richard White is a member of that radical, pseudo-Christian, cop-hating Covenant of the New Commandment, and isn't it true that he lives in the same building as you?"

Sanders appeared exasperated, confused, and about to laugh, all at the same time. "I don't know anyone named Richard White. I have no idea what you're talking about."

Erlickson looked directly at the jury. The black jury member seemed to shrink as the defense attorney continued his tirade.

"This is a black and white fight!" Erlickson roared, slamming his hand down on a nearby lectern. "This man Sanders is an unmitigated liar. Any man who would sit here and lie a man's life away is not entitled to a fair trial—he should be taken out and shot!"

Morehouse threw her hands in the air. "Objection, your honor, what is counsel talking about? David Sanders isn't on trial, Michael Patrick is. This is absolutely the crudest form of questioning___"

"Objection overruled."

During the exchange, an Erlickson note-taking aide signaled him. The attorney hurried over, bent and listened, and began looking across the visitors. He stood suddenly and pointed.

"What's your name? Stand up, *boy!*"

"My name is not 'boy.' My name is Richard White," the man shouted back. He was young, tall, and angry. Two friends restrained him as he tried to stand. He wore a red, black and green flag in his lapel.

Judge Bass struck his gavel twice, trying to still the increasing hubbub. "Order in the court!" he said.

Erlickson stared at the tall, rangy White. "Why don't you lock him up?"

"I'm sure you didn't mean to offend anybody, Mister Erlickson," Judge Bass said, his tone unmistakably deferential.

"Some black people seem to think it disgraceful to be called 'boy.' My grandfather and father called me that. What's wrong with it? I don't understand this childish, infantile feeling. I have defended these people many times without fee. I have no hatred for these people, no feeling at all. But I won't take any back talk out of them either!"

White was so astonished he shook his head, smiled despite himself, and sat down. Andy thought he saw one juror smile slightly in what appeared to be unconscious approval.

Even Judge Bass looked uncomfortable. "The jury will disregard these remarks," he said. Then, apologetically, to Erlickson, "I did not mean to imply earlier that you meant offense to anyone."

"No further questions," Erlickson said to Sanders without looking at him.

The courtroom buzzed with opinions, conjecture, criticism, and support for what had been witnessed. Some in the courtroom, enthralled with Ike Erlickson's histrionics, had forgotten David Sanders.

"Mister Sanders, how long have you lived on Dock Street?" Arlene Morehouse asked after the courtroom settled down.

"This is my third year," he said. "I moved in during my senior year, and this is my second year in grad school."

"Did you know George Bascomb?"

"I knew him to speak and say hello, that was about it."

"Did you know Michael Patrick?"

"No. I did see him once parking his trailer."

"Then you didn't know Mister Patrick was a police officer?"

"No, ma'am, I didn't."

"Was what you saw that night a police officer trying to keep the peace?"

"What I saw was an argument between Mister Patrick and some neighbors," Sanders said.

Maybe we've caught a break, Andy thought as he scribbled notes. Morehouse was facing the press in their jury box; Andy thought her face brightened.

"Was Mister Patrick wearing a police badge or any police identification?"

"I didn't see any police identification until Mister Patrick took his badge from his pocket after he shot Mister Bascomb."

"Did he say he was a police officer?"

"No."

"Did he behave like a police officer?"

"Well, I thought he was abusive and abrasive with his language. I have seen police officers behave like that, if that's what's you're asking me."

"Objection!" Isaac Erlickson stood, his face livid. "Witness is expressing an opinion. Move to have that struck from the record."

"I withdraw the question, your honor," Arlene Morehouse said. "No further questions."

Andy thought she looked pleased with herself, and also with her friendly and honest "hostile" witness. As she reached the prosecution table she froze, then tapped her partner on the shoulder and pointed. Hugh Fuego turned and seemed equally surprised.

Morehouse turned around. "Your honor, may we have a ten-minute recess?"

"Very well," Bass said, pounding his gavel. "The court will stand in recess for ten minutes."

Andy tried to see what had surprised the two young attorneys. Then a tall, dark-skinned man stood up.

Carvel Thomas! Where in the hell had he been?

Fuego and Morehouse stood at the wooden rail dividing the courtroom and talked animatedly with Thomas. Andy stood and worked his way toward the three people. When he got close, he still couldn't hear what the conversation was about. He managed to catch Thomas' eye; the detective nodded acknowledgement that he saw Andy.

Erlickson watched the conversation with a scowl. Then Fuego and Morehouse walked over to the bailiff. The bailiff went to the judge's chambers and knocked. Erlickson headed toward the front of the courtroom, too. The three attorneys disappeared into the judge's chambers.

Andy gestured to Thomas, who didn't look happy.

"Hey Carvel, what's all this is about?"

"How you doing? You're Butler's friend. Bascomb's brother." They shook hands.

"You're not going to believe what happened," Thomas said.

"Maybe not, but I'm going to write it down anyway," Andy said. He flipped to a clean page in his notebook.

Thomas exhaled deeply. "I put in for vacation for this week a couple months back. When the trial started with jury selection a few weeks ago, I realized I might be needed to testify and tried to re-schedule my vacation. So I tell my supervisor and he said he'd get right on it. The next day he tells me I'm locked into this time period, there's nothing he can do. Well, I was a little pissed off, but I knew this case is what it is and thought I should stay in town so I could testify. I canceled my vacation plans and told my supervisor to tell the D.A. I'd be here when they wanted me. When I didn't hear anything, I came down today only to learn Arlene and Fuego didn't even know I was in town. When they tried to get me on the witness list, they were told not to bother because I was on vacation. Nobody told them I was in town."

"Sounds like somebody don't want to hear what you have to say."

"Sounds like it, huh?"

"You want to tell me?"

Thomas frowned. "Look, if they get me on the stand, you'll get it anyway. If they don't, we'll talk."

When the four officers of the court came out, Andy saw on their faces that he had an exclusive. Fuego and Morehouse wore scowls; Bass was impassive; Erlickson did what he could to look saintly. Fuego and Morehouse called Thomas to the rail for another animated conversation. The prosecutors glanced toward Andy and shrugged. Before they could say anymore, Bass gaveled the courtroom back to order. Thomas motioned with his head toward the door.

They sat on the same bench where Andy had counseled young Jon Gardiner. Andy started to ask a question and stopped himself. It might be best to let this brother just start talking, and then ask questions, he thought. Clearly, he was trying to compose his thoughts.

Finally, Thomas spoke. "I've been trying to hold on to get my pension. But I think I'm going to have to hang it up. Take a payout and get the hell out. I don't like what I'm seeing." He looked at Andy. "The night your brother was killed, myself and another officer had to rewrite our reports three times. Under orders. We were told to mention only the statements of police who had been at the scene. My statement they didn't like at all. I quoted too many people there, they said. By midnight the commissioner had decided justifiable homicide. It was only then that they took statements from Mister Harris and the others. I had to fight like hell to get the charges dropped against them."

Suddenly he pounded on the bench. "I'm a good cop, Blackman. I know I'm a good cop. I wanted to vomit in that courtroom when I saw what that man Erlickson is doing. And Bass is letting him get away with it."

"How do you think I feel?" Andy said. "At one point I was ready to go over to the defense table and snatch Patrick and his asshole attorney."

Andy scribbled furiously. Thomas took a deep breath. "Obviously Bass denied their request to let me testify. He said it was their negligence that I wasn't on their list. They've rested their case; Erlickson's calling witnesses now. They asked Erlickson if he knew I was here. He wouldn't say, which means he knew. But he sure as hell wasn't going to call me."

He stood up. "You got your story?"

"Yeah, I've got enough for now. Give me your card in case I have follow questions." Andy stood up and shook his hand. "Thanks, man. Romeo said you're a stand up guy."

"Say hello for me." He looked Andy directly in the eye. "I can't do this shit anymore."

FIFTY-FOUR

ichael Patrick's friends and enemies agreed that he personified "the typical American" even if they didn't agree on what that meant.

Typical in believing that America was the greatest country on the planet; typical in working hard for the things he wanted; typical in viewing the Super Bowl as the premier sporting event in the world.

Typical in agreeing with the way the U.S. government defined its role in the world; typical in his world view of people who were not of European descent; typical in accepting white privilege as so normal he was oblivious to having it.

He was the grandson of immigrants in a nation that prided itself on being a nation of immigrants, indigenous people and the descendants of Africans notwithstanding. As the grandson of a self-made man, he believed strongly in individualism. Sean Patrick, Michael's father, became the highest-ranking Irishman in the Boston Police Department before retiring as an inspector. Michael was the first Patrick to go to college and become an "educated law enforcement officer." He majored in criminal justice for two years before marrying his pregnant high school sweetheart. Their child was stillborn six months after their wedding. After passing the police examination, Michael decided against returning to school. He and his wife separated a year before he shot George Bascomb to death.

Now, on the witness stand, Isaac Erlickson wanted the jury to see Michael Patrick, from the tip of Michael Patrick's newly barbered black hair to the heels of his highly polished shoes, as a prototype of what the country stood for, a man who represented the American Dream, a man being dragged through a nightmare not of his making.

"Uncle Ike" questioned his client in the avuncular manner of a man wanting to get at the truth about rumors maligning his nephew.

"Mike, it's been rumored that you were drunk on the night George Bascomb met his death," Erlickson said, standing as close as he could to the witness stand. "Is that true?"

"No, Mister Erlickson, I wasn't drunk."

"Had you been drinking at all?"

"Aw, I'd had a few nips of Red Mountain burgundy, but I wasn't drunk."

"There's been another rumor, Mike, and I know you've heard it. We may as well confront it for the jury and show that we're not hiding anything. It's been said that when you were on the boat earlier with your lady friend, you threatened her with a walk home from the dock if she didn't, uh, "cooperate." Is *that* true?"

"Oh, no, sir. I'd never do a thing like that. I was a little upset because she'd gotten moody and it was supposed to be a 'fun day,' you know, but I didn't threaten her with anything like walking home, no."

"In fact, you were on your way back to see her when this unfortunate incident occurred, isn't that right?"

"Yes, sir."

Erlickson morphed from concerned uncle into a father knowing he would be told the truth. His voice softened, so that those in the courtroom became quiet and attentive.

"Mike, in your own words, I want you to tell me what happened the night George Bascomb met his death."

Patrick looked out over the courtroom. "Well, while I was talking to Carl Harris, this fellow Bascomb attacked me with a stick. I pulled my service Glock and I tried to shoot him between the knee and the thigh, but the gun clicked and didn't go off. I thought it was empty."

"Objection!" The voice belonged to Arlene Morehouse. "A police officer's service weapon is never empty unless he or she is cleaning it."

"Overruled."

"Here's this man with a club, he made a real lunge at me. I backed away but he caught me across the right side of the head. I stumbled backward. As I stumbled backward the gun discharged."

Erlickson leaned close. "How did you feel when you heard that Bascomb was dead?"

"I, I was at the precinct when I heard. I couldn't talk anymore. I was crying."

Stifling sobs, Marian Bascomb walked hurriedly from the room, triggering an undercurrent of murmurs. "Order in the court," Bass said, slamming his gavel twice.

Andy felt the knot in his stomach feeding on his pain. Unbidden, his mind went back to something he had heard at WiTHWA: *You must transform your rage into energy you can use against your opponent. Rage can consume you and get you killed.* He breathed deeply, forced himself to focus.

Erlickson tried to regain the moment, patting his client on the arm. "Thank you, Officer Patrick." He walked back to the defense table in a manner meant to preserve the somberness of the moment. "Your witness."

Tactically, they decided to go with Fuego. The prosecutor stood and looked directly at the defendant after checking his notes.

"Mister Patrick, does the name Malik Al-Amin mean anything to you?"

"Yeah, he's that cop killer on death row," Patrick said.

"Have you heard the slogan, 'Malik should be out'?"

"Sure. There are some people who think he shouldn't be in jail. But___"

"Isn't it true that you have a T-shirt that says, 'Malik should be under —Six feet under'?"

"Yeah, but that's only a joke. Lots of officers have them."

Patrick looked toward his defense attorney for help. Erlickson, in a rare momentary lapse, was taking notes. Fuego picked up a large photograph, large enough to be seen three or four rows back in the courtroom. He held it up; a red mark circled the head of a dark-haired man. Fuego kept stringing questions together, happy that he had apparently caught the legendary lawyer flatfooted. Erlickson finally looked up. Apoplectic, he roared to his feet.

"Objection!"

"Is this you in the photograph wearing a 'six feet under' shirt, and aren't three of the men in this picture wearing what are known as I.N.K. shirts. And doesn't I.N.K. stand for, 'I'm a nigger killer'? And don't you own one, too?"

"Objection, your honor! This testimony is irrelevant, it has nothing___"

"I want this picture in evidence. It has everything to do___"

"Sustained. Order! Order! I'll have the room cleared if you don't quiet down! Strike Mister Fuego's comments from the record. Will you both approach the bench?"

Judge Bass leaned over. "We can't have you two yelling at each other. I'm going to run an orderly courtroom, is that clear? And no, that photo is not admissible."

"Your honor, in the video we heard the defendant saying that___"

"I said no, counselor. That's final. Take it up on appeal."

Bass called a ten-minute recess.

Andy and Claudia looked at each other as they headed for the door.

"It's Simi Valley and Rodney King all over again. The video doesn't matter. He's going to win." Andy wondered which brigade would get the assignment.

"Simi Valley? Rodney King?"

Andy nodded. "The men who beat Rodney King were tried in Simi Valley because of a change of venue. Videotape or no videotape, Erlickson told the jury that we didn't see what we saw. On the King tape, many whites saw a man resisting arrest. Most blacks saw a man resisting an ass whipping. Patrick thinks they'll believe him over their own eyes."

"I want to change the subject," Claudia said. "This trial is depressing. I'm so glad the school's giving F.L. the two days off to see her mommy get married."

"Straight A students have it like that," Andy said. "And next week's spring break for her anyway, so they saw it made sense."

"I wish we could wait. But with our . . . work, I think we're doing the right thing. Maybe you'll get to know her a little bit while she's here. I told her about you when I went out there before I went on assignment. She hardly listened. She said, 'Mommy, if you say he's nice, that's good enough.'"

"She knows her mother has good taste."

Claudia placed a hand on one ample hip. "Listen at you. You're all that, are you?" Then she grinned. "Yeah, you are." They looked around and kissed each other quickly.

They looked at each other, knowing they might have days or years together. Which was true of anybody. But they walked back to the courtroom knowing that the adage, "Tomorrow's not promised," meant more to them than most.

Fuego remained at the prosecution table as he spoke. "Mister Patrick, I'd like you to demonstrate exactly how you backed away from George Bascomb the night you shot him," he said. "You may use the area in front of the witness stand. And may I remind you that you are still under oath."

Andy had the image of George's murder burned into his brain. He kept a running tally of the discrepancies as Patrick testified.

Patrick glanced at his attorney, who nodded. The former police officer stepped down, unbuttoned his suit coat, bent his knees, and extended his right arm. "Well, I was in a crouch, like this, and my arm was out, like this, and he was charging at me and when he hit me on the head I stumbled backward and started to fall. And the gun discharged."

You lying sack of shit, Andy thought. Despite the video . . . . He closed his eyes.

As Patrick demonstrated his version of events, his right arm tilted upward from the horizontal.

"Hold that position, Mister Patrick, just like that." Fuego moved around the prosecution table and started toward Patrick. "How far away was Mister Bascomb when the gun discharged?"

"He was right on top of me, maybe a foot, no more than two feet." Patrick's legs trembled slightly from the awkward position but he maintained it.

Fuego had a small pointer in his hand. He stopped next to Patrick, turned toward the jury.

"I'd like to point out to the jury that, in Mister Patrick's present position, his arm is pointing upward at an angle of almost forty degrees relative to the horizontal," Fuego said, pointing. "I'd also like to point out that a police firearm will spray powder into clothing at a distance of *three* feet. Mister Bascomb was killed with a bullet that traveled *downward*, there were no powder burns on his clothing, and the stick that he allegedly used to 'club' the defendant was only twenty-three inches long. Assuming an error in the defendant's judgment of distance, it's pretty hard to strike a man on the head with a two foot stick when you're more than three feet away." He gave Patrick a "gotcha" look. "The witness may step down."

Between scribbles, Andy glanced at the jury. Most of their faces were impassive; at least two appeared slightly angry. If he was right about their feelings, Andy didn't think they were angry with the defendant.

And so ended testimony in the *State v. Patrick*.

FIFTY-FIVE

The Reverend Al Scott's ad hoc committee did not have the ecumenical breadth he wanted. Time constraints had forced him to settle for another Baptist minister like himself, two conservative Church of God in Christ preachers, plus his mentor, Bishop William Rivers. Less than forty-eight hours earlier, Bishop Rivers had called and said that Mayor Liotta wanted a meeting. Rivers had called the mayor about a $250,000 federal grant awarded to the city's Faith Based Initiatives Commission (FBI) for a tutoring program. The grant was being administered through the city; Rivers wanted to know when the funds would be released. The eighty-one-year old bishop, past president and now president emeritus of the Alliance of African-American Ministers, agreed to make some calls on the mayor's behalf.

"Al, we need some responsible leadership in our community to speak out against the Walkers," Rivers said during a fifty-minute telephone conversation after his talk with the mayor. "Johnnie Walker was a hoodlum when he started and he's a hoodlum now. And he knows more about those terrorists, this Unit 2236, than he's letting on. And some black people are listening to him. I'm hoping I can count on AAAM to speak out, too."

"Of course you can, Bishop," Scott replied. "I expressed some of the same concerns to the mayor about a week ago. If this Patrick is acquitted, you can bet Unit 2236 will go after him. That won't be good for the city or for race relations."

And so it came to pass that Bishop Rivers, the Reverend Scott, and three other pillars of the faith community sat down in the mayor's City Hall conference room with John Edgar, a black FBI official with a nasal-sounding, reedy voice; police Captain Danis Burton; and Mayor Alfonse Liotta. They were in search of a strategy that would neutralize their longtime nemesis, Minister Johnnie "Black Label" Walker.

Liotta knew Patrick had a fair chance of being acquitted. The move to Levyville was good for that much. If his police force could keep Patrick alive (and take credit for it instead of those hicks up in Levyville), if they could thwart and maybe even catch Unit 2236, Liotta knew he had a good shot at the governor's mansion the next time around. If Patrick was convicted, he'd point out how well the system worked for everyone, regardless of race, gender or creed. Although he couldn't really take credit, he could indirectly point out that justice was served on his watch.

He knew, too, that the feds had more resources than he did to handle the Covenant and this mess with Unit 2236. Even if they had fucked up the raid on Walker's house. So he needed them at this meeting.

The mayor's people on the street were hearing the same thing. A considerable amount of black folks were cheering this Unit 2236 on, even if they were keeping those cheers muted. Whether Walker was involved with the killers or not, some of his own people nevertheless wanted him out of the way.

"Thanks for coming on such short notice, gentlemen," the mayor said as his administrative assistant placed coffee cups, a pot of coffee, a tray with glasses, and a pitcher of ice water on the conference table. "I'm very interested in what you have to say, and in finding ways we can address a serious problem before it rages out of control in our city. Yes, Al."

"We appreciate you taking time from your busy schedule, Mister Mayor," Scott said. The ad hoc committee had named him spokesman. "To get right to the point, we have serious concerns about Johnnie Walker and the growing crisis in our community. Walker's speeches are stirring up the people and arousing passions."

"Unfortunately, much of that's protected by the First Amendment, Al," Liotta said. "We need to nail him on something more concrete than his rhetoric."

"May I interject something here?" John Edgar said. Scott found the speaker's voice irritating. "I'm glad to see some responsible leaders are ready to step up."

"Certainly, Agent Edgar." Liotta smiled at his other guests. "Gentlemen, this is John Edgar. He's with the FBI. And, forgive me; I didn't introduce Captain Dan Burton. I thought law enforcement should be represented here. I hope you don't mind."

Rivers was glad to see an African-American, and a well-spoken one at that, doing such important work for the FBI. "Of course not, Mister Mayor," said Bishop Rivers. "We're glad you invited them. These are serious matters we're dealing with."

"Indeed they are, gentlemen," Edgar said. "There are some things I'm not at liberty to disclose to you, but, to use the mayor's phrase, we may be able to nail Walker soon. We're fortunate to have a strong man in the White House, and I can tell you that President Bruder has asked lawyers at Justice to give him a ruling on whether or not the Covenant churches can be closed under the provisions of PATRIOT Act III. If they say no, he will request new legislation from Congress directed at the Covenant, who are undoubtedly the biggest domestic threat today to the internal security of the United States.

"What we need from you is public condemnation of what they're doing," Edgar continued. "If Mike Patrick is convicted, we imagine it will keep things quiet. But if he's acquitted, your congregations need to know that, first and foremost, the rule of law is what's important.

"I'm suggesting that you hold a news conference with the mayor and Chief Kaheel," the FBI official continued. "If I'm not there, we'll have someone else from Justice attend. Walker denies it, but you know and I know that he's linked in some way to these cop killers. We hope you can reinforce that, and stress the dangers in supporting these people. I appreciate your perspective, Reverend. Walker is indeed stirring up the people and arousing their passions. We need people to be calm and sensible, regardless of how the trial turns out."

"I'll get started on it right away, Agent Edgar," Scott said. "We all know that most of our people are both God-fearing and law abiding. Walker's always been an anomaly. He refuses to call his congregation a church, refuses to identify as a Christian, insisting that he's only a student of Yahshua, whatever that means, and says almost nothing about our Savior's death and resurrection."

"Speaking of Christians," the FBI agent said, "I'm going to invite representatives from the Conservative Christian Crusaders to stand with you. The CCC represents some of the president's most ardent supporters. It will show a diverse presence and be good for everybody." He noticed Scott's crestfallen face. "What's wrong?"

"Uh, you must know the CCC is not well-liked in much of the black community," Scott said. "I mean, I know we agree with them on abortion, and homosexual marriage, and terrorism, and even on fighting fundamentalist Islam, but they are seen as racist even by many in my congregation."

"I think the president will want them there," the cinnamon-colored FBI agent said. "Tell you what. Go with me on this, try and educate your people as best you can, and I'll do all I can to arrange a luncheon meeting for this fine committee with President Bruder. That's a promise."

"Well, even *I* haven't met the president yet," Liotta said, only half-feigning envy. He noticed that the palliative worked instantly on his guests. He chuckled. "John, I hope you can squeeze me into that luncheon." He looked at Burton. "Did you have anything you wanted to say, captain?"

"No, I'm basically here as an observer for the commissioner," Burton said. "I'm filling in for a deputy inspector who called in sick."

The mayor stood up, indicating the meeting was over. "Thank you, gentlemen," he said. "It's good to know there's still responsible leadership in your community."

They shook hands all around. "God bless America," the mayor said as he embraced Scott.

In the hallway, Burton approached the man calling himself Edgar. "Are you new in the local office? I know the SAC there, and I didn't hear anything about him being transferred."

John Edgar was flattered; Burton saw that he was no ordinary field agent. "I'm here on special assignment from Justice." He looked around. "Just between us crime fighters, are you familiar with COINTELPRO?"

"Of course I am," Burton said. "They shut down the Panthers back in the Seventies. Congress ended the program shortly thereafter."

"So they thought. We've been low profile, but there's a new and improved version. I was tapped to head it up." He tried, unsuccessfully, to keep pride from his voice.

Burton smiled. "That's good to hear," he said. "It's just what we need to get this Unit 2236."

"We will," the agent said. "Believe me, no one wants them worse than me. They are doing so much to hurt race relations in this country."

The two men shook hands and exchanged business cards. "With the Covenant headquartered here, if I can ever be of help, don't hesitate to call me," John Edgar said.

Burton smiled again. "I'll do that."

FIFTY-SIX

The silver-haired defense attorney placed a reassuring hand on his client's shoulder as he stood to begin his summation.

Earlier, while smoking a cigarette on the courthouse steps, Mike Patrick's anxiety had been evident. (The occasional dinner meetings with Bulldog Hudson and his attorney, coupled with the trial, had caused him to resume the habit.) Uncle Ike told the younger man not to worry.

"It was pretty rough in there yesterday, Mister Erlickson," Patrick said between puffs.

"I know it, Mike, I know it was rough," Erlickson said. "That's why you have me. It's time for me to dazzle the jury into giving Uncle Ike what he wants, son. When I finish, they won't know what hit them, I promise. Look, Mike, that hussy Morehouse is being considered for a job in Washington. Winning an impossible case would make her look good, like she's got more talent than she actually has. The woman was an affirmative action hire, everybody knows it, and so was Fuego."

He had placed both hands on Patrick's arms. "Son, you're a *policeman*. Nobody wants to see you convicted. Can you understand that? They need a reason to acquit you, and that's where I come in. I'm going to convince them that they won't be able to live with themselves if they send you to jail. I know this trial's been rough for you, but we have to go through the motions. Thank God the American people still believe in their policemen. I came along at a time when the youngsters and the blacks called them pigs and had people thinking they were the enemy. Mike, you are a cop. You're a good cop. Now, I'm going in there and wrap this thing up so we can go home, and you can get your job back."

For Isaac Erlickson, the summation was the crème de la crème of moments in a jury trial. It brought him center stage, where, in his mind, he belonged. In a bench trial, he received pleasure, too, but because he directed his argument at another legal mind, he often had the victory before he "wrapped it all in one package," as he put it. With a jury, he performed. In his mind, he became an Olivier, a Barrymore, coaxing his audience to accept his words as Truth.

329

He clapped Michael Patrick on the shoulder twice and stood up. He said nothing until he stood directly before the jury of his client's peers.

Andy felt churning in his stomach. He knew that something important was being decided for his life, and for the lives of those who would come after him. He looked at his soon-to-be bride; she squeezed his hand.

He realized he was holding his breath for no reason. As he exhaled, he sensed, for a moment, his brother's presence. There were no words in Andy as he sat there, only a warmth, a tingling, a belief that George appreciated what he was doing, and what he might have to do if the trial followed long standing historical precedent: police officers, especially white police officers, did not receive punishment for killing black Americans.

"Ladies and gentlemen of the jury, let's first consider the videotape you saw." Erlickson's forefinger of his right hand touched the little finger of his left hand, itemizing the many ways that his client had been wronged. "Let's get that out of the way because some people would have you believe that what's on that tape is the *complete* story of what happened that night, that tragic night when, not one, but *two* people were victimized on Dock Place.

"What you saw comes in on events already in progress. Some people tell you that Mike Patrick didn't identify himself as a policeman that night. How do you know? How do you know he hadn't already showed his policeman's shield before this young boy turned on his camera? You don't know, you really don't, and neither does the boy with the camera.

"I'll tell you what I believe," Erlickson said. "I believe they knew Mike was an officer and just didn't give a damn, that's what I believe. I believe that you hear anger in Mike's voice that night because some of these people had already started to taunt him and give him a problem, that's what I believe. Don't let that soft voice of Carl Harris fool you. I'm going to come back to him a little later, but don't let it fool you. I believe you should understand that the videotape does not tell the *whole* story of what my client, Mike Patrick, faced that night on Dock Place. Which brings me to my next point."

His right forefinger touched his left ring finger. "Next, let's consider the area in which the defendant, in defense of his life, caused the death, inadvertently, of George Bascomb. Let's consider Dock Place. As residents of Antelope County, you probably know very little about Dock Place. Which is a good thing.

"Dock Place," Erlickson said, his voice rising in degrees. "Do you know what Dock Place is? It's a hellhole, with nearly two hundred hyenas in there, that's what it is. You saw the video tape!"

Audible gasps arose in the audience. Andy looked at the jury. Several looked like deer caught in headlights as they focused totally on Isaac Erlickson. Andy closed his eyes. *He's just started and he's telling the world that we're hyenas.*

"And Michael Patrick was in there, being attacked, and he had to defend himself." Erlickson thrust his hands into his pants pockets, turned and walked away from the jury box. "Mike didn't do what I would have done. I would have shot him then and there." Whirling, he pointed at the jury. "But Mike backed away, remembering his policeman's training.

"There shouldn't have been a trial, we shouldn't even be here now," Erlickson said, thrusting a forefinger in the air. "The mayor ordered this trial for one reason and one reason only."

??? WHAT'S HE TALKING ABOUT? A MAYOR CAN'T ORDER TRIAL! , Andy scribbled. He showed it to Claudia; her face was tight, her full lips set in a straight line.

"The mayor's looking for the minority vote," Erlickson continued. "That's the only reason we're here. Let's look at the witnesses. Let's look at Amanda Harris. Let's look at her testimony."

He walked up close to the jury bench, his face a mask of righteous anger. "That woman should be in jail for perjury. The blood of Bascomb is on her hands. I don't know how she can sleep at night.

"All of those people have manufactured a false façade of lies, chicanery and trickery and the prosecuting attorneys have patched up all these stories to make them fit one mold." Strutting like a bantam rooster, he exuded confidence. Even his adversaries, already repulsed, felt it.

Across the room, both Arlene Morehouse and Hugh Fuego looked ready to vomit.

"But you know, we should expect this—this litany of lies," Erlickson said. "You must realize we're dealing here with people of little or no moral integrity. Take Mister Carl Harris. I told you I'd come back to Mister Holier-than-Thou. The Deacon. He reminds me of the old prayer meetings down home. That Mister Holier-than-Thou is nothing but a sanctimonious little liar!"

He suddenly smiled broadly, as if he and the jury shared a private joke. "But I'd better stick to the record; otherwise, I'll be accused . . . of being a racist or something." He paused. "Let's talk about David Sanders. It will turn my stomach but let's talk about him. This boy is almost certainly a terrorist sympathizer and hates police as sure as I'm standing here."

TERRORIST SYMPATHIZER???? Andy scribbled. WHY IS

2236

BASS ALLOWING THIS? Andy looked at Judge Bass. The jurist was paying rapt attention to the summation.

Standing next to the defense lectern, Erlickson slapped it. "He hates police and would shoot them if he had a chance . . . he is a vicious young punk who wants to destroy our government, our homes, our children, two hundred years of American democracy, and the flag and all that stands for.

"Now I can realize our black brethren sticking together. They, uh, do things I don't approve of, but I can understand." He slapped the lectern again. "What I don't understand, what I refuse to understand, is Sanders coming apparently from a good home and selling his soul to prove his hatred for a policeman, what he calls a pig.

"But, Sanders aside, there's something that must be understood and understood in this court. What we must understand is this: these people would have killed Michael Patrick and they would have killed you, too, if you'd been there. They have absolutely no respect for an oath, they have no respect for the truth, and they have no respect for common decency."

Erlickson stood at the defense table next to Michael Patrick. He placed a hand on his client's shoulder. "These people would just as soon sacrifice you as they did this boy here. Don't sacrifice this boy on the altar of chicanery to get a few lousy, dirty votes. If you don't find Michael Patrick not guilty, there is only one answer—the Thomas Jefferson Bridge!"

The room remained hushed as Isaac Erlickson walked the few steps to the defense table and took his seat.

Andy and Claudia exchanged glances. Then he looked at Erlickson, looked at Judge Bass, looked at the jury, looked at the prosecutors, and scribbled in his notebook:

IF I HADN'T SEEN IT, I WOULDN'T BELIEVE IT. BASS LOOKS PROUD. SOME OF THE JURORS LOOK REVERENTIAL. THE PROSECUTORS LOOK DEFEATED.

"Is the prosecution ready with its summation?" Judge Bass asked into the quiet of the stunned courtroom.

They had decided on Fuego getting Patrick, and Morehouse doing the summation. Morehouse, summa cum laude from Howard Law School, stood quietly, gathering her thoughts. She walked to the prosecution lectern, her face pensive. A short, attractive woman, she looked first at the jury, and then at Judge Bass, whose face had returned from rapt interest to inscrutability.

"Your honor, I . . . after hearing the summation of the defense, and hearing such a statement permitted in this court, I . . . there's really not much to say."

Bass' face darkened at the implied criticism but quickly returned to impassivity.

"I would, however, like to make one point, for whatever importance it may have. Most of the police witnesses made an effort to reflect what the . . . what their superiors thought should be reflected, not what the facts were. We're talking about credibility. We have to keep our eyes open. We have to see what happened, not what some people may want us to believe. In essence, we should look at the facts, and only the facts."

She looked down, then at the jurors. "I want to say, too, that you *saw* what happened. You then saw the defendant present another version of what happened in this courtroom. And, quite simply, his version doesn't fit the facts, even if you hadn't seen the tape.

"When you deliberate, take your time going over the testimony and comparing it with what you *saw*. Then come back with the only verdict that is honestly possible, and that's a verdict that declares the defendant, Michael Patrick, guilty."

TALK ABOUT CAVING IN, Andy wrote slowly beneath his shorthand notes of Morehouse's brief summation. IT'S PROBABLY AS GOOD AN INDICATOR AS ANY OF THE TRIAL.

Judge Alvin O. Bass looked with grave demeanor at the jury of Michael Patrick's peers. "We'll recess for thirty minutes," he said. "When we return, I'll instruct you on the rules that will govern your deliberations. Let me warn you again, you are not to speak . . ."

Andy and Claudia looked at each other. "What do you think?" Andy asked.

Claudia was thoughtful. "I don't want to believe—I don't believe that kind of summation goes on all the time," she said finally. "I would tell you that you made this up if you told me about it without me having been here. But what scares me is that the rest of this trial, I suspect, was rather ordinary. The distortions here probably happen all the time when the victim's poor, black—or brown—and unprotected." She shrugged. "I don't care if I never, ever see another trial again in my life."

FIFTY-SEVEN

oltrane's saxophone prayed through his "Psalm," the sacred song filling Andy's car with his worship. Claudia's presence in his life enveloped everything else, he thought as they headed down the freeway toward the airport. They were going to pick up F.L.

They were picking someone else up, too. It hadn't been difficult getting them on the same flight. He knew Claudia would be surprised. But then, she had helped create a rather seismic shift inside him. This was his way of showing her.

In the past six months, he'd lost his half-brother, become a trained assassin, and steeled himself to sit, for more days than he cared to count, in a courtroom infected with the virus of racism and look at the son-of-a-bitch who had killed George. Thankfully, that was nearing an end. Depending on the length of jury deliberations, the farce would finally be over.

If they acquitted him, he knew in his heart that he wanted the assignment. It was personal. But with Unit 2236, it was business, at least in the philosophical sense. They might think it best that the assignment go to another agent. Of course, a guilty verdict and fair sentence would eliminate the necessity for extra-systemic justice. Although, even with the jury doing the right thing, it was hard to see Judge Bass giving Patrick a lengthy sentence, what with his own life membership in POBA.

Qué será, será.

"You're thinking about George, aren't you?" He felt her hand touch his forearm.

"Indirectly, yes," Andy said. "You're getting to know me too well."

"*Too* well? Isn't that what the next—the rest of our lives are supposed to be about?"

"I'm glad you're getting to know me too well. How did you know?"

"Something happens in your eyes and your mouth tightens a certain way. It's the only time I see you look like that. I know it's going to hurt for a while."

After a few moments, Claudia spoke again. "I started to say 'what the next forty or fifty years are supposed to be about,' and I caught myself. In our new

334

line of work, I'd think the odds are against us, you know?"

"Before I started thinking about George, I was thinking about you and how grateful I am for you," Andy said. "With you, the rest of it seems somehow manageable."

Her hand squeezed his arm again, warm and firm, and then he felt the softness of her mouth kiss his arm after she drew it to her.

"So after we pick up F.L., you said we're picking up someone else. Who are we meeting?" Claudia asked as they stood just beyond the security checkpoint where deplaning passengers exited. "And what time?"

"Actually, I got them to take the same flight," he said. "I'll give you a hint. It's someone I thought you'd say needs to be at our wedding tomorrow night."

Claudia frowned. "Someone . . . ?" Her mouth dropped open; she tugged his sleeve and made him stop. "Look at me," she said. "Did you invite Mary Bascomb?"

"Yes. I felt as if my mother should see her surviving son take a wife," Andy said. "When I made the decision, it felt like a burden lifted and flew away." As he said "mother" to Claudia, what emotional residue remained evaporated.

Claudia moved close, touched his cheek with one hand. "Andrew Blackman, you are a wonderful man." She kissed him with a delicious sweetness. "Thank you. That is a wonderful wedding present."

"No, thank you, my brown-eyed bride-to-be. You planted the seed. I've had to think so much about love in recent months. Loving you, loving my brother, *really* loving the Covenant and not just giving lip service, loving our people even, or especially, with all the damage we're carrying. I think I just reached a place where I saw what the resentment was doing, saw how destructive it really was to me. We'll be doing some ugly things in the days ahead, and I guess I want as little ugly in my life as possible. This new beginning with us just felt like the right time." This time he kissed her.

Fannie Lou Greene-Benjamin and Mary and Grady Bascomb saw them that way as they came through the door.

The five of them took a while holding each other.

The next evening, they took their vows before Minister Johnnie Walker in his study. Romeo stood with Andy as his best man; Lucinda Allen, a lifelong friend who had come into the Covenant at the same time as Claudia had, was her matron of honor; F.L. was her maid of honor.

Time constraints helped to keep the guest list small. Still, the minister's study was crowded, and joyfully so. The visitors called the Creator of the universe by many names: Yahweh, God, Jesus, and Allah, and, on this day, rejoiced as friends seeing unity in their diversity.

Garfield and Gladys Greene were in from Detroit. Both told their daughter it was the grandest moment in their lives, except for the births of her and her siblings, since their days in the movement with Kwame Ture (when he was Stokely Carmichael) and Jamil Al-Amin, (when he was H. Rap Brown) in the Student Non-Violent Coordinating Committee of the early Sixties. Claudia saw her brother Glenn have tears in his eyes for the first time she could remember. "I got something in it," he mumbled with a trace of a smile.

The Reverend Grady Bascomb reminded his wife Mary that God was good *all* the time; they both thanked Him for the blessing.

Marian, beautifully swollen at seven months of her pregnancy, sat through the ceremony. Her parents, Isaac and Vera Muhammad, had flown in from Des Moines for a more joyful visit than their last.

"Ministering to you, Sister Claudia, and to you, Andy, have been blessings in my life," Minister Johnnie said. "Claudia, I have watched you blossom during your years in the Covenant into a flower of strength, extraordinary competence, and exceptional loveliness. You work as hard as anyone I know for our people.

"And you, Brother Andy," Minister Johnnie said. "Until recently, I knew you mostly by the fruits of your labor for our newspaper. You are a quiet brother, but you exemplify all that is righteous and good about black manhood.

"Aside from our professional interactions, up close and personal, you are both good, decent human beings," Minister Johnnie said. "Thank you for allowing me to be your minister. I am honored to bring you together, two who on this special day are becoming one."

He looked up. "Who gives this woman to be married?"

Garfield Greene stepped forward and smiled at the couple. "I do," he said, and stepped back.

Mary Bascomb made no attempt to wipe away her tears. The loss of her youngest son had plummeted her into a level of pain she didn't know existed. It even eclipsed her self-inflicted wound of surrendering her firstborn to another. Now, that firstborn's forgiveness melted guilt that had ossified over four decades.

Minister Johnnie held the hands of Andy and Claudia after they had recited their vows and offered a prayer that the union would be long and filled with Holy Breath:

"I bless your marriage in the name of Yahweh, who is All There Is, in whom we live and walk and breathe and have our very being; I bless your marriage in the name of His/Her son Yahshua, who taught us that we are all sons and daughters of Yahweh, that we are all his brothers and sisters; I bless your marriage in the essence of the Holy Breath that fills us when we follow the Commandment to love."

"It's been a pleasure to meet you, Mister Andy," Claudia's daughter said after the ceremony. "Mommy summed you up pretty good when she came to see me. You guys really do seem like half of each other, like she said, and I hope you keep it up. She's a nice person and you seem real good for her. I hope you'll be good to her."

Andy looked at his stepdaughter, then at Claudia. "Did you really say that, Mrs. Blackman?"

Claudia looked at her daughter, then at Andy. "She wasn't supposed to tell you, Mister Blackman. But yes, I did. And you are."

He kissed F.L. on one cheek and her mother kissed her on the other. "Don't you two stay up all night, okay?" F.L. said with a mischievous smile.

They took a long time. Despite the aching excitement of newness, they refused to rush. They made a ritual of playfulness and teasing, wallowing in their exhilaration. They turned their anticipation into an obedient companion.

Sitting in the suite's spacious hot tub, the Blackmans bathed each other slowly, both, they told each other later, amazed by their patient ardor. Kisses and touches went everywhere: gentle ones, greedy ones, demanding ones.

And when their arousal became unbearable, ready to burst, they loved each other into exhaustion, falling asleep still coupled.

They awoke before dawn and made love again.

FIFTY-EIGHT

It quickly became a working honeymoon. When the Blackmans awoke a second time just before noon, they ordered and enjoyed a leisurely breakfast in bed. There was a text message, sent twice, when Andy turned his cell phone on after showering.

Minister Johnnie had laughingly given them a command when they parted. "You are both ordered to miss Saturday morning lecture," he said. They had saluted and promised to obey. Now, here was an urgent text message the first thing in the morning.

It was succinct: *Need to see u ASAP. Pretty important. 2000 hrs sat. Miss Jones.* He realized that he had never mentioned Miss Jones to Claudia. It was separate from Unit 2236 although Miss Jones was aware of the operation. He would tell her as much of the truth as he could right now and check with Minister Johnnie. He didn't know the man's identity so he didn't see the harm.

"Yo, Mrs. Blackman," he said, kissing her on the stomach. "The bad news is, I have to do something urgent for the Covenant at eight P.M. The good news is, it shouldn't take more than hour."

"If you keep messing with my stomach, you'll be too tired to go anywhere by eight o'clock." She caressed the back of his head. "Can't talk about it?"

"I'll find out if I can. I'll let you know when I get back." His lips kissed below her navel, just above her hairline.

She sighed. "Mister Blackman, you have been warned."

"Yeah, yeah, whatever." His words were muffled as his mouth moved lower; her full thighs opened and surrendered her moistness.

The sun was low in the afternoon sky when they awoke.

The night was dry, unusually windy, and cold for late March. Good snuggling weather for one's first night of marital bliss, Andy mused. He arrived at the garage first. Shoulders hunched, the collar of his brown wool-lined leather jacket turned up, he stood near the closet where they usually met. When Miss Jones arrived, his face was grim and unsmiling as he strode across the garage in an old-fashioned dark plaid mackinaw.

"You guys are up shit's creek if what I have is true," he said. "I got lucky on this one. I happened to attend a meeting with a guy from Justice." He described him to Andy. "As usual, the feds want local assistance and I got wind of a special ops. What do you know about a stash of weapons at Romeo's and some kind of operation he's got planned?"

The enormity of the comment hit Andy like a punch in the solar plexus. "David," he said.

The police officer frowned, confused, when he saw Andy's reaction.

"I know enough about it to know it's not true," Andy said. "They've infiltrated us at the highest level." He told Miss Jones about the phony intelligence they had given David Walker on a hunch. "We want the raid to happen," he said. "Do you know when?"

"I have my ear to the ground. I'd guess you have at least three or four days, maybe as much as a week. They're putting together a major operation. The only thing that might move it up is if the trial looks like it's coming to an end. The jury could come back at any time. Another thing. Apparently David provided his FBI controller with information on you and Romeo as the ones heading up Unit 2236. They think they're close on Romeo with this; they'll be coming for you, too. Be careful."

"I'll be okay. This will break Minister Johnnie's heart," Andy said. "He thought David had straightened out after he went into rehab."

"You just never know how stuff is going to shake out, do you?" Miss Jones shook his head. "Betraying his own father. But then, some folks, if they knew, would say I'm a traitor. And I feel real good about what I'm doing."

He looked at Andy. Somehow it felt like the right time to tell him about his old friend Darryl, the man he knew long before he adopted the code name "Robert" ...

They met at Fort Knox in 1972 and somehow hit it off immediately, an unlikely friendship between recruits from disparate backgrounds. "Darryl" was twenty-year-old Darryl Moore way back then, a young blood who ran with the Slausons, a hard core street gang from Slauson Avenue in South Central Los Angeles. He was Danny Burton, straight out of the hills of Kentucky. In basic training, both he and Darryl were selected as acting squad leaders for teams of ten raggedy-ass recruits each. The drill sergeant said he picked them because Darryl had a year of Los Angeles Community College under his belt and a shitload of street smarts; Danny, on the other hand, was gung ho for the military razzle-dazzle from day one and let the sergeant know he was good with a rifle. Brothers in the Slausons with Darryl had learned from dudes like Bunchy Carter, one of their leaders, that you could be tough and get some education, too. Even though Bunchy had been killed three years earlier, he'd made an impact on Darryl, who had almost followed Bunchy into the newly-formed Black Panther Party. Although they were buck privates, as "acting squad leaders," Darryl and Danny wore armbands with corporal stripes throughout basic training.

They stayed in one of a group of barracks the recruits dubbed "pink palaces." Built a decade earlier, their red brick exteriors and air-conditioned interiors were light years from the aging shotgun-style wooden barracks that dated back to World War Two. Acting squad leaders bunked in semi-private rooms while the rank-and-file lived dormitory style. Darryl and Danny agreed that it wasn't a bad perk when you wanted some quiet, or when you wanted to have late night bullshit sessions and solve the problems of the world as they did on a regular basis. Danny gave Darryl the nickname "Soapbox Sam" because of his fiery and rebellious rhetoric; Darryl returned the favor by labeling Danny first "Hillbill" and then "Bill Hill."

They went to radio school together, spending five hours a day studying Morse code even though Teletype was being used in real-life assignments. Go figure, they both said.

Danny was a patriot and thought they were doing the right thing in Vietnam; Darryl had been influenced by the Black Power thinking that saturated South Central. Danny had joined to kill gooks and keep the world safe from godless communism; Darryl joined because his lousy grades at LACC didn't match his intellect and he couldn't find a decent job.

Then, just like that, they were both headed to the Nam. Despite their Military Occupational Specialty, both men ended up as replacements in an infantry battalion.

They were part of a recon patrol, slogging along double file, when it happened.

A Viet Cong sniper sighted in on Danny. Darryl saw something in the trees move, saw sunshine glint ever so briefly on the rifle barrel, and dove to knock Danny out of harm's way.

Their squad got the sniper. At first Darryl didn't know he was hit. But Danny would never forget the look on his friend's face when he said, "I can't feel my legs."

Darryl decided to stay on the East Coast with an aunt and uncle after the VA discharged him in a government-issue wheelchair. Danny, aware by then that he was an invader and not a rescuer in Nam, bailed out when his enlistment and the war both ended about the same time in 1975. He looked Darryl up and became the "white dude" frequently seen on Darryl's porch over on Cambridge where it dead-ended into the city park. A year passed, then two, then two more.

The two men talked about the repression and escuadrones de la muerte *in El Salvador; Darryl educated Danny about the Sandinistas deposing a brutal dictator in Nicaragua and angering President Reagan; Danny looked back and re-analyzed the U.S. overthrow of democracy in Chile at about the time Darryl was saving his life; they looked at the ongoing "Troubles" in Belfast and how the Catholics saw themselves as the "niggers" of Ireland in their struggle with the British and Irish Protestants. The two men conducted armchair revolutions.*

Danny met a woman, married, and divorced. He liked city life but grew tired of waiting tables. Still believing the system worked despite its many problems, he joined the police force in 1984 and at 30 was the oldest in his class at the academy. He was also in better physical condition than most of his youthful classmates.

The savage beating of Rodney King started him thinking about things. When he heard most of his colleagues defend it, Danny began to wonder if change for the better was possible. When the officers were acquitted, it made him think some more. The Reginald Denny beating made him think more, too.

Danny understood that the two vicious acts of violence symbolized and summarized the deep, unspoken subconscious of white America and black America. White America's deepest fear; black America's repressed rage. His reaction to an acquittal for King's assailants and a ten-year sentence for Denny's attacker was quiet outrage.

By the time of the King beating, Darryl had been a Covenant member for about a decade. He became close to Black Label, who was definitely his kind of preacher. He became a social worker in the Covenant, running a community outreach program that helped veterans renew their lives and showed broken and disabled men how to develop independent skills and self-esteem. He continued the outreach work as a cover after he assumed the identity of "Robert" at the Teacher's request.

The formative stage of Unit 2236 was kindled when four police officers fired forty-one shots and murdered Amadou Diallo. The spark became a flame a year later when the police killed Patrick Dorismond. Although they didn't know either man personally, both the Teacher and Darryl agreed that the slayings at the hands of law enforcement represented an Americanism: it was okay to kill black people. Even black people had bought into this centuries-old American custom and now killed each other in record numbers.

When Dan went to work in the police department's information technology section, he became aware of how widespread police surveillance was. For all its fiery rhetoric, the Covenant of the New Commandment had no history of violence. But to the police department, they were dangerous. One day he and his old friend Darryl were talking, and one thing led to another . . .

*

Miss Jones was able to smile now. "Because of his choice, I'm alive today," he said. "I will never, ever forget that."

Choices.

Andy saw that these two men, who never saw each other anymore, were as tight as he and Romeo were, maybe tighter. Yes, life was about relationships, but it was also about choices. People make choices, even, or especially, when they "don't want to get involved."

George made a choice. George's choice pushed Andy to a choice.

"How long do you think you can do what you're doing?" Andy asked.

"Probably not much longer," Miss Jones answered without missing a beat. "I'm more valuable to the Covenant where I am than any other way I can think of. If I'm caught, they'll find a way to kill me way before I can get sent to jail. This thing has escalated. If I can see them closing in, I'll try to get to one of your safe houses and hope some black folks, not knowing anything about me, don't shoot me first, " He looked at his watch. "Minister Johnnie has to know about the pending raid, and David, right away. I don't know when I'll see you again."

They shook hands and embraced. This time Miss Jones left first.

Andy and Minister Johnnie walked side by side along his tree-lined street. Several yards behind, two watchful Swords followed. On the other side of the street, a third Sword walked parallel to them at their pace.

Minister Johnnie's black ankle-length overcoat swayed like a priest's cassock as he walked. He wore a black Kangol cap to keep the chill off his head. The minister had listened without interruption as they walked. Now they had gone almost a block without speaking.

"I came this close to telling him the identity of the Fourth Star," Minister Johnnie said, holding up the forefinger and thumb of his right hand pressed together. "But I listened to my gut. As I told him about Unit 2236, my stomach kept tightening. I pushed myself to trust him because he had cleaned up."

"It's been over ten days since you gave him the Romeo story," Andy said. "Somehow I think he might not have said everything. I mean, about you being the Third Star. In fact, it sounds like he's betraying our work and trying to shield you at the same time. If he's trying to save you, why is he trying to destroy your work?"

"Andy, they may be paying him, they may have something on him, who knows? He's always had a hair up his ass about Romeo."

"Which is why he lied to them and said Romeo's running Unit 2236, I guess. It sounds like he was forced to tell them *something,* and he lied to them to save you."

They walked. "I understand a mystery now, something I've pondered throughout the forty years of my ministry." He stopped walking and looked at Andy. "After they executed the Great Teacher, we've always been shown the persecution of his early followers. We've never seen them portrayed as fighting back. But they were probably a lot like us, or like we're getting ready to be. Defending themselves as best they could. I mean we're talking about them surviving for a few hundred years before Constantine. Some of them had to resist.

"Where am I going with this? Andy, the empire wants an excuse to sell the American people on a bloodbath. They know the Covenant will fight to the death. And in a conventional toe-to-toe, we can't possibly win. They know that, too."

Minister Johnnie's next words stunned Andy. "We have to let this Romeo thing play out, but I'm going to surrender before they can wipe us out."

"Minister Johnnie, I don't understand."

"They believe in cutting off the head. I'm the head. Without the head, they will still come after us but they can't use me as an excuse. I could go underground but then they'd have an excuse for a manhunt." He paused. "I'm going in. I'll call Raphael when I get home and see if he can arrange something."

"But they haven't charged you with anything."

Minister Johnnie chuckled. "They'll think of something." His mind made up, he decided to turn back toward home.

He heard Minister Johnnie, and he didn't want to hear him. He wondered if his proposal, the one he'd discussed with Claudia up on King Drive, would help or hinder what the Teacher wanted to do. There was only one way to find out.

He talked; Minister Johnnie listened.

"It may be a hard sell," Minister Johnnie said when Andy was finished. "We're going to have casualties regardless of what we do. Even with my surrender there'll be casualties, but hopefully not a bloodbath. What you suggest may save some lives."

By now, they stood in front of Minister Johnnie's home. They knew they were being watched, and not just by Swords. Now that they were back, they were probably being listened to as well.

"Tell you what," Minister Johnnie said. "Find us a place to eat tomorrow evening that's probably not bugged. Certain ones of us need to hear your idea, along with a few other things I have to say. Get on it first thing in the morning and then call me." He smiled at Andy and placed a hand on his shoulder. "Needless to say, you and Mrs. Blackman must be there. You've been more valuable in the past six months than many have been who have been with me for years. Thank you." His smile broadened. "This is a heck of a way to spend a honeymoon, isn't it?"

FIFTY-NINE

Danis Burton liked libraries. He thought of reading a book as holding a conversation with someone he was unlikely to meet, and having to be a really good listener in that conversation. When he wanted quiet time, he would often take a long lunch and sit in one of the main branch's many high-vaulted reading rooms for an hour or so. He would often look up from a magazine (all that he usually had time for) and marvel at the sheer immensity of information. He had a standing cliché that always came to mind: so many books, so little time. His workload kept him from spending nearly as much time as he wished in what he referred to as "bibliographic temples for bibliophiles."

This was one of those days when he regretfully had no time to spend. He went in and walked directly to the bank of computer terminals lining the library's second-floor hallways. He registered with a second library card he had under an assumed name and sat down at a terminal.

He logged on as "gdamiano" and sent a brief e-mail to Andy's cell phone. It read:

A wicked april fool's day trick is planned for you. You better stay up because it will happen early. I'll check my messages for questions later today. All the best, miss jones.

SIXTY

"They are ready to kill me."

The peacefulness beneath the words unsettled everyone listening. There was an absolute absence of fear in the Teacher's statement. He was not speaking generically, they knew; he meant his death was imminent.

Andy, sitting two seats away from Minister Johnnie, looked up from the notes he had written on two-by-five cards. If this was setting the tone of the meeting, it was clear why they were at Giovanni's Vegetarian Restaurant instead of at the meetinghouse.

"Chaz, we need a place where we can sit, eat, and talk privately for an hour or two," Andy had told the proprietor, an old college friend. He couldn't give the real reason: Minister Johnnie's inner circle needed to gather where it was unlikely to encounter electronic listening devices. As far as he knew, none of them were vegetarians, but Andy knew the cuisine would satisfy even die-hard carnivores. He'd eaten jumbo "shrimp" a few years back at Giovanni's and had been unwilling to believe the soy product wasn't actually seafood.

After returning to the hotel, he and Claudia had talked well past midnight and fallen asleep in a warm spoon-like embrace. He'd called Chaz early, gone back to sleep for an hour. Then Claudia suggested they "practice" and they did.

Now, in the restaurant's second-floor dining area—the first floor was buffet—they listened to Minister Johnnie's stark opening words.

Downstairs, several Swords ate and watched the street, noting that a patrol car circled with some regularity.

Minister Johnnie watched his loved ones react to his opening comment. He was immaculate and street sharp in a collarless white silk shirt open at the throat, a black leather vest, and charcoal grey slacks. His spirit felt full as he looked at some of the best fruit of his four decades of work.

After asking the elders present, David and Roxanne Cook, for permission to begin, Minister Johnnie's prediction had stunned them all.

"I have selected text to fashion a prayer to give thanks for this extraordinary fellowship and for this meal," Minister Johnnie said. "We who have

346

been through so much must discuss some serious matters. Because we have never been here, except for Andy, there's a good chance we are not being eavesdropped on. Speak freely; you are the most trustworthy in the Covenant."

He looked across the round table to David. "I want David to bless us with a prayer based on Matthew 10:34 through 37," he said. "Will you do that for us, son?"

Andy wondered what was going on. He had lied to David, at his father's insistence, and told him that Romeo had been ordered to bring his wife back from her vacation and leave his daughter with her grandparents. Romeo was still planning the attack, he said. David was asking Romeo about a non-existent operation, again at Minister Johnnie's insistence, and ordered to report back to his father. Now, judging by the look on David's face, he, too, sensed that something was amiss. He looked almost nauseous. Andy bowed his head, as did the others.

David wanted to run from the room. Romeo had admitted being in charge of a renegade operation. He seemed upset and fearful that David knew.

"You can't tell Minister Johnnie, he'll be furious at me," Romeo had told David. "Let me tell him, maybe he'll understand. Give me twenty-four hours to go tell him." And now this meeting had suddenly happened. As he looked at the Bible verse, he felt a stirring of panic. He sensed this prayer was directed at him. Something was wrong. He was trying to control things and things were controlling him.

"Yahweh, our Creator, we gather in the spirit of the words of Yahshua, who told those who followed him: 'think not that I am come to send peace on earth: I came not to send peace, but a sword. For I am come to set a man at variance against his father, and the daughter against her mother, and the daughter-in-law against her mother-in-law. And a man's foes shall be they of his own household. He that loves father or mother more than me is not worthy of me: and he that loves son or daughter more than me is not worthy of me.'

"Yahweh, we pray that as we face these difficult times ahead, we ask Your strength in our lives, that we may be an example to those who have not found You. We ask your blessings on this meal and our serious deliberations today. We say Amen, so let it be done."

"Amen," said those gathered with Minister Johnnie. David knew that he was more afraid than he had ever been in his life.

"Thank you, David," Minister Johnnie said. He signaled to a Giovanni employee that they were ready to eat.

They dined sumptuously on vegetarian jumbo shrimp scampi, several pastas, spinach, collard greens, and yams prepared in a wonderfully exotic sauce.

There was nary a murmur of dissent at the absence of meat in the meal.

"Before I say some things, I want us to hear from our dear brother, Andy Blackman," Minister Johnnie announced when they all had finished eating and were sipping on tea or an organic coffee substitute. "I truly believe Andy has been given a spiritual insight that may have eluded me all these years. Then again, maybe it hasn't. Andy wants to synthesize ideas that most of us have always assumed existed as a dichotomy. Whatever we decide, I believe he's worth hearing out. Andy?"

Andy looked around at the remarkable assemblage. Minister Johnnie's wife Ila, glowed with the quiet certainty a person has who knows inwardly they have almost always done their best; his new bride, Claudia, had transformed her looks at him from merely attractive dark brown eyes into pure orbs of unconditional love as they faced whatever dangers were around the corner; Romeo and Malikah seemed almost as peaceful as their Teacher, holding hands; Glennville Greene, his face stoic, sat at a table by the door (thinking of his gang banging days and how it seemed little had changed, that the gangs were just bigger now); Robert sat in a chair that few knew was equipped with a semi-automatic weapon in each wheelchair arm; David and Judith—she, as always, a study in quiet seriousness, and he the least comfortable person in the room, a solitary dissonant energy; and, finally, Elders Roxanne and David Cook, Malikah's parents, regarded by all as the spiritual mother and father of the Covenant of the New Commandment.

David Cook and Roxanne Smith had met each other at the same Black Power conference that Johnnie Walker had attended in 1968. They had been founding members of the Covenant, so impressed had they been with the brash young man who, to them, "just seemed different from other preachers."

"Thank you, Minister Johnnie." Andy shuffled the note cards in his hands, knowing he probably wouldn't need them. "A lot has happened in such a short space of time. A year ago, we were angry about the upsurge in murders of black people by police, and the immunity given to the wrongdoers. Today, we're under siege. You all know the president will address the nation in the next few days announcing what will amount to martial law without calling it that. We have reason to believe they will try and shut down our meetinghouses. In my opinion, we have almost everything against us, but, *maybe,* a couple of things going for us.

"One thing going for us, *maybe*: the empire has always prided itself on its so-called Bill of Rights, even before they started pretending it applied to us. So, the freedom of religion they espouse *may*—and I stress that word—keep us from being annihilated. Although, under Bruder, we have fewer legal guarantees than usual. And we must not forget that so-called Middle America loves this man.

"The other thing is trickier. I once thought nonviolent direct action was the best way to fight, especially if you professed to being a spiritual person. Then, after I lost my brother, I was stopped by a STOP cop who assumed I had a police record, and something changed inside me. I knew he'd blow me away just as soon as look at me, whether I was doing anything or not. Especially today. I'm now convinced that, given the climate, armed struggle is necessary. Like Minister Johnnie, I won't denounce whoever's started arming themselves." Even though they felt the room was secure, and everyone in the room knew of Unit 2236's relationship to the Covenant, Minister Johnnie had instructed everyone to still speak as if a nosy waiter or electronic device was observing them.

"Having said that, I'm proposing that the Swords of the Master abandon their mission of self defense in favor of nonviolent direct action," Andy said. He felt no surprise at the buzz and murmurs that followed. He looked at Glenn; he was frowning.

"Glenn, your input will be critical, but everybody should weigh in," Andy said. "My reasoning goes like this. To battle the empire, we need both philosophies instead of thinking either/or. These folks known as Unit 2236 are battling from underground; the Swords are not underground. Even if the Swords arm themselves to the teeth, we face being annihilated if we try and defend the meetinghouses. We cannot hold off any concerted military effort for long without being wiped out. And they will happily wipe us out. Again, this Unit 2236 faction that's been in contact with us is fighting a guerilla military operation, which is different.

"However, if we move to Martin Luther King's assertive kind of direct action, the secret to winning will be getting the rest of the world to see us defending our places of worship by being civilly disobedient and refusing to cooperate with the authorities, but without weapons. We must remind the world that nonviolent is an adjective, and that they have taught people to drop the noun, as in nonviolent *resistance*."

Andy saw understanding start to glimmer on the faces of some of his beloved comrades. *Places of worship. Defending. Direct action. Resistance.*

"In all probability, private security from OneCorporation International will be used against us, along with regular police," Andy continued. "Television is no longer new. Fifty years ago, they unwittingly aided and abetted civil rights protestors in their resistance by flashing the images across the country and around the world. It's unreasonable to believe that OCI television stations and newspapers will show anymore than they must to maintain the 'free and open press' illusion. We will have to get our message out by the Internet, DVDs, cell phones, and any other way we can think of, and we must make the communication effort international.

"I'm not naïve. The Covenant will lose lives whether we use weapons or whether we use nonviolence. Nonviolent direct action is most effective against a brutal fascist type. Unless they're psychotic, they will stop hurting you not because they come to love you, as King believed, but simply because they will look immoral and bad and see they can't get what they want. People forget that King said you must create tension, a crisis, when people won't negotiate, and continue and increase that tension until they will negotiate.

"In conclusion, I'm telling you that we must continue to advocate support for the armed resistance of Unit 2236, wherever and whoever they are," he said, winking to those around the table. "And I will stand with the Swords nonviolently as well as continuing my other duties, since you cannot ask others to do what you won't do. It will be dangerous against these crazies, but I feel it's our only chance to survive without going underground." They translated the meaning of his words: he would continue to fight in Unit 2236 as well as struggle at the meetinghouses.

"Magnificent, Brother Andy," Minister Johnnie said. "We sometimes think we're in a dichotomy in life when we aren't. In all my years in this ministry, I have tended to think one or the other, even when I saw nonviolent tactics were more efficient, as when we used them during the assault on my home. Glenn, as Swords captain, let's hear from you first. Then, I want the testosterone in the room to defer briefly to some response from our mates."

Glenn was succinct as always. "I understand and accept the logic. Maybe for the first time, I see the courage needed to fight without weapons. The Swords will obey orders because of our military discipline, but I think many of them will find it hard at first to internalize the rightness of this approach."

Minister Johnnie looked at his wife of nearly thirty-seven years. "Ila?"

Those who knew his wife knew that she preferred a non-spotlight role not because she was uncertain, inarticulate, or old-fashioned. Ila Walker simply felt the *yin yang* approach was healthier for her relationship with a man who excelled in the spotlight. Those who knew her called her an "iron warrior."

"When I married our Teacher, I subordinated any allegiance to Caesar to my allegiance to Yahweh," she said in her quiet but strong voice. "I knew we were signing death warrants then; having thirty-seven years is more than I bargained for. I say, dare to struggle, dare to win."

The Cooks were extremely brief. "In loving each other, we cannot lose although some lives will be lost. They're killing us anyway," Roxanne Cook said.

"I'm glad we lived to see this day," David Cook said.

When David Walker spoke, he was choked up. "I never thought it would come to this," he said. "My father is an awesome man to have brought us this far. I don't know why he feels he's going to die, but I feel overwhelmed and am glad the mighty strength in this room will be with us if I am called to lead as he suggests."

Minister Johnnie nodded to his wife. She opened her bag and produced a large bottle. It took a moment for understanding to sink in at what they saw. They had all noticed shot glasses at their place settings but had no context for knowing why they were there.

Minister Johnnie uncapped the fifth of Johnnie Walker Black Label Scotch whisky. He had owned it for more than forty-one years. He poured a shot and passed it to Ila. She did the same and passed it.

As the bottle reached his son, he said, "David, you may just symbolically hold it and drink water, if you prefer." Every member of the inner circle knew that David had gone to rehab.

"No sir, it's okay," David said. Since drinking bourbon with his handler, he had bought and drank two pints, which were "to be his last." "This is a special occasion."

Minister Johnnie said nothing, but it wasn't the answer he wanted or expected to hear. After everyone's shot glass had been filled, Minister Johnnie held his own high in salute; his family and friends did the same.

They drank.

"I guess it's a little strong after forty-one years, knowwhatI'msaying?" Minister Johnnie said, making a face, smiling. "I think our Creator understands old friends having a drink together to remember forty-one and a half years of service."

"I began our meeting by saying they're going to kill me. I say it because I understand the evil that is our enemy. Like empires before them, and empires that will follow them, they believe if you cut off the head, the body will die. They don't understand, and will never understand, that in a just cause, the body will regenerate a new head.

"I'm going to die because I'm the leader of the Covenant. They can't find the leader of Unit 2236 and I'm the next best thing." He paused. "To avoid a bloodbath, I'm going to turn myself in to them once they make it overtly clear that they're going to attack us. If I don't, nonviolence or no nonviolence, they will attack in full force. With me on the street, they will not back down again as they did before. With me in custody, they may back down as long as they can't connect us to Unit 2236, like they tried to do in Memphis. You notice that was a public relations failure; no one believed them.

"I am not a dumb man. Once I'm in their custody, they will kill me. It's that simple. How, I don't know."

The Teacher opened a book. "We began with a scripture and we'll end with one. But before we do, I want to read something to you that I first read during the infancy of the Covenant. I used it for a sermon on our fifth anniversary. And, to be honest, it sounded so romantic and unlikely I couldn't visualize it. The Black Power Movement was no longer on the ascendancy, Nixon was president, and black folks were licking their wounds. Plus, the man who wrote it was two years in his grave. He, too, knew, they would kill him. This is what he wrote:

" 'We must accept the eventuality of bringing the U.S.A. to its knees; accept the closing off of critical sections of the city with barbed wire, armored pig carriers crisscrossing the streets, soldiers everywhere, tommy guns pointed at stomach level, smoke curling black against the daylight sky, the smell of cordite, house-to-house searches, doors being kicked in, the commonness of death,"

He closed the book. "That was Soledad Brother George Jackson speaking in his book, *Blood in My Eye,* completed just days before he was assassinated. It seems less romantic now. If I'm not with you physically, my spirit will be with you at the barricades."

He stretched his hands out. "As a benediction, let's recite Luke, the twenty-second chapter and the thirty-sixth verse."

Ila took his right hand; Romeo Butler took his left. The others followed suit until they had an unbroken circle. They spoke in one voice:

"Then said he unto them, But now, he that hath a purse, let him take it, and likewise his scrip: and he that hath no sword, let him sell his garment, and buy one."

SIXTY-ONE

ister Jake struggled to restrain himself. It took a mighty effort. To aid his self-control, he quietly placed his stockinged feet back in his aged rundown sandals. That way, he knew he wouldn't pick up a shoe and hurl it at the television set. As much as she loved the Checkers Gang, the administrator at Butler Center had come close to banning them years earlier when Mister Jake had, in fact, thrown a shoe at the set (and fortunately missed) when George W. Bush was selected to serve as forty-third president and gave his first inaugural address.

The red and black checkers sat on their scruffy board, forgotten by Mister Jake and the others. The Reverend Doctor Aloysius "Al" Scott III, his gang of three, Mayor Liotta, two exquisitely coiffed Conservative Christian Crusaders, and an assemblage of federal "suits" were having a grand old time "skinning and grinning," as Mister Jake called it, as a news reader's voiceover introduced a "deputy special assistant to the president." The federal official was an unexpected last minute addition to the Scott news conference. Scott and the others shook hands, smiled, and looked important.

The square-jawed, blue-eyed, blow-dried deputy special assistant to the president wore a navy blue suit, white shirt, and red foulard tie. He stepped to the microphone. The banner at the bottom of the screen had changed to red with white letters, bordered with blue. The OC EYE logo sat in the left corner; the other corner was adorned with a small American flag. The caption read, THE COVENANT CULT CRISIS: THE U.S. RESPONDS.

"What fucking Covenant crisis?" asked Big Larry. "I didn't know there was a Covenant crisis."

"When did they become a cult?" Varnell wanted to know. "I didn't know they were no cult."

"The big white folks say they're a cult," Mister Jake said. "I try to tell you, white folks ain't gonna treat you right regardless."

"Good morning," the presidential aide said. "I'm Stuart Breissinger, deputy special assistant to the president. I bring greetings from President Hugh

Bruder who, as we speak, is preparing an executive order to mobilize and deputize OneCorporation International's new elite security division, the Governmental Oversight Division, which the president has aptly nicknamed the GOD Squad. He will ask Congress for an immediate $2 billion appropriation so that additional hires can be made in the fifteen cities where the Covenant of the New Commandment has offices. The GOD Squad will supplement the overtaxed FBI teams already in the field combating this new and formidable threat to national security. This is a direct quote from President Bruder: 'The forces of the right will be triumphant in this battle to preserve our American way of life.'"

"It really is happening here," Mister Otis said, awed by the thought.

"Hell, 'it' has been happening here for some time now," Mister Jake groused. "For us, it's never stopped happening. We just ain't done a damn thing about it."

". . . The president's order has a six-point plan designed to crush this violence before it gets out of hand, effective immediately. We fear that the bold robbery in Memphis is only a harbinger of things to come. We know that Unit 2236 is violent; we now know that the Covenant of the New Commandment not only endorses their vicious killing spree but are committed to violent criminal behavior, too. Both organizations are bands of thugs who will be brought under the control of law by President Bruder.

"The six-points are as follows: First, Johnnie Walker, the leader of the Covenant, has forty-eight hours to surrender to law enforcement authorities, with or without his attorney. Second, all meetinghouses of the Covenant will be sealed by authorized law enforcement agencies in seven days and become the property of the U.S. government until further notice. Third, the apprehension of all members of Unit 2236 will become the top priority of the Federal Bureau of Investigation. In conjunction with this, our efforts will be coordinated with law enforcement agencies nationwide, who will be asked to make this a top priority. Fourth, additional security will be present in Levyville until the end of the trial there for former police Officer Michael Patrick. Fifth, we are searching our database for the last five years to see if other officers might be in jeopardy who have participated in justifiable homicides in which African-Americans were the deceased. Security measures will be put in place where appropriate. And finally, the president will request immediate emergency passage of the African-American Short-term Emergency Protection and Identification Act, also known as S.E.P.I.A. This bill will facilitate the conversion of driver's licenses and identification cards into national identity cards for people of African descent, complete with locator microchips. Until further notice, citizens identifiable as African-Americans would be required to have the card on their persons at all times. Failure to have the card or produce it on demand for a duly authorized federal, state, or local law enforcement officer would be grounds for arrest and indeterminate detention. Under this act, writs of Habeas Corpus are inapplicable. For the purposes of this act, all security personnel employed by OneCorporation International would be considered duly deputized and authorized persons to request identification. The president expects emergency passage of the bill within forty-eight hours and recommends that citizens of African-American descent report to any state department of motor vehicles or Internal Revenue Service facility within seven days of the bill's passage to have their cards adjusted.

"A sub-section of this act asks the Congress to disband the Congressional Black Caucus as an organization. Former CBC members who vote for this bill and comply with its requirements will continue in their duties. Any CBC member who refuses to comply will be in violation of the law and dealt with accordingly.

"President Bruder understands that these measures are strong and may appear harsh to some. He assures the public that once the threats to national security have been eliminated, these measures will be rescinded."

Breissinger assured viewers that the six-point plan had support from "diverse recognized national religious leaders," meaning the CCC and the black leaders on the rostrum with him. Scott and his crew had never heard themselves called national leaders by anyone of Breissinger's stature. They looked appropriately solemn behind him.

"Thank you for listening," Breissinger said. "We won't be taking any questions. God bless America."

"I don't want you all to get me wrong with what I'm about to say," Mister Jake said as he lit a cigarette. His upper lip curled as if he had just smelled an overripe pile of human feces. "I've known Black Label longer than most all of you, except maybe Otis. Black Label would be the first to tell you he ain't hardly no Jesus. But damned if those no good for nothing niggers standing there ain't just like the Sadducees and Pharisees that killed Jesus." He cleared his throat and spit into a nearby trash can. "I'll be damned if at my age I'm going to carry some damn identification card like they did in South Africa."

They knew Mister Jake meant what he said. The other men were silent. They were doing what almost every dusky-hued citizen free under the sanctions of the Fourteenth Amendment was doing: deciding what their options were.

Four

We hold these truths to be self-evident, that all men are created equal, that they are endowed by their Creator with certain unalienable Rights, that among these are Life, Liberty and the pursuit of Happiness. --That to secure these rights, Governments are instituted among Men, deriving their just powers from the consent of the governed. --That whenever any Form of Government becomes destructive of these ends, it is the Right of the People to alter or to abolish it, and to institute new Government, laying its foundation on such principles and organizing its powers in such form, as to them shall seem most likely to effect their Safety and Happiness. Prudence, indeed, will dictate that Governments long established should not be changed for light and transient causes; and accordingly all experience hath shewn, that mankind are more disposed to suffer while evils are sufferable than to right themselves by abolishing the forms to which they are accustomed. But when a long train of abuses and usurpations, pursuing invariably the same Object evinces a design to reduce them under absolute Despotism,

. . . it is their right, it is their duty . . .

to throw off such Government, and to provide new Guards for their future security.

SIXTY-TWO

pril began with a pre-dawn light drizzle that made it colder than it should have been.

At precisely 0300 hours, with lights off, eight Special Weapons And Tactics wagons and five FBI-registered vehicles rolled quietly onto the tree-lined street where Romeo Butler, deputy director of the Swords of the Master (and, as the Second Star, deputy commander of Unit 2236), lived with his wife and twelve-year-old daughter. They had two battering rams, forty-eight semiautomatic rifles, a box of flash grenades, and more than four dozen side arms. They also had a search warrant to recover four dozen high-powered rifles, an assortment of hand grenades, and a cache of equipment and material for making explosives.

If unarmed Swords were there and didn't surrender, the SWAT teams had orders: take them down. If the Swords were armed, they had the same orders and an additional one: call in two helicopters carrying several cases of explosives.

FBI personnel had quietly and inconspicuously evacuated the home attached to Butler's earlier in the day. Without even being told, the family, a retired couple, knew it had to be about their quiet but militant neighbor.

Wardell Keyes was no longer undercover. His request had been granted to lead one of the FBI teams. With his last test scores, he knew a promotion to Special-Agent-in-Charge was certain once they saw his role in bringing down this pseudo-church bunch. Becoming a SAC had been a remote dream when he joined the Bureau, but not anymore. He and Jhanae could live openly after this, without the pressures he'd put her under while on loan to the police here.

At 0309 hours, with Romeo Butler's semi-detached house surrounded and sharpshooters on a nearby roof, Butler's telephone rang. The Special Agent-in-Charge waited for an answer. Because of Butler's wife and child, they were ordered to try and acquire a peaceful surrender. Their intelligence said he had taken them away, but best to be safe rather than sorry. Hurting a woman and child would be bad public relations. They had no reason to believe anyone else was there. Surveillance by a circling patrol car had shown Butler arriving home, apparently from work, about seven P.M. No one had been seen entering or leaving since.

No one answered. Despite the inconvenience to Butler's neighbors, at 0315 hours, a baritone male voice barked instructions through a loudspeaker.

"Romeo Butler, this is the Federal Bureau of Investigation and the police. We have your house surrounded. We have a search warrant for your home. We are asking you to surrender peacefully. We don't want to bring harm to your family. We are giving you ten minutes to come out with your wife and child. You are to place your hands on your head and come out peacefully."

Lights winked on along the block. Keyes had argued for no-knock but had been overruled. This was a middle-class neighborhood; it might prove good for the reputation of the department if some consideration was given before force was used. Unless Butler had somehow gotten men inside, a firefight was unlikely. The man was fierce, but surely he wouldn't jeopardize his family and his neighbors.

Nothing.

They waited fifteen minutes. At 0330 hours, as neighbors watched, the battering ram was readied at the front door; a SWAT team took positions at the rear door.

At 0332 hours, they swarmed Butler's house. Flash grenades went off; the elite SWAT teams moved in during the commotion. One room at a time, they cleared each room and closet in the two-story brick façade porch home.

"Move! Move, move, move, move!" Keyes shouted as they charged inside. Laser scope assault rifles pointed at each nook and cranny.

"Clear!" Keyes said, his adrenaline pumping. They moved into the dining room: "Clear!" And so it went.

By 0340 hours, it became clear that neither Butler nor his family were in the house. Keyes felt a sinking feeling in his stomach. The search for weapons and explosives ended in the basement at about the same time Romeo Butler walked up on the other side of the street, accompanied by two Swords. He had watched the proceedings through binoculars from a parked car two blocks away. The police cars blocking entrance to his street had never noticed him.

He wore an off-white baseball cap pulled low, and the collar of his white windbreaker pulled up, but one or two neighbors still recognized him right away. As they started toward him, Romeo quietly waved them away, and then placed his hands on his head. Both Swords did likewise. They wore baseball caps like their leader, along with denim jackets and pants.

Johnnie Walker's orders had been explicit to two of his best warriors, who had volunteered, and to his Unit 2236 field commander. Under no circumstances should Butler in any way resist arrest, even if attacked physically. He should obey any and all commands from law enforcement, including surrender. Likewise, if he *was* attacked physically, the two unarmed Swords should fight physically to defend him with their very lives, while Butler remained utterly passive.

Andy Blackman received a signal of two rings on his cell phone just before Romeo left his vehicle. Wearing his press pass, he drove as close as he could and parked just as Romeo walked into the block where he lived.

Minister Johnnie gave the order believing—correctly—there would be witnesses. Witnesses hadn't seemed to help much in the Bascomb case, but other eyes might help here. Romeo's block was racially diverse. Minister Johnnie felt that white witnesses would be treated differently.

Romeo and his bodyguards watched quietly for some time as agents carried out three desktop computers, two laptops, and dozens of boxes. None of the boxes contained rifles or explosives or grenades.

Romeo waited until he saw Wardell Keyes. When he spotted him, he ducked under the yellow police tape and started slowly across the street with his hands on his head. He ordered the two Swords to remain three steps behind him unless there was a need to obey Walker's superseding order.

Then, a strange thing happened. One of the neighbors who had first noticed Romeo started to applaud, along with his family. Others looked, saw their neighbor, and began clapping, too. It took startled police officers a few moments to assess what was happening.

The SAC saw him first. He placed his hand on his sidearm reflexively, and then realized Butler's posture of surrender would make him look bad.

"How you doing, Wardell?" Romeo said loudly.

Keyes turned and cursed when he saw the expression on Romeo's face. He walked up to him.

"There aren't any weapons, are there?" he said with a scowl. His angry face glistened with rain.

"I reserve the right to remain silent until I can have an attorney present," Romeo said. Then, for a split second, Romeo forgot he was a leader in a religious organization. "You jive ass motherfucker," he added.

It was hard, but Keyes resisted the urge to punch Romeo out. He knew he wouldn't be able to help David Walker. Whether or not the Covenant had known that he, Keyes, was undercover, for some reason they had suspected David and set him up.

The SAC watched the exchange with puzzlement at first. Then he remembered Keyes had been undercover. "Where are the weapons, Butler?" he asked.

Romeo smiled, keeping his hands on his head the entire time. "I don't have an attorney present, but you'll be hearing from him first thing in the morning," he said. "I know you think you had probable cause, so we'll see how it shakes out when I sue your fat ass, and everyone associated with this debacle."

Neighbors had moved closer despite the police tape. "Watch your mouth, Butler," the SAC said.

"You tear up my home and you want me to watch my mouth? Fuck you and the horse you rode in on! You are out of your mind! If I am under arrest, handcuff me and take me in. If I'm not, I want you out of my home now. Unless, of course, you still want to look for the guns you think I have."

They knew he was taunting them. Keyes cursed under his breath. One thing bothered him far more than not finding the weapons. What bothered Keyes was that, all along, they thought they were one up on Romeo Butler and the Covenant. Instead, the Covenant was one up on them.

The operation had been well planned and well executed, but with one underlying, and obviously false, premise. Somehow their source, David, had been found out, or had been suspected, and so the source turned out to be utterly unreliable. It was inconceivable that he had set them up for ridicule. He had too much to lose.

Keyes grimaced. Now they had no physical evidence at all that Johnnie Walker or Butler was doing anything they could bring Walker down for. Without evidence, the conspiracy charges under the new Short-term Emergency Protection and Identification Act would have to suffice.

Keyes turned away and came face to face with Andy Blackman. "Hey Wardell," Andy said. "Looks like you're having a bad night. Can you give me a statement for my story? For instance, would you address how you've been an undercover cop in a religious organization, and maybe even an agent provocateur? And can you say anything about the so-called Covenant robbery in Memphis? By the way, when did you start smoking, or do you only smoke in airports?"

"Get out of my face, Blackman," Keyes snarled. "I don't have any comment, none at all."

Carvel Thomas' phone rang. Blinking sleep away, he looked at his nightstand. 4:30 A.M. *Shit.*

It was attorney Raphael Roper, lead counsel for the Covenant of the New Commandment. His client, Johnnie Walker, had to surrender no later than noon of the following day. He would bring him in. If he failed to do so, they would look for him and arrest him, beginning at 12:01.

"Why are you calling me?"

"If anything goes wrong, Minister Johnnie wanted at least one decent cop to know the truth, that he was willing to surrender," Roper said. "He trusts you," he added.

"What can I do?" Thomas started to ask, but Roper had hung up.

Thomas sat on the side of his bed, elbows on his knees, his face in his hands. His wife rolled over. "What's wrong?" she asked with sleep in her voice.

"Let's talk in the morning," he replied. "I'll tell you about it then." He got back under the covers. *I want to know how you feel about me filing for retirement*, he thought as he adjusted his pillow. *I don't want to do this anymore.*

Thomas knew Walker would keep his word. He picked up the phone and called Commissioner Kaheel.

By the next morning, the drizzle had given away to an overcast day struggling to maintain supremacy as sunshine fought its way through the clouds.

At 10:15 A.M. a black Jeep, a black sedan, and a second black Jeep pulled into the semi-circular driveway at the entrance to the Horseshoe. About two dozen reporters and photographers stood poised behind a police barricade just to the right of the front door. Lined the entire length and perimeter of the driveway were police officers in riot gear, their visors up, their faces immobile.

In the sedan sat the Teacher, Minister Johnnie Walker; Ila Walker, pain etched on her face—mixed oddly with a preternatural serenity; the Teacher-Designate, David Walker, thinking (mistakenly) that no one knew he had downed several shots of bourbon earlier that morning; Romeo Butler, resisting an urge to cry; and Raphael Roper, the Covenant's lean, mean principal attorney. Other Covenant attorneys were in court at that moment asking for a hearing to appeal a federal court order that gave the *Scabbard* and the meetinghouses seven days to close their doors.

Eight members of the Swords of the Master alighted from the two Jeeps. Andy Blackman and Glenn Greene also got out of the lead Jeep. Glenn and his Swords squad wore full dress black military uniforms trimmed in red and green; Andy wore a blue jeans waist jacket and pants reminiscent of the civil rights activists fighting for political rights before he was born. Others were there to cover the story; Andy knew that, if he lived, he was there so he could write the *entire* story one day.

They walked to the sedan and Glenn opened the door for the Teacher. Minister Johnnie got out slowly, stood up, looked around, and smiled. Andy looked at his leader, feeling many things, but not feeling like a reporter.

"Is there anything we can say to change your mind, Minister Johnnie?" Andy asked, knowing the question was futile.

The minister's smile was broad. There was no bravado in it, only warmth. "Why in the world would I change my mind, Brother Andy?" he said. "Some things must unfold the way they must." He placed both of his large hands on Andy's shoulders. "The work is in capable hands, and it must move to another level."

Warmth suffused Andy's body. He would miss this man. Romeo approached them, his face somber..

"Minister, you really believe they will kill you?" Romeo's voice cracked as he asked the question.

"I've never been more certain of anything," Minister Johnnie said. He looked at Glenn and nodded.

Glenn Greene and two Swords turned and walked through the double doors into the lobby of the Horsehoe. Alerted to the spectacle unfolding, Chief Kaheel and an assortment of aides arrived almost simultaneously. Glenn walked directly to Kaheel who, without realizing it, came to attention to greet his guest.

"Chief Kaheel, our Teacher, Minister Johnnie Walker, is here to surrender to arrest. We are his escorts, and we are requesting permission to remain parked in the driveway until he is booked."

The two men stood eyeball to eyeball. "Why did you think an escort was necessary?" Kaheel asked. "All he needed was his lawyer."

"I will be explicit," Glenn said, his voice soft and even. "I have low expectations of your security for our Teacher. Very low. Being placed in your custody is something I oppose strongly. And until the moment he's in your custody, I have taken a vow to stop anyone who so much as raises a hand to harm him. By any means necessary."

"Permission granted," Chief Kaheel said. He was mildly annoyed that, despite himself, he felt respect for these people. He admired discipline in anyone.

"Thank you, Chief," Glenn said. He did an about face; his aides followed suit. They went to the double doors and signaled.

The six remaining Swords came to the doors, paired off and faced each other, and stood at attention. The Teacher and his entourage got out of the sedan and walked into the building through the honor guard. Andy and Romeo stood together at the doors. It was a family moment; Minister Johnnie wanted to address his son's betrayal before he surrendered to Caesar.

An OC Eye television reporter watched the unfolding pageantry with one side of her mouth curled in a smirk. "They treat this guy like he's a frigging head of state," she said.

"Maybe he is," said the black reporter standing behind her. "Maybe he is."

"Heshimu, you really like these people, don't you?" she asked.

The dark-skinned man looked at her, saw the incomprehension in her eyes, and smiled. "Yeah, I really like 'these people.'"

Raphael Roper was not a happy man when he briefed the Covenant leadership. The charges, all federal, were incitement to commit sedition, conspiracy to commit sedition, incitement to commit treason, conspiracy to commit treason, conspiracy to commit armed robbery, aiding and abetting armed robbery, and a variety of minor charges. He would be held without bail. After processing, he would be driven to a federal facility the next day.

The armed robbery charges stemmed from the CP2-engineered holdup in Memphis. The other charges cited several "inflammatory" statements made publicly, either to the media or in sermons/lectures. The most damaging evidence of treason and sedition had come, the indictment said, in his last meetinghouse talk five days earlier—quoted at length in the arrest warrant from a transcription of an informant's surreptitious recording—when the Teacher had spoken to his congregation:

"This nation has a document written by men who held African men and women in captivity who survived the murderous Middle Passage from our homeland. Because these kidnappers and captors wrote it, I sometimes get criticism from my nationalist brethren for quoting it. But I use anything that will help me be free. And I like watching them squirm when faced with words they *say* they hold sacred. See, some things are eternally true, and even kidnappers and slaveholders recognize this, even if they don't apply it to anyone but themselves.

"Now this document tells people they have the right to life, liberty, and the pursuit of happiness. It says that a government that prevents any part of this triune of freedom—the document says 'destructive of these ends'—should be 'altered or abolished.'

"It don't say how, it just says it ought to be done, and that people have a right to do it. And it makes a point of saying it means *any* form of government. [Laughter] Not just the British. Not just communists, or Nazis, or Muslims. [Laughter] Not just people they don't like, but *any* form of government.

"It goes on to say to folks that they shouldn't just up and rebel or resist for what they call 'light and transient causes.' You know, paying us less wages is not as serious as paying us no wages at all; giving us third-rate resources for our schools may not be as bad as making education illegal for us; segregating us may be a lighter and more transient cause than dumping us, or forcing us to jump, in uncounted numbers into the frigid vastness of the Atlantic Ocean. Of course I'm being facetious because none of it was light or transient to us, or to our ancestors.

"Still, this document they wrote—I didn't write none of this—counsels patience 'while evils are sufferable.' It says they are no longer sufferable when there's a long train of abuses. Not a short train, a *long* train, it says. I didn't write it; that's what they wrote. When there's a long train of abuses, this document says, and when that train of abuses has a pattern, a pattern to reduce them under 'absolute despotism'—I had to look that one up [laughter]—then they have certain rights and duties. My dictionary said despotism means 'rule by a tyrant' or 'cruel and arbitrary use of power.'

"What rights and duties do a people have when there has been a long train of abuses, and when they have decided evils are no longer sufferable? Well, actually, this document only lists two rights and duties. First, they have a right and duty to 'throw off such government.' Second, it says they have a right and duty to provide 'new guards for their future security.' Again, it don't say how, just that it ought to be done.

"Now, I've told you what it says. I have a few questions for you. Have we suffered evils? [Shouts of "yes."] Are we still suffering evils? [Shouts of "yes."] Are those evils still sufferable? [Shouts of "no."] Have there been abuses? [Shouts of "yes."] A long train of abuses? [Shouts of "yes."] Is there still, today, right now, a long, long train of abuses that have not been corrected? [Shouts of "yes."]

"Well, they're coming after us. I don't know how much longer I'll be among you. But I want to be clear. Pray for the protection of Unit 2236. Support them in spirit, and any other way you can. Keep the Covenant in your heart, regardless of what they do to the physical structures.

"And resist, resist, resist! [Shouts and applause] Alter it! Abolish it! Throw it off! They have never protected you, they will never protect you; you must protect yourself or die! Love one another, as you are loved by your Creator! And resist!"

Inside the Horseshoe, Minister Johnnie asked his lawyer to summon Romeo and Andy. When they arrived, he looked at his family and friends. And smiled.

"I knew exactly what I was doing in my last talk," he said. ""I've done what Paul Robeson did when he said that artists must choose to fight for freedom or slavery, and that he had made his choice. Preachers got to choose, too. And the people they preach to must choose, as you have chosen." He turned to Andy. "As long as you live, record our story and tell it. People must know we weren't cowards and didn't go willingly. I'm surrendering to prevent a bloodbath we can't win. We will lose fewer warriors this way, I'm sure of it. If I asked, the Swords would be fierce and unyielding."

"Only now do I realize how very much you've given me, Minister Johnnie," Andy said. They embraced.

The Teacher looked at Romeo and then at David. "You are no longer Teacher-Designate," he said to his son. "The board will receive letters today making my wishes known. Have you seen the morning newspaper?"

David frowned, shook his head.

"You may have my copy," Minister Johnnie said, handing his newspaper to the former Teacher-Designate. "After the raid on Romeo's home, I didn't know if you'd have the courage to come this morning. I believe I understand now why you betrayed the Covenant. Now that you may have helped destroy us, I don't think you'll feel very welcome ever again."

No one in the group had seen the paper except David's mother, who had picked it up from the doorstep at dawn as coffee brewed. When David opened it, he cringed and lowered his head. A hush fell over the group. Under the word EXTRA, there were two headlines in large black type. COVENANT OFFICIAL IN SEX SCANDAL, the top headline read. Below it: RED-FACED FBI BUNGLES RAID, COVENANT LEADER WILL SURRENDER. Andy turned away. How much did David know, he wondered. How much had he told them?

"Romeo, you will always be my son," Andy heard the Teacher say behind him. "You are now the Teacher-Designate. I know you'll do what you can in these terrible times."

"Teacher, I love you and thank you," Romeo said, his voice faltering. They embraced.

"God damn you! I tried! I tried to save you! I did!" Unable to contain himself any more in this final humiliating moment, David knew his life was as wrong as it could ever be, with no way out that he could see. He looked at Ila Walker. "Mom, it wasn't supposed to turn out like this." He realized that he sounded like a little boy. He needed a drink.

Ila Walker looked at the man she had carried in her womb and let her tears fall without a sound. With the man she loved so completely going into the bowels of the empire, possibly never to return, and with her only child so utterly lost, she knew this Friday morning would scar her soul for all of her remaining days on earth. She had always believed that no one received more than they could bear; now, on this day, she felt near collapse and was no longer certain that was true. She turned away from her son.

Minister Johnnie looked David directly in the eye. "I left something for you in your middle desk drawer." When David had walked to the sedan, he saw his father give a large envelope to Judith, even as he implored her not to join them. He'd said his good-byes and kissed her gently on the cheek, knowing how much sorrow lie ahead for his lovely daughter-in-law. "It's the kindest thing I could do for you at this point."

The Teacher turned to his wife and touched her tear-stained cheek. "Well, Pooky, I think we knew it would always come to something like this."

Ila touched his cheek in return as she stepped close. "What did I tell you when I met you forty-five years ago and learned your nickname was 'Black Label?' I said, 'Well, Mister Black Label, I will call you 'Top Shelf' as long as you earn it. I've never stopped calling you that, have I?" She kissed him. "I will miss you so very much but, because of you and for you, I will get through this. A few more black men like you and we might have a chance of making this sick country do right."

"Maybe we've found a few," he said softly. They kissed again, transmitting thirty-seven years of marital joy and pain and struggle and triumph as best they could.

The area was quiet with an ethereal stillness. Even his adversaries sensed that they were looking at someone different.

The Teacher looked at a somber Raphael Roper. "I'm ready," he said. He straightened his shoulders and looked at his personal door of no return. Those who loved him watched until he disappeared behind the tall glass doors.

David had disappeared. Ila Walker returned to the sedan with her private thoughts and pain. Andy and Romeo stood apart from the others, engulfed by the awfulness of the moment. "I can't believe he's going to die," Andy said, his voice thick. "I just can't."

"He's definitely going to die," Romeo said. He had been fighting tears only minutes earlier. Now his voice carried the calm they had heard in their leader before he left them. "He will join the ancestors before this day is over."

The statement startled Andy. "How can you possibly know that?"

Romeo looked directly at his old friend. "Our Teacher has been so effective keeping us focused on the life and teachings of the Great Teacher, and on the New Commandment, that many of us hardly think about all the traditional, orthodox dogma about blood and death and dying for our sins. And we don't do all the holiday stuff that others do. Andy, he's going to die because today, April second, is Good Friday. Good men die on this day."

SIXTY-THREE

avid sat in his driveway for some time. Sunshine had claimed at least a temporary victory; it was turning into a shirtsleeves kind of day. A humiliated wife waited for him inside. And a mysterious package from his father.

His cell phone rang. Although his readout said "private," he knew who it was.

"You son of a bitch," David hissed into the phone "You fucking rotten son of a bitch."

"Spoken like a true man of God," the nasal, reedy voice of John Edgar snarled back. "Don't you dare say too much to me because I'm not in a very good mood at this moment. I may yet come over to wreak more vengeance on your sorry ass, you understand me? I have been utterly humiliated in the Bureau because of the bogus information you gave me. My career is probably ruined and it's your fault."

"I was set up."

"You're stating the obvious, you asshole. This is a bad time for another embarrassment for the Bureau, can you understand that?"

"What do you want?"

"Watch your tone, Walker. I released your fuck pictures because I was angry and you deserved it for giving us bullshit. If you didn't know, you should have known. 'What I want' is some better information is what I want. I need to redeem myself, and in the process I may be able to help your father if you provide something good on the two names you gave me, Blackman and Butler. I assume they'll be running things now with you disgraced and your old man in jail."

"You can't help my father. He's a dead man. He knows it if you don't."

"I'm telling you, Walker__"

David clicked "end" and turned his phone off.

Judith looked at him through their large picture window as he walked up the walkway. He stood in the doorway to the living room and looked at her; she kept looking out the window.

"I'm sorry," he said after a while. "I really am."

She turned to look at him and tilted her head. "You're talking about screwing that slut, aren't you?" Her voice didn't sound hurt, it sounded angry.

He looked at her.

"Only at this moment do I realize that I've never known you," Judith said. "Yes, I have a little ego bruise." She held up a large manila envelope. "A note with these pictures says that you've been an FBI informant. And you stand there apologizing for screwing a slut who set you up. All these years I thought you were an admirable man doing admirable things. And now I learn you may have helped destroy something that may not have been perfect, but was one of the few decent things our people have. You don't have enough apology in you for that."

Judith turned away from the window and tossed the envelope on their marble top coffee table. She'd been holding her coat, a small gray leather waist length jacket. She walked over to him.

"I wish there was something I could say to help you but I'm too angry," she said. "You look quite the lover with her," Judith said, gesturing with her head toward the pictures. "Too bad you never wanted to do some of those things at home with me. Or at least you never asked."

She pushed past him and walked out the front door. The engine of her Volvo started and she drove off. He walked to his study.

Seated behind his desk, he poured three fingers of bourbon, tossed it down, poured three fingers more, and then sat back. He couldn't remember ever feeling so tired. Somehow the weight of the package didn't surprise him when he picked it up. He took the silver chrome revolver out, inspected it, and opened the cylinder. All the chambers were empty except one. He sat for several minutes, thinking about his options.

Damn. Once again, his father was right.

When Judith returned, she found her late husband slumped forward, his mutilated head resting on the desk next to the chrome pistol with its spent shell.

SIXTY-FOUR

Just before sunset, they brought Minister Johnnie "Black Label" Walker in handcuffs through the basement to the inside of the curve of the Horseshoe. Federal authorities had ordered his immediate transfer to federal jurisdiction.

He walked erect and proud. Remarkably, it was the first time he had been arrested since his days of civil disobedience during the unruliness of the Sixties.

The federal van was not at the door as they exited into a cool, fine spray of rain. Instead, it sat at the curb between the two ends of the 'Shoe. Several television cameras and a slew of photographers formed a corridor behind yellow wooden police barricades erected specifically for this photo-op.

As Minister Johnnie looked across the courtyard, he had a premonition. An epiphany permeated his being; a leap of knowing that he understood would be his last. What he saw in the walk-across-the-yard tableau before him took on the appearance of artifice; it resembled a film set, a stage setting. The message must be sent to his people: every time you raise one up, we will get him.

He walked forward behind two uniformed STOP cops, between two plainclothes detectives, and in front of two more STOP cops.

Twelve yards out, the crouching man—so perfect an image he seemed sent from central casting—sprang out of the crouching position he had assumed when his target appeared. He was young, bald, blue-eyed, unshaven, pale, snarling, and dressed in a fatigue jacket, jeans and dirty sneakers.

Despite his handcuffs, Minister Johnnie's body moved without thinking. His years of aikido training responded as the long hunting knife tore a jagged line across his abdomen above his navel. His coat took some of the blow but not enough; his yielding movement away from the blade helped, but not enough. One hand reached for the assassin's attacking wrist but grabbed the cutting edge of the knife instead. Summoning all his *ki* into his circular move, the Teacher dipped low. One foot swept his attacker's legs at the ankles, lifting him in the air. Just before Minister Johnnie made contact, the knife struck him again high on his thigh. The man fell backwards, striking his head on the pavement.

372

The two detectives on either side of their prisoner appeared startled in the frozen news images that flashed around the country within the hour, recoiling in the opening moments of the attack. The man yelled things at first indecipherable, later sorted out from replays as "You gutless traitor! America doesn't need niggers like you!"

The words were difficult to make out at first because the man spoke them as he made his first punching motion at Minister Johnnie's midsection. The two officers in front turned and reached for the man as he punched. Devotees of the prisoner would say later that slow motion videotaped replays capturing the assassination showed one officer actually pushing the assailant's elbow forward as he purportedly grabbed him. These critics would be called conspiracy theorists.

After Minister Johnnie was slashed on his thigh, the man was subdued and his bloody hunting knife taken away from him. None of the officers were injured; the suspect sustained a concussion and bruises.

An investigation later determined that the suspect acted alone, although he had past connections to an obscure white supremacist organization.

Minister Johnnie "Black Label" Walker was pronounced dead on arrival in the emergency room of City Hospital a half mile away twenty-five minutes after the attack. An artery at the juncture of his thigh had been severed; his stomach wound had allowed blood to flood his abdominal cavity.

Andy and Romeo looked out across the water at the Teacher's favorite spot, greenish with the reflection of the panoply of trees on the opposite bank. Andy wasn't good at such things, but he thought they were mostly sycamores and oaks. The verdant display extended in both directions as far as he could see, up beyond the Richardson-Jones Bridge. All of it looked like a three-dimensional mural that was indeed the work of a Master Painter. Somehow, He had thought this time of sorrow would feel different, would have more drama.

"He really did know," Andy said.

"Yeah."

"Even when he walked into the Horseshoe, I thought Roper would have him out on bail in no time."

Looking across at the other bank, Andy felt the uncertainty and slight disorientation that comes with déjà vu. Had he dreamed being here at this moment? A vague sense of someone on the other bank gripped him. He'd been here in fact several times but it had never felt like this. It was probably his grief. And fatigue, since neither he nor Romeo had slept since Mother Ila's tearful call from the city morgue. Claudia and Malikah had accompanied her.

"They didn't take long, did they?" she said before hanging up.

An unmarked dark blue Ford sat at the end of the parking lot. Two men in it watched them. Ten yards away from the Ford sat a black four-door Hyundai. Inside sat four Swords watching the men watching Romeo and Andy. It was hard to go anywhere in the city and not see patrol cars, most manned with three and four officers.

Romeo threw a stone, skimming it across the surface of the water. "The thing about war and its insanity—and the Teacher tried to tell me this," he said, "is how quickly the killing gets out of hand. The Teacher was obsessed with trying to prevent us from suffering casualties for as long as we could. And he became the first." He threw another stone. "I want to do the same. But Unit 2236 can't go much longer without losing somebody."

They were quiet for some moments. "When we were coming up, I tried so hard not to get into being a thug," Andy said. He wanted to jump in the water, start swimming—somewhere—and just never come back. "And one day I watched the Secret Service doing something to protect Reagan, or the first Bush, or Clinton, I don't even remember. I saw that they were just thugs in suits. Thugs with discipline and training, but thugs trained to hurt without even thinking about it. And I saw that armies, anybody's armies, are the same thing, thugs with discipline. Great big street gangs fighting over great big streets, you know? Taking stuff from people if they're told. I held onto the idea of nonviolence for a long time after that, but I guess I started understanding back then that it's hard to survive in this world without some thug in you. It's how you use it and how much ass you can whip. The brothers on the block fuck it up by preying on their own and thinking they have turf that they really don't, but they understand the concept."

Romeo snorted a laugh. "That's what Tupac may have been trying to say. If you don't have some thug in you, the world will kick your ass, then blame you and say it's your fault you're getting your ass kicked."

"Speaking of thugs, this man may be one of their biggest," Andy said. "Miss Jones gave us this." He handed a small snapshot of John Edgar to Romeo. "He doesn't know his real name. What aliases he could get are listed on the back. He said David gave him our names specifically. He speculates that David was trying to save his father."

"He didn't do a real good job, did he?"

The geese idling on the bank took off in a noisy V formation, honking loudly as they ascended over the river. An athletic-looking woman rowed by in a long, narrow kayak with strong, confident strokes, moving her boat noiselessly to an unknown destination.

A trio of ducks floated toward them in a line, their ebony necks erect, just being ducks. The quiet motion of the river melded with an eerie stillness inside Andy. Somewhere in his mind he heard Robert saying, "Lock and load . . ."

Both men felt a long way from Seventeenth and Cambridge, in the heart of the 'hood where they grew up, and yet they weren't far at all. They had never left home. The now Beirut-like ravaged intersection of their youth stood as a perverse contradictory symbol of the "progress of your people" trumpeted by self-serving politicians. It was fifteen minutes away by car from where they stood on King Drive. It was over a score of years away by the living each of them had done. But it was only moments away when they looked at who they were in their inner core.

They were the six-year-olds playing cops and gangstas, always wanting to be the gangstas; the nine-year-olds running like crazy after kissing a girl on the cheek; the twelve-year-olds playing stickball and reviving a game their parents had played called "Running Bases"; the thirteen-year-olds finally not afraid to rumble to protect their movie money; the fifteen-year-olds watching Sonny Butler gunned down by the clichés of racism that reasoned the only black people in the bank must be the bad guys; and the eighteen-year-olds deciding on school over dealing drugs, even if they did smoke some weed some time.

Andy especially liked to tell people, "I'm from Cambridge Street," even those who had no idea where it was. It grounded him, reminded him of essential things he had discovered, forgotten, learned, loved, hated, feared, fought, and been molded by. It told him he was more than President Hugh Bruder's equal because he would walk anywhere but Bruder wouldn't bring his little punk ass anywhere near Seventeenth and Cambridge by himself even before he became president, *especially* before he became president. The three-story tenement Andy grew up in was long gone, a ghost structure that only he saw, a weed-strewn rectangle meagerly protected by a chain link fence. But it was only a building. All of what had happened since had brought him to see he was now a warrior on behalf of those who lived on Cambridge Streets anywhere, everywhere. He was duty bound to wreak havoc on their behalf. It was his right; it was his duty.

Evils were no longer sufferable. He looked at his lifelong friend and had another thought, a sudden one, springing up from those back-in-the-day days on Cambridge Street when they were first discovering the rhetoric of resistance.

"Rome, you remember a speech we used to listen to by Malcolm about the odds of winning?"

"I'm not sure."

"I don't remember the exact words, but he was talking about either Korea or Vietnam, or both." Andy smiled at the memory of the shining black prince's wry humor. "Malcolm was talking about folks here, black folks and white folks both, talking about how people said black people shouldn't fight the government because numerically we're outnumbered and can't win. 'And then they draft you,' Malcolm said, 'and they send you overseas with a rifle and a bayonet to face eight hundred million Chinese, and tell you to defend their democracy, because it's sure not yours. And you're good Americans, so you do it. Well, hell,' he said, 'if you're not afraid of those odds, don't be afraid of these odds.'"

They laughed. "Like Minister Johnnie likes to say, we win by not losing," Romeo said. He fell silent when he realized that he'd used the present tense.

Evils were no longer sufferable, Andy thought.

The long train of abuses—the undeclared war against their homeland four hundred years ago, the kidnappings, beatings, murders, rapes, humiliations, starvation, deprivations, loss of fathers, mothers, daughters, sons, wives, husbands, tribes, teachers, leaders; and then the evil demons with ships that steered the dreaded inhuman murderous genocidal abomination now benignly called the Middle Passage, the bottomless fear, stench, disease, suicides, mutilation, loss of names, languages, religions, histories, the foreign shores, psychological dislocation, dehumanizing disfiguring into chattel, forced labor, unholy night visits, whips, dogs, guns, degradation, debasement, psychological tearing ripping scarring, outlawing of education, rupture of families, the forced and hollow citizenship, the meaningless constitutional amendments, the Klan, the infidelity to their own legal codes, disgracing of their own religion, the inventing and institutionalizing and enforcement of segregation/apartheid, the hypocrisy of democracy, the inferior homes, food, education, jobs, the unjust courts, taxation without representation, the scarring of souls, the lie of white supremacy transformed into an unholy custom masquerading as truth, the lie of inferiority force fed day after day after day after day after day, the Orwellian use of language that said Assimilation is Integration and Segregation is Separation and Unequal is Equal and Neo-slavery is Freedom, conducting a pogrom with all this, and with the Dred Scott decision, and with *Plessy v. Ferguson,* and for having a Supreme Court refuse to hear Cornelius Jones' case in 1915 demanding $65 million in unpaid wages, and for using the Bakke case to take back a so-called commitment to change just as the Rutherford Hayes Compromise/Betrayal took back the first so-called commitment to change, and the thousands and thousands and thousands and thousands and thousands and thousands of lynchings (that we know of) that flowed from that betrayal, and the refusal of pensions for ex-slaves because "it would be too much of a burden on the taxpayer" and the persecution of Callie House and Isaiah Dickerson for daring to campaign for those pensions, and the persecution of Marcus Garvey and Elijah Muhammad and Paul Robeson and Robert F. Williams and Malcolm X and Ella Baker and Martin Luther King, Jr., and Fannie Lou Hamer and Stokely Carmichael and H. Rap Brown and Huey P. Newton and Bobby Seale and Eldridge Cleaver and Geronimo Pratt and the Panther 21 and Assata Shakur and Angela Davis and Ruchell Magee and Fleeta Drumgo and John Clutchette and Maulana Karenga and Mumia Abu-Jamal and the murders of Emmett Till and Jimmie Lee Jackson and Denise McNair and Carole Robertson and Addie Collins and Cynthia Wesley and James Chaney and Andy Schwerner and Mickey Goodman and Viola Liuzzo and Malcolm and Li'l Bobby Hutton and Mark Clark and Fred Hampton and Cleveland Edwards and "Sweet Jugs" Miller and W.L. Nolen and Jonathan Jackson and William Christmas and James McClain and George Jackson and the thirty-nine at Attica Penitentiary and the unnamed we didn't hear of or read about and the martyrdom of the ancestors who resisted, who resisted unto death like Cinque and Nat Turner and Denmark Vesey and Gabriel Prosser and the ongoing unjust murdering of innocents like George Baskett and Eula Love and the infant of Delois Young and Tyesha Miller and Ron Settles and Amadou Diallo and Patrick Dorismond and Donta Dawson and Eleanor Bumpers and Alberta Spruill and Ousmane Zongo and the ones we are fighting to avenge, and the imprisonment/re-enslavement of most of the two million languishing in prisons since the Civil Rights Movement that flowed from the second betrayal of a so-called commitment to change, and for a refusal to discuss reparations/restitution to repair the damage because "it's unfair to pay now because we didn't enslave anybody"—stretching back over centuries and uncounted generations was interminable and a very long train indeed, and would no longer be accepted by those who believed in Johnnie "Black Label" Walker as their Teacher and Yahshua as their Great Teacher.

Put simply, they would fight as long as any of them had breath in their bodies.

What the men who first wrote "long train of abuses" suffered pales by comparison, Andy thought as he and Romeo looked over the water. Water would always remind him of the Teacher.

Judith had called Romeo with the news of David's suicide.

"I wish it could have been different with David," Andy said.

"It is what it is," Romeo said. "Minister Johnnie thought he could trust him when he cleaned up, and he was wrong. He betrayed us. We've got to do all we can to stay alive, and we don't need traitors in our midst. And we must have Unit 2236 both become more aggressive and gain more recruits. Many of the Swords are ready now. We just have to be careful about security and bringing in informants. As of now, if there is irrefutable information that someone's an informant, a Star should be informed. The Star Command may now give execution orders on an informant after reviewing evidence.

"We have less than forty-eight hours before the announced shutdown of the meetinghouses. We've got a lot of work to do." For a moment, Romeo was far away. "I'll miss him," he said.

"Yes."

"Andy, I'll be spending the rest of the day with Glenn, now that he's Second Star. We've got to expand our military operation. The August 21st Brigade has been slipping into town individually for some time. I've also sent for December 4th; they'll be nearby in the next day or so.

"Also, if Patrick's acquitted, we've got to take him down."

"To show our people that the crackdown hasn't had an effect."

"Exactly. Patrick may be the first executive action in phase two. Security is tight in Levyville. Glenn and I will put something together to get him. We've been watching his hotel almost since the trial started. In the meantime, we have to see if the rest of the world lets them shut down our places of worship without saying anything. We'll keep the above ground struggle going as long as we possibly can. It's an urban street fight now. Here's what I want you to do . . ."

Andy used e-mail and followed with phone calls, assuming that both were probably under surveillance. He had no choice. Confusion and trauma threatened to rip the Covenant asunder as word spread that both Walkers had joined the Ancestors within a twenty-four hour period. Discipline would crumble altogether if Romeo—the new Teacher and Third Star—didn't exert leadership, and quickly.

The small band known as Unit 2236, Andy hoped, would be different. They were trained to be killing machines. It was time to see what they knew.

So far, they had at least two helpful situations. First, Robert had called Romeo shortly after the death of Minister Johnnie.

"A house is not a home, my friend," Robert said. The code phrase meant —until they were told differently—that the place known to Andy's brigade as

WiTHWA was secure. How to get people there and not blow the cover of the Fourth Star was another matter. They were working on it, Romeo said. And safe houses were being activated.

Andy learned with pleasant surprise that Covenant Academy students had been communicating with each other for weeks. All fifteen schools were committed to waging civilly disobedient sit-ins, locking the doors and living at the schools unless told to do otherwise by their elders, for as long as the elders could supply them with food. They had taught them well.

His shrouded message to the fifteen leaders of Swords units was the same: "The best I can say in this e-mail is that those whom you admire will reach out to you. They will tell you to read 'Letter From Birmingham Jail' during the day and study the twenty-second chapter of Luke at night. They will explain what this means. May the blessings of Yahweh be with you all."

Unit 2236 would be in touch. Nonviolent resistance was still the order of the day for Swords until further notice. At night, it would be another matter.

SIXTY-FIVE

Romeo Butler's news conference the day after the Teacher's death, and on the eve of the meetinghouse seizure deadline, had one odd element. Registering for the new identification cards would be a matter of conscience for members of the Covenant, Butler said. The draconian measure had come so suddenly; Covenant leadership had debated the matter intensely. They might refine the decision at a later date; those who wanted to comply could do so. Some found the announcement strange; others said the Covenant was feeling the pressure of the crackdown.

The truth of the matter was simpler and not for public consumption. Members of Unit 2236 had to be able to move about and thus needed identification cards. They used the fake identities created for them at WiTHWA. The Covenant majority needed to refuse to register as a demonstration of civil disobedience to their communities. Out of this grew their seemingly strange pronouncement.

Neutralizing the locator chips in the cards had been problematic until Andy remembered a young man named Jonathan Gardiner. Could he make counterfeit cards with locator chips that didn't work? Once Jon saw the real thing, he had a counterfeit prototype ready in less than two days. He knew he was doing something important, and probably for Unit 2236. He didn't ask questions.

With Jon Gardiner making placebo chips for their false names, Unit 2236 members on assignment would simply leave their active cards at home and travel with the non-working chips. If law enforcement had some way to test them, and tried to do so during a stop, the entire unit was under orders to take executive action.

Despite a persistent chill, the news conference took place on the Covenant meetinghouse parking lot before the 11 a.m. Saturday lecture. It was the only way to accommodate both the press and the standing room only attendance of Covenant members and supporters. The first lecture had been cancelled. A quickly improvised temporary entrance was created with the metal detector for the heightened security on meetinghouse grounds.

Andy passed out a news release announcing the death of Minister

Johnnie Walker. In addition, it provided the Covenant's official response to President Bruder's six points.

Romeo's voice was hoarse and strained as he addressed the reporters with a prepared statement from behind a phalanx of Swords. He wore small gold triangles on the collar of his shirt.

After announcing the identification card freedom-of-choice decision, Romeo addressed the other five points in President Bruder's executive order.

"With the issuance of Executive Order 10-2223 earlier this week, all pretense of democracy disappeared and returned this nation to the overt criminality that passed for democracy in the eighteenth, nineteenth and the first two-thirds of the twentieth century. Citizens of all races are expressing shock at the president's draconian actions. Because Covenant members know our history well, we know the nation has been here before, and never has been far from here even when it pretended to change.

"First, the president ordered our beloved Teacher, Minister Johnnie Walker to surrender. To minimize needless bloodshed around this issue, the Minister complied. In less than twenty-four hours, we witnessed the return of the so-called 'lone, crazed assassin.' The lone, crazed assassin phenomenon has been largely absent from our culture for more than thirty years; I guess we thought they were in a retirement home for lone, crazed assassins. But we see that whenever forces of resistance to repression appear in this society, lone crazed assassins seem to crawl out of the woodwork. We will take measures to protect ourselves from lone, crazed assassins.

"Second, the government has said they will close our meetinghouses. We say publicly that, in the spirit of Martin Luther King's 'Letter From Birmingham Jail,' we categorically refuse to obey an unjust law, a law that suspends both freedom of religion and freedom of peaceful assembly. In the spirit of Doctor King, we say publicly that we will not be violent at our meetinghouses. We have every expectation that the police and OCI forces will be violent unless the public helps us. In any case, we will not cooperate in the closings. We will resist and, as King taught, create a crisis and build on the tension brought about by our government. We hope those who believe in being free will assist us.

"Third, the government has repeatedly pressured us to denounce the armed resistance of Unit 2236, and has made their apprehension a top priority. We have not denounced them in the past; we will not do so now. We do not intend to denounce them in the future. This government cannot tell us who we should like or dislike.

"The president's fourth point about additional security for the murderer, Michael Patrick, and others like him, has nothing to do with the Covenant. Nor does his fifth point concerning his desire to protect police officers involved in other wrongful deaths.

"We will announce funeral arrangements for our Teacher when they have been completed. The widow of David Walker announced today that her late husband, who died two days ago, was cremated yesterday in a private ceremony. There will be no memorial service; she thanks you for your prayers.

"We will not be taking questions. Thank you for coming out."

As the reporters began to leave, and Covenant members headed inside, Romeo gestured to his friend Heshimu Kenyatta. The veteran reporter stayed for the lecture and then joined the new Teacher for an exclusive interview in the late Minister Johnnie's study.

SIXTY-SIX

Ward Keyes crushed his cigarette out. He clenched his teeth. I am going to hurt this silly bitch if she doesn't shut up, he thought. "Jhanae, this is not a good time to have this conversation. You knew what I did for a living, so don't start getting weepy and difficult on me now, okay?"

Jhanae felt glued to the black leather couch. Her hands were clenched almost in a prayer position. She wanted to run and felt paralyzed. "Wardell, I didn't know what you did, you know I didn't," she said. She was trying to say everything without saying too much, without pissing him off. "By the time I knew, I was in love with you, and you were saying that you were just gathering information. I didn't know it was going to be like this!"

Ward whirled toward her, making her flinch. "Well, it is like this, okay?" he said. "I don't want to talk about this anymore because I am two minutes from knocking the shit out of you. Now, I'm going to the office. When I get back, you can be here or not be here, I don't give a damn. And I have too much on my mind to pay attention to you whining. If you didn't like what I did, you should have left a long time ago."

"You wouldn't let me leave!" Her voice was high; she tried to keep anger out of it.

"Well, I have changed my mind!" he shouted as he grabbed his baseball cap from the glass coffee table. "I am really tired of your wimpy ass." He slammed the door hard as he left.

Two men sitting across the street in a compact car watched Ward Keyes go to his vehicle and get in. "Now," one of them said. He pressed a button on a remote control device in his lap.

The explosion was loud. Jhanae jumped, screaming, then ran to the picture window overlooking the street. Bright orange flames engulfed what was left of Ward Keyes' car. Jhanae stared in disbelief at her late fiancée's funeral pyre, unable to decipher the jumble of emotions that overwhelmed her senses.

SIXTY-SEVEN

The jury deliberated for six days and most of a seventh. Andy looked at the faces of the jurors as they filed in. Both housewives looked glum. So did the linguistics professor. The jury foreman's countenance remained neutral.

Andy scribbled something on his notepad, showed it to Claudia. *They're going to let him off.* She looked at him but said nothing.

The walls on either side of the courtroom were lined two deep with uniformed police officers supportive of their colleague. Mike Patrick was not a "former" officer to them, Andy noted on his pad. They wanted him back; their eyes said so.

Judge Albert O. Bass allowed a bank of television cameras into the room for the verdict. They stood, one-eyed sentinels, waiting.

"Please rise, Mister Foreman," Judge Bass said.

The jury foreman stood.

"Has the jury reached a verdict?"

"Yes, we have, your honor." One of the housewives looked down, placed her forehead in one hand.

"Please announce the verdict to the Court."

"Your honor, the jury in the case of the State versus Patrick, finds the defendant, Michael Patrick, not guilty of the charges brought against him."

Very few heard anything after "not." Reporters opened cell phones as they headed for the door. Cheers and applause erupted from both sides of the room as police officers shouted, "Way to go, Mike." Contrapuntal shouts of "No!" arose from friends and family of George Bascomb. Judge Bass' banging gavel only contributed to the bedlam.

Andy patted Claudia's hand. He needed to call Marian. Having struggled to court every day through the benevolent chauffeuring of neighbors, especially Mister Harris, Marian had been a stoic presence in the courtroom. It was probably best that she had missed the trial's all-American denouement. The day before, her son, whom she named George Andrew Bascomb (and eventually nicknamed "Little Johnnie" because he started talking precociously at sixteen months), decided it was time to enter the world and had done so kicking and screaming shortly before dawn.

Because he was a professional, he made his way to the mob outside the courtroom door where Erlickson held forth with his exonerated client.

"... all along that this trial was for political reasons. I told you that this fine police officer was being raked over the coals."

"Do you think the change of venue helped?"

"The courts made that decision, obviously in the interest of my client getting a fair trial."

"How do you feel, Mike?"

"I'm glad it's over. And I hope I can go back to work."

Erlickson seized the moment. "We will petition immediately to have Mike returned to the police force. Now that he's acquitted, they have no right to deprive him of a job doing what he loves."

"Mike, given the recent assassinations of policemen, are you afraid for your life?" The voice obviously belonged to a black reporter. The mob of reporters quieted.

"First of all, the police department in this city will protect Mike Patrick," Erlickson said before his client could open his mouth. "Second, I know that all of you heard what President Bruder had to say. I predict that between the police, the FBI, and the newly deputized OCI security forces, those scum who call themselves Unit 2236 will be erased within 30 days. Mike, are you afraid for your life?"

Mike Patrick smiled. "I'll be fine," he said.

Andy clicked his tape recorder off, turned and walked away.

SIXTY-EIGHT

Shortly after Michael Patrick's acquittal, the Third Star told all Unit 2236 teams that they were now in Phase Two. The new operational level meant they would do what was necessary to complete a mission, except kill civilians. Two brigades, including Andy's, were activated to take executive action against Michael Patrick. The all-women's unit was placed on ready standby.

The three-story Levyville Inn sat in regal elegance less than three hundred yards south of the exit from the bustling freeway that linked it to urban areas and other points north and south. The stately hotel's white marble colonnade front hinted at antebellum aspirations despite its location well above the Mason-Dixon Line. The inn successfully mingled the charm of a bed and breakfast with the efficiency and amenities of an urban mega-chain, a melding carefully nurtured during its thirty years as the premier hostelry for the "Town That Thinks Like A City."

Michael Patrick and Isaac Erlickson stayed at the Levyville Inn on weekdays for the length of the trial, commandeering two luxury suites. "I'm an old man; I don't like the wear and tear of fighting rush hour every day," the barrister had groused. Both men enjoyed the genteel hostelry; it made the ordeal of the trial bearable. Going home on weekends was enough. For security reasons, other rooms on the floor weren't rented, although an obvious exception was made on the final night of the trial for Bulldog Hudson. The Levyville finance director added the cost of lost revenue for the empty rooms to the reimbursement report.

Court proceedings were still in the jury selection stage when Unit 2236's Star Command decided on an investment. If Michael Patrick were found guilty, they would not consider it money wasted. But if they let him off, the investment would pay invaluable dividends with the intelligence gleaned during that time which would help them complete their mission. Executive action had been unanimously decreed for Patrick, pending a jury verdict of guilty that would automatically set the Star Command decision aside. Through an intermediary, a room was rented at the Levyville Inn for the duration of the trial.

The manager wondered at first about the man named "Clarence" (who had been 123 at WiTHWA with Andy) when he registered and said he was working on a book about the trial. Not many black people had extended stays at the Levyville Inn. But when Clarence paid $6,000 up front for his room for four weeks, it evaporated the manager's doubts. His publisher was picking up the tab, Clarence said. He was an earnest, bookish-looking young man and the manager thought no more about it. Clarence, picked precisely because he had an ingrained quiet manner, became inconspicuous despite his color and faded into the inn's expensive cherry woodwork paneling.

Clarence actually took copious notes at the trial. He and Andy nodded at each other, speaking as if they were strangers, the way black people do in strange settings when they're seriously outnumbered.

In Clarence's day job, he served as minister at the Covenant of the New Commandment meetinghouse in Monroe, North Carolina. Never one of the biggest congregations, it was always one of the most prestigious because of their native son, Minister Johnnie. Clarence took an immediate leave of absence with pay when Romeo called with the assignment. He knew now he faced a sorrowful congregation when he returned, especially the old-timers who had grown up with Minister Johnnie. He wondered if he would finish in Levyville in time to attend the Teacher's funeral. Brother Butler said they were definitely taking the body home to Monroe after the meetinghouse memorial service.

In this way, the Star command learned that OCI security hired to protect Michael Patrick's room around the clock kept four officers at the room, and two in the lobby on the day and swing shifts. In addition, there were two-person teams at the hotel's front and rear entrances at all times. On weekends, a guard was posted round the clock until Patrick returned.

When the trial ended, it was late afternoon. Mike Patrick wanted to leave but Ike Erlickson and Bulldog Hudson talked him into a celebration drink in the Levyville Inn's sumptuous lounge. An overturned truck on the freeway lengthened rush hour by three hours and convinced them to stay the night. Bulldog rented a room next to theirs, and the three men ordered dinner and several more drinks.

Clarence sat in the lobby and read. He knew all the clerks by now. It was a little after 5 P.M. when he ambled over to the front desk. He and Natalie, one of the hotel's two black front desk employees, had become friendly.

"Hey Nat, how you doing?" he asked.

"Clarence, good evening, I'm fine," Nat said. "How are you?" She smiled a lot, revealing a gap between her front teeth that made her smile more attractive. A diminutive woman with a husky voice, she wondered about this quiet brother living large, but who wasn't making any moves. Too bad, too, because she liked the strong silent type.

"I guess you heard the trial ended." Clarence said.

"Sure did." She looked around in both directions. "It's a damn shame they let that man off," she said *sotto voce*. Her eyebrows lifted. "I bet that Unit 2236 tears him a new asshole. You watch."

"I guess he and his attorney have checked out, huh?"

"Oh no, they're going to stay over until morning." She hooked a finger toward the lounge. "They're in there celebrating like they did something good."

"Thanks, Nat." He placed a two-pound box of chocolates on the desk. "Look, I've only got another two days myself. I know you can't fraternize with guests, or I'd treat you to dinner. So it's just a small token to say thanks for being nice. Maybe I'll get up this way again sometime."

She cocked her head to one side, beaming. "That's really sweet. Thank you so much." Damn, she thought. A brother who just wants to be nice, and don't want nothing. Isn't that something?

"You know, it's damn good to see the court system really works," Mike Patrick said after his second martini.

Bulldog Hudson held up his drink. "Here's to the best judicial system in the world," he said by way of a toast.

The three men clinked glasses. "And here's to the best defense attorney in the world," Mike Patrick said.

"Hear, hear," said Bulldog Hudson. Ike Erlickson smiled his appreciation.

"I figured I owe the Benevolent Association one; they'd probably say more than one," Erlickson said with a wink to Bulldog. "This will probably be my last case."

"Oh c'mon, Ike," Bulldog said. "You can't retire. You don't know how."

Uncle Ike pulled out an expensive cigar for himself, handed two others to his friends, and lit up everyone with a two hundred dollar cigar lighter. After quickly wreathing their area of the room in acrid but expensive cigar smoke, he sat back.

"I had to reach down deep for this one, and some of it was unpleasant." The attorney wrinkled his brow. "None of what I'm about to say leaves this table." He looked at his former client. "You shouldn't have shot that boy, Mike. You didn't have to do it, and you shouldn't have."

An uneasy silence descended. "That's pretty harsh, Ike," Bulldog said. "We're supposed to be celebrating. Lighten up."

"Hell, we are celebrating. We won, didn't we? Never again can

Mike Patrick be tried for the death of George Bascomb. And thanks to an administration that has the balls to say we've got to stand up to these colored or black vigilantes, whatever they want to be called, we'll keep you alive. But now that we *can* celebrate, I'm talking about the truth." He took a big puff on his cigar. "I learned early in life what I wanted. I wanted to be a winner, and I wanted to live well. I've done both by being honest with myself, even if I have to lie to you. When I saw what I was up against in this case, I couldn't worry about truth, justice and the American Way, not if I wanted to win.

He chuckled. "I didn't worry about the American Way, I used it." He puffed again and looked admiringly at the long, dark tube. "Helluva smoke, this is." He looked up at them. "Both of you know about the Malik Al-Amin case, the reporter on death row, right?"

They nodded. "I saw a case much like it early in my career. It wasn't my case." He puffed on the cigar. "It looked like this young black kid had done it but there were some real questions. Like Al-Amin, a cop had wounded the kid and then been shot to death. Some people said they saw someone run from the scene. The evidence I saw didn't say the kid was innocent but it showed without a doubt the prosecutors were fucking him over.

"A police inspector said he heard the kid admit he did it on the night of the shooting. They pretty much held the kid without bail at his prelim based on the inspector's testimony. Well, wouldn't you know, the feds indicted the inspector two weeks after the prelim for taking about fifty or sixty large in bribes from pimps to let their hookers stay on the street. So a month after the prelim, they bring in this cop who was with the kid for hours right after the shooting and had said the kid had said nothing. Mind you, they're bringing him in two months after the shooting. Well, the frigging cop, when asked by Internal Affairs why he took so long to say he heard the kid admit shooting the cop, said the kid's statement had disgusted him, and he didn't realize how important the confession was until right then, that moment, when they're asking him. According to the cop, the kid had said something like, 'Yeah, I shot the motherfucker, so what?' This is a *street cop* who's disgusted, right? Well, once IA wrote that up that way, they couldn't use that bonehead to testify. Can you believe they found another cop two weeks after *that*, in fact, the dead cop's partner, to say he'd heard the confession, too? I pulled the ADA aside who was prosecuting the case and asked him what the hell was going on. I'll never forget his answer. 'Ike,' he said, 'justice is all well and good but I'm trying to win this thing. We're convinced the kid did it and we know a jury will believe a cop over the kid if he testifies. Especially the dead cop's partner."

Erlickson leaned forward and held up his drink again. "Here's to the American Way."

They clinked glasses again. "Thanks for saving my life, Uncle Ike," Mike Patrick said. "I mean that with all my heart."

The aging attorney smiled. "Just don't forget to invite me to your wedding, son. I like weddings."

They turned in around eight-thirty so they could get an early start the next morning.

There were two operational plans, one for Levyville and one for the city. Once the Star Command learned Patrick was staying overnight, the Levyville "Milk and Cookies" offensive was activated.

Most people meeting 116 for the first time—"Lynn" was her code name—thought she was white. Lynn's British expatriate mother was, in fact, white, as was her grandmother on her father's side; her father was a light-skinned North Carolinian pale enough to pass as white.

On this April night, Lynn looked like a typical soccer mom, quietly stunning in jeans, loafers, a white shirtwaist blouse buttoned just so over her full breasts, driving gloves, and a windbreaker that remained open. More importantly, she looked like a *Levyville* soccer mom with her blonde-brownish hair in a ponytail, fashionable rimless glasses, and a perky smile. She had been selected for the assignment because of her complexion and because she could radiate seductiveness without being flashy about it. If the unforeseen happened, a nine- millimeter was stored in her waistband, concealed under her windbreaker in the small of her back.

Even with the hullabaloo of the trial, Levyville went to sleep about nine o'clock. At 9:29 P.M., Lynn pulled up in the driveway of the Levyville Inn and parked her black Subaru station wagon directly across from the OCI security team guard post at the front door. She got out carrying a large plate of chocolate chip cookies and a box of coffee from a nearby fast food donut shop.

"Hi fellas," she said. Sunshine saturated her voice. "How you doing?"

"Good evening, m'am," the guard in charge said. He was a swarthy man who enjoyed authority. "What can we do for you?"

"I drive by here often and I've seen you young men out here protecting that fine officer ever since the trial started," Lynn said. "And I've been meaning to find a way to say thank you for, I don't know, helping him, and helping Levyville and helping the country, and I'm the biggest procrastinator in the world, and when I saw the trial ended today, I thought I had lost my chance. But then I saw you all around dinnertime and saw that you were still here and I said the least I can do is bake those fine fellows some cookies. It's not much but my family says I bake the best chocolate chip cookies they've ever tasted." She held the box of coffee up. "And I brought you some coffee. I didn't make it but they have good coffee."

The guard in charge smiled. "That's a really nice gesture, it really is," he said. "It will sure help us get through the night."

"My name's Lynn," she said, flashing her megawatt smile. "I tried to bring enough for you and the fellows in the back."

"I'm Sergeant John Obram. Pleased to meet you." He looked in the box. "Wow. You sure made a lot of cookies. We'll even be able to share these with the men inside."

Lynn looked surprised. She made a face. "Oh dear, I thought it was just the four of you. I didn't know there were others," she lied. "I'm glad I made enough. Well, again, I just wanted to thank you all for what you're doing. These are some terrible times with those black agitators terrorizing our country the way they are. We're really safer with you fine men here."

"Thank you, m'am," Obram said. "It is a terrible time but you'll be okay with us here. Your husband's a lucky man."

Lynn pursed her lips just so. "I'm divorced," she said, looking the sergeant directly in his eyes.

"Oh. Well, I'm sorry this is our last night." Obram bit into a cookie. "These are really good. I sure wish I could have bought you a drink, Miss Lynn." He winked.

She thought for a few moments. "Tell you what. There's no harm in having a drink with one of our security soldiers. That's what they call you here in town, security soldiers." She took a pen from her jeans pocket. "Do you have something I can write on?"

He handed her a tablet and she scribbled her phony telephone number on it: 555-6322. Obram was so busy staring at her hint of cleavage as she bent over to write that he didn't even look at the paper. He placed it in his pocket and stared at her butt as she walked back to her car.

"Call me tomorrow," she called back over her shoulder.

"Yes, Miss Lynn, I am going to do that little thing," he said as he took another bite of the cookie in his hand. He winked at his smiling partner as he handed the box to him. "Damn, these cookies are good!" he exclaimed.

"Now don't forget to share them," she called out. She smiled at Sergeant Obram, then waved and drove off.

They all used their canteens for the coffee and washed the cookies down with it. Sergeant Obram fantasized about how many ways he would put it to Miss Lynn if she wanted to play.

All fourteen OCI employees were fucked up on Sweetness within thirty minutes. As a result, they didn't notice the heavy smoke swirling skyward from a seven-passenger van's engine just after it exited the freeway at Levyville shortly before ten o'clock.

The Sweetness-laced coffee and cookies were designed thus: anybody who ate more than two bites of a cookie at all would get seriously stoned and have impaired reflexes and hallucinations; the ingestion of two cookies would provide an overdose; three cookies would probably kill the person who ate them. Lynn provided the four OCI "security soldiers" with twenty-four cookies, enough to incapacitate all ten men they expected to be on duty, and possibly kill one or two greedy ones. Drugwise, one cup of coffee was the same as eating a cookie.

As it turned out, four additional OCI guards were assigned to the lobby for the last night because of the verdict, which kept the cookies from killing anyone except Sergeant John Obram.

The smoking van carried seven black male passengers. When the first of Levyville's three police cruisers responded, accompanied by a volunteer fire team, one passenger was cussing up a storm.

"Y'all won't listen to me! I told you this goddamned van would not make the trip. Ain't this some shit? We ain't gonna get there in time for the game! I told you, I told you but no, nobody would listen! Ain't this some shit?"

"C'mon Fred, be cool, man, we'll get there," the tallest passenger said. "You got to calm down. Hi, how are you, officer? As you can see, we have a little problem.

"We're the Hampton-Clark College basketball team," the tall one continued. "It's in upstate New York. We have a playoff game tomorrow night in Seaford, Delaware."

Smoke shot almost fifteen feet in the air as the firefighters sprayed water and foam onto the vehicle. "It's not looking good for you fellows," one of the officers said.

All three police officers felt the barrels of pistols in their backs at the same time. "It's not looking good for you either unless you do exactly as we say," the tall man said. He glanced at the three fire volunteers. "Keep doing your work," he said. With the other three "basketball players" pointing pistols at them, they didn't have much choice.

A large U-Haul truck pulled into the driveway of the Levyville Inn. Danis Burton was driving. He wore the beginning of a blonde mustache and beard about the color of what hair he had left. He wore a black watch cap over his baldness, a black sweater, and black jeans. He got out after ascertaining the two uniformed men by the door had very little control of their bodies. As he approached the door, one guard slid from his chair to the ground, unconscious.

"Hi Nat, how are you?" Burton said as he approached the front desk. He looked at the six OCI guards. Two were trying to function; the other four were slumped in their chairs.

"Do I know you?" the startled woman asked. She'd been trying to figure what the hell the guards were drinking. They had never acted like this.

"It's not important. What is important is that right about now, you don't feel well, and you really should take the rest of the night off."

"Are you crazy? I can't do that. There's no one here to relieve me."

"Nat, trust me, take the money in the register for safekeeping, and anything else you need to take, or else we'll have to tie you up and blindfold you."

"You'll have to do *what*?"

"Nat, do what he says, please." She recognized Clarence's voice coming from the corridor to the first floor rooms. When she looked up, the man she knew stood wearing a black ski mask with goggles on his forehead, a black sweater, and black sweat pants. He wore two semiautomatic pistols, one on each hip. When she looked back, the white man had rolled his watch cap down to cover his face, except for the eyeholes. He pulled goggles from his breast pocket and placed them on his forehead.

The two guards had eaten only one cookie each. Bleary-eyed, they stumbled to their feet and tried to unholster their weapons.

"Wha' the hellshgoing on here? Who are you?" asked one, his words almost illegible.

"Unit 2236," Dan Burton answered. The pistols on Clarence's hips came quickly from their specially constructed holsters that accommodated silencer attachments. Both guns whooshed once; wet red circles appeared on the guards' foreheads; they crumbled to the floor with their eyes open.

"Oh shit!" Nat, eyes wide, didn't bother with the register. She grabbed her purse and rushed to the door, passing six masked and similarly attired people coming in. The team commander remained in the vestibule.

The OCI guards she passed sprawled outside the door had rivulets of blood leaking from one ear, the ear with a knitting needle driven into it. (The next day, Nat's employers received a tearful, frightened recounting of that night's activities. She regaled family and friends for years with how "them brothas were baaaad and took care of much business, you hear me? I ain't never seen no shit like that!")

While Clarence disabled the switchboard, the other four—three men and "Lynn"—broke the necks of the four incapacitated guards. Both 121—Andy—and 122 took the steps three at a time as Clarence pulled fuses and the lights went out. *I'm playing this fly ball to the wall, George,* 121 thought as he raced up the steps to his moment of destiny with Mike Patrick.

Upstairs, Bulldog Hudson hadn't been able to sleep. He decided to see if it was too late for room service. He couldn't get a dial tone. When his nightstand light and the television set went out moments later, Hudson's police instincts kicked in. Like most retired police officers, he still had a carry permit. He took his pistol from his nightstand, clicked off the safety, and slid a round into the chamber as he moved toward the door.

122 recognized the sound of the gun being readied and posted by Hudson's door on the right side. The retired inspector first looked to his left in the darkened hallway. When he turned to his right, the last thing he saw was a flash of light as 122 shot him between the eyes.

The two guards by Mike Patrick's door had overdosed into comas. One had fallen to the floor. Andy checked their pulses and knew they'd be still for some time. He heard movement in the room. But they had night goggles; Patrick didn't.

121 kicked the door to the darkened room. Both 121 and 122 ducked as Mike Patrick's gun boomed loud. Patrick was a green specter crouched by his bed pointing his revolver at the door. 122 squeezed off repeated shots from both his pistols as cover, making Patrick cringe beside the bed. 121 rolled into the room and fired both of his pistols as he came up in a crouch. Patrick's gun boomed again as 121's guns whooshed. Both rounds struck the clearly delineated green shape. One hit him in the neck; the other shattered his nose before entering his brain.

They knew the noise of two gunshots only gave them seconds to get out. The two men scampered past a horrified Ike Erlickson and other frightened guests awakened by the commotion and raced down the steps.

At the Levyville freeway exit, a police barricade instructed vehicles to detour. It kept them from seeing the disarmed and blindfolded police officers and fire volunteers and the seven members of Unit 2236's December Fourth Brigade. One member picked up a police radio beside a disarmed and blindfolded police officer.

"Alpha One, please respond," said the voice over the radio in a monotone. "Alpha One, do you copy?"

Two other Unit members knew they had a problem even before they removed the soaked smoke grenades from the engine of the van. "The engine's damaged, we can't use this thing," one man said. "Did everyone have gloves on?"

"Affirmative," the other one replied. "I checked. The van's clean."

The man code named "Fred" punched a speed dial number on his cell phone. "August two one, your partners need pickup. We're at the freeway exit. Y'all need to hurry!"

"Alpha One, we're sending a car to your last location, do you copy that?" the radio voice said. "Alpha One, please respond."

Dan Burton drove up in his U-Haul just as two Unit 2236 members removed the phony police barricades. He saw the red and white lights on the approaching police car in his rear view mirror.

When the patrol car arrived, the two officers saw three police cars, a fire truck, a U-Haul truck, and a foam-logged van. All but one was empty; a white man, seemingly unconscious, sat in the driver's seat of the U-Haul. Both Levyville officers drew their pistols, got out, and cautiously approached the U-Haul. As they trained their guns on Dan Burton, they felt guns at the back of their heads.

"All you have to do to live is slowly drop your weapons," a voice behind them said. "Any other move at all will be considered a hostile one." Amazed and frightened, the Levyville cops let their pistols drop to the ground as several ski-masked men dressed in black emerged from the bushes.

The officers in the third patrol car joined their bound comrades on the side of the road. The two Unit 2236 brigades got in the U-Haul and hauled ass.

SIXTY-NINE

The first action in Phase Two for Unit 2236 was page one the next day in newspapers, and led most radio and television accounts across the country. Versions of the action, both accurate and distorted, flew back and forth on the Internet. Most described the action as the "Levyville Massacre."

No mainstream media received information directly from the assassin team. Radio stations, television stations, and newspapers were reduced to lifting information from the Internet. Those who covered it showed a brief sound byte of a masked man who said he was the leader of Unit 2236. This was big news because he was the first visible person claiming association.

It was another story on the streets of black communities across the country; the entire contents of the broadcast became quickly available on both CDs and DVDs. The disks appeared on street corners, in barber shops, beauty parlors, schools, bars, and anywhere else black folks gathered. And there were bootleg Internet accounts.

As Big Larry strolled down the Avenue to meet the Checkers Gang that morning, he passed two well-dressed young men handing out CDs and DVDs to passersby from two briefcases. Oddly, they weren't hustling because they took no money from their customers.

"We have a message for you from people who care about you," one of them said as if he were hawking newspapers or bean pies. The taller of the two looked familiar in a vague way to Big Larry. He approached them.

"What you got?" he asked. The young men looked at him and also kept their eyes scanning passing vehicular traffic.

"A message for the people," the taller youth said. He held up the cover of the DVD.

"Oh, hell yes," Big Larry said. "Thank you. Y'all are taking a big risk handing these out. You're with the Swords of the Master, aren't you?"

"Yes, sir, we are," the young man said. "As far as the risk, well, being black and living in this country is a big risk all day, every day, you know what I'm saying? Especially these days."

The vague familiarity of the young man jostled Big Larry's memory.

"I don't mean no harm, but what's your name, young brother?" he asked with a slight smile.

The young man looked at him first with wariness, then relaxed. "Willis Richardson, sir. They used to call me Cornbread the Third on the street." He nodded to his companion. "This is Farik Frazier."

"The artist formerly known as Bugeye," Frazier chimed in. They all laughed. "I'm training to draw cartoons for the *Scabbard*. Brother Butler says I have a lot of talent." Farik scanned the street as he spoke.

"I'll be damned! I knew there was something about you. Is an oldhead who called himself Cornbread related to you?

Willis smiled. "Yes, sir, that's my grandfather. Do you know him?"

Big Larry looked pleased with himself. "Nah, I didn't really know him all that well. We ran in the same circles, you know? We knew each another to nod at each other, but we weren't tight or nothing. He might remember my name. Cornbread was a bad brother. Boy, you look just like him."

"Yes, sir, a lot of people say that," Willis said.

"I'm glad to see you're doing some good things, Willis." Big Larry extended his hand; Richardson shook it. "You tell your grandfather that Big Larry Palmer said hello. He might remember me."

Both Willis and Farik were snapping their briefcases shut. They moved away in different directions. "Yes, sir, I'll do that," Richardson said over his shoulder.

Big Larry looked around. A police car, still a block away from the Avenue, moved in his direction.

Big Larry bounced into the Butler Center, a grin splitting his face almost ear to ear. "Wait until y'all see what I got," he said when he reached his longtime comrades. He waved the DVD in a black cardboard jacket at them. The front bore the name, "Unit 2236," in blood red type. Beneath the name were the words, "Greater love has no man than this, that a man lay down his life for his friends.."

"When's this man gonna stop being a day late and a dollar short?" Mister Jake asked. "We were just going to go find the player." He held up his own disk in an identical jacket, except for the words below the name: "Love one another; protect one another."

They moved to another room in the center that housed the center's DVD player and another television set. After all four were seated, Big Larry pressed the buttons on the remote control device.

A close-up of a man wearing a black ski mask came into focus. Other than a light blue backdrop, little background was visible. There was a flag visible above the man's right shoulder: the red, green and black tri-color created by Marcus Mosiah Garvey. When the masked man spoke, his words sounded robotic; his voice had obviously been altered.

"I bring greetings to all people who love freedom," the man said. "I am the commander of Unit 2236. I will be brief.

"What they are calling the Levyville Massacre we identify as the Battle of Levyville. The government calls us subversive, and we are. We are subversive to the horrors directed at our people in the form of police shootings, drug shipments, fifth-rate educations, inadequate health care, and so on. We will resist and we will either win or die. Now that this has started, we will never surrender. We ask you to join us by refusing to cooperate with the authorities every chance you get. Non-cooperation was the essence of the civil rights struggle, and it must be at the heart of this fight, too. As they fought for human dignity, so must we do the same. And we must do so without compromise.

"Drugs are no longer permitted in our community. We assume responsibility for enforcing this edict. If you are dealing and we find you, execution is the penalty for selling drugs; you have been warned.

"We live among you; we *are* you. Form your own teams of resistance and join us." He raised his right hand in a fist. "Freedom or death." The screen went dark.

"That's what I'm talking about!" Big Larry said. "Man, these niggas are the real deal, you hear me? It's about time somebody started doing something."

Mister Jake exposed his nicotine-stained teeth in a grin. "I guess Brother Garvey has come back on that whirlwind he promised," he said. "You saw them colors in the background, didn't you?"

Varnell snorted. "I don't care if they are Garveyites, which they ain't, or black Jews, which they ain't neither, or Muslims or Christians, which they also ain't, these mammy-jammers are taking care of much business. That Patrick got what he deserved."

"This is about way more than Patrick now," Mister Otis said. "You know Bruder and his OCI troopers will come down on us hard. You see what they doing to the Covenant of the New Commandment."

"Yeah, well, nobody's saying so, but you know as well as I do that Unit 2236 is hooked up with the Covenant more than they are letting on," Mister Jake said. "These men are underground, and the Covenant is above ground, out in the open, doing what they can to wake us up." He cocked his head. "You know something?

I just might go to the Covenant meeting next Saturday."

"You know something else? I just might go with you, Jake," Mister Otis said.

SEVENTY

Two bungled raids were inexcusable. By the time John Edgar returned to Washington, his office had been cleaned out. His belongings, including a prized oil painting of the late FBI director, J. Edgar Hoover, sat in several boxes by the door, and the locks had been changed. His desktop computer, considered government property, remained in the office with a freshly scrubbed hard drive. The envelope posted on the door contained a curt note to see his superior as soon as possible.

"I don't think you're cut out for anything as sensitive as this CP2 assignment," the Bureau's deputy director for clandestine operations said. He was a blond, Nordic type with a weathered face. "You let a bunch of dumb, cultish niggers outsmart you, not once but twice. Obviously you're no smarter than they are."

John Edgar knew the harshness and the epithet were calculated and deliberate; his visceral dislike for the man's use of the "N" word surprised him. Humiliation washed through his being, followed by the heat of resentment. Not for the deputy director, but for those goddamned people who had humiliated the Bureau and, by extension, him.

"Sir, I am abjectly sorry," the cinnamon-colored man said. He felt his face burning. In some perverse way, he was glad his superior could see that he was light enough to blush in his embarrassment. "I promise you to do all I can for the Bureau in this war to neutralize the Covenant."

"That remains to be seen," the deputy director said, pursing his lips. "Take a week or two off to clear your head. You're being assigned to the field office in Butte, Montana, as the assistant SAC."

He hated to beg. "With all due respect, sir, I'd like to stay in the fight against the Covenant, even as a field agent. They don't have a meetinghouse anywhere in Montana. If it's possible—"

"Butte."

"Yes, sir."

He'd kill Blackman first, then Butler. He wished he could bring that fucking son of a bitch David Walker back to life just so he could kill him again, too. A lifetime of service to his country crashed in flames. Someone had to pay.

Both Blackman and Butler resisted arrest, he would say. Even though he was on leave, the Bureau surely wouldn't cry if he took down two of the Covenant's top men. Now that Butler had replaced the Walkers as the so-called Teacher, they would thank him for cutting off the head. And Blackman. The things he'd been writing about the country were as treasonous as the things Johnnie Walker had been saying.

He knew an agent in the local office who was a good man to have watch his back. Within the Bureau, the man was big on advocacy for the Conservative Christian Crusaders. Although Bob Jones didn't like black people, John Edgar had personally been able to establish a relationship with him. He had even convinced Jones that CCC should open African-American Auxiliaries to avoid accusations of being a white racist organization. There were enough black conservatives around to make the concept work. As a devout churchgoer himself, he was a charter member of the first CCC-AAA chapter.

He'd go to see Butler and Blackman about their identification cards. And although he didn't expect truthful answers, he would ask them what they knew about the leadership of Unit 2236.

Andy rubbed the hard rubber ball, squeezed it, tossed it from one hand to the other. Bob Jones and John Edgar. No warrant. A flimsy ass excuse. "An informal visit," they called it. He looked just as he did in the photograph that Miss Jones had given him, Andy thought.

Bob Jones had an ordinary, blend-into-a-crowd kind of face. Dark hair, slicked back and combed to the right, a high forehead, blue-gray eyes that were not expressive, lips neither narrow nor full, and a slight cleft in his chin. His clothes were neat and without imagination.

On the other hand, this Uncle Tom with the irritating voice who called himself "John Edgar" could barely contain the rage in his eyes. He tried to act as if he were in charge of the visit.

When Andy had cracked his door, both men held their leather wallets high to display their badges and identification.

"Can I help you?" he'd asked.

"FBI," John Edgar had said. "Are you Andrew Sherman Blackman?"

Andy knew that they already knew his identity. "Yes. What can I do for you?"

"May we come in?"

Claudia had stepped from their bedroom at that moment. Quickly, Andy held up one finger, then two, then one again. Then he rapidly flashed one finger three times. 121. 111. She disappeared back into the bedroom.

"Do you have a search warrant?"

"Mister Blackman, this is an informal visit," the white agent had said. "I'm Bob Jones and this is John Edgar. We're new in the local office and thought we might have a chat with you and other local Covenant leaders to see if we can keep the escalating violence from getting out of hand. If you have a few minutes, we'd appreciate it. May we come in?"

Now the three of them sat, wary and pretending to be cordial. Andy exercised his fingers around the hard rubber ball.

"Is your wife here?"

"No."

"Mind if we look around?"

"If you don't have a warrant, I mind very much."

John Edgar and Bob Jones looked at each other. If they exchanged any signal, Andy didn't see it. "Well, may we sit down?" Jones asked.

"Sure." Andy gestured toward two chairs facing the sofa, chairs with their backs to the bedroom.

"Have you registered and obtained an identification card yet?"

Shit. They knew who he was; his pseudonymic card would do no good. "I'm going to get one today. In fact, I'm waiting for my wife to come back, and then we're going together," Andy said. "We still have a few hours before deadline."

"Yes, that's true," John Edgar said. Jones had agreed to take his lead on shooting them. "As we said, this is informal. Unfortunately, we have to close your meetinghouse tomorrow. We hope the Swords of the Master won't fight back and cause a lot of people to die."

"There's no need for me to give you rhetoric about self-defense," Andy said. "And I'm sure you're aware of Romeo's statement about our decision to engage in nonviolent civil disobedience. The Swords and all law-abiding Covenant members will attend a special service tomorrow expressly to argue their right to freedom of religion and freedom of peaceful assembly. If there's any violence, it will come from the government."

The cinnamon-colored man tried not to make a face, but was only partially successful. "The Bureau must carry out the president's wishes," he said. "Which reminds me, what can you tell us about Unit 2236?"

"What you already know. They've claimed responsibility for the deaths of several police officers," Andy replied. "They send their communiqués to the Covenant of the New Commandment. And the government is attacking the Covenant because we refuse to denounce them. That's about it."

"David Walker gave up your name, and that of your lifelong friend, Romeo Butler, as key leaders of these killers."

"David Walker was being blackmailed and he was suicidal. I think that speaks loudly to his credibility."

The black FBI agent stood up; Jones followed his lead. "We're going to take a look around," he said.

"You said you don't have a search warrant," Andy said.

"I lied. We do have search warrants," John Edgar said, reaching inside his suit jacket.

The hard rubber ball crushed his right eyeball before his gun cleared its holster. Screaming in agony, he grabbed his bloody face as his weapon clambered to the floor. Andy's kick to his solar plexus knocked the wind from him and he collapsed.

"We lied, too," Claudia said. Instinctively, Jones turned, drawing his weapon as he did so. The ball hit dead center on his Adam's apple with the force of a major league pitcher's fastball. He couldn't scream as he fell to his knees, unable to breathe.

Claudia took two knitting needles from a ball of yarn sitting benignly on a bookcase against the wall and handed one to her husband.

They called Claudia's brother. Glenn quickly dispatched four Swords to Andy's apartment to remove the bodies and dispose of them. Andy had no way of knowing they had caught half a break: the black agent was on vacation and wouldn't be missed for several days. Although a hunt for Jones would begin the next day, he and John Edgar were never found.

They called Romeo. "We need to see you right away, it's extremely urgent," Claudia said.

"The parking lot of the meetinghouse is about as safe as it gets," Romeo said. "In two hours."

They packed quickly and drove to the meetinghouse. Romeo had apparently deemed it safe because people were everywhere. A couple dozen reporters were camped across the street from the front entrance behind several wooden horses. Police cars sat at both ends of the block in an uneasy truce. Uniformed Swords lined the sidewalk in front of the wrought iron fence running the length of the parking lot. The new Teacher stood in the middle of the lot talking to several congregants. Covenant members milled about, moving in and out of the building.

"How are the newlyweds?" Romeo asked. Claudia and Andy smiled. They had been married two frantic, painful, loving, turbulent weeks. He hugged each of them. Andy looked at the grief and weariness etched on Romeo's face. He wondered if he looked the same way, knew that he probably did, and knew it was just beginning.

"We don't have much time, so let me update you and then you give me your urgent news," Romeo said. "Bruder may have dug a hole for himself that will buy us some time, 'us' meaning the Covenant. After Levyville night before last, they are pulling their hair out looking for leads. Robert trained you well.

"But the Covenant has some breathing room. Not much, but some. You know Minister Johnnie used to say that if a nonpartisan judge not aligned with either party could be found, Roper would find him. He called Roper our 'courtroom assassin.' Well, incredibly, Roper found one, a sassy sister named Gwendolyn Cornwall-Hill. Takes no tea for the fever from *anybody*. More incredibly, he's got some amicus briefs being filed from folks who don't even like us that much, mostly white progressive and liberal churches who like our ugly president even less for crossing the lines on church and state. None of your faith-based types. The judge has issued an order keeping us open for at least thirty days while both sides write opinions. Bruder wants to kick our ass but he doesn't want a constitutional crisis.

"So here's the deal," Romeo said. "We have only one executive action pending; we'll get him, we just don't have to rush. The Unit will be fine because the government doesn't know who or where, and we have to keep it like that. I'll be mapping out an underground plan for the Covenant and will be ready by the time we go to court. Maybe we'll move in and live in the meetinghouses, I don't know yet.

"We leave in the morning for Monroe with the Teacher's body. We're allowing three days so we can stop for viewings in the Baltimore and D.C. meetinghouses. Depending on how the next days shake out, I'm considering something I know you two won't like, but my options are limited. I may have to split the two positions I hold and have someone else serve as Teacher. If it happens, I want you to become the Teacher, Claudia. Having been my right hand, the members will accept and respect you. The way things are going, my other work will call for every bit of energy I've got."

The Blackmans stood open-mouthed even as they understood the logic of it.

"I'm honored at your trust," Claudia said. Her voice cracked. "And I'm a bit overwhelmed."

"It may not happen, I'm just giving you a heads up," he said. "So what is the 'extremely urgent'?"

They told him about the two agents. "I don't know who the white boy was, but the Uncle Tom was definitely the CP2 chief."

No one said anything at first. Finally, Romeo looked at each of them and then spoke. "You two head for Memphis now. Immediately. Someone will meet you, and you'll know who by the time you get there. I'm sorry you have to miss the funeral, but we can't afford having you caught. I'll join you as soon as I can. May Yahweh's blessings go with you."

They embraced. Romeo held each of them for a while. His eyes were moist when he released his lifelong friend.

"They make some strong niggas at Seventeenth and Cambridge," Romeo said.

"Yeah they do," Andy said. "We play all fly balls to the wall."

Even though there were two safe houses between them and WiTHWA, Romeo's orders were explicit: don't stop until they arrive at the remote location. Remain until further notice. Some in the Battle of Levyville would be there; others were dispersed at safe houses. They had time.

The couple slept at the meetinghouse and left Thursday afternoon for Memphis. They let the 1,000-mile trip take twenty-two hours. At a rest stop early Friday, they watched a news report as they ate lunch.

As the United Nations Security Council met in emergency session, President Bruder announced that U.S. troops were en route to South Africa. Thousands of demonstrators were protesting in Paris, London, Berlin, Stockholm, Rome, Havana, and Caracas.

They also saw five hundred police officers from across the U.S. give Michael Patrick a hero's funeral in a closed casket ceremony. Because of the acquittal, Isaac Erlickson had urged—successfully—that Patrick be reinstated to his job posthumously; he was buried in uniform.

Andy chewed on his turkey club sandwich. He looked around to see if anyone sat close to him and Claudia; the booths nearby were empty. Claudia picked at her Cobb salad.

"It didn't feel like I thought it would to kill someone," he said. "Until afterward."

Claudia nodded. "You're too busy trying to stay alive."

"I'm grateful for the First Star and his training."

"Indeed." Claudia's eyes remained on the eulogistic ceremony unfolding on television for George Bascomb's murderer. "As I watch this, this–" she hesitated. "This pageantry. I'm just realizing that I should know better, but I'm still surprised."

"It shows how they feel about us," Andy said. "And about him." His adrenalin no longer pumped; he was tired. "George is already forgotten by the people who bring us this." He waved a hand as he bit into his sandwich. "From now on, my brother will be an obligatory sentence to journalists, when he's mentioned at all, as 'the man who assaulted Michael Patrick, the officer who was acquitted after a controversial trial.' Plaques will be forged that memorialize Patrick and subtly demonize George. And, needless to say, that demonize us."

"I get scared sometime when I realize there are only forty-nine of us," she said, her voice low. "Against an empire."

Andy looked around again. "Forty-nine trained assassins are formidable when the enemy doesn't know who or where they are. Plus, we have some Swords who we're going to take a chance with, I think."

"The word on the street is that the checkpoints and identification cards are really pissing people off," Claudia said. She looked at her watch and pushed her salad aside. "We'd better go."

They stood up. "It's funny, I just had this feeling," Andy said. "As long as public pressure keeps the meetinghouses open, I think our special work has a chance. On the other hand, if people let them shut us down, all bets are off because I really think they'll start street-to-street searches."

"Do you think our people will put up with that?"

Andy's smile was tight. "I hope not."

124 met Andy and Claudia in Memphis Friday afternoon; they arrived at the estate they called WiTHWA that night, had a late dinner, and slept for twelve hours. In the morning, they joined a fast with those who had already arrived. The fast lasted from Saturday morning until after the memorial service in Monroe the next day.

The rites for the Teacher were broadcast on a twenty-four hour cable news station. The coverage lasted for three hours. Thousands from all over the country—Covenant members, friends of the Covenant, natives of Monroe and surrounding towns (and some agents/enemies)—packed the Monroe meetinghouse and flooded the city's streets to say good-bye to the Teacher, Johnnie "Black Label" Walker.

They took his remains to the cemetery on an open flatbed truck similar to one he had used for street sermons during the late Sixties. "When I leave here and return to the Creator," a twenty-five year old Minister Johnnie said at the time, "take me to the cemetery in one of these and bury me next to my parents." Escorted by Romeo and Malikah Butler and a ceremonial guard from Swords of the Master, Ila Walker followed her husband by foot to his final resting place.

Two squads of Swords in full dress uniforms accompanied the truck and stood on each side of the grave, their ceremonial blades raised and gleaming in the Sunday sun over the casket of their fallen Teacher.

On the large screen at WiTHWA, Andy looked at the inscription on the coffin: John 15:13 – "Greater love has no man than this, that a man lay down his life for his friends." He didn't try and wipe the tears as they came. This warm, lovable, rowdy, vain, and fierce man had brought him to himself. Whatever waited for him tomorrow, Andy knew he was a free man today. *And before he'd be a slave, he'd be buried in his grave* . . . He looked at his wife. She was crying, too. They squeezed each other's hands.

Suddenly Andy felt himself back on the day he had first joined the Covenant of the New Commandment, listening to this fierce, proud firebrand of a man. Not being a Bible thumper, he hadn't thought of the experience in years; the words meant far more this Sunday morning than they had on that Saturday morning eight years ago. He felt almost as if he were having a vision, so long ago had it been since he'd thought of the words.

"These things I command you, that you love one another," Andy heard himself say aloud. "If the world hate you, you know that it hated me before it hated you."

"If you were of the world, the world would love its own," Claudia joined in.

"But because you are not of the world, but I have chosen you out of the world, therefore the world hates you," they said together. "Remember the word that I said unto you, 'the servant is not greater than his Master. If they have persecuted me, they will also persecute you; if they have kept my sayings, they will keep yours also.'"

Claudia cocked her head and looked at her husband. "Facing this madness won't be as hard with you next to me," she said. "Whatever happens, I'll feel you with me."

"I guess we're getting to know each other because I was going to say the same thing," Andy replied. He kissed her softly. "If I have to do it, I'm glad a tough broad like you is doing it with me." They fell silent again when they saw the Teacher's coffin was at the gravesite, sitting over the hole that would return him to dust.

As they lowered Minister Johnnie's body into the ground, they honored the last request in his instructions. ("I'm going to run my mouth until the very last," he told Romeo when he recorded it.) His voice boomed out over the gravesite from a recording made days before his death.

"Although I am speaking primarily to my people, I really speak to anyone who professes to love freedom, justice and righteousness,' the Teacher said. "Anyone who truly loves these values will stand with us as we fight to make them long overdue realities for everyone living under the thumb of the empire. I record this as the Covenant is under siege, and as a small band of freedom fighters known as Unit 2236 dare to struggle against an empire of repression.

"My message is brief and comes in the form of a true story. It's a story a now successful attorney tells who, when I was a teenager, was a struggling civil rights attorney, just out of law school. One of his first cases was in Mississippi in 1960 or 1961, for the NAACP. This was during the days when Mississippi was a criminal state running amok without any regard for the Thirteenth, Fourteenth and Fifteenth Amendments to the Constitution. Things were unimaginably bad in Mississippi then, real bad. White folks could kill black folks just because they felt like it. Just because they woke up in a bad mood.

"After court each day, the white lawyers went to lunch in the town's restaurant while this young lawyer and his two colleagues ate bologna sandwiches and drank a soda in their car. On about the third day of the trial, a black woman in the segregated balcony got their attention. The civil rights attorney telling the story went to see what she wanted. She told them not to eat the sandwiches that day and invited them to her home when the court session ended.

"When they arrived, the attorney said, the woman had laid out her finest linen, china settings and silverware for dinner. She had invited neighbors over and they all sat down for some magnificent Southern cooking. Her husband said a prayer over the food. The now wealthy attorney said the man prayed so long they were afraid the food had gotten cold. It seemed like he prayed for ten minutes and the attorney remembers none of it, except for two sentences he said he'd never forget.

" 'Lord, down here we can't join the NAACP,' the man said. 'But we can feed the NAACP lawyers.'"

"I know most of you aren't going to pick up guns like Unit 2236 has. And most of you aren't even going to join the Covenant. But wherever you are, and whatever you're doing, make up your mind to *do something* to change things.

As King taught, don't cooperate with repression; *do something* to change things. As Malcolm taught, if you find an organization committed to fighting for the liberation of black people, then join that organization.

"I am not with you physically, but if you're struggling to be free, I'm there. If you're at war with the empire, I'm with you. Keep on keeping on."

The Teacher's recording ended. Someone clicked the remote, replacing the transmission with a closed circuit inscription on the screen:

John 15:12

Matthew 22:37   John 15:13   Matthew 22:39

Andy and Claudia looked at each other. "Let's make as many little Johnnies as we still can," she said, placing her head on his chest. "Let's keep our Teacher alive."

"Let's do that," Andy said.

EPILOGUE

As Mister Jake took Mister Otis' last checker, the younger man looked up and cursed. Mister Jake, thinking he was being cussed, looked up, too, surprised. He followed his old friend's eyes to the window.

A squad of OCI troops alighted from a white van with red and blue lettering. Two OCI patrol cars pulled up behind the van. Children in the neighborhood had nicknamed the OCI troops with a nonsense name: "Ockey Knockeys." Two patrol cars, and a wagon. Identification card time.

Mister Jake set up the checkers. Mister Otis turned the window chair over to Big Larry. "I knew I should have followed my first mind," Mister Jake said to no one in particular.

"What's that, Jake?" Mister Otis said.

"Oh, I was going to stop and see my grandkids, spend some time with them, and then go on down to Belize to see if I liked it," Jake said. "Didn't want to live my last years under this mess we got now. This man Bruder has lost his mind. He's worse than his predecessor, and all this mess has just been getting on all my nerves. Looks like I waited too long."

Mister Jake had never mentioned moving, even to them. But he'd been thinking.

Minutes later, the Butler Center administrator, a petite, energetic bespectacled woman the color of currant opened the door to the game room. Her manner, usually a mixture of amiable and acerbic banter, was stiff and affected this warm May morning. Behind her walked three white men in gray fatigues, military boots, and black baseball caps with American flags on them. The shortest one wore a sidearm; the other two had carbines slung over their shoulders.

"Excuse me, gentlemen, I've been asked to escort these men around the building," she said. Her glasses hung on a chain around her neck. The chain framed her national identification card hanging on a shorter chain, optional and provided at no additional cost by the government for those who chose to wear the card in view. "They want to see your identification cards."

The short white man wearing sergeant stripes walked over to the checkers table. He looked first at Mister Jake, then at Big Larry, and finally at Mister Otis

411

and Varnell. "Good afternoon, gentlemen. May I see your NICs, please?" His manner was pleasant and oozed public relations.

Varnell took out his wallet. He took out his now red-bordered white driver's license with blue lettering, his photograph, and a tiny silver disk embedded on the back and handed it to the sergeant. A legend next to the disk reminded the bearer that tampering with the device was a federal crime punishable by ten years in jail, a $50,000 fine, or both.

Mister Otis took his out and did the same. The sergeant looked at them and handed them back. "Thank you, gentlemen." He looked at Big Larry, who was scowling. He reached in his shirt pocket and handed the sergeant his card.

The sergeant looked at Mister Jake. Mister Jake looked back at him through his coke bottle glasses.

"Sir, may I see your NIC, please?" the sergeant said. He had a smooth face, blonde hair and electric blue eyes.

"Don't have one," Mister Jake said.

"Excuse me? What do you mean, you don't have one?"

Mister Jake looked at the man as if he were stupid. "I mean I haven't registered, and I don't have one of your cards," he said.

"Sir, all of you people are required to have the cards. It's illegal not to have a card."

Mister Jake looked back at the board. He picked up a black checker and moved. *Whap!* Again. *Whap!* And again. *Whap!* He smiled his nicotine-stained smile at Big Larry. "Still can't play." He looked his friend straight in the eye. "Maybe you'll be able to win some games now."

He looked up at the sergeant. "I don't have a what-do-you-call-it? An NIC? I don't have one, don't intend to get one, and know that you or nobody else can make me get one. Now, what's next?"

"Sir, I'll have to place you under arrest for violation of the African-American Short-term Emergency Protection and Identification Act. You have the right to remain silent—"

Mister Jake stood up with the energy of a man half his age. "Son, I don't need to hear all that. I'll be eighty years old next month. I was born a race man and I'll die a race man, even if it's in one of your fancy private jails. Which means I ain't going to carry one of your damn cards. Ever." He held his arms in front of him so they could place handcuffs on him.

The room was still. The handcuffs clicked loudly in the silence as they locked. The remaining three checker players stared at the floor. Mister Jake looked at his three friends. "I hear there's no bail because they say that only a certain type won't get the card. So if I don't see you no more, y'all learn to play some checkers, okay?" He turned to Mister Otis. "Some chess, too."

The two carbine carrying soldiers flanked him and headed for the door.

"Sergeant."

The sergeant turned. Otis held his friend's cigarette lighter and his own identification card. He flicked the lighter. The chip emitted a humming noise as the flames engulfed the plastic.

"Sir, defacing an NIC—"

Mister Otis stood up and held his arms in front of him. "Spare me the bullshit, okay?" he said.

The others watched the two men and their guards walk to the wagon. The administrator coughed. When the two men looked at her, two thin tracks of tears streaked her dark face.

"I'm getting ready to retire. I've got to think about my family," Varnell said, trying, and failing, to keep shame out of his voice. Big Larry and the administrator said nothing.

The two men never played checkers there again.

II

The Fourth Star sat in the pre-dawn stillness, alone with their private thoughts. Although there were two of them, they preferred referring to themselves with singular rank.

They were en route to a celebration in Omaha on the anniversary of Malcolm X's birthday. If he had lived to be eighty-five, what would the world he lived in be like, they wondered. As the Fourth Star remembered him, they remembered other things.

She remembered the words of a young Turk who had emerged as a leader and scholar about the time Malcolm was cut down. "History is a people's memory," the youthful Ron Karenga used to say. "If you lose your history, you lose your memory. If you lose your memory, you lose your mind." Through their personal success, through the gains of their people, through the madness, through the setbacks, through loyalties and betrayals, through love and hurt and pain and joy and loss, they kept their memories intact.

He remembered a long ago thought from a long dead Lebanese poet, Kahlil Gibran, and the multi-layered meaning it had for him during the various stages of his

413

remarkable life: *One may not reach the dawn save by the path of the night.*

The woman remembered that horrible wonderful long ago day, as teenagers, when the two of them made a silent vow with their eyes, a vow fleshed with words later. The welding of their love began in pain and terror and shock at a funeral for someone they didn't even know. And yet, they both said to each other later, in a very real way, the dead boy was both of them. He was their son, their brother, their uncles; he was any black woman or man, he was *them*.

The man and woman sat quietly in the sleek black limousine parked on the tarmac at Los Angeles International Airport. Their private jet was being refueled. For as long as they could remember, both enjoyed the stillness of the hours just before dawn. For meditation . . . for creativity . . . for lovemaking . . . for planning an insurrection . . .

The Fourth Star looked out across the tarmac, their thoughts going back to that fall day in 1955. *Someone must protect and defend our people. This government won't.* When a fifteen-year-old hears those words from loving parents, they remember.

Their parents were friends and Garveyites. Four fierce, proud people, two couples passionate about the vision of black people standing on the world stage again as equals, a vision their leader, the Honorable Marcus Mosiah Garvey had articulated. Both couples wanted, more than life itself, that their children not grow up with what they called "the mentality of slaves."

Someone must protect and defend our people. This government won't. When these two fifteen-year-olds heard that, and then stood at the bier holding the unrecognizable remains of Emmett Till, they remembered. When they looked down at young Emmett's bloated and mutilated countenance, a man-child disfigured beyond anything any mother should witness, when they looked at him lying in his casket, they said they would remember.

When they read that the courts set the killers free, they remembered.

Before they were husband and wife, even before they were lovers, they verbalized the silent pact at Emmett Till's bier: Until the killers of innocents like Emmett Till received justice at the hands of the state, they would find a way to defend their people with whatever talents and resources God bestowed on them. Emmett Till was them, and as long as the government failed to protect them, they would find a way to protect themselves.

They were young enough and idealistic enough and foolish enough and courageous enough to believe they could do it.

And then, not long after, an Alabama black woman stood up by refusing to give up her seat on a bus. Not many years after that, four young black men stood up by sitting down at a lunch counter in South Carolina. And it wasn't too long after that before some young lions—panthers, actually—armed themselves in a West Coast city and started facing down racist cops.

For several years, the childhood friends' busy lives moved away from each other. They stayed in touch and maintained a long distance friendship.

He became a star athlete, a fleet and powerful running back, both in college and as a professional. He became Phi Beta Kappa and because the times they were a-changing, was tokened into the secret society called Skull and Bones. The timing was good. The U.S. government reluctantly began enforcing its own laws, and mercurial athletes like him became financial assets to professional teams, valuable regardless of their hue. Some referred to him as the second coming of Paul Robeson, although, they said, "he's not as militant as Robeson was." He was glad they thought that he wasn't as forceful about race as his idol. Carefully, he cultivated that public image.

She became a dancer with breathtaking skills and audacious flair. A Chicago troupe ended a tour in Los Angeles and she stayed. A self-assurance that radiated from stage and screen brought roles. She, too, became a financial asset, valuable to others precisely because of her color.

He shamelessly exploited his athletic name recognition into acting roles, too. To the surprise of many, he had skills. The two assets in tandem, name and talent, translated into big box office.

Their careers brought them together as co-stars in a film, and they fell deeply in love, building on the trust of an already strong friendship. They married and invested well. They became icons of entertainment, fashionable philanthropists for worthy causes, and responsible leaders.

And they remembered their youthful vows and renewed them.

When civil rights workers were murdered and no one was punished, they remembered. When J. Edgar Hoover ran amok, they remembered. They returned to Chicago to walk through the apartment where cops shot Black Panther Party member Mark Clark to death while answering the door, and murdered his comrade, Deputy Chairman Fred Hampton, in his bed.

And they remembered.

Thirty years later, the list was still growing. By now, they knew Johnnie "Black Label" Walker. The three had met in Hampton's bloody apartment on that awful December day in 1969. Black Label's congregation still met in his apartment then; the couple loaned him money to rent a building. They liked preachers who sounded like Nat Turner must have sounded.

Thirty years later, forty-one shots were fired at Amadou Diallo for the crime of reaching for his wallet. They remembered their vow. Thirty years later, Patrick Dorismond got angry with an undercover cop who insulted the young man by asking him to sell him drugs. His anger cost him his life. When both men were blamed for their own deaths, it tilted the balance for the couple. The voices of their Ancestors reached across the years to them: *Someone must protect and defend our people. This government won't.*

The cell phone on the seat between them rang. The man opened it, clicked on.

"Yes?"

"The two-movie deal is dead for now," the voice said. "A man and wife couple is being considered for the lead roles but, as executive producer, the deal needs your okay."

His wife watched tenseness flicker on her loved one's face.

"They'll be fine," the male half of the Fourth Star said. "Keep the two-movie deal alive."

"I'll be in touch."

The phone clicked off, and then rang again. An aide said their plane was ready.

"Glennville Greene is dead," the man said. "He was arrested and died while in custody. I'm sure Roper is trying to get more details. Because we've already discussed it, I told the caller that the Blackmans should both assume the position of Second Star."

"May Yahweh guide their efforts," the woman said.

Greene's death must be Covenant-related, the male Fourth Star thought, because no Unit 2236 actions were ordered. Litigation had kept the meetinghouses open temporarily; an uneasy truce existed between the Covenant and the federal government. Meanwhile, tension was growing in several cities because of the hated checkpoints.

The chauffeur opened the door; the Fourth Star alighted, and, hand in hand, walked toward the plane. Whenever he looked at the plane, he felt grateful for having the earning power to own it. But each and every time he got on it, he remembered the fun he had as a boy taking the El to the South Side of Chicago. *You can take the brotha out of the 'hood,* he mused, *but you can't take the 'hood out of the brotha.*

They would help Unit 2236 do what they could for as long as they could, and for as long as they had breath in their bodies. If the Unit died, they hoped new warriors would replace them. As others around the world had learned, this empire, like all empires, was striking back. But, like others, they would win by not losing. Ruchell Magee knew that. It seemed significant that only one black citizen had been killed by law enforcement under questionable circumstances in the last eight months.

All these years later, and so little has changed, the male Fourth Star thought quietly, contemplatively. He took the old CD from the case he carried. At contemplative moments like this one, he liked to hear Ruchell Magee's rough-hewn, seemingly smoke-scarred, craggy Southern voice. He had been recorded for a radio program remembering the murder of Soledad Brother George Jackson. The Fourth Star played the recording regularly. They never tired of being reminded of something basic, something elemental, that had sustained Magee since he was a young blood. The man slid the disk in the player next to his oversized leather seat and pushed the button for track five:

. . . As long as I keep fighting, nobody know how the fight gonna turn out . . . It's a possibility I might win . . . But I know if I stop fighting, or follow a foolish one, I cannot win . . . I also believe that one man—one man—can make a difference if he's sincere . . . .

LOVE YAHWEH
YOUR ELOHIM
WITH ALL YOUR
HEART, AND

WITH ALL
YOUR SOUL,
AND WITH ALL
YOUR MIND

LOVE YOUR NEIGHBOR AS YOURSELF

THIS IS MY COMMANDMENT: LOVE ONE ANOTHER, AS I HAVE LOVED YOU